GREAT CALIFORNIA STORIES

Dearest Mimi,

For your
California Dreamin'...

Love Gevry

GREAT
CALIFORNIA
STORIES

Edited by A. Grove Day

UNIVERSITY OF NEBRASKA PRESS   *Lincoln and London*

Publication of this volume was assisted by
The Virginia Faulkner Fund, established in
memory of Virginia Faulkner, editor-in-chief
of the University of Nebraska Press

Acknowledgments for the use of copyrighted
material appear on pages 267–68, which constitute an
extension of the copyright page.

The paper in this book meets the minimum
requirements of American National Standard for
Information Sciences—Permanence of Paper
for Printed Library Materials, ANSI Z39.48–1984.

Library of Congress Cataloging-in-Publication Data
appear on the last printed page of this book.

CONTENTS

PREFACE

A Spanish romancer, García Ordóñez de Montalvo, published in 1510 a popular novel of fairyland chivalry, *The Deeds of Esplandián,* which proclaimed that "on the right hand of the Indies there is an island called California, very close to the side of the Terrestrial Paradise." The place was inhabited solely by Amazons led by a queen named Calafia. "Their island was the strongest in all the world, with its steep cliffs and rocky shores. Their arms were all of gold, and so was the harness of the wild beasts which they tamed to ride, for in the whole island there was no metal but gold." Thus began the rich literature of California.

The contents of *Great California Stories* have been selected to convey the breadth and variety of the state. Careful attention has been paid to each of the following features:

Settings. "California literature," according to the nature writer David Rains Wallace, "is full of articulate thinking about the diverse, exacting landscape." Settings range from ocean beaches to snowy ranges, from groves of gigantic sequoias to below-sea-level deserts of sand, from isolated ranches to teeming urban stretches.

Eminent authors. Since territorial days California has attracted the attention of world-renowned writers, including two Nobel Prize recipients—Henryk Sienkiewicz and John Steinbeck—and a Pulitzer Prize winner—Wallace Stegner. Many of the other authors are legendary: Mark Twain, Bret Harte, Ambrose Bierce, and Evelyn Waugh, for example.

Chronological arrangement. The stories are presented in a

roughly chronological sequence based on the period in which the action takes place. The reader who starts at the beginning glimpses the periods of settlement and development of the region. Starting with short selections from the oral tradition of the oldest inhabitants—the Native Americans—the stories recall the Hispanic settlement, the gold rush of the 1850s that brought immigrants from many parts of the world, the agricultural epoch, the growth of cities like San Francisco and Los Angeles, and the foibles of Hollywood.

Characterizations. California is famously polyracial and so is this anthology. Its characters represent a multiplicity of cultures and perspectives: Californios and mission fathers, forty-niners and prospectors, European immigrants, Chinese workers, farmers from many of the eastern states seeking free land, Russian emigrés, Mexican Americans and blacks, Hollywood screenwriters, and even a hero from the animal kingdom.

For the convenience of the reader, each selection is preceded by a biographical sketch of the author and a note on the story itself.

MIWOK TALE

Mouse Steals Fire

Hundreds of generations before the coming to California of Hispanics from Mexico or Euro-Americans from the east, the sole human inhabitants of the region were Native Americans. They were largely hunters and gatherers who lived peacefully and in deep harmony with their environment. At the time of white settlement, beginning in the late eighteenth century, they numbered some three hundred thousand and occupied perhaps five hundred villages, each politically and territorially independent of the others. The newcomers saw them largely as subjects for conversion, enslavement, and, finally, annihilation. In less than a decade and a half the Indians' numbers were reduced by more than ninety percent.

Fortunately, enough of their culture was recorded to give insight into their rich mythology. Like much of North American tribal lore, it often sought to explain the cosmos in terms of the society's own observations and experience, to ponder the origins of humankind, and to propound ethical dilemmas. Animals, viewed as beings with intelligence, emotions, and souls or spirits much like those of humans, played a large role in the stories. The following brief folk tale was told by the Miwok group of present Marin County—whose inhabitants today, ironically, are famous as a model of modern civilization's conspicuous consumption and insistence on immediate material gratification.

"Mouse Steals Fire" first appeared in Californian Indian Nights Entertainments *(1930), compiled by Edward W. Gifford and Gwendoline Harris Block of the Museum of Anthropology, University of California.*

A long time ago, in the very beginning of things, the people in the hills were freezing, for they had no fire with which to keep warm. They gathered in their assembly house to talk over what they could do. There were Black Goose, White Goose, Lizard, Coyote, Mouse, and many others. It was Lizard, sitting on the rock outside of the assembly house, who discovered fire emerging from an assembly house in the valley below.

Later, Mouse, the Flute-player, slipped away unnoticed to go and steal some of the fire from the valley people. He took with him four of his flutes. When he arrived at the assembly house in the valley he found Bear, Rattlesnake, Mountain Lion, and Eagle guarding all the entrances. But Mouse managed, nevertheless, to get into the house. He climbed on top of the house, and while Eagle slept he cut two of his wing feathers which were covering the smoke hole, and slipped in.

Once in, he began to play his flute for the people. The music soon lulled them to sleep, and, when they were all snoring, Mouse safely filled his four flutes with fire and escaped.

When the people awoke they searched all over the hills for the one who had stolen fire from them.

Eagle sent Wind, Rain, and Hail in pursuit, for they were considered the swiftest travelers among the valley people. Finally Hail came up to Mouse, but Mouse had concealed his flutes under a buckeye tree just before Hail overtook him, and so denied having the fire. Hail believed him and departed.

Because Mouse placed his flutes of fire under the buckeye tree, there remains to this day fire in the buckeye tree, and people today obtain their fire with a drill of buckeye wood.

After Hail's departure, Mouse resumed his journey with his four flutes of fire. He met Coyote, who had become impatient fearing some dreadful fate had befallen Flute-player, and had gone out to find him.

Arrived home, Mouse sat on top of the assembly house, playing his flutes and dropping coals through the smoke hole.

Coyote interrupted him, however, before he was finished, and so it is that the people who sat in the middle of the house received fire. Those people now cook their food and talk correctly. The people who sat around the edge of the room did not get any fire and today when they talk their teeth chatter with the cold. That is the way the languages began. If Coyote had not interrupted and Mouse had been able to finish playing all his flutes of fire, everyone would have received a share of fire and all would have spoken one language.

Indians today talk many different languages for the reason that all did not receive an equal share of fire.

THEODORA KROEBER

Dance Mad

In her foreword to the book from which this story is taken, Theodora Kroeber wrote that the California Indian "was an introvert, reserved, contemplative, and philosophical. He lived at ease with the supernatural and the mystical, which were pervasive in all aspects of life. . . . The ideal was the man of restraint, dignity, rectitude, he of the Middle Way. Life proceeded within the limits of known and proper pattern from birth through death and beyond. Its repetitive rhythm was punctuated with ritual, courtship, dance, song, and feast, each established according to custom going back to the beginning of the world." Her story from the Wintu tribe that inhabited the Sacramento Valley and the mountains surrounding the Trinity Alps reveals the power that such ritual could have over the earliest settlers of the middle region of the future state.

Theodora Kroeber frequently accompanied her husband, the anthropologist A. L. Kroeber, on many of his field trips. She is best known for her psychological study of "the last wild Indian," Ishi in Two Worlds (1961). "Dance Mad" is taken from her earlier volume, The Inland Whale (1959).

It sometimes happens when many people are gathered together for dancing and singing and feasting that one or another of those who are dancing does not stop when the others stop, does not eat or sleep or rest, but goes on dancing and dancing. He goes dance mad.

Once long ago a whole people went dance mad, dancing

while the moons and seasons came and went, dancing all around the world.

It began one day of spring after the heavy winds had quieted and the bare ground was green with young clover, in a village on Swift Creek, midway between the top edge of the world where the three principal rivers are small streams and the lower edge of the world where these rivers, wide and deep, flow together to make the Nom-ti-pom—that is, the Sacramento River—and empty into the sea. This village, like the sea and the rivers, was old, its people unchanged in their ways since the world was made.

The occasion was a feast celebrating the initiation into full womanhood of Nomtaimet, the daughter of one of the village families. Nomtaimet's father and mother had neglected nothing of the customary observances and training belonging to this period in a girl's life. They knew that it is an important and indeed a dangerous time for her, and for others, too, if she does not learn to keep its prohibitions, to follow its complex ritual, and to behave with decorum.

Nomtaimet's mother built for her daughter a little house. Here, separated from the family but close by, she lived alone during the moons of her initiation. She fasted and kept to herself, seeing only her mother and her mother's mother, who brought her food, bathed her, combed her hair, and cared for her, for she was not allowed, by old custom, to touch herself. She left the little house only after dark, and then briefly, keeping her head covered and her face screened from sight all the time she was outside. She spent the long days and nights inside and alone, doing only those tasks appropriate to her state, learning from her mother and her grandmother the role and behavior of a good woman and wife.

She learned that on the day and the night before her husband should go to hunt or fight or gamble, she must help him to avoid her and by no means tempt him to sleep with her, for this would spoil his luck. She learned that she must again help him to avoid her during all of her moon periods until she was an old woman unable to bear him children, that she must live in her own separate house during these times, apart from her husband. There were further rules of continence and food prohibitions which she must faithfully follow each time she should be with child. Each rule and prohibition came embedded in ritual, song, and story, and these, too, she learned.

When the long moons of learning and fasting and praying came to an end, her mother and her grandmother were more than satisfied with her behavior and her knowledge. They and her father, and her mother's and her father's brothers and sisters, made a feast in her honor, sending runners to invite the people from villages all up and down Swift Creek to come to feast and dance and sing with them.

Her young friends, boys and girls, had sung to her often in the evening outside her little house to let her know she was not forgotten, but she never broke the rule—she neither looked out nor showed herself nor answered them. They were as happy to have her back as she was to be there, and now the young married women came up and talked to her as if she was already a grown woman and one of their group.

Nomtaimet emerged from her long seclusion pale, much changed, and very beautiful. The old as well as the young exclaimed at her beauty, while the old recalled that a girl is never so beautiful as at this time when she is newly returned to the world from her long initiation. She was carefully dressed for her great day. Her new buckskin shirt was elaborately ornamented with shells and beads. In her ears were enormous polished shell earrings and about her neck many strings of beads which half covered her breasts. Her hair, washed and shining, hung in two thick braids tied with mink. She carried rattles made from deer's hooves and a slender willow staff given her by the young married women to symbolize her coming of age.

The women who were not taken up with cooking or caring for children gathered around Nomtaimet, admiring her. First one man and then another joined them until someone said, "We should dance—we are enough to make a circle dance." Holding hands and singing, they formed a moving circle around Nomtaimet, dancing the old circle dance which had been the coming of age dance for girls since the beginning of time.

Hearing the singing and the familiar rhythm of the shuffling side step of the dance, the old men and women came from their fires and their houses, and the children who were big enough to dance came with them, all of them joining the moving circle which grew bigger and bigger. The only ones not dancing were the women who were pounding acorns or stirring the food which was being cooked in large baskets in preparation for the feast. One by one even they put down their pestles and their stirring paddles and became part of the circle. They circled and sang until above the stamp of their dancing feet came the echo of distant voices and the silken sound of arrows flying swiftly overhead. The dancing stopped while the people from the neighboring villages appeared from behind the hills, running, shouting, and singing, the young men among them releasing arrows to whir, level, over the heads of the dancers.

In this way the guests came to the village, and there were greetings and talking and laughing until Nomtaimet's father invited them all to eat.

It was a great feast. For ten days and ten nights they ate and sang and danced. At last the feasting was over. The tenth night of singing and dancing came and went. But the pale dawn of the eleventh day found all those people still dancing. They kept right on dancing, all of them. They went dance mad.

In a long line, singing as they went, they danced up the trail leading out of the village to the east. Soon the last house was left behind and they were dancing among the hills they knew, the hills of home, up and over them until they could no longer see their houses. Through briars and chaparral, over rocks and rough ground, up and down hill, they danced on and on.

It is possible to retrace much of their dancing journey around the world, for it is known that they came to the Trinity River, the first of the great rivers, and that they forded this river as they forded all streams—by dancing straight across them. On the far side of the Trinity there is a flat, open and bare today as it was then, where the dancers again formed in a circle and danced the round dance. In a line once more, they danced on east through a gap in the hills to the Hayfork and across it and up the steep ridge beyond. At the top of the ridge they found a spring,

Paukaukunmen. Here they stopped to rest and drink from the spring. You can still see the large basins in the rocks where they sat. This was their first resting place.

From Paukaukunmen, they danced down the other side of the ridge. They might have become faint from hunger, except that they learned to gather berries and to catch small animals without breaking the rhythm of their dance, crossing ridge after ridge, fording small streams, and so finding themselves at last on the banks of Middle River, the McCloud. Here they made their second resting place.

By this time their moccasins were cut to pieces and nothing much but belts and a few maple bark and buckskin shreds of aprons remained of their clothes. They did not try to replace their worn-out clothing; instead they filled their pouches with clays and dyes for face and body paint, and for the rest of their dancing trip they wore no clothes at all, keeping their faces and bodies freshly painted.

The dancers were far, far from home now, farther than any of them had ever been, in country they knew only from the tales told them by the old ones. The old ones themselves knew only so much as was learned from an occasional meeting with strangers who had, rarely and at some earlier time, wandered west as far as Swift Creek—strangers who spoke in the same tongue and observed the same way of life, but who nonetheless lived far from the center of the world and close to the border-land of peoples of other ways and tongues. The dancers found the Middle River Country much as they had been told it was, that is to say, a rich country of many people and many deer, of bushes loaded with hazelnuts and berries of many sorts. There was an abundance for all, and they hunted and gathered and ate there by the river, growing fat and sleek while they made friends with the people of the Middle River. One of the things they learned from their new friends was to catch and cook salmon—something which, strange as it seems now, they had not known about.

With this fresh salmon diet they felt new strength and new power, and they set off dancing again. They were no longer interested in hunting and gathering; they wished only to dance and dance, and then to fish and cook and eat more salmon. So now they danced close beside one stream or another, wherever the salmon were best, learning the names of the many different kinds of salmon, their size and appearance and their favorite rivers. Dancing and fishing, they went farther and farther downstream as the season drew on and the salmon swam shorter distances upstream to spawn.

Having left home in the time of winds and new clover, they had by now passed the warm moons dancing and spearing salmon. As the leaves began to dry and fall from the trees, the dancers were on the banks of the third great river, the Pitt; and dancing far, far to the south, they came where the rivers join for their trip to the sea. They were in country different from any they knew even by report from the old ones, a country whose people spoke in a tongue they did not understand. The land on both sides of the lower Sacramento River stretches as far as eye can see, marshy, swampy, full of water birds. They danced through the marshes and swamps and among the water birds until there came to them the smell of salt on the air. Leaving the marshes behind, they danced down the Sacramento where it broadens at its mouth. And they stood and watched it empty into the sea.

Wearied at last of watching, they danced again, this time on the lower rim of the earth where the river meets the sea. Keeping to the rim, they turned their backs to the river, dancing away from the Nom-ti-pom toward the north. The time of the dead leaves was past. The fog moon came and went, and it was already the time of the mud moon and of frosts. They saw all about them storms and rain and floods, but there on the lower rim of the earth there were no storms, and they continued to dance along its sometimes rocky, sometimes sandy shore.

The season of storms and cold, like the other seasons, came and went, blown away by the big winds of the awakening earth. And now the dancers turned inland, away from the sea, dancing and half blown towards home. They reached Swift Creek as the new clover was making a green mat over the earth, just as it had done when Nomtaimet first came out of her seclusion at the beginning of the dance journey.

The dancers were home, and the dance madness was no longer on them. It had lasted through all the moons and seasons and had carried them all around the world. As long as she lived, Nomtaimet told her children, as her children's children tell even today, of the feast her father made for her, and of the dance madness that came after it.

BRET HARTE

The Right Eye of the Commander

One of Mark Twain's rival taletellers was Francis Brett Harte (1836–
1902), born in Albany, New York, of English, Dutch, and Jewish
descent. His father was an impoverished schoolteacher, and the family
wandered from city to city in the eastern states.

The boy left school at thirteen to earn his living, but he had early
ransacked his father's collection of English literature (his favorite
authors were to be Irving, Dickens, and Hawthorne), and at the age of
eleven he had published a poem in a New York newspaper. His
mother, widowed in 1845, went to California in 1853 and remarried
there. Young Frank followed by way of Nicaragua, and thus entered
the region that was to be the background of his most famous writings,
published under the name of Bret Harte.

Harte drifted about, working at odd jobs, tutoring, serving as an
express messenger, and visiting the mining camps, although—frail
and delicate—he probably never wielded a pick for a living. At Arcata
he learned to set type on the town newspaper and practiced the writer's
trade, but in 1860 his condemnation in that paper of the brutal massacre
of some sixty peaceful Indians so aroused the ire of the local populace
that he was forced to leave that town and fled to San Francisco.

During the next three years more than a hundred of his poems and
sketches appeared in the Golden Era, a monthly tabloid. He was
given a sinecure in the branch mint of the United States Treasury and
became a literary leader in the city by the Golden Gate, where he
helped establish the Overland Monthly in 1868.

"The Right Eye of the Commander" evokes the earlier period of
Spanish missions along the Camino Real, the main coastal thor-
oughfare. The missions were often close to ports frequented by New

*England trading ships. Here the shrewdness of a Yankee peddler causes
dismay among the Indians of the mission when the appearance of the
"Señor Commandante" is markedly transformed.*

The year of grace 1797 passed away on the coast of California
in a southwesterly gale. The little bay of San Carlos, albeit
sheltered by the headlands of the blessed Trinity, was rough
and turbulent; its foam clung quivering to the seaward wall of
the Mission garden; the air was filled with flying sand and
spume, and as the Señor Commandante, Hermenegildo Salvatierra, looked from the deep embrasured window of the
Presidio guardroom, he felt the salt breath of the distant sea
buffet a color into his smoke-dried cheeks.

The Commander, I have said, was gazing thoughtfully from
the window of the guardroom. He may have been reviewing
the events of the year now about to pass away. But, like the
garrison at the Presidio, there was little to review; the year, like
its predecessors, had been uneventful—the days had slipped by
in a delicious monotony of simple duties, unbroken by incident
or interruption. The regularly recurring feasts and saints' days,
the half-yearly courier from San Diego, the rare transport ship
and rarer foreign vessel, were the mere details of his patriarchal
life. If there was no achievement, there was certainly no failure.
Abundant harvests and patient industry amply supplied the
wants of Presidio and Mission. Isolated from the family of
nations, the wars which shook the world concerned them not
so much as the last earthquake; the struggle that emancipated
their sister colonies on the other side of the continent to them
had no suggestiveness. In short, it was that glorious Indian
summer of California history around which so much poetical
haze still lingers—that bland, indolent autumn of Spanish rule,
so soon to be followed by the wintry storms of Mexican independence and the reviving spring of American conquest.

The Commander turned from the window and walked toward the fire that burned brightly on the deep ovenlike hearth.
A pile of copybooks, the work of the Presidio school, lay on the
table. As he turned over the leaves with a paternal interest, and
surveyed the fair round Scripture text—the first pious pot-

hooks of the pupils of San Carlos—an audible commentary fell from his lips: " 'Abimelech took her from Abraham'—ah, little one, excellent!—'Jacob sent to see his brother'—body of Christ! that upstroke of thine, Paquita, is marvelous; the Governor shall see it!" A film of honest pride dimmed the Commander's left eye—the right, alas! twenty years before had been sealed by an Indian arrow. He rubbed it softly with the sleeve of his leather jacket, and continued: " 'The Ishmaelites having arrived—' "

He stopped, for there was a step in the courtyard, a foot upon the threshold, and a stranger entered. With the instinct of an old soldier, the Commander, after one glance at the intruder, turned quickly toward the wall, where his trusty Toledo hung, or should have been hanging. But it was not there, and as he recalled that the last time he had seen that weapon it was being ridden up and down the gallery by Pepito, the infant son of Bautista, the tortilla-maker, he blushed and then contented himself with frowning upon the intruder.

But the stranger's air, though irreverent, was decidedly peaceful. He was unarmed, and wore the ordinary cape of tarpaulin and sea boots of a mariner. Except a villainous smell of codfish, there was little about him that was peculiar.

His name, as he informed the Commander, in Spanish that was more fluent than elegant or precise—his name was Peleg Scudder. He was master of the schooner *General Court,* of the port of Salem in Massachusetts, on a trading voyage to the South Seas, but now driven by stress of weather into the bay of San Carlos. He begged permission to ride out the gale under the headlands of the blessed Trinity, and no more. Water he did not need, having taken in a supply at Bodega. He knew the strict surveillance of the Spanish port regulations in regard to foreign vessels, and would do nothing against the severe discipline and good order of the settlement. There was a slight tinge of sarcasm in his tone as he glanced toward the desolate parade ground of the Presidio and the open unguarded gate. The fact was that the sentry, Felipe Gomez, had discreetly retired to shelter at the beginning of the storm, and was then sound asleep in the corridor.

The Commander hesitated. The port regulations were severe, but he was accustomed to exercise individual authority, and beyond an old order issued ten years before, regarding the American ship *Columbia,* there was no precedent to guide him. The storm was severe, and a sentiment of humanity urged him to grant the stranger's request. It is but just to the Commander to say that his inability to enforce a refusal did not weigh with his decision. He would have denied with equal disregard of consequences that right to a seventy-four-gun ship which he now yielded so gracefully to this Yankee trading schooner. He stipulated only that there should be no communication between the ship and shore. "For yourself, Señor Captain," he continued, "accept my hospitality. The fort is yours as long as you shall grace it with your distinguished presence"; and with old-fashioned courtesy, he made the semblance of withdrawing from the guardroom.

Master Peleg Scudder smiled as he thought of the half-dismantled fort, the two moldy brass cannon, cast in Manila a century previous, and the shiftless garrison. A wild thought of accepting the Commander's offer literally, conceived in the reckless spirit of a man who never let slip an offer for trade, for a moment filled his brain, but a timely reflection of the commercial unimportance of the transaction checked him. He only took a capacious quid of tobacco as the Commander gravely drew a settle before the fire, and in honor of his guest untied the black-silk handkerchief that bound his grizzled brows.

What passed between Salvatierra and his guest that night it becomes me not, as a grave chronicler of the salient points of history, to relate. I have said that Master Peleg Scudder was a fluent talker, and under the influence of divers strong waters, furnished by his host, he became still more loquacious. And think of a man with a twenty years' budget of gossip! The Commander learned, for the first time, how Great Britain lost her colonies; of the French Revolution; of the great Napoleon, whose achievements, perhaps, Peleg colored more highly than the Commander's superiors would have liked. And when Peleg turned questioner, the Commander was at his mercy. He gradually made himself master of the gossip of the Mission and Presidio, the "small-beer" chronicles of that pastoral age, the conversion of the heathen, the Presidio schools, and even asked the Commander how he had lost his eye! It is said that at this point of the conversation Master Peleg produced from about his person divers small trinkets, kickshaws, and newfangled trifles, and even forced some of them upon his host. It is further alleged that under the malign influence of Peleg and several glasses of aguardiente, the Commander lost somewhat of his decorum, and behaved in a manner unseemly for one in his position, reciting high-flown Spanish poetry, and even piping in a thin, high voice divers madrigals and heathen canzonets of an amorous complexion; chiefly in regard to a "little one" who was his, the Commander's, "soul"! These allegations, perhaps unworthy the notice of a serious chronicler, should be received with great caution, and are introduced here as simple hearsay. That the Commander, however, took a handkerchief and attempted to show his guest the mysteries of the *semicuacua,* capering in an agile but indecorous manner about the apartment, has been denied. Enough for the purposes of this narrative that at midnight Peleg assisted his host to bed with many protestations of undying friendship, and then, as the gale had abated, took his leave of the Presidio and hurried aboard the *General Court.* When the day broke the ship was gone.

I know not if Peleg kept his word with his host. It is said that the holy fathers at the Mission that night heard a loud chanting in the plaza, as of the heathens singing psalms through their noses; that for many days after an odor of salt codfish prevailed in the settlement; that a dozen hard nutmegs, which were unfit for spice or seed, were found in the possession of the wife of the baker, and that several bushels of shoe pegs, which bore a pleasing resemblance to oats, but were quite inadequate to the purposes of provender, were discovered in the stable of the blacksmith. But when the reader reflects upon the sacredness of a Yankee trader's word, the stringent discipline of the Spanish port regulations, and the proverbial indisposition of my countrymen to impose upon the confidence of a simple people, he will at once reject this part of the story.

A roll of drums, ushering in the year 1798, awoke the Commander. The sun was shining brightly, and the storm had ceased. He sat up in bed, and through the force of habit rubbed his left eye. As the remembrance of the previous night came back to him, he jumped from his couch and ran to the window. There was no ship in the bay. A sudden thought seemed to strike him, and he rubbed both of his eyes. Not content with this, he consulted the metallic mirror which hung beside his crucifix. There was no mistake; the Commander had a visible second eye—a right one—as good, save for the purposes of vision, as the left.

Whatever might have been the true secret of this transformation, but one opinion prevailed at San Carlos. It was one of those rare miracles vouchsafed a pious Catholic community as an evidence to the heathen, through the intercession of the blessed San Carlos himself. That their beloved Commander, the temporal defender of the Faith, should be the recipient of this miraculous manifestation was most fit and seemly. The Commander himself was reticent; he could not tell a falsehood—he dared not tell the truth. After all, if the good folk of San Carlos believed that the powers of his right eye were actually restored, was it wise and discreet for him to undeceive them? For the first time in his life the Commander thought of policy—for the first time he quoted that text which has been the lure of so many well-meaning but easy Christians, of being "all things to all men." Infeliz Hermenegildo Salvatierra!

For by degrees an ominous whisper crept through the little settlement. The Right Eye of the Commander, although miraculous, seemed to exercise a baleful effect upon the beholder. No one could look at it without winking. It was cold, hard, relentless, and unflinching. More than that, it seemed to be endowed with a dreadful prescience—a faculty of seeing through and into the inarticulate thoughts of those it looked upon. The soldiers of the garrison obeyed the eye rather than the voice of their commander, and answered his glance rather than his lips in questioning. The servants could not evade the ever watchful but cold attention that seemed to pursue them. The children of the Presidio school smirched their copybooks under the awful supervision, and poor Paquita, the prize pupil, failed utterly in that marvelous upstroke when her patron stood beside her. Gradually distrust, suspicion, self-accusation, and timidity took the place of trust, confidence, and security throughout

San Carlos. Whenever the Right Eye of the Commander fell, a shadow fell with it.

Nor was Salvatierra entirely free from the baleful influence of his miraculous acquisition. Unconscious of its effect upon others, he only saw in their actions evidence of certain things that the crafty Peleg had hinted on that eventful New Year's eve. His most trusty retainers stammered, blushed, and faltered before him. Self-accusations, confessions of minor faults and delinquencies, or extravagant excuses and apologies met his mildest inquiries. The very children that he loved—his pet pupil, Paquita—seemed to be conscious of some hidden sin. The result of this constant irritation showed itself more plainly. For the first half-year the Commander's voice and eye were at variance. He was still kind, tender, and thoughtful in speech. Gradually, however, his voice took upon itself the hardness of his glance and its skeptical, impassive quality, and as the year again neared its close it was plain that the Commander had fitted himself to the eye, and not the eye to the Commander.

It may be surmised that these changes did not escape the watchful solicitude of the Fathers. Indeed, the few who were first to ascribe the right eye of Salvatierra to miraculous origin and the special grace of the blessed San Carlos, now talked openly of witchcraft and the agency of Luzbel, the evil one. It would have fared ill with Hermenegildo Salvatierra had he been aught but Commander or amenable to local authority. But the reverend father, Friar Manuel de Cortes, had no power over the political executive, and all attempts at spiritual advice failed signally. He retired baffled and confused from his first interview with the Commander, who seemed now to take a grim satisfaction in the fateful power of his glance. The holy Father contradicted himself, exposed the fallacies of his own arguments, and even, it is asserted, committed himself to several undoubted heresies. When the Commander stood up at mass, if the officiating priest caught that skeptical and searching eye, the service was inevitably ruined. Even the power of the Holy Church seemed to be lost, and the last hold upon the affections of the people and the good order of the settlement departed from San Carlos.

As the long dry summer passed, the low hills that surrounded the white walls of the Presidio grew more and more to resemble in hue the leathern jacket of the Commander, and Nature herself seemed to have borrowed his dry, hard glare. The earth was cracked and seamed with drought; a blight had fallen upon the orchards and vineyards, and the rain, long-delayed and ardently prayed for, came not. The sky was as tear-less as the right eye of the Commander. Murmurs of discon-tent, insubordination, and plotting among the Indians reached his ears; he only set his teeth the more firmly, tightened the knot of his black-silk handkerchief, and looked up his Toledo.

The last day of the year 1798 found the Commander sitting, at the hour of evening prayers, alone in the guardroom. He no longer attended the services of the Holy Church, but crept away at such times to some solitary spot, where he spent the interval in silent meditation. The firelight played upon the low beams and rafters, but left the bowed figure of Salvatierra in darkness. Sitting thus, he felt a small hand touch his arm, and looking down, saw the figure of Paquita, his little Indian pupil, at his knee. "Ah, littlest of all," said the Commander, with something of his old tenderness, lingering over the endearing diminutives of his native speech—"sweet one, what doest thou here? Art thou not afraid of him whom everyone shuns and fears?"

"No," said the little Indian, readily, "not in the dark. I hear your voice—the old voice; I feel your touch—the old touch; but I see not your eye, Señor Commandante. That only I fear—and that, O señor, O my father," said the child, lifting her little arms towards his—"that I know is not thine own!"

The Commander shuddered and turned away. Then, re-covering himself, he kissed Paquita gravely on the forehead and bade her retire. A few hours later, when silence had fallen upon the Presidio, he sought his own couch and slept peacefully.

At about the middle watch of the night a dusky figure crept through the low embrasure of the Commander's apartment. Other figures were flitting through the parade ground, which the Commander might have seen had he not slept so quietly. The intruder stepped noiselessly to the couch and listened to the sleeper's deep-drawn inspiration. Something glittered in the firelight as the savage lifted his arm; another moment and the sore perplexities of Hermenegildo Salvatierra would have been over, when suddenly the savage started and fell back in a paroxysm of terror. The Commander slept peacefully, but his right eye, widely opened, fixed and unaltered, glared coldly on the would-be assassin. The man fell to the earth in a fit, and the noise awoke the sleeper.

To rise to his feet, grasp his sword, and deal blows thick and fast upon the mutinous savages who now thronged the room was the work of a moment. Help opportunely arrived, and the undisciplined Indians were speedily driven beyond the walls, but in the scuffle the Commander received a blow upon his right eye, and, lifting his hand to that mysterious organ, it was gone. Never again was it found, and never again, for bale or bliss, did it adorn the right orbit of the Commander.

With it passed away the spell that had fallen upon San Carlos. The rain returned to invigorate the languid soil, harmony was restored between priest and soldier, the green grass presently waved over the sere hillsides, the children flocked again to the side of their martial preceptor, a *Te Deum* was sung in the Mission Church, and pastoral content once more smiled upon the gentle valleys of San Carlos. And far southward crept the *General Court* with its master, Peleg Scudder, trafficking in beads and peltries with the Indians, and offering glass eyes, wooden legs, and other Boston notions to the chiefs.

GERTRUDE ATHERTON

The Vengeance of Padre Arroyo

Gertrude Horn Atherton (1857–1948) was the author of some of the best stories about the decade when the placid, colorful life of the Hispanic Californios was overturned by the invasion of gold seekers.

Born on Rincon Hill in San Francisco, she was the daughter of quarrelsome, spoiled parents, and was reared in luxury. She married a wealthy older man, George Atherton, who died at sea and left her a lovely blonde widow with a bent toward writing. Her first novel, published when she was twenty-five, appeared anonymously. The shocking secret of her authorship was soon out, and Atherton was launched on a career that was touched with scandal: even a novel published when she was in her mid-sixties, Black Oxen, a tale about treatment by glandular therapy for rejuvenation, was widely denounced and as widely read. Her most enduring work is The Conqueror (1902), a biographical novel based on the life of Alexander Hamilton.

Living in England at a time in the late 1880s when she was not writing, Atherton read a comment on the lack of fiction about the Spanish period of California. She hurried back to her native state and carefully prepared herself to present the era of caballeros and rancheros, bullfights and horse races, mission friars, fiestas, and beauteous señoritas. At her death sixty years later she was the gracious dean of California's writers.

When her volume of stories Before the Gringo Came (1894) was to be reissued in 1902 in enlarged format, she read the question of one of her critics: "Why doesn't Mrs. Atherton give us more stories of the splendid idle forties . . . ?" She immediately wrote to her publisher, "Change book's title to The Splendid Idle Forties." Thus was

*named the best collection of her short stories, most of which can still be
read with full enjoyment. Among them is this happy tale of mission
life, "The Vengeance of Padre Arroyo."*

I

Pilar, from her little window just above the high wall surrounding the big adobe house set apart for the women
neophytes of the Mission of Santa Ines, watched, morning and
evening, for Andreo, as he came and went from the rancheria.
The old women kept the girls busy, spinning, weaving, sew-
ing; but age nods and youth is crafty. The tall young Indian
who was renowned as the best huntsman of all the neophytes,
and who supplied Padre Arroyo's table with deer and quail,
never failed to keep his ardent eyes fixed upon the grating so
long as it lay within the line of his vision. One day he went to
Padre Arroyo and told him that Pilar was the prettiest girl
behind the wall—the prettiest girl in all the Californias—and
that she should be his wife. But the kind stern old padre shook
his head.

"You are both too young. Wait another year, my son, and if
thou art still in the same mind, thou shalt have her."

Andreo dared to make no protest, but he asked permission to
prepare a home for his bride. The padre gave it willingly, and
the young Indian began to make the big adobes, the bright red
tiles. At the end of a month he had built him a cabin among the
willows of the rancheria, a little apart from the others: he was in
love, and association with his fellows was distasteful. When the
cabin was builded his impatience slipped from its curb, and
once more he besought the priest to allow him to marry.

Padre Arroyo was sunning himself on the corridor of the
mission, shivering in his heavy brown robes, for the day was
cold.

"Orion," he said sternly—he called all his neophytes after the
celebrities of earlier days, regardless of the names given them at
the font—"have I not told thee thou must wait a year? Do not
be impatient, my son. She will keep. Women are like apples:
when they are too young, they set the teeth on edge; when ripe

and mellow, they please every sense; when they wither and turn brown, it is time to fall from the tree into a hole. Now go and shoot a deer for Sunday: the good padres from San Luis Obispo and Santa Barbara are coming to dine with me."

Andreo, dejected, left the padre. As he passed Pilar's window and saw a pair of wistful black eyes behind the grating, his heart took fire. No one was within sight. By a series of signs he made his lady understand that he would place a note beneath a certain adobe in the wall.

Pilar, as she went to and fro under the fruit trees in the garden, or sat on the long corridor weaving baskets, watched that adobe with fascinated eyes. She knew that Andreo was tunnelling it, and one day a tiny hole proclaimed that his work was accomplished. But how to get the note? The old women's eyes were very sharp when the girls were in front of the gratings. Then the civilizing development of Christianity upon the heathen intellect triumphantly asserted itself. Pilar, too, conceived a brilliant scheme. That night the padre, who encouraged any evidence of industry, no matter how eccentric, gave her a little garden of her own—a patch where she could raise sweet peas and Castilian roses.

"That is well, that is well, my Nausicaa," he said, stroking her smoky braids. "Go cut the slips and plant them where thou wilt. I will send thee a package of sweet pea seeds."

Pilar spent every spare hour bending over her "patch"; and the hole, at first no bigger than a pin's point, was larger at each setting of the sun behind the mountain. The old women, scolding on the corridor, called to her not to forget vespers.

On the third evening, kneeling on the damp ground, she drew from the little tunnel in the adobe a thin slip of wood covered with the labour of sleepless nights. She hid it in her smock—that first of California's love-letters—then ran with shaking knees and prostrated herself before the altar. That night the moon streamed through her grating, and she deciphered the fact that Andreo had loosened eight adobes above her garden, and would await her every midnight.

Pilar sat up in bed and glanced about the room with terrified delight. It took her but a moment to decide the question; love had kept her awake too many nights. The neophytes were asleep; as they turned now and again, their narrow beds of hide, suspended from the ceiling, swung too gently to awaken them. The old women snored loudly. Pilar slipped from her bed and looked through the grating. Andreo was there, the dignity and repose of primeval man in his bearing. She waved her hand and pointed downward to the wall; then, throwing on the long coarse gray smock that was her only garment, crept from the room and down the stair. The door was protected against hostile tribes by a heavy iron bar, but Pilar's small hands were hard and strong, and in a moment she stood over the adobes which had crushed her roses and sweet peas.

As she crawled through the opening, Andreo took her hand bashfully, for they never had spoken. "Come," he said; "we must be far away before dawn."

They stole past the long mission, crossing themselves as they glanced askance at the ghostly row of pillars; past the guard-house, where the sentries slept at their post; past the rancheria; then, springing upon a waiting mustang, dashed down the valley. Pilar had never been on a horse before, and she clung in terror to Andreo, who bestrode the unsaddled beast as easily as a cloud rides the wind. His arm held her closely, fear vanished, and she enjoyed the novel sensation. Glancing over Andreo's shoulder she watched the mass of brown and white buildings, the winding river, fade into the mountain. Then they began to ascend an almost perpendicular steep. The horse followed a narrow trail; the crowding trees and shrubs clutched the blankets and smocks of the riders; after a time trail and scene grew white: the snow lay on the heights.

"Where do we go?" she asked.

"To Zaca Lake, on the very top of the mountain, miles above us. No one has ever been there but myself. Often I have shot deer and birds beside it. They never will find us there."

The red sun rose over the mountains of the east. The crystal moon sank in the west. Andreo sprang from the weary mustang and carried Pilar to the lake.

A sheet of water, round as a whirlpool but calm and silver, lay amidst the sweeping willows and pine-forested peaks. The snow glittered beneath the trees, but a canoe was on the lake, a hut on the marge.

II

Padre Arroyo tramped up and down the corridor, smiting his hands together. The Indians bowed lower than usual, as they passed, and hastened their steps. The soldiers scoured the country for the bold violators of mission law. No one asked Padre Arroyo what he would do with the sinners, but all knew that punishment would be sharp and summary: the men hoped that Andreo's mustang had carried him beyond its reach; the girls, horrified as they were, wept and prayed in secret for Pilar.

A week later, in the early morning, Padre Arroyo sat on the corridor. The mission stood on a plateau overlooking a long valley forked and sparkled by the broad river. The valley was planted thick with olive trees, and their silver leaves glittered in the rising sun. The mountain peaks about and beyond were white with snow, but the great red poppies blossomed at their feet. The padre, exiled from the luxury and society of his dear Spain, never tired of the prospect: he loved his mission children, but he loved Nature more.

Suddenly he leaned forward on his staff and lifted the heavy brown hood of his habit from his ear. Down the road winding from the eastern mountains came the echo of galloping footfalls. He rose expectantly and waddled out upon the plaza, shading his eyes with his hand. A half-dozen soldiers, riding closely about a horse bestridden by a stalwart young Indian supporting a woman, were rapidly approaching the mission. The padre returned to his seat and awaited their coming.

The soldiers escorted the culprits to the corridor; two held the horse while they descended, then led it away, and Andreo and Pilar were alone with the priest. The bridegroom placed his arm about the bride and looked defiantly at Padre Arroyo, but Pilar drew her long hair about her face and locked her hands together.

Padre Arroyo folded his arms and regarded them with lowered brows, a sneer on his mouth.

"I have new names for you both," he said, in his thickest voice. "Antony, I hope thou hast enjoyed thy honeymoon. Cleopatra, I hope thy little toes did not get frost-bitten. You both look as if food had been scarce. And your garments have gone in good part to clothe the brambles, I infer. It is too bad you could not wait a year and love in your cabin at the rancheria, by a good fire, and with plenty of frijoles and tortillas in your stomachs." He dropped his sarcastic tone, and, rising to his feet, extended his right arm with a gesture of malediction. "Do you comprehend the enormity of your sin?" he shouted. "Have you not learned on your knees that the fires of hell are the rewards of unlawful love? Do you not know that even the year of sackcloth and ashes I shall impose here on earth will not save you from those flames a million times hotter than the mountain fire, than the roaring pits in which evil Indians torture one another? A hundred years of their scorching breath, of roasting flesh, for a week of love! Oh, God of my soul!"

Andreo looked somewhat staggered, but unrepentant. Pilar burst into loud sobs of terror.

The padre stared long and gloomily at the flags of the corridor. Then he raised his head and looked sadly at his lost sheep.

"My children," he said solemnly, "my heart is wrung for you. You have broken the laws of God and of the Holy Catholic Church, and the punishments thereof are awful. Can I do anything for you, excepting to pray? You shall have my prayers, my children. But that is not enough; I cannot—ay! I cannot endure the thought that you shall be damned. Perhaps"—again he stared meditatively at the stones, then, after an impressive silence, raised his eyes. "Heaven vouchsafes me an idea, my children. I will make your punishment here so bitter that Almighty God in His mercy will give you but a few years of purgatory after death. Come with me."

He turned and led the way slowly to the rear of the mission buildings. Andreo shuddered for the first time, and tightened his arm about Pilar's shaking body. He knew that they were to be locked in the dungeons. Pilar, almost fainting, shrank back as they reached the narrow spiral stair which led downward to the cells. "Ay! I shall die, my Andreo!" she cried. "Ay! my father, have mercy!"

"I cannot, my children," said the padre, sadly. "It is for the salvation of your souls."

"Mother of God! When shall I see thee again, my Pilar?" whispered Andreo. "But, ay! the memory of that week on the mountain will keep us both alive."

Padre Arroyo descended the stair and awaited them at its foot. Separating them, and taking each by the hand, he pushed Andreo ahead and dragged Pilar down the narrow passage. At its end he took a great bunch of keys from his pocket, and raising both hands commanded them to kneel. He said a long prayer in a loud monotonous voice which echoed and reëchoed down the dark hall and made Pilar shriek with terror. Then he fairly hurled the marriage ceremony at them, and made the couple repeat after him the responses. When it was over, "Arise," he said.

The poor things stumbled to their feet, and Andreo caught Pilar in a last embrace.

"Now bear your incarceration with fortitude, my children; and if you do not beat the air with your groans, I will let you out in a week. Do not hate your old father, for love alone makes him severe, but pray, pray, pray."

And then he locked them both in the same cell.

MARK TWAIN

The Celebrated Jumping Frog of Calaveras County

More than a century and a half after the birth of America's greatest storyteller, Samuel Langhorne Clemens (1835–1910), better known as Mark Twain, every American knows something of his life. The lad's boyhood, much like that of his own Tom Sawyer and Huckleberry Finn, was spent in Hannibal, Missouri, on the Mississippi River. When his father died, Sam was apprenticed to his elder brother Orion, who ran a country newspaper. After wandering about the eastern states as a journeyman printer, he mastered the glamorous vocation of Mississippi steamboat pilot.

In 1861, following an interlude of aimless soldiering, he joined his brother, who was secretary to the governor of Nevada Territory. Tiring of a fling at prospecting, Sam became a reporter on the Virginia City Enterprise. He went on to practice his trade in San Francisco, where he wrote his "Jumping Frog" story. It was widely reprinted and made him a national figure. After a roving assignment in the Hawaiian Islands, he went to New York and joined the steamship cruise to the Holy Land that resulted in his first important book, The Innocents Abroad *(1869). The remainder of his life is literary history.*

"The Celebrated Jumping Frog of Calaveras County," a classic example of the straight-faced frontier tall tale, first appeared in the New York Saturday Press on November 18, 1865. A jumping contest for frogs is now an annual event in Calaveras County. Another example of frontier humor, almost equally celebrated, is "Jim Baker's Blue-Jay Yarn," which was collected in A Tramp Abroad *(1880). It appears to discuss the habits of California birds, but readers will discover parallels between them and insatiable human dollar-gatherers.*

In compliance with the request of a friend of mine, who wrote me from the East, I called on good-natured, garrulous old Simon Wheeler, and inquired after my friend's friend, *Leonidas* W. Smiley, as requested to do, and I hereunto append the result. I have a lurking suspicion that *Leonidas* W. Smiley is a myth; that my friend never knew such a personage; and that he only conjectured that, if I asked old Wheeler about him, it would remind him of his infamous *Jim* Smiley, and he would go to work and bore me nearly to death with some infernal reminiscence of him as long and tedious as it should be useless to me. If that was the design, it certainly succeeded.

I found Simon Wheeler dozing comfortably by the barroom stove of the old, dilapidated tavern in the ancient mining camp of Angel's, and I noticed that he was fat and baldheaded, and had an expression of winning gentleness and simplicity upon his tranquil countenance. He roused up and gave me good-day. I told him a friend of mine had commissioned me to make some inquiries about a cherished companion of his boyhood named *Leonidas* W. Smiley—*Rev. Leonidas* W. Smiley—a young minister of the Gospel, who he had heard was at one time a resident of Angel's Camp. I added that, if Mr. Wheeler could tell me anything about this Rev. Leonidas W. Smiley, I would feel under many obligations to him.

Simon Wheeler backed me into a corner and blockaded me there with his chair, and then sat me down and reeled off the monotonous narrative which follows this paragraph. He never smiled, he never frowned, he never changed his voice from the gentle-flowing key to which he tuned the initial sentence, he never betrayed the slightest suspicion of enthusiasm; but all through the interminable narrative there ran a vein of impressive earnestness and sincerity, which showed me plainly that, so far from his imagining that there was anything ridiculous or funny about his story, he regarded it as a really important matter, and admitted its two heroes as men of transcendent genius in *finesse*. To me, the spectacle of a man drifting serenely along through such a queer yarn without ever smiling was exquisitely absurd. As I said before, I asked him to tell me what he knew of Rev. Leonidas W. Smiley, and he replied as follows. I let him go on in his own way, and never interrupted him once:

There was a feller here once by the name of *Jim* Smiley, in the winter of '49—or maybe it was the spring of '50—I don't recollect exactly, somehow, though what makes me think it was one or the other is because I remember the big flume wasn't finished when he first came to the camp; but anyway, he was the curiousest man about always betting on anything that turned up you ever see, if he could get anybody to bet on the other side; and if he couldn't, he'd change sides. Any way what suited the other man would suit him—any way just so's he got a bet, *he* was satisfied. But still he was lucky, uncommon lucky—he most always come out winner. He was always ready and laying for a chance; there couldn't be no solit'ry thing mentioned but that feller'd offer to bet on it, and take any side you please, as I was just telling you. If there was a horserace, you'd find him flush, or you'd find him busted at the end of it; if there was a dog-fight, he'd bet on it; if there was a cat-fight, he'd bet on it; if there was a chicken-fight, he'd bet on it; why, if there was two birds setting on a fence, he would bet you which one would fly first; or if there was a camp meeting, he would be there reg'lar, to bet on Parson Walker, which he judged to be the best exhorter about here, and so he was, too, and a good man. If he even seen a straddle-bug start to go anywheres, he would bet you how long it would take him to get wherever he was going to, and if you took him up, he would foller that straddle-bug to Mexico but what he would find out where he was bound for and how long he was on the road. Lots of the boys here has seen that Smiley, and can tell you about him. Why, it never made no difference to *him*—he would bet on *any*thing—the dangdest feller. Parson Walker's wife laid very sick once, for a good while, and it seemed as if they warn't going to save her; but one morning he came in, and Smiley asked how she was, and he said she was considerable better— thank the Lord for his inf'nit mercy—and coming on so smart that, with the blessing of Prov'dence, she'd get well yet; and Smiley, before he thought, says, "Well, I'll risk two-and-a-half that she don't, anyway."

Thish-yer Smiley had a mare—the boys called her the fifteen-minute nag, but that was only in fun, you know, because, of course, she was faster than that—and he used to win money on that horse, for all she was so slow and always had the asthma, or the distemper, or the consumption, or something of that kind. They used to give her two or three hundred yards start, and then pass her under way; but always at the fag-end of the race she'd get excited and desperate-like, and come cavorting and straddling up, and scattering her legs around limber, sometimes in the air, and sometimes out to one side amongst the fences, and kicking up m-o-r-e dust, and raising m-o-r-e racket with her coughing and sneezing and blowing her nose—and always fetch up at the stand just about a neck ahead, as near as you could cipher it down.

And he had a little small bull pup, that to look at him you'd think he wan't worth a cent but to set around and look ornery and lay for a chance to steal something. But as soon as money was up on him, he was a different dog; his under-jaw'd begin to stick out like the fo'castle of a steamboat, and his teeth would uncover, and shine savage like the furnaces. And a dog might tackle him, and bullyrag him, and bite him, and throw him over his shoulder two or three times, and Andrew Jackson— which was the name of the pup—Andrew Jackson would never let on but what *he* was satisfied, and hadn't expected nothing else—and the bets being doubled and doubled on the other side all the time, till the money was all up; and then all of a sudden he would grab that other dog jest by the j'int of his hind leg and freeze to it—not chaw, you understand, but only jest grip and hang on till they throwed up the sponge, if it was a year. Smiley always come out winner on that pup, till he harnessed a dog once that didn't have no hind legs, because they'd been sawed off by a circular saw, and when the thing had gone along far enough, and the money was all up, and he come to make a snatch for his pet holt, he saw in a minute how he'd been imposed on, and how the other dog had him in the door, so to speak, and he 'peared surprised, and then he looked sorter discouraged-like, and didn't try no more to win the fight, and so he got shucked out bad. He give Smiley a look, as much to say his heart was broke and it was *his* fault for putting up a dog that hadn't no hind legs for him to take holt of, which was his main dependence in a fight, and then he limped off a piece and laid down and died. It was a good pup, was that Andrew

Jackson, and would have made a name for hisself if he'd lived, for the stuff was in him, and he had genius—I know it, because he hadn't no opportunities to speak of, and it don't stand to reason that a dog could make such a fight as he could under them circumstances, if he hadn't no talent. It always makes me feel sorry when I think of that last fight of his'n, and the way it turned out.

Well, thish-yer Smiley had rat-tarriers, and chicken-cocks, and tomcats, and all them kind of things, till you couldn't rest, and you couldn't fetch nothing for him to bet on but he'd match you. He ketched a frog one day, and took him home, and said he cal'klated to edercate him; and so he never done nothing for these three months but set in his back yard and learn that frog to jump. And you bet you he *did* learn him, too. He'd give him a little punch behind, and the next minute you'd see that frog whirling in the air like a doughnut—see him turn one summerset, or maybe a couple, if he got a good start, and come down flat-footed and all right, like a cat. He got him up so in the matter of catching flies, and kept him in practice so con- stant, that he'd nail a fly every time as far as he could see him. Smiley said all a frog wanted was education, and he could do most anything—and I believe him. Why, I've seen him set Dan'l Webster down here on this floor—Dan'l Webster was the name of the frog—and sing out, "Flies, Dan'l, flies!" and quicker'n you could wink, he'd spring straight up, and snake a fly off'n the counter there, and flop down on the floor again as solid as a gob of mud, and fall to scratching the side of his head with his hind foot as indifferent as if he hadn't no idea he'd been doin' any more'n any frog might do. You never see a frog so modest and straightfor'ard as he was, for all he was so gifted. And when it come to fair and square jumping on the dead level, he could get over more ground at one straddle than any animal of his breed you ever see. Jumping on a dead level was his strong suit, you understand; and when it come to that, Smiley would ante up money on him as long as he had a red. Smiley was monstrous proud of his frog, and well he might be, for fellers that had traveled and been everywhere all said he laid over any frog that ever *they* see.

Well, Smiley kept the beast in a little lattice box, and he used to fetch him downtown sometimes and lay for a bet. One day a feller—a stranger in the camp, he was—come across him with his box, and says:

"What might it be that you've got in the box?"

And Smiley says, sorter indifferent like, "It might be a parrot, or it might be a canary, maybe, but it ain't—it's only just a frog."

An' the feller took it, and looked at it careful, and turned it round this way and that, and says, "H'm—so 'tis. Well, what's *he* good for?"

"Well," Smiley says, easy and careless, "he's good enough for *one* thing, I should judge—he can outjump ary frog in Calaveras county."

The feller took the box again, and took another long, particular look, and give it back to Smiley, and says, very deliberate, "Well, I don't see no p'ints about that frog that's any better'n any other frog."

"Maybe you don't," Smiley says. "Maybe you understand frogs, and maybe you don't understand 'em; maybe you've had experience, and maybe you ain't only a amature, as it were. Anyways, I've got *my* opinion, and I'll risk forty dollars that he can outjump any frog in Calaveras county."

And the feller studied a minute, and then says, kinder sad like, "Well, I'm only a stranger here, and I ain't got no frog; but if I had a frog, I'd bet you."

And then Smiley says, "That's all right—that's all right—if you'll hold my box a minute, I'll go and get you a frog." And so the feller took the box, and put up his forty dollars along with Smiley's, and set down to wait.

So he set there a good while thinking and thinking to hisself, and then he got the frog out and pried his mouth open and took a teaspoon and filled him full of quail shot—filled him pretty near up to his chin—and set him on the floor. Smiley he went to the swamp and slopped around in the mud for a long time, and finally he ketched a frog, and fetched him in, and give him to this feller, and says:

"Now, if you're ready, set him alongside of Dan'l, with his forepaws just even with Dan'l, and I'll give the word." Then he says, "One—two—three—jump!" and him and the feller touched up the frogs from behind, and the new frog hopped off, but Dan'l give a heave, and hysted up his shoulders—so—like a Frenchman, but it wasn't no use—he couldn't budge; he was planted as solid as an anvil, and he couldn't no more stir than if he was anchored out. Smiley was a good deal surprised, and he was disgusted too, but he didn't have no idea what the matter was, of course.

The feller took the money and started away; and when he was going out at the door, he sorter jerked his thumb over his shoulder—this way—at Dan'l, and says again, very deliberate, "Well, *I* don't see no p'ints about that frog that's any better'n any other frog."

Smiley he stood scratching his head and looking down at Dan'l a long time, and at last he says, "I do wonder what in the nation that frog throw'd off for—I wonder if there ain't something the matter with him—he 'pears to look mighty baggy, somehow." And he ketched Dan'l by the nap of the neck, and lifted him up and says, "Why, blame my cats, if he don't weigh five pounds!" and turned him upside down, and he belched out a double handful of shot. And then he see how it was, and he was the maddest man—he set the frog down and took out after that feller, but he never ketched him. And—

Here Simon Wheeler heard his name called from the front yard, and got up to see what was wanted. And turning to me as he moved away, he said: "Just set where you are, stranger, and rest easy—I ain't going to be gone a second."

But, by your leave, I did not think that a continuation of the history of the enterprising vagabond *Jim* Smiley would be likely to afford me much information concerning the Rev. *Leonidas* W. Smiley, and so I started away.

At the door I met the sociable Wheeler returning, and he buttonholed me and recommenced:

"Well, thish-yer Smiley had a yeller one-eyed cow that didn't have no tail, only jest a short stump like a bannanner, and—"

"Oh, hang Smiley and his afflicted cow!" I muttered, good-naturedly, and bidding the old gentleman good-day, I departed.

Jim Baker's Blue-Jay Yarn

Animals talk to each other, of course. There can be no question about that; but I suppose there are very few people who can understand them. I never knew but one man who could. I knew he could, however, because he told me so himself. He was a middle-aged, simple-hearted miner who had lived in a lonely corner of California, among the woods and mountains, a good many years, and had studied the ways of his only neighbors, the beasts and the birds, until he believed he could accurately translate any remark which they made. This was Jim Baker. According to Jim Baker, some animals have only a limited education, and use only very simple words, and scarcely ever a comparison or a flowery figure; whereas, certain other animals have a large vocabulary, a fine command of language and a ready and fluent delivery; consequently these latter talk a great deal; they like it; they are conscious of their talent, and they enjoy "showing off." Baker said, that after long and careful observation, he had come to the conclusion that the blue-jays were the best talkers he had found among birds and beasts. Said he:—

"There's more *to* a blue-jay than any other creature. He has got more moods, and more different kinds of feelings than other creatures; and mind you, whatever a blue-jay feels, he can put into language. And no mere commonplace language, either, but rattling, out-and-out book-talk—and bristling with metaphor, too—just bristling! And as for command of language—why *you* never see a blue-jay get stuck for a word. No man ever did. They just boil out of him! And another thing: I've noticed a good deal, and there's no bird, or cow, or anything that uses as good grammar as a blue-jay. You may say a cat uses good grammar. Well, a cat does—but you let a cat get excited, once; you let a cat get to pulling fur with another cat on a shed, nights, and you'll hear grammar that will give you the lockjaw. Ignorant people think it's the *noise* which fighting cats make that is so aggravating, but it ain't so; it's the sickening grammar they use. Now I've never heard a jay use bad grammar but very seldom; and when they do, they are as ashamed as a human; they shut right down and leave.

"You may call a jay a bird. Well, so he is, in a measure—because he's got feathers on him, and don't belong to no church, perhaps; but otherwise he is just as much a human as you be. And I'll tell you for why. A jay's gifts, and instincts, and feelings, and interests, cover the whole ground. A jay hasn't got any more principle than a Congressman. A jay will lie, a jay will steal, a jay will deceive, a jay will betray; and four times out of five, a jay will go back on his solemnest promise. The sacredness of an obligation is a thing which you can't cram into no blue-jay's head. Now on top of all this, there's another thing: a jay can out-swear any gentleman in the mines. You think a cat can swear. Well, a cat can; but you give a blue-jay a subject that calls for his reserve-powers, and where is your cat? Don't talk to *me*—I know too much about this thing. And there's yet another thing: in the one little particular of scolding—just good, clean, out-and-out scolding—a blue-jay can lay over anything, human or divine. Yes, sir, a jay is everything that a man is. A jay can cry, a jay can laugh, a jay can feel shame, a jay can reason and plan and discuss, a jay likes gossip and scandal, a jay has got a sense of humor, a jay knows when he is an ass just as well as you do—maybe better. If a jay ain't human, he better take in his sign, that's all. Now I'm going to tell you a perfectly true fact about some blue-jays.

"When I first begun to understand jay language correctly, there was a little incident happened here. Seven years ago, the last man in this region but me, moved away. There stands his house,—been empty ever since; a log house, with a plank roof—just one big room, and no more; no ceiling—nothing between the rafters and the floor. Well, one Sunday morning I was sitting out here in front of my cabin, with my cat, taking the sun, and looking at the blue hills, and listening to the leaves rustling so lonely in the trees, and thinking of the home away yonder in the States, that I hadn't heard from in thirteen years, when a blue-jay lit on that house, with an acorn in his mouth, and says, 'Hello, I reckon I've struck something.' When he spoke, the acorn dropped out of his mouth and rolled down the

roof, of course, but he didn't care; his mind was all on the thing
he had struck. It was a knot-hole in the roof. He cocked his
head to one side, shut one eye and put the other one to the hole,
like a 'possum looking down a jug; then he glanced up with his
bright eyes, gave a wink or two with his wings—which sig-
nifies gratification, you understand,—and says, 'It looks like a
hole, it's located like a hole,—blamed if I don't believe it *is* a
hole!'

"Then he cocked his head down and took another look; he
glances up perfectly joyful, this time; winks his wings and his
tail both, and says, 'O, no, this ain't no fat thing, I reckon! If I
ain't in luck!—why it's a perfectly elegant hole!' So he flew
down and got that acorn, and fetched it up and dropped it in,
and was just tilting his head back, with the heavenliest smile on
his face, when all of a sudden he was paralyzed into a listening
attitude and that smile faded gradually out of his countenance
like breath off'n a razor, and the queerest look of surprise took
its place. Then he says, 'Why I didn't hear it fall!' He cocked his
eye at the hole again, and took a long look; raised up and shook
his head; stepped around to the other side of the hole and took
another look from that side; shook his head again. He studied a
while, then he just went into the *details*—walked round and
round the hole and spied into it from every point of the com-
pass. No use. Now he took a thinking attitude on the comb of
the roof and scratched the back of his head with his right foot a
minute, and finally says, 'Well, it's too many for *me,* that's
certain; must be a mighty long hole; however, I ain't got no
time to fool around here, I got to 'tend to business; I reckon it's
all right—chance it, anyway.'

"So he flew off and fetched another acorn and dropped it in,
and tried to flirt his eye to the hole quick enough to see what
become of it, but he was too late. He held his eye there as much
as a minute; then he raised up and sighed, and says, 'Consound
it, I don't seem to understand this thing, no way; however, I'll
tackle her again.' He fetched another acorn, and done his level
best to see what become of it, but he couldn't. He says, 'Well, *I*
never struck no such a hole as this, before; I'm of the opinion
it's a totally new kind of a hole.' Then he begun to get mad. He
held in for a spell, walking up and down the comb of the roof

and shaking his head and muttering to himself; but his feelings got the upper hand of him, presently, and he broke loose and cussed himself black in the face. I never see a bird take on so about a little thing. When he got through he walks to the hole and looks in again for half a minute; then he says, 'Well, you're a long hole, and a deep hole, and a mighty singular hole altogether—but I've started in to fill you, and I'm d—d if I *don't* fill you, if it takes a hundred years!'

"And with that, away he went. You never see a bird work so since you was born. He laid into his work like a nigger, and the way he hove acorns into that hole for about two hours and a half was one of the most exciting and astonishing spectacles I ever struck. He never stopped to take a look any more—he just hove 'em in and went for more. Well at last he could hardly flop his wings, he was so tuckered out. He comes a-drooping down, once more, sweating like an ice-pitcher, drops his acorn in and says, '*Now* I guess I've got the bulge on you by this time.' So he bent down for a look. If you'll believe me, when his head come up again he was just pale with rage. He says, 'I've shoveled acorns enough in there to keep the family thirty years, and if I can see a sign of one of 'em I wish I may land in a museum with a belly full of sawdust in two minutes!'

"He just had strength enough to crawl up on to the comb and lean his back agin the chimbly, and then he collected his impressions and begun to free his mind. I see in a second that what I had mistook for profanity in the mines was only just the rudiments, as you may say.

"Another jay was going by, and heard him doing his devotions, and stops to inquire what was up. The sufferer told him the whole circumstance, and says, 'Now yonder's the hole, and if you don't believe me, go and look for yourself.' So this fellow went and looked, and comes back and says, 'How many did you say you put in there?' 'Not any less than two tons,' says the sufferer. The other jay went and looked again. He couldn't seem to make it out, so he raised a yell, and three more jays come. They all examined the hole, they all made the sufferer tell it over again, then they all discussed it, and got off as many leather-headed opinions about it as an average crowd of humans could have done.

"They called in more jays; then more and more, till pretty soon this whole region 'peared to have a blue flush about it. There must have been five thousand of them; and such another jawing and disputing and ripping and cussing, you never heard. Every jay in the whole lot put his eye to the hole and delivered a more chuckle-headed opinion about the mystery than the jay that went there before him. They examined the house all over, too. The door was standing half open, and at last one old jay happened to go and light on it and look in. Of course that knocked the mystery galley-west in a second. There lay the acorns, scattered all over the floor. He flopped his wings and raised a whoop. 'Come here!' he says, 'Come here, everybody; hang'd if this fool hasn't been trying to fill up a house with acorns!' They all came a-swooping down like a blue cloud, and as each fellow lit on the door and took a glance, the whole absurdity of the contract that that first jay had tackled hit him home and he fell over backwards suffocating with laughter, and the next jay took his place and done the same.

"Well, sir, they roosted around here on the house-top and the trees for an hour, and guffawed over that thing like human beings. It ain't any use to tell me a blue-jay hasn't got a sense of humor, because I know better. And memory, too. They brought jays here from all over the United States to look down that hole, every summer for three years. Other birds too. And they could all see the point, except an owl that come from Nova Scotia to visit the Yo Semite, and he took this thing in on his way back. He said he couldn't see anything funny in it. But then he was a good deal disappointed about Yo Semite, too."

BRET HARTE

The Outcasts of Poker Flat

Bret Harte's great chance came when, as first editor of the Overland
Monthly *(see above, p. 11), he decided to make the magazine a
reflection of the booming life of the Pacific slope. In the second number
(1868) he printed "The Luck of Roaring Camp," the first story in his
new local-color style. It was an immediate hit—especially in the East
and in Europe, where the California gold mines were a romantic
setting. But soon it was attacked as immoral, and Harte prudently held
back for six months the publication of "The Outcasts of Poker Flat,"
which finally appeared in the January 1869 issue.*

*His worldwide reputation as a humorist came in 1870 with the
appearance of the comic ballad "Plain Language from Truthful James"
("The Heathen Chinee"). In the same year, his first important book,*
The Luck of Roaring Camp and Other Sketches, *was published
in Boston. He made a triumphal progress to the East and was given a
generous ten-thousand-dollar contract for twelve contributions to the*
Atlantic Monthly.

*Thus he left California after seventeen years and became the literary
lion of America and Europe. He wrote steadily and slaved as a lecturer
to support the expensive tastes of his wife and children, and left the
United States in 1878, to live abroad for the rest of his life. He turned
out stories, sketches, and plays on the old formula, but the magic was
gone. Harte's best work had been done before he was thirty-five: the
invention of the dramatic Wild West story by adapting the Dickens
method to the colorful and fresh locale of the California gold camps.*

*Gamblers and prostitutes are usually lacking hearts of gold in the
western saga, but ironically, and with more than a few humorous*

sidelights, Harte transforms the sinning outcasts into something ap-
proaching sainthood.

As Mr. John Oakhurst, gambler, stepped into the main street of Poker Flat on the morning of the twenty-third of November, 1850, he was conscious of a change in its moral atmosphere since the preceding night. Two or three men, conversing earnestly together, ceased as he approached, and exchanged significant glances. There was a Sabbath lull in the air, which, in a settlement unused to Sabbath influences, looked ominous.

Mr. Oakhurst's calm, handsome face betrayed small concern of these indications. Whether he was conscious of any predisposing cause was another question. "I reckon they're after somebody," he reflected; "likely it's me." He returned to his pocket the handkerchief with which he had been whipping away the red dust of Poker Flat from his neat boots, and quietly discharged his mind of any further conjecture.

In point of fact, Poker Flat was "after somebody." It had lately suffered the loss of several thousand dollars, two valuable horses, and a prominent citizen. It was experiencing a spasm of virtuous reaction, quite as lawless and ungovernable as any of the acts that had provoked it. A secret committee had determined to rid the town of all improper persons. This was done permanently in regard to two men who were then hanging from the boughs of a sycamore in the gulch, and temporarily in the banishment of certain other objectionable characters. I regret to say that some of these were ladies. It is but due to the sex, however, to state that their impropriety was professional, and it was only in such easily established standards of evil that Poker Flat ventured to sit in judgment.

Mr. Oakhurst was right in supposing that he was included in this category. A few of the committee had urged hanging him as a possible example, and a sure method of reimbursing themselves from his pockets of the sums he had won from them. "It's agin justice," said Jim Wheeler, "to let this yer young man from Roaring Camp—an entire stranger—carry away our money." But a crude sentiment of equality residing in the breasts of those who had been fortunate enough to win from Mr. Oakhurst overruled this narrower local prejudice.

Mr. Oakhurst received his sentence with philosophic calmness, none the less coolly that he was aware of the hesitation of his judges. He was too much of a gambler not to accept Fate. With him life was at best an uncertain game, and he recognized the usual percentage in favor of the dealer.

A body of armed men accompanied the deported wickedness of Poker Flat to the outskirts of the settlement. Besides Mr. Oakhurst, who was known to be a coolly desperate man, and for whose intimidation the armed escort was intended, the expatriated party consisted of a young woman familiarly known as "The Duchess"; another, who had gained the infelicitous title of "Mother Shipton"; and "Uncle Billy," a suspected sluice-robber and confirmed drunkard. The cavalcade provoked no comments from the spectators, nor was any word uttered by the escort. Only, when the gulch which marked the uttermost limit of Poker Flat was reached, the leader spoke briefly and to the point. The exiles were forbidden to return at the peril of their lives.

As the escort disappeared, their pent-up feelings found vent in a few hysterical tears from the Duchess, some bad language from Mother Shipton, and a Parthian volley of expletives from Uncle Billy. The philosophic Oakhurst alone remained still. He listened calmly to Mother Shipton's desire to cut somebody's heart out, to the repeated statements of the Duchess that she would die on the road, and to the alarming oaths that seemed to be bumped out of Uncle Billy as he rode forward. With the easy good humor characteristic of his class, he insisted upon exchanging his own riding-horse, Five Spot, for the sorry mule which the Duchess rode. But even this act did not draw the party into any closer sympathy. The young woman readjusted her somewhat draggled plumes with a feeble, faded coquetry; Mother Shipton eyed the possessor of Five Spot with malevolence, and Uncle Billy included the whole party in one sweeping anathema.

The road to Sandy Bar—a camp that, not having as yet experienced the regenerating influences of Poker Flat, consequently seemed to offer some invitation to the emigrants—lay over a steep mountain range. It was distant a day's severe journey. In that advanced season, the party soon passed out of the moist, temperate regions of the foothills into the dry, cold bracing air of the Sierras. The trail was narrow and difficult. At noon the Duchess, rolling out of her saddle upon the ground, declared her intention of going no farther, and the party halted.

The spot was singularly wild and impressive. A wooded amphitheater, surrounded on three sides by precipitous cliffs of naked granite, sloped gently toward the crest of another precipice that overlooked the valley. It was undoubtedly the most suitable spot for a camp, had camping been advisable. But Mr. Oakhurst knew that scarcely half the journey to Sandy Bar was accomplished, and the party were not equipped or provisioned for delay. This fact he pointed out to his companions curtly, with a philosophic commentary on the folly of "throwing up their hands before the game was played out." But they were furnished with liquor, which in this emergency stood them in place of food, fuel, rest, and prescience. In spite of his remonstrances, it was not long before they were more or less under its influence. Uncle Billy passed rapidly from a bellicose state into one of stupor, the Duchess became maudlin, and Mother Shipton snored. Mr. Oakhurst alone remained erect, leaning against a rock, calmly surveying them.

Mr. Oakhurst did not drink. It interfered with a profession which required coolness, impassiveness, and presence of mind, and, in his own language, he "couldn't afford it." As he gazed at his recumbent fellow-exiles, the loneliness begotten of his pariah-trade, his habits of life, his very vices, for the first time seriously oppressed him. He bestirred himself in dusting his black clothes, washing his hands and face, and other acts characteristic of his studiously neat habits, and for a moment forgot his annoyance. The thought of deserting his weaker and more pitiable companions never perhaps occurred to him. Yet he could not help feeling the want of that excitement which, singularly enough, was most conducive to that calm equanimity for which he was notorious. He looked at the gloomy walls that rose a thousand feet sheer above the circling pines around him; at the sky, ominously clouded; at the valley below, already deepening into shadow. And, doing so, suddenly he heard his own name called.

A horseman slowly ascended the trail. In the fresh, open face of the newcomer Mr. Oakhurst recognized Tom Simson, otherwise known as "The Innocent" of Sandy Bar. He had met him some months before over a "little game," and had, with perfect equanimity, won the entire fortune—amounting to some forty dollars—of that guileless youth. After the game was finished, Mr. Oakhurst drew the youthful speculator behind the door and thus addressed him: "Tommy, you're a good little man, but you can't gamble worth a cent. Don't try it over again." He then handed him his money back, pushed him gently from the room, and so made a devoted slave of Tom Simson.

There was a remembrance of this in his boyish and enthusiastic greeting of Mr. Oakhurst. He had started, he said, to go to Poker Flat to seek his fortune. "Alone?" No, not exactly alone; in fact—a giggle—he had run away with Piney Woods. Didn't Mr. Oakhurst remember Piney? She that used to wait on the table at the Temperance House? They had been engaged a long time, but old Jake Woods had objected, and so they had run away, and were going to Poker Flat to be married, and here they were. And they were tired out, and how lucky it was they had found a place to camp and company. All this the Innocent delivered rapidly, while Piney—a stout, comely damsel of fifteen—emerged from behind the pine tree, where she had been blushing unseen, and rode to the side of her lover.

Mr. Oakhurst seldom troubled himself with sentiment, still less with propriety; but he had a vague idea that the situation was not felicitous. He retained, however, his presence of mind sufficiently to kick Uncle Billy, who was about to say something, and Uncle Billy was sober enough to recognize in Mr. Oakhurst's kick a superior power that would not bear trifling. He then endeavored to dissuade Tom Simson from delaying further, but in vain. He even pointed out the fact that there was no provision, nor means of making a camp. But, unluckily, the Innocent met this objection by assuring the party that he was provided with an extra mule loaded with provisions, and by the discovery of a rude attempt at a loghouse near the trail.

"Piney can stay with Mrs. Oakhurst," said the Innocent, pointing to the Duchess, "and I can shift for myself."

Nothing but Mr. Oakhurst's admonishing foot saved Uncle Billy from bursting into a roar of laughter. As it was, he felt compelled to retire up the canyon until he could recover his gravity. There he confided the joke to the tall pine trees, with many slaps of his leg, contortions of his face, and the usual profanity. But when he returned to the party, he found them seated by a fire—for the air had grown strangely chill and the sky overcast—in apparently amicable conversation. Piney was actually talking in an impulsive, girlish fashion to the Duchess, who was listening with an interest and animation she had not shown for many days. The Innocent was holding forth, apparently with equal effect, to Mr. Oakhurst and Mother Shipton, who was actually relaxing into amiability. "Is this yer a d—d picnic?" said Uncle Billy, with inward scorn, as he surveyed the sylvan group, the glancing firelight, and the tethered animals in the foreground. Suddenly an idea mingled with the alcoholic fumes that disturbed his brain. It was apparently of a jocular nature, for he felt impelled to slap his leg again and cram his fist into his mouth.

As the shadows crept slowly up the mountain, a slight breeze rocked the tops of the pine trees, and moaned through their long and gloomy aisles. The ruined cabin, patched and covered with pine boughs, was set apart for the ladies. As the lovers parted, they unaffectedly exchanged a kiss, so honest and sincere that it might have been heard above the swaying pines. The frail Duchess and the malevolent Mother Shipton were probably too stunned to remark upon this last evidence of simplicity, and so turned without a word to the hut. The fire was replenished, the men lay down before the door, and in a few minutes were asleep.

Mr. Oakhurst was a light sleeper. Toward morning he awoke benumbed and cold. As he stirred the dying fire, the wind, which was now blowing strongly, brought to his cheek that which caused the blood to leave it—snow!

He started to his feet with the intention of awakening the sleepers, for there was no time to lose. But turning to where Uncle Billy had been lying, he found him gone. A suspicion leaped to his brain and a curse to his lips. He ran to the spot where the mules had been tethered; they were no longer there. The tracks were already rapidly disappearing in the snow.

The momentary excitement brought Mr. Oakhurst back to the fire with his usual calm. He did not waken the sleepers. The Innocent slumbered peacefully, with a smile on his good-humored, freckled face; the virgin Piney slept beside her frailer sisters as sweetly as though attended by celestial guardians, and Mr. Oakhurst, drawing his blanket over his shoulders, stroked his mustachios and waited for the dawn. It came slowly in the whirling mist of snowflakes, that dazzled and confused the eye. What could be seen of the landscape appeared magically changed. He looked over the valley, and summed up the present and future in two words—"Snowed in!"

A careful inventory of the provisions, which, fortunately for the party, had been stored within the hut, and so escaped the felonious fingers of Uncle Billy, disclosed the fact that with care and prudence they might last ten days longer. "That is," said Mr. Oakhurst, *sotto voce* to the Innocent, "if you're willing to board us. If you ain't—and perhaps you'd better not—you can wait till Uncle Billy gets back with provisions." For some occult reason, Mr. Oakhurst could not bring himself to disclose Uncle Billy's rascality, and so offered the hypothesis that he had wandered from the camp and had accidentally stampeded the animals. He dropped a warning to the Duchess and Mother Shipton, who of course knew the facts of their associate's defection. "They'll find out the truth about us *all,* when they find out anything," he added, significantly, "and there's no good frightening them now."

Tom Simson not only put all his worldly store at the disposal of Mr. Oakhurst, but seemed to enjoy the prospect of their enforced seclusion. "We'll have a good camp for a week, and then the snow'll melt, and we'll all go back together." The cheerful gayety of the young man and Mr. Oakhurst's calm infected the others. The Innocent, with the aid of pine boughs, extemporized a thatch for the roofless cabin, and the Duchess directed Piney in the rearrangement of the interior with a taste and tact that opened the blue eyes of that provincial maiden to their fullest extent.

"I reckon now you're used to fine things at Poker Flat," said Piney. The Duchess turned away sharply to conceal something that reddened her cheek through its professional tint, and Mother Shipton requested Piney not to "chatter." But when Mr. Oakhurst returned from a weary search for the trail, he heard the sound of happy laughter echoed from the rocks. He stopped in some alarm, and his thoughts first naturally reverted to the whisky, which he had prudently *cached*. "And yet it don't somehow sound like whisky," said the gambler. It was not until he caught sight of the blazing fire through the still blinding storm, and the group around it, that he settled to the conviction that it was "square fun."

Whether Mr. Oakhurst had *cached* his cards with the whisky as something debarred the free access of the community, I cannot say. It was certain that, in Mother Shipton's words, he "didn't say cards once" during the evening. Haply the time was beguiled by an accordion produced somewhat ostentatiously by Tom Simson, from his pack. Notwithstanding some difficulties attending the manipulation of this instrument, Piney Woods managed to pluck several reluctant melodies from its keys, to an accompaniment by the Innocent on a pair of bone castinets. But the crowning festivity of the evening was reached in a rude camp-meeting hymn, which the lovers, joining hands, sang with great earnestness and vociferation. I fear that a certain defiant tone and Covenanter's swing to its chorus, rather than any devotional quality, caused it speedily to infect the others, who at last joined in the refrain:

> I'm proud to live in the service of the Lord,
> And I'm bound to die in His army.

The pines rocked, the storm eddied and whirled above the miserable group, and the flames of their altar leaped heavenward, as if in token of the vow.

At midnight the storm abated, the rolling clouds parted, and the stars glittered keenly above the sleeping camp. Mr. Oakhurst, whose professional habits had enabled him to live on the smallest possible amount of sleep, in dividing the watch with Tom Simson, somehow managed to take upon himself the greater part of that duty. He excused himself to the Innocent, by saying that he had "often been a week without sleep." "Doing what?" asked Tom. "Poker!" replied Oakhurst, sententiously. "When a man gets a streak of luck—real luck—he don't get tired. The luck gives in first. Luck," continued the gambler, reflectively, "is a mighty queer thing. All you know about it for certain is that it's bound to change. And it's finding out when it's going to change that makes you. We've had a streak of bad luck since we left Poker Flat—you come along, and slap you get into it, too. If you can hold your cards right along you're all right. For," added the gambler, with cheerful irrelevance,

> "I'm proud to live in the service of the Lord,
> And I'm bound to die in His army."

The third day came, and the sun, looking through the white-curtained valley, saw the outcasts divide their slowly decreasing store of provisions for the morning meal. It was one of the peculiarities of that mountain climate that its rays diffused a kindly warmth over the wintry landscape, as if in regretful commiseration of the past. But it revealed drift on drift of snow piled high around the hut; a hopeless, uncharted, trackless sea of white lying below the rocky shores to which the castaways still clung. Through the marvelously clear air, the smoke of the pastoral village of Poker Flat rose miles away. Mother Shipton saw it, and from a remote pinnacle of her rocky fastness, hurled in that direction a final malediction. It was her last vituperative attempt, and perhaps for that reason was invested with a certain degree of sublimity. It did her good, she privately informed the Duchess, "Just to go out there and cuss, and see." She then set herself to the task of amusing "the child," as she and the Duchess were pleased to call Piney. Piney was no chicken, but it was a soothing and ingenious theory of the pair thus to account for the fact that she didn't swear and wasn't improper.

When night crept up again through the gorges, the reedy notes of the accordion rose and fell in fitful spasms and long-drawn gasps by the flickering campfire. But music failed to fill entirely the aching void left by insufficient food, and a new diversion was proposed by Piney—storytelling. Neither Mr. Oakhurst nor his female companions caring to relate their personal experiences, this plan would have failed, too, but for the Innocent. Some months before he had chanced upon a stray copy of Mr. Pope's ingenious translation of the Iliad. He now proposed to narrate the principal incidents of that poem—having thoroughly mastered the argument and fairly forgotten the words—in the current vernacular of Sandy Bar. And so for the rest of that night the Homeric demigods again walked the earth. Trojan bully and wily Greek wrestled in the winds, and the great pines in the canyon seemed to bow to the wrath of the son of Peleus. Mr. Oakhurst listened with quiet satisfaction. Most especially was he interested in the fate of "Ash-heels," as the Innocent persisted in denominating the "swift-footed Achilles."

So with small food and much of Homer and the accordion, a week passed over the heads of the outcasts. The sun again forsook them, and again from leaden skies the snowflakes were sifted over the land. Day by day closer around them drew the snowy circle, until at last they looked from their prison over drifted walls of dazzling white, that towered twenty feet above their heads. It became more and more difficult to replenish their fires, even from the fallen trees beside them, now half-hidden in the drifts. And yet no one complained. The lovers turned from the dreary prospect and looked into each other's eyes, and were happy. Mr. Oakhurst settled himself coolly to the losing game before him. The Duchess, more cheerful than she had been, assumed the care of Piney. Only Mother Shipton—once the strongest of the party—seemed to sicken and fade. At midnight on the tenth day she called Oakhurst to her side. "I'm going," she said, in a voice of querulous weakness, "but don't say anything about it. Don't waken the kids. Take the bundle from under my head and open it." Mr. Oakhurst did so. It contained Mother Shipton's rations for the last week, untouched. "Give 'em to the child," she said, pointing to the sleeping Piney. "You've starved yourself," said the gambler. "That's what they call it," said the woman, querulously, as she lay down again, and, turning her face to the wall, passed quietly away.

The accordion and the bones were put aside that day, and Homer was forgotten. When the body of Mother Shipton had been committed to the snow, Mr. Oakhurst took the Innocent aside, and showed him a pair of snowshoes, which he had fashioned from the old packsaddle. "There's one chance in a hundred to save her yet," he said, pointing to Piney; "but it's there," he added, pointing toward Poker Flat. "If you can reach there in two days she's safe." "And you?" asked Tom Simson. "I'll stay here," was the curt reply.

The lovers parted with a long embrace. "You are not going, too?" said the Duchess, as she saw Mr. Oakhurst apparently waiting to accompany him. "As far as the canyon," he replied. He turned suddenly, and kissed the Duchess, leaving her pallid face aflame, and her trembling limbs rigid with amazement.

Night came, but not Mr. Oakhurst. It brought the storm again and the whirling snow. Then the Duchess, feeding the fire, found that some one had quietly piled beside the hut enough fuel to last a few days longer. The tears rose to her eyes, but she hid them from Piney.

The women slept but little. In the morning, looking into each other's faces, they read their fate. Neither spoke; but Piney, accepting the position of the stronger, drew near and placed her arm around the Duchess's waist. They kept this attitude for the rest of the day. That night the storm reached its greatest fury, and, rending asunder the protecting pines, invaded the very hut.

Toward morning they found themselves unable to feed the fire, which gradually died away. As the embers slowly blackened, the Duchess crept closer to Piney, and broke the silence of many hours: "Piney, can you pray?" "No, dear," said Piney, simply. The Duchess, without knowing exactly why, felt relieved, and putting her head upon Piney's shoulder, spoke no more. And so reclining, the younger and purer pillowing the head of her soiled sister upon her virgin breast, they fell asleep.

The wind lulled as if it feared to waken them. Feathery drifts of snow, shaken from the long pine boughs, flew like white-winged birds, and settled about them as they slept. The moon through the rifted clouds looked down upon what had been the camp. But all human stain, all trace of earthly travail, was hidden beneath the spotless mantle mercifully flung from above.

They slept all that day and the next, nor did they waken

when voices and footsteps broke the silence of the camp. And when pitying fingers brushed the snow from their wan faces, you could scarcely have told, from the equal peace that dwelt upon them, which was she that had sinned. Even the Law of Poker Flat recognized this, and turned away, leaving them still locked in each other's arms.

But at the head of the gulch, on one of the largest pine trees, they found the deuce of clubs pinned to the bark with a bowie knife. It bore the following, written in pencil, in a firm hand:

BENEATH THIS TREE

LIES THE BODY

OF

JOHN OAKHURST,

WHO STRUCK A STREAK OF BAD LUCK

ON THE 23D OF NOVEMBER, 1850,

AND

HANDED IN HIS CHECKS

ON THE 7TH OF DECEMBER, 1850.

And pulseless and cold, with a derringer by his side and a bullet in his heart, though still calm as in life, beneath the snow lay he who was at once the strongest and yet the weakest of the outcasts of Poker Flat.

AMBROSE BIERCE

The Secret of Macarger's Gulch

Master of the witty, cynical, and horrible, Bierce (1842–1914?) hated most of his family and most of humanity. He was born into a puritanical household in a log cabin on Horse Cave Creek in Ohio. His uncle Lucius paid for the only schooling young Ambrose had—a year at Kentucky Military Institute before that school burned down.

The outbreak of the Civil War gave Bierce a release from home. He enlisted as a drummer boy, fought bravely throughout four years, was severely wounded at Kennesaw Mountain, and emerged as a brevet major. His years in the army inspired one of his most celebrated volumes, Tales of Soldiers and Civilians (1891).

After the war, he obtained his discharge from service in San Francisco, entered journalism as a cartoonist and writer of political squibs, and by 1868 was editor of the News-Letter. His first story was published in 1871 in Bret Harte's Overland Monthly. In the same year he married and went to join the literary life of London.

He did not return to California until 1876, when he announced: "It is my intention to purify journalism in this town by instructing such writers as it is worth while to instruct, and assassinating those that it is not." For more than a decade thereafter, he was the literary dictator of the Pacific Coast, as editor of the Wasp, a satirical weekly. He befriended many a young writer, but his work became more bitter as his disillusion with life mounted. From 1897 to 1909 he was a Washington correspondent for the Hearst newspapers.

"Bitter Bierce" returned to California for the last time in 1913, on his way to Mexico to find another war. There he disappeared in 1914, probably murdered in the revolution then raging between Venustiano Carranza and Pancho Villa.

Aside from his tales of war, Bierce's short stories appear in Can
Such Things Be? *(1893), collected from the* San Francisco Examiner. *"The Secret of Macarger's Gulch," included in the 1903 revi-
sion, is an outstanding example of the "ghost story" still popular a
century later.*

Northwestwardly from Indian Hill, about nine miles as the
crow flies, is Macarger's Gulch. It is not much of a gulch—
a mere depression between two wooded ridges of inconsider-
able height. From its mouth up to its head—for gulches, like
rivers, have an anatomy of their own—the distance does not
exceed two miles, and the width at bottom is at only one place
more than a dozen yards; for most of the distance on either side
of the little brook which drains it in winter, and goes dry in the
early spring, there is no level ground at all; the steep slopes of
the hills, covered with an almost impenetrable growth of manzanita and chemisal, are parted by nothing but the width of the
water course. No one but an occasional enterprising hunter of
the vicinity ever goes into Macarger's Gulch, and five miles
away it is unknown, even by name. Within that distance in
any direction are far more conspicuous topographical features
without names, and one might try in vain to ascertain by local
inquiry the origin of the name of this one.

About midway between the head and the mouth of Macarger's Gulch, the hill on the right as you ascend is cloven by
another gulch, a short dry one, and at the junction of the two is
a level space of two or three acres, and there a few years ago
stood an old board house containing one small room. How the
component parts of the house, few and simple as they were,
had been assembled at that almost inaccessible point is a problem in the solution of which there would be greater satisfaction
than advantage. Possibly the creek bed is a reformed road. It is
certain that the gulch was at one time pretty thoroughly pros-
pected by miners, who must have had some means of getting in
with at least pack animals carrying tools and supplies; their
profits, apparently, were not such as would have justified any
considerable outlay to connect Macarger's Gulch with any center of civilization enjoying the distinction of a sawmill. The

house, however, was there, most of it. It lacked a door and a window frame, and the chimney of mud and stones had fallen into an unlovely heap, overgrown with rank weeds. Such humble furniture as there may once have been and much of the lower weatherboarding, had served as fuel in the camp fires of hunters; as had also, probably, the curbing of an old well, which at the time I write of existed in the form of a rather wide but not very deep depression near by.

One afternoon in the summer of 1874, I passed up Macarger's Gulch from the narrow valley into which it opens, by following the dry bed of the brook. I was quail-shooting and had made a bag of about a dozen birds by the time I had reached the house described, of whose existence I was until then unaware. After rather carelessly inspecting the ruin I resumed my sport, and having fairly good success prolonged it until near sunset, when it occurred to me that I was a long way from any human habitation—too far to reach one by nightfall. But in my game bag was food, and the old house would afford shelter, if shelter were needed on a warm and dewless night in the foothills of the Sierra Nevada, where one may sleep in comfort on the pine needles, without covering. I am fond of solitude and love the night, so my resolution to "camp out" was soon taken, and by the time that it was dark I had made my bed of boughs and grasses in a corner of the room and was roasting a quail at a fire that I had kindled on the hearth. The smoke escaped out of the ruined chimney, the light illuminated the room with a kindly glow, and as I ate my simple meal of plain bird and drank the remains of a bottle of red wine which had served me all the afternoon in place of the water, which the region did not supply, I experienced a sense of comfort which better fare and accommodations do not always give.

Nevertheless, there was something lacking. I had a sense of comfort, but not of security. I detected myself staring more frequently at the open doorway and blank window than I could find warrant for doing. Outside these apertures all was black, and I was unable to repress a certain feeling of apprehension as my fancy pictured the outer world and filled it with unfriendly entities, natural and supernatural—chief among which, in their respective classes, were the grizzly bear, which I knew was occasionally still seen in that region, and the ghost, which I had reason to think was not. Unfortunately, our feelings do not always respect the law of probabilities, and to me that evening, the possible and the impossible were equally disquieting.

Everyone who has had experience in the matter must have observed that one confronts the actual and imaginary perils of the night with far less apprehension in the open air than in a house with an open doorway. I felt this now as I lay on my leafy couch in a corner of the room next to the chimney and permitted my fire to die out. So strong became my sense of the presence of something malign and menacing in the place, that I found myself almost unable to withdraw my eyes from the opening, as in the deepening darkness it became more and more indistinct. And when the last little flame flickered and went out I grasped the shotgun which I had laid at my side and actually turned the muzzle in the direction of the now invisible entrance, my thumb on one of the hammers, ready to cock the piece, my breath suspended, my muscles rigid and tense. But later I laid down the weapon with a sense of shame and mortification. What did I fear, and why?—I, to whom the night had been

> a more familiar face
> Than that of man—

I, in whom that element of hereditary superstition from which none of us is altogether free had given to solitude and darkness and silence only a more alluring interest and charm! I was unable to comprehend my folly, and losing in the conjecture the thing conjectured of, I fell asleep. And then I dreamed.

I was in a great city in a foreign land—a city whose people were of my own race, with minor differences of speech and costume; yet precisely what these were I could not say; my sense of them was indistinct. The city was dominated by a great castle upon an overlooking height whose name I knew, but could not speak. I walked through many streets, some broad and straight with high, modern buildings, some narrow, gloomy, and tortuous, between the gables of quaint old houses whose overhanging stories, elaborately ornamented with carvings in wood and stone, almost met above my head.

I sought someone whom I had never seen, yet knew that I should recognize when found. My quest was not aimless and fortuitous; it had a definite method. I turned from one street into another without hesitation and threaded a maze of intricate passages, devoid of the fear of losing my way.

Presently I stopped before a low door in a plain stone house which might have been the dwelling of an artisan of the better sort, and without announcing myself, entered. The room, rather sparely furnished, and lighted by a single window with small diamond-shaped panes, had but two occupants; a man and a woman. They took no notice of my intrusion, a circumstance which, in the manner of dreams, appeared entirely natural. They were not conversing; they sat apart, unoccupied and sullen.

The woman was young and rather stout, with fine large eyes and a certain grave beauty; my memory of her expression is exceedingly vivid, but in dreams one does not observe the details of faces. About her shoulders was a plaid shawl. The man was older, dark, with an evil face made more forbidding by a long scar extending from near the left temple diagonally downward into the black mustache; though in my dreams it seemed rather to haunt the face as a thing apart—I can express it no otherwise—than to belong to it. The moment that I found the man and woman I knew them to be husband and wife.

What followed, I remember indistinctly; all was confused and inconsistent—made so, I think, by gleams of consciousness. It was as if two pictures, the scene of my dream, and my actual surroundings, had been blended, one overlying the other, until the former, gradually fading, disappeared, and I was broad awake in the deserted cabin, entirely and tranquilly conscious of my situation.

My foolish fear was gone, and opening my eyes I saw that my fire, not altogether burned out, had revived by the falling of a stick and was again lighting the room. I had probably slept only a few minutes, but my commonplace dream had somehow so strongly impressed me that I was no longer drowsy; and after a little while I rose, pushed the embers of my fire together, and lighting my pipe proceeded in a rather ludicrously methodical way to meditate upon my vision.

It would have puzzled me then to say in what respect it was worth attention. In the first moment of serious thought that I gave to the matter I recognized the city of my dream as Edinburgh, where I had never been; so if the dream was a memory it was a memory of pictures and description. The recognition somehow deeply impressed me; it was as if something in my mind insisted rebelliously against will and reason on the importance of all this. And that faculty, whatever it was, asserted also a control of my speech. "Surely," I said aloud, quite involuntarily, "the MacGregors must have come here from Edinburgh."

At the moment, neither the substance of this remark nor the fact of my making it, surprised me in the least; it seemed entirely natural that I should know the name of my dreamfolk and something of their history. But the absurdity of it all soon dawned upon me: I laughed aloud, knocked the ashes from my pipe and again stretched myself upon my bed of boughs and grass, where I lay staring absently into my failing fire, with no further thought of either my dream or my surroundings. Suddenly the single remaining flame crouched for a moment, then, springing upward, lifted itself clear of its embers and expired in air. The darkness was absolute.

At that instant—almost, it seemed, before the gleam of the blaze had faded from my eyes—there was a dull, dead sound, as of some heavy body falling upon the floor, which shook beneath me as I lay. I sprang to a sitting posture and groped at my side for my gun; my notion was that some wild beast had leaped in through the open window. While the flimsy structure was still shaking from the impact I heard the sound of blows, the scuffling of feet upon the floor, and then—it seemed to come from almost within reach of my hand, the sharp shrieking of a woman in mortal agony. So horrible a cry I had never heard nor conceived; it utterly unnerved me; I was conscious for a moment of nothing but my own terror! Fortunately my hand now found the weapon of which it was in search, and the familiar touch somewhat restored me. I leaped to my feet, straining my eyes to pierce the darkness. The violent sounds had ceased, but more terrible than these, I heard, at what seemed long intervals, the faint intermittent gasping of some living, dying thing!

As my eyes grew accustomed to the dim light of the coals in the fireplace, I saw first the shapes of the door and window, looking blacker than the black of the walls. Next, the distinction between wall and floor became discernible, and at last I was sensible to the form and full expanse of the floor from end to end and side to side. Nothing was visible and the silence was unbroken.

With a hand that shook a little, the other still grasping my gun, I restored my fire and made a critical examination of the place. There was nowhere any sign that the cabin had been entered. My own tracks were visible in the dust covering the floor, but there were no others. I relit my pipe, provided fresh fuel by ripping a thin board or two from the inside of the house—I did not care to go into the darkness out of doors—and passed the rest of the night smoking and thinking, and feeding my fire; not for added years of life would I have permitted that little flame to expire again.

Some years afterward I met in Sacramento a man named Morgan, to whom I had a note of introduction from a friend in San Francisco. Dining with him one evening at his home I observed various "trophies" upon the wall, indicating that he was fond of shooting. It turned out that he was, and in relating some of his feats he mentioned having been in the region of my adventure.

"Mr. Morgan," I asked abruptly, "do you know a place up there called Macarger's Gulch?"

"I have good reason to," he replied; "it was I who gave to the newspapers, last year, the accounts of the finding of the skeleton there."

I had not heard of it; the accounts had been published, it appeared, while I was absent in the East.

"By the way," said Morgan, "the name of the gulch is a corruption; it should have been called 'MacGregor's.' My dear," he added, speaking to his wife, "Mr. Elderson has upset his wine."

That was hardly accurate—I had simply dropped it, glass and all.

"There was an old shanty once in the gulch," Morgan resumed when the ruin wrought by my awkwardness had been repaired, "but just previously to my visit it had been blown down, or rather blown away, for its *débris* was scattered all about, the very floor being parted, plank from plank. Between two of the sleepers still in position I and my companion observed the remnant of a plaid shawl, and examining it found that it was wrapped about the shoulders of the body of a woman, of which but little remained besides the bones, partly covered with fragments of clothing, and brown dry skin. But we will spare Mrs. Morgan," he added with a smile. The lady had indeed exhibited signs of disgust rather than sympathy.

"It is necessary to say, however," he went on, "that the skull was fractured in several places, as by blows of some blunt instrument; and that instrument itself—a pick-handle, still stained with blood—lay under the boards near by."

Mr. Morgan turned to his wife. "Pardon me, my dear," he said with affected solemnity, "for mentioning these disagreeable particulars, the natural though regrettable incidents of a conjugal quarrel—resulting, doubtless, from the luckless wife's insubordination."

"I ought to be able to overlook it," the lady replied with composure; "you have so many times asked me to in those very words."

I thought he seemed rather glad to go on with his story.

"From these and other circumstances," he said, "the coroner's jury found that the deceased, Janet MacGregor, came to her death from blows inflicted by some person to the jury unknown; but it was added that the evidence pointed strongly to her husband, Thomas MacGregor, as the guilty person. But Thomas MacGregor has never been found nor heard of. It was learned that the couple came from Edinburgh, but not—my dear, do you not observe that Mr. Elderson's boneplate has water in it?"

I had deposited a chicken bone in my finger bowl.

"In a little cupboard I found a photograph of MacGregor, but it did not lead to his capture."

"Will you let me see it?" I said.

The picture showed a dark man with an evil face made more forbidding by a long scar extending from near the temple diagonally downward into the black mustache.

"By the way, Mr. Elderson," said my affable host, "may I know why you asked about 'Macarger's Gulch'?"

"I lost a mule near there once," I replied, "and the mischance has—has quite—upset me."

"My dear," said Mr. Morgan, with the mechanical intonation of an interpreter translating, "the loss of Mr. Elderson's mule has peppered his coffee."

HENRYK SIENKIEWICZ

A Comedy of Errors

In the early spring of 1876 a group of Polish intellectuals seeking to flee Russian tyranny sent two of its members to Southern California to locate a site for a commune modeled on Thoreau's Brook Farm. One of the two was Henryk Sienkiewicz (1846–1916), who later was awarded the Nobel Prize in literature, and the site selected was near Anaheim, an area that had already attracted many German-speaking settlers. Sienkiewicz's companion returned to Poland with glowing accounts; from a shack at Anaheim Landing, Sienkiewicz wrote letters no less enticing.

Helena Modjeska, Poland's most famous actress and the most illustrious member of the incipient commune, rhapsodized in a letter at the prospect: "After a day of toil, to play the guitar and sing by moonlight, to recite poems, or to listen to the mocking bird! And listening to our songs would be charming Indian maidens, our neighbors, making wreaths of luxuriant wild flowers for us! . . . And oh, we should be so far away from everyday gossip and malice, nearer to God, and better."

The nine other members of the commune joined Sienkiewicz in late summer and they all took up residence in a two-bedroom farmhouse. But after six months of homesickness and high thinking the experiment went the way of Brook Farm and fell into bankruptcy. Madame Modjeska returned to the stage and became one of California's leading actresses. Sienkiewicz, after a short residence in Los Angeles, returned to his native land, having acquired material for several amusing short stories. There he began a novelist's career that included the famous Quo Vadis? *(1895) as well as other historical works.*

"A Comedy of Errors," first published in a Polish periodical before the turn of the century, is a delightful tale of rival grocers, male and female, in a pioneer Southern California village. This translation, by H. E. Kennedy and A. Uminska, first appeared in Tales from Henryk Sienkiewicz *(1931).*

Five or six years ago, in the Mariposa district, an oil well was discovered in a certain locality. The immense profits which similar wells bring with them in Nevada induced some company promoters to form a company for the purpose of exploiting the newly-discovered springs. Various machines, pumps, cranes, ladders, tuns, barrels, bores, and boilers were conveyed there. Houses were built for the workmen, the locality was christened "Struck-Oil," and after a while, in this empty, unpeopled neighbourhood which a year before had been inhabited only by coyotes, there was a settlement consisting of some fifty to sixty houses, inhabited by a few hundred workmen.

Two years later Struck-Oil was already called "Struck-Oil City," and indeed it was already a "city" in the fullest sense of the word. Please note that now there lived there a shoemaker, a tailor, a carpenter, a blacksmith, a butcher, and a French doctor who, in his time, had shaved chins in France, but anyhow was a "learned man" and harmless, which is a great deal to say of an American doctor.

The doctor, as most frequently happens in small towns, also kept the chemist's shop and the post office. So he had three professions. He was as harmless a pharmacist as he was a doctor, for in his pharmacy there were to be found but two medicines, namely, julep and laurel drops. This quiet, gentle old man was wont to say to his patients:

"Never be afraid of my medicines. My custom when I give a sick person medicine is to take the same dose myself, for I argue that if it doesn't hurt a healthy man it won't hurt a sick one either. Eh?"

"That's so," would reply the reassured citizens, to whom it never occurred that it's a doctor's duty not only not to harm a patient, but to cure him.

Mr. Dasonville—for such was the doctor's name—had, however, special faith in the wonderful effects of laurel drops. Often at meetings he took off his hat and, turning to the public, said: "Ladies and gentlemen, give laurel drops a trial! I'm seventy years of age; I've been taking laurel drops for forty years: and look, I haven't one grey hair on my head!"

The ladies and gentlemen might have observed again that the doctor hadn't indeed a single grey hair, but then, he had none at all, for his head was as bald as a lamp-shade. But as a remark of the kind would in no way have tended to increase the growth of Struck-Oil City, it was not made at all.

Meanwhile Struck-Oil City grew and grew. At the end of two years a branch railway was constructed to it. The town now had its elected officials. The doctor, who was universally liked, became, as representing the educated class, the judge. The shoemaker, who was a Polish Jew, Mr. Devis (David), was the sheriff, that is, the chief of police, which force was composed of the sheriff and no one else. A school was built, which was presided over by a "school marm," a maiden of uncertain age, who had a perpetually swollen face. Finally, the first hotel was built, and named "The United States Hotel."

"Business" became extremely brisk. The export of petroleum brought in fine profits. It was observed that Mr. Devis had a glazed shop-front, like those of the San Francisco shoemakers, erected before his stall. At the next meeting the citizens bestowed public thanks upon Mr. Devis for this "new ornament to the town," upon which Mr. Devis replied with the modesty of a great citizen: "Thank you, thank you! Aï vaï!"

Where a judge and a sheriff are there are cases. That necessitates writing and paper, so at the corner of Coyote Street, at number one, there arose a stationery shop, in which there were also sold political newspapers and caricatures, representing Grant under the form of a boy milking a cow, which, in its turn, was to represent the United States. The sheriff's duties did not in any way compel him to forbid the sale of drawings of this kind, for that was not the business of the police.

But that wasn't the end. An American town can't live without a newspaper. So when another year had passed, a journal called the *Saturday Weekly Review* came into being, and it had as many subscribers as there were inhabitants of Struck-Oil City. The editor of this paper was also its publisher, printer, manager, and distributor. This latter duty was the more easy to him inasmuch as he kept cows besides, and every morning had to bring milk round to the houses. Nor did it prevent him from beginning the leading articles with the words: "If our vile President of the United States took the advice we gave him in our last issue"; and so forth.

So, as we see, there was nothing lacking in that blessed Struck-Oil City. Moreover, as oil-miners are not characterized by either violence or the rude manners proper to gold-miners, it was quiet in the town. Nobody fought with anybody, lynching wasn't even mentioned. Life flowed on quietly; one day was as like another as one drop of water is to another. In the morning everybody was engaged in business, in the evening they burned rubbish in the streets, and, if there was no meeting, went to bed, knowing that they would burn rubbish next day too.

The only thing that worried the sheriff was that he couldn't teach the citizens not to shoot off their guns at the wild geese which, in the evening, flew over the town. The urban laws forbade shooting off guns in the streets. "If it had been some lousy little town," the sheriff would repeat, "I'd not say a word. But to have 'pif paf, pif paf' in such a big town, is most unfitting."

The citizens listened, nodded, replied "Oh, yes!" but when in the evening on the rosy sky the grey and white lines of geese appeared, making their way from the mountains to the ocean, every one forgot his promise, seized his gun, and the fusillade began in full strength. Mr. Devis could, indeed, have brought each culprit before the judge, and the judge could have fined him, but we mustn't forget that the culprits were also the patients of the doctor and, in case of shoes wearing out, the customers of the sheriff. And as one hand washes the other, so one hand does not injure the other.

So it was as quiet in Struck-Oil City as in heaven. But suddenly those halcyon days came to an end. The man-grocer conceived a mortal hatred for the woman-grocer, and the woman-grocer for the man-grocer.

Here we must explain what is called a grocery. A grocery, then, or grocer's store, is a shop where everything is sold. You can get there flour, hats, cigars, brooms, buttons, rice, sardines, shirts, bacon, seeds, blouses, trousers, lamp-shades, hatchets, biscuits, plates, paper collars, and dried fish—in a word, everything a man can require. In the beginning there was only one grocery in Struck-Oil City. It was kept by a German, Hans Kasche by name. He was just a phlegmatic German, a native of Prussia. He was thirty-five and had goggle eyes. He was not corpulent, but just fairly stout. He always went about without his coat, and he was never without a pipe in his teeth. He knew just as much English as he required for business, and not a jot more. Still, he did a good trade, so that at the end of a year it was already said in Struck-Oil City that he "was worth several thousand dollars."

But suddenly a second grocery made its appearance.

And, strangely enough, while the first was kept by a German man, the second was founded by a German woman. "*Kunegunde und Eduard, Eduard und Kunegunde!*" So at once war broke out between the parties, and it began by Miss Neuman, or, as she called herself, Newman, serving at her housewarming lunch cakes baked with flour mixed with soda and alum. This would have injured Miss Neuman herself most had she not maintained and produced witnesses to prove that, since her flour was not yet unpacked, she had bought it from Hans Kasche. So the result was that Hans Kasche was envious and a villain, who wished at the very outset to ruin his rival in public opinion. Anyhow it was to be foreseen that the two groceries would be rivals to each other, but nobody foresaw that this rivalry would become a terrible personal hatred. This hatred soon went so far that Hans only burnt rubbish when the wind blew the smoke into his adversary's shop, and the adversary never called Hans anything but "Dutchman," which the latter looked upon as the greatest of insults. At the beginning the inhabitants laughed at them both, the more so because neither of them knew English; but gradually, as the result of daily dealings with the groceries, two parties were formed in the town: Hansists and Neumanists, who began to look askance at one another, which fact might well be a hindrance to the happiness and quietude of Struck-Oil City, and might cause menacing complications in the future. That profound politician, Mr. Devis, wished to cure the evil at its source, so he tried to reconcile the German with his fellow-countrywoman. He would stand in the middle of the street and say to them in their native language:

"There, why should you quarrel? Don't you buy your shoes from the same shoemaker? I have some now, than which you will find no better in the whole of San Francisco."

"It's useless to praise shoes to one who'll soon go barefoot," Miss Neuman would interrupt sourly.

"I don't make capital out of my feet," replied Hans phlegmatically.

Now you must know that Miss Neuman, although she was a German, had really pretty feet; so sneers of this kind filled her heart with mortal anger.

In the town the two parties had already begun to moot the matter of Hans and Miss Neuman at meetings. But since in America nobody with a case against a woman will get justice, the majority were on Miss Neuman's side.

Soon Hans perceived that his grocery barely paid him.

But neither did Miss Neuman do too successful business, for again all the women in the town took Hans's side. For they noticed that their husbands were too frequent customers of the beautiful German woman, and that each time when they went to buy they stayed too long in her shop.

When there was nobody in either of the groceries Hans and Miss Neuman would stand in their doorways opposite each other, casting at each other looks full of fury. Miss Neuman would then hum to the tune of *Mein lieber Augustin:*

"Dutchman, Dutchman, Du-Dutchman, Du-Dutchman-man!"

Mr. Hans would look at her feet, then at her figure, then at her face, with the same expression with which he would have looked at a coyote which had been killed a month ago; then, bursting into demoniac laughter, he would cry:

"By God!"

Hatred reached such a height in that phlegmatic man that when in the morning he appeared in the doorway and Miss

Neuman wasn't there, he would fidget about as if he missed something.

There would long ago have been active hostilities between the two, had it not been for the fact that Hans was certain he would lose in any law case, and the more so because Miss Neuman had an adherent in the person of the editor of the *Saturday Weekly Review*. Hans found this out when he spread the news that Miss Neuman had an artificial bust. It was a probable enough thing, for it was a universal custom in America. But the next week there appeared in the *Saturday Weekly Review* a thundering article in which the editor, writing in general of slanders by "Dutchmen," concluded with a solemn assurance that the bust of a certain calumniated lady was real.

Thenceforth Mr. Hans drank every morning black coffee instead of coffee with milk, for he didn't wish to take milk from the editor, but, on the other hand, Miss Neuman took twice as much milk as usual. Besides this she ordered a frock from the tailor, the bodice of which was so formed as finally to convince every one that Hans was a slanderer.

Hans felt himself helpless in the face of feminine hatred; and meanwhile his lady compatriot, standing before the shop every morning, would sing ever louder:

"Dutchman, Dutchman, Du-Dutchman, Du-Dutchman-man."

"What can I do to her?" thought Hans. "I have poisoned wheat for rats; maybe I might poison her chickens. No! They'd make me pay! But I know what I'll do!"

And in the evening Miss Neuman, to her great surprise, perceived Mr. Hans carrying bunches of wild sunflowers and arranging them so as to form a path to the barred window of his cellar. "I'm curious what that's going to be," she thought to herself. "Certainly something against me!" Meanwhile it grew dark. Mr. Hans had placed the sunflowers in two lines, so that there only remained in the middle a free path to the window of the cellar. Then he carried out some object covered with linen, turned his back to Miss Neuman, took the linen off the mysterious object, covered it with sunflower leaves, then approached the wall and began to trace some letters on it.

Miss Neuman was dying of curiosity.

"He's certainly writing something against me," she thought. "But as soon as ever everybody goes to bed, I'll go and see, even if I were to die for it."

Hans, having finished his work, went upstairs and soon put the light out. Then Miss Neuman hastily threw on a dressing-gown, put slippers on her bare feet, and set forth across the street. Having reached the sunflowers, and wanting to read the inscription on the wall, she went straight up the path to the window. Suddenly her eyes bulged, she threw the upper part of her body backwards, and there issued from her mouth first of all a painful "Ow! Ow!" and then a despairing cry: "Help! Help!"

The upper window was raised.

"*Was ist das?*" sounded quietly in Hans's voice. "*Was ist das?*"

"Accursed Dutchman," screamed the young lady. "You've murdered me, ruined me! You shall hang to-morrow. Help! Help!"

"I'll be down in a minute," said Hans.

And in a moment he appeared, candle in hand. He looked at Miss Neuman, who stood as if rooted to the earth, then put his hands on his hips and began to laugh.

"What's this? Is it Miss Neuman? Ha! Ha! Ha! Good evening, miss. Ha! Ha! Ha! I set a trap for skunks and I caught you! Why did you come to look into my cellar? I specially wrote a warning on the wall to prevent any one coming near. Now shout! Let folk come running. Let every one see that you come at night to look into the Dutchman's cellar! *O mein Gott!* Shout, but stand there till the morning. Good night, miss, good night!"

Miss Neuman's position was frightful. Shout? Folk would come running. She would be compromised. Not shout? To stand all night in a trap and to be a sight for every one next day! And besides her foot hurt more and more. She got giddy, the stars mingled with each other, the moon with Mr. Hans's menacing face. She fainted.

"*Herr Je!*" exclaimed Hans to himself. "If she dies they'll lynch me to-morrow without a trial!"

And his hair stood on end with fright.

There was no way out. Hans sought the key as quickly as he could to open the trap, but it was difficult to open, for Miss Neuman's dressing-gown was in the way. It had to be undone a little and . . . in spite of all his hatred, Hans couldn't restrain himself from casting a glance at the beautiful little feet of his enemy that looked, in the light of the red moon, as if carved in marble.

One might have said that there was now pity mingled with his hatred. He quickly opened the trap and, as the young lady did not move, he lifted her up in his arms and bore her quickly to her house. On the way he again felt pity. Then he went back to his own place, and couldn't shut an eye the whole night.

Next morning Miss Neuman didn't appear before her grocery to sing "Dutchman, Dutchman, Du-Dutchman, Du-Dutchman."

Perhaps she was ashamed, and perhaps she was silently plotting vengeance.

It became evident that she was plotting vengeance. The evening of that very day the editor of the *Saturday Weekly Review* challenged Hans to box with him, and, at the very beginning of it, gave him a black eye. But Hans, driven to despair, gave him so many terrible blows, that after a short and vain resistance, the editor fell full length on the ground crying, "Enough! Enough!"

In some unknown way, for not through Hans, the whole town got to know about Miss Neuman's nocturnal accident. After the fight with the editor, pity for his enemy disappeared from Hans's heart and hatred alone remained.

Hans had a feeling that some unexpected blow from the hated hand would fall upon him. And really he hadn't long to wait for it. The owners of groceries often stick up before their establishments advertisements of various kinds of goods, and these usually have the heading: "Notice!" Again you must know that groceries usually sell ice, without which no American drinks either whisky or beer. Well, suddenly Hans observed that people had completely stopped buying ice from him. The immense chunks he brought from the railway melted in the cellar in which he had placed them. The damage amounted to about fifteen dollars. Why? How? What? Hans saw that even his partisans daily bought ice from Miss Neuman; so he couldn't understand what it meant, the more because he hadn't fallen out with any public-house keeper.

He decided to clear the matter up.

"Why don't you buy ice from me?" he asked in broken

English of the public-house keeper, Peters, who was just passing his shop.

"Because you don't keep it."

"What? I don't keep it?"

"Well, I know you don't."

"*Aber* I do keep ice."

"Then what's that?" asked the public-house keeper, pointing
to a notice which was stuck up on the house.

Hans looked, and went green with rage. Somebody had
scratched out from the advertisement the letter "t" in the word
"notice," so that "notice" became "no ice."

"*Donnerwetter!*" shouted Hans, and, blue in the face, and
trembling, he rushed into Miss Neuman's shop.

"This is villainy!" he cried, foaming. "Why did you scratch
me out a letter from the middle?"

"What did I scratch out of your middle?" asked Miss Neuman, mischievously pretending to be stupid.

"The letter 't', I say. You scratched out 't.' *Aber Goddam,* this
can't go on. You must pay me for the ice! *Goddam!*"

And losing his usual cold-bloodedness, he began to scream
like one possessed. Upon this Miss Neuman began to shout.
People came running.

"Help!" called Miss Neuman. "The Dutchman has gone
mad! He says I scratched something out of his inside. And I
didn't scratch anything. What should I scratch? I didn't scratch
anything. Oh, Lord, I'd have scratched out his eyes if I could,
but nothing more. I'm a poor woman, alone! He'll kill me,
murder me on the spot!"

Thus shouting, she dissolved into floods of tears. The Americans didn't understand what was the matter, but they can't
bear woman's tears. So they went for the German and put him
out of doors. He would have resisted, but he hadn't a chance.
He was shot out like a stone from a sling, across the street and
through his own door, and he fell full length.

A week later an immense pictorial signboard hung over his
shop. This signboard showed a monkey dressed in a striped
frock and a white apron with shoulder-straps. Just like Miss
Neuman! Underneath there was an inscription in great, yellow
letters:

"At the sign of the monkey!"

People assembled to look. Laughter lured Miss Neuman to her door. She came out, looked, paled, but not losing her presence of mind cried out at once:

"At the sign of the monkey! Nothing strange in that, since Mr. Kasche lives there. Ha!"

But the blow had struck her to the heart. At noon she would hear crowds of children passing the shops on their way home from school stop before the sign, crying:

"Oh, that's Miss Neuman! Good evening, Miss Neuman!"

It was too much. When the editor came to see her in the evening, she said to him:

"That monkey's I. I know it's I, but I won't give in. He must take it down and lick out that monkey with his own tongue before me."

"What are you going to do?"

"I'm going to the judge at once."

"What? At once?"

"To-morrow."

She went out early in the morning and, approaching Hans, said:

"Listen, Mr. Dutchman! I know that monkey's I. But come with me to the judge. Let's see what he'll say."

"He'll say I can paint whatever I like over my shop."

"We'll soon see about that."

Miss Neuman could scarcely breathe.

"And how do you know that that monkey is you?"

"My conscience tells me so. Come, come to the judge, or the sheriff'll bring you to him in chains."

"All right, I'll come," said Hans, sure he would win.

They closed their shops and went, abusing each other on the way. It was only at Judge Dasonville's very door that they remembered that neither of them knew enough English to explain the matter. What was to be done? Oh, the sheriff, being a Polish Jew, knew both German and English. Forward to the sheriff!

But the sheriff had just got into a cart and was about to drive away.

"Go to the devil!" he shouted quickly. "The whole town is

disturbed through you. You wear the same shoes for years on end! I'm off for lumber. Good-bye!"

And he drove off.

Hans put his hands on his hips.

"You'll have to wait till to-morrow, miss," he said phlegmatically.

"I'll have to wait? I'll die first! Unless you take down the monkey."

"I won't take down the monkey."

"Then you'll hang! You'll hang, you Dutchman, you! We'll do without the sheriff. The judge knows what it's about anyhow."

"Then let's go and do without the sheriff," said the German.

But Miss Neuman was mistaken. Of all the townsfolk the judge alone knew nothing whatever of their quarrel. The innocent old man was mixing his laurel drops and thinking he was saving the world. He received them, as he was wont to receive every one, kindly and courteously.

"Show me your tongues, my children!" said he. "I'll prescribe for you at once."

They both began to make signs that they didn't want medicine. Miss Neuman repeated: "It's not that we want—not that."

"Then what?"

They both talked together. For every word Hans said the lady said ten. Finally, the woman thought of pointing to her heart as a sign that Mr. Hans had pierced it with sorrow.

"I understand. Now I understand!" said the doctor.

Then he opened a book and began to write. He asked Hans how old he was. "Thirty-five." He asked the young lady— she didn't remember exactly. "Oh, somewhere about twenty-five." "All right!" "What were their Christian names?" "Hans." "Lora." "All right!" "What was their profession?" "They had groceries." "All right!" Then some other questions. Neither understood, but they answered: Yes. The doctor nodded. It was all over.

He finished writing, stood up and suddenly, to Lora's great surprise, clasped her round the waist and kissed her.

She took it for a good omen and, full of rosy hopes, went home. On the way she said to Hans:

"I'll show you what!"

"You'll show it to someone else," rejoined the German quietly.

Next morning the sheriff came and stood before their shops. Both shop-keepers stood before their doors. Hans was puffing at a pipe. The young lady was singing:

"Dutchman, Dutchman, Du-Dutchman, Du-Dutchman-man!"

"Do you want to go to the judge?" asked the sheriff.

"We've been already."

"Well, and what happened?"

"My dear sheriff! My dear Mr. Devis!" cried the young lady. "Go and ask. I just require a pair of shoes. And say a word there for me to the judge. You see, I'm a poor girl . . . alone!"

The sheriff went and returned in a quarter of an hour. But, for no known reason, he came back surrounded by a crowd of people.

"Well, what? Well, how goes it?" they both started asking.

"Everything's all right—oh!" said the sheriff.

"Well, what did the judge do?"

"Why should he have done anything bad? He married you."

"Married us!"

"People do get married, don't they?"

If a thunderbolt had suddenly fallen Hans and Miss Neuman wouldn't have been so frightened. Hans opened his eyes wide, opened his mouth, hung out his tongue, and looked like a fool at Miss Neuman, while Miss Neuman opened her eyes wide, opened her mouth, hung out her tongue, and looked like a fool at Mr. Hans. They were struck dumb, turned to stone! Then they both started shouting:

"I'm supposed to be his wife?"

"I'm supposed to be her husband?"

"Help! Help! Never! A divorce at once! I won't!"

"No, I won't have it."

"I'll die first! Help! Divorce, divorce, divorce! Whatever's going on here!"

"My dear people," said the sheriff quietly; "what's the use of shouting? The judge marries but he doesn't divorce. What's the good of shouting? Are you San Francisco millionaires to get a divorce? Don't you know what it costs? *Aï!* What're you shouting for? I've beautiful children's shoes. I sell them cheap. Good-bye!"

So saying he went off. The people, laughing, also dispersed. The newly-married couple remained alone.

"'Twas that Frenchman," cried the maiden-wife. "He did it on purpose because we're Germans."

"*Richtig!*" replied Hans.

"But we'll apply for a divorce."

"I'll do it first. You scratched me out a 't' from the middle."

"No, I'll be the first. You caught me in a trap."

"I don't want you."

"I can't bear you."

They separated and shut up their shops. She sat in her house meditating the whole day, and so did he. Night came. It brought no peace with it. Neither of them could think of sleep. They lay down, but no sleep came to their eyes. He thought: "There sleeps my wife!" She thought: "There sleeps my husband!" And strange feelings arose in their hearts. Those feelings were hatred and anger, together with a sense of loneliness. Besides this, Mr. Hans thought of his monkey over the shop. How could he keep it there when it was a caricature of his wife? And it occurred to him that he had done a very horrid thing, having that monkey painted. But then, again, that Miss Neuman! Why, he hated her! It was her fault that his ice had melted. Why, he'd caught her by moonlight in a trap! Then again there came into his mind her form as seen by moonlight. "Well, truth to tell, she's a fine girl!" thought he. "But she can't bear me, nor I her." What a position! *Ach, Herr Gott!* He was married? And to whom? To Miss Neuman! And a divorce cost so much. His whole grocery wouldn't pay for it.

"I'm that Dutchman's wife," said Miss Neuman to herself. "I'm a spinster no longer . . . that is, I mean, I'm a spinster, but I've got married! To whom? To Kasche, who caught me in a trap! It's true, of course, that he took me round the waist and carried me up the stairs. How strong he is! He took me round the waist, just like that! . . . What's that? Something's rustling!"

There was no rustling, but Miss Neuman began to be afraid, though she'd never been afraid before.

"But if he dared now . . . Lord!" But then she added, in a voice in which there was a strange tone of disappointment:

"But he won't dare. He! . . ."

For all that her fear grew. "A woman's always so lonely!" she thought further. "If there were a man here it would be safer. I heard of robberies in the neighbourhood." (She hadn't.) "They'll kill me here some time or another. Ah, that Kasche! That Kasche! He's shut the way to me. I must take advice, anyhow, about a divorce."

So thinking, she tossed about sleeplessly in her wide American bed and really did feel very lonely. Suddenly she jumped up again. This time her fear had a real reason. Blows with a hammer were distinctly audible in the silence of the night.

"Lord!" cried the young lady. "They're breaking into my grocery!"

So saying, she jumped out of bed and ran to the window, but, looking through it, she at once calmed down. By the moonlight a ladder was visible and on it the rounded, white figure of Hans, beating out with the hammer the nails that kept the signboard in place.

Miss Neuman noiselessly opened the window.

"Anyhow he's taking down the monkey. That's kind of him," she thought.

And suddenly she felt as if something round her heart melted.

Hans slowly drew out the nails. The sheet of tin fell with a clatter to the ground. Then he climbed down, hammered off the frame, rolled the sheet of tin in his veiny hands and began to remove the ladder.

The young lady followed him with her eyes. . . . The night was a quiet one, warm.

"Mr. Hans," the maiden suddenly whispered.

"Then you're not asleep, miss?" Hans whispered, just as softly.

"No. Good evening, sir!"

"Good evening, miss!"

"What are you doing?"

"Taking down the monkey."

"Thank you, Mr. Hans."

A moment's silence ensued.

"Mr. Hans!" murmured the maiden's voice again.

"What, Miss Lora?"

"We must talk over the divorce."

"Yes, Miss Lora."

"To-morrow?"

"To-morrow."

A moment of silence, with the moon smiling, and no dogs barking.

"Mr. Hans!"

"What, Miss Lora?"

"I'm anxious to get that divorce."

The maiden's voice sounded mournfully.

"So'm I, Miss Lora."

Hans's voice was sad.

"And you see, sir, so as not to delay . . ."

"Better not delay."

"The quicker we talk it over the better."

"The better, Miss Lora."

"Then we might talk it over at once."

"With your permission."

"Then you'll come to my place?"

"I'll just dress myself."

"No ceremony, please."

The hall door opened. Mr. Hans disappeared into the darkness and, in a moment, found himself in the maiden's little room, which was quiet, warm and tidy. Miss Lora was clothed in a white dressing-gown and was charming.

"I'm listening," said Hans, in a soft, broken voice.

"Well, you see, sir, I should like very much to get a divorce, but . . . I'm afraid somebody in the street might have seen us."

"Why, the windows were dark," said Hans.

"Oh, yes, of course," rejoined Miss Lora.

Then began a council about divorce which has nothing to do with our story.

Peace returned to Struck-Oil City.

JACK LONDON

All Gold Canyon

Jack London (1876–1916) was born in San Francisco, spent his boyhood in Oakland, and all his life dreamed of owning a ranch in the northern part of California, the scene of more than a few of his novels and stories.

This native son, after an adventurous youth as an oyster pirate in San Francisco Bay, sailor on a sealing ship to the Bering Sea, hobo, student for one semester at the University of California, budding socialist, and prospector in the Alaska gold rush, taught himself to write by daily effort. Later, as a war correspondent, he covered the Russo-Japanese War (1904–5) and, in 1914, the Mexican Revolution.

His first stories, tales of the Yukon, were published in the Over-land Monthly, and his collection The Son of the Wolf: Tales of the Far North *(1900) established his reputation. Before his early death he became the best-known, highest-paid, and most popular writer of his time. On the* Snark, *a yacht he had designed, he and his second wife, Charmian, cruised for two years around the Hawaiian and other Pacific islands, and he wrote some of his best books about this ocean region, although he is most remembered today for* The Call of the Wild *(1903), his novel about a Klondike sled dog.*

Of London's California tales, one of the most outstanding has a setting in the Sierra. "All Gold Canyon," first published in the Century Magazine *in 1905, dramatizes the lonely life of the gold prospector and the immense labor required to discover and grasp a hoard of treasure from the earth. The story offers, moreover, a classic example of the plot in which a successful trickster must be eternally vigilant against rivals and robbers.*

It was the green heart of the canyon, where the walls swerved back from the rigid plan and relieved their harshness of line by making a little sheltered nook and filling it to the brim with sweetness and roundness and softness. Here all things rested. Even the narrow stream ceased its turbulent down-rush long enough to form a quiet pool. Knee-deep in the water, with drooping head and half-shut eyes, drowsed a red-coated, many-antlered buck.

On one side, beginning at the very lip of the pool, was a tiny meadow, a cool, resilient surface of green that extended to the base of the frowning wall. Beyond the pool a gentle slope of earth ran up and up to meet the opposing wall. Fine grass covered the slope—grass that was spangled with flowers, with here and there patches of color, orange and purple and golden. Below, the canyon was shut in. There was no view. The walls leaned together abruptly and the canyon ended in a chaos of rocks, moss-covered and hidden by a green screen of vines and creepers and boughs of trees. Up the canyon rose far hills and peaks, the big foothills, pine-covered and remote. And far beyond, like clouds upon the border of the sky, towered minarets of white, where the Sierra's eternal snows flashed austerely the blazes of the sun.

There was no dust in the canyon. The leaves and flowers were clean and virginal. The grass was young velvet. Over the pool three cottonwoods sent their snowy fluffs fluttering down the quiet air. On the slope the blossoms of the wine-wooded manzanita filled the air with springtime odors, while the leaves, wise with experience, were already beginning their vertical twist against the coming aridity of summer. In the open spaces on the slope, beyond the farthest shadow-reach of the manzanita, poised the mariposa lilies, like so many flights of jewelled moths suddenly arrested and on the verge of trembling into flight again. Here and there that woods harlequin, the madrone, permitting itself to be caught in the act of changing its pea-green trunk to madder-red, breathed its fragrance into the air from great clusters of waxen bells. Creamy white were these bells, shaped like lilies-of-the-valley, with the sweetness of perfume that is of the springtime.

There was not a sigh of wind. The air was drowsy with its weight of perfume. It was a sweetness that would have been cloying had the air been heavy and humid. But the air was sharp and thin. It was as starlight transmuted into atmosphere, shot through and warmed by sunshine, and flower-drenched with sweetness.

An occasional butterfly drifted in and out through the patches of light and shade. And from all about rose the low and sleepy hum of mountain bees—feasting Sybarites that jostled one another good-naturedly at the board, nor found time for rough discourtesy. So quietly did the little stream drip and ripple its way through the canyon that it spoke only in faint and occasional gurgles. The voice of the stream was a drowsy whisper, ever interrupted by dozings and silences, ever lifted again in the awakenings.

The motion of all things was a drifting in the heart of the canyon. Sunshine and butterflies drifted in and out among the trees. The hum of the bees and the whisper of the stream were a drifting of sound. And the drifting sound and drifting color seemed to weave together in the making of a delicate and intangible fabric which was the spirit of the place. It was a spirit of peace that was not of death, but of smooth-pulsing life, of quietude that was not silence, of movement that was not action, of repose that was quick with existence without being violent with struggle and travail. The spirit of the place was the spirit of the peace of the living, somnolent with the easement and content of prosperity, and undisturbed by rumors of far wars.

The red-coated, many-antlered buck acknowledged the lordship of the spirit of the place and dozed knee-deep in the cool, shaded pool. There seemed no flies to vex him and he was languid with rest. Sometimes his ears moved when the stream awoke and whispered; but they moved lazily, with foreknowledge that it was merely the stream grown garrulous at discovery that it had slept.

But there came a time when the buck's ears lifted and tensed with swift eagerness for sound. His head was turned down the canyon. His sensitive, quivering nostrils scented the air. His eyes could not pierce the green screen through which the stream rippled away, but to his ears came the voice of a man. It was a steady, monotonous, singsong voice. Once the buck heard the harsh clash of metal upon rock. At the sound he snorted with a sudden start that jerked him through the air from water to meadow, and his feet sank into the young velvet, while he pricked his ears and again scented the air. Then he stole across the tiny meadow, pausing once and again to listen, and faded away out of the canyon like a wraith, soft-footed and without sound.

The clash of steel-shod soles against the rocks began to be heard, and the man's voice grew louder. It was raised in a sort of chant and became distinct with nearness, so that the words could be heard:

> "Tu'n around an' tu'n yo' face
> Untoe them sweet hills of grace
>   (D' pow'rs of sin yo' am scornin'!).
> Look about an' look aroun'
> Fling yo' sin-pack on d' groun'
>   (Yo' will meet wid d' Lord in d' mornin'!))."

A sound of scrambling accompanied the song, and the spirit of the place fled away on the heels of the red-coated buck. The green screen was burst asunder, and a man peered out at the meadow and the pool and the sloping side-hill. He was a deliberate sort of man. He took in the scene with one embracing glance, then ran his eyes over the details to verify the general impression. Then, and not until then, did he open his mouth in vivid and solemn approval:

"Smoke of life an' snakes of purgatory! Will you just look at that! Wood an' water an' grass an' a side-hill! A pocket-hunter's delight an' a cayuse's paradise! Cool green for tired eyes! Pink pills for pale people ain't in it. A secret pasture for prospectors and a resting-place for tired burros. It's just boooful!"

He was a sandy-complexioned man in whose face geniality and humor seemed the salient characteristics. It was a mobile face, quick-changing to inward mood and thought. Thinking was in him a visible process. Ideas chased across his face like wind-flaws across the surface of a lake. His hair, sparse and unkempt of growth, was as indeterminate and colorless as his complexion. It would seem that all the color of his frame had gone into his eyes, for they were startlingly blue. Also, they were laughing and merry eyes, within them much of the naiveté and wonder of the child; and yet, in an unassertive way, they contained much of calm self-reliance and strength of purpose founded upon self-experience and experience of the world.

From out the screen of vines and creepers he flung ahead of him a miner's pick and shovel and gold-pan. Then he crawled out himself into the open. He was clad in faded overalls and black cotton shirt, with hobnailed brogans on his feet, and on his head a hat whose shapelessness and stains advertised the rough usage of wind and rain and sun and camp-smoke. He stood erect, seeing wide-eyed the secrecy of the scene and sensuously inhaling the warm, sweet breath of the canyon-garden through nostrils that dilated and quivered with delight. His eyes narrowed to laughing slits of blue, his face wreathed itself in joy, and his mouth curled in a smile as he cried aloud:

"Jumping dandelions and happy hollyhocks, but that smells good to me! Talk about your attar o'roses an' cologne factories! They ain't in it!"

He had the habit of soliloquy. His quick-changing facial expressions might tell every thought and mood, but the tongue, perforce, ran hard after, repeating, like a second Boswell.

The man lay down on the lip of the pool and drank long and deep of its water. "Tastes good to me," he murmured, lifting his head and gazing across the pool at the side-hill, while he wiped his mouth with the back of his hand. The side-hill attracted his attention. Still lying on his stomach, he studied the hill formation long and carefully. It was a practised eye that traveled up the slope to the crumbling canyon-wall and back and down again to the edge of the pool. He scrambled to his feet and favored the side-hill with a second survey.

"Looks good to me," he concluded, picking up his pick and shovel and gold-pan.

He crossed the stream below the pool, stepping agilely from stone to stone. Where the side-hill touched the water he dug up a shovelful of dirt and put it into the gold-pan. He squatted down, holding the pan in his two hands, and partly immersing it in the stream. Then he imparted to the pan a deft circular motion that sent the water sluicing in and out through the dirt and gravel. The larger and the lighter particles worked to the surface, and these, by a skilful dipping movement of the pan, he spilled out and over the edge. Occasionally, to expedite matters, he rested the pan and with his fingers raked out the large pebbles and pieces of rock.

The contents of the pan diminished rapidly until only fine dirt and the smallest bits of gravel remained. At this stage he began to work very deliberately and carefully. It was fine washing, and he washed fine and finer, with a keen scrutiny and delicate and fastidious touch. At last the pan seemed empty of everything but water; but with a quick semi-circular flirt that sent the water flying over the shallow rim into the stream, he disclosed a layer of black sand on the bottom of the pan. So thin was this layer that it was like a streak of paint. He examined it closely. In the midst of it was a tiny golden speck. He dribbled a little water in over the depressed edge of the pan. With a quick flirt he sent the water sluicing across the bottom, turning the grains of black sand over and over. A second tiny golden speck rewarded his effort.

The washing had now become very fine—fine beyond all need of ordinary placer mining. He worked the black sand, a small portion at a time, up the shallow rim of the pan. Each small portion he examined sharply, so that his eyes saw every grain of it before he allowed it to slide over the edge and away. Jealously, bit by bit, he let the black sand slip away. A golden speck, no larger than a pin-point, appeared on the rim, and by his manipulation of the water it returned to the bottom of the pan. And in such fashion another speck was disclosed, and another. Great was his care of them. Like a shepherd he herded his flock of golden specks so that not one should be lost. At last, of the pan of dirt nothing remained but his golden herd. He counted it, and then, after all his labor, sent it flying out of the pan with one final swirl of water.

But his blue eyes were shining with desire as he rose to his feet. "Seven," he muttered aloud, asserting the sum of the specks for which he had toiled so hard and which he had so wantonly thrown away. "Seven," he repeated, with the emphasis of one trying to impress a number on his memory.

He stood still a long while, surveying the hillside. In his eyes was a curiosity, new-aroused and burning. There was an exultance about his bearing and a keenness like that of a hunting animal catching the fresh scent of game.

He moved down the stream a few steps and took a second panful of dirt.

Again came the careful washing, the jealous herding of the golden specks, and the wantonness with which he sent them flying into the stream. His golden herd diminished. "Four, five," he muttered, and repeated, "five."

He could not forbear another survey of the hill before filling the pan farther down the stream. His golden herds diminished. "Four, three, two, two, one," were his memory tabulations as he moved down the stream. When but one speck of gold rewarded his washing, he stopped and built a fire of dry twigs. Into this he thrust the gold-pan and burned it till it was blue-black. He held up the pan and examined it critically. Then he nodded approbation. Against such a color-background he could defy the tiniest yellow speck to elude him.

Still moving down the stream, he panned again. A single speck was his reward. A third pan contained no gold at all. Not satisfied with this, he panned three times again, taking his shovels of dirt within a foot of one another. Each pan proved empty of gold, and the fact, instead of discouraging him, seemed to give him satisfaction. His elation increased with each barren washing, until he arose, exclaiming jubilantly:

"If it ain't the real thing, may God knock off my head with sour apples!"

Returning to where he had started operations, he began to pan up the stream. At first his golden herds increased—increased prodigiously. "Fourteen, eighteen, twenty-one, twenty-six," ran his memory tabulations. Just above the pool he struck his richest pan—thirty-five colors.

"Almost enough to save," he remarked regretfully as he allowed the water to sweep them away.

The sun climbed to the top of the sky. The man worked on.

Pan by pan, he went up the stream, the tally of results steadily decreasing.

"It's just booful, the way it peters out," he exulted when a shovelful of dirt contained no more than a single speck of gold.

And when no specks at all were found in several pans, he straightened up and favored the hillside with a confident glance.

"Ah, ha! Mr. Pocket!" he cried out, as though to an auditor hidden somewhere above him beneath the surface of the slope. "Ah, ha! Mr. Pocket! I'm a-comin', I'm a-comin', an' I'm shorely gwine to get yer! You heah me, Mr. Pocket? I'm gwine to get yer as shore as punkins ain't cauliflowers!"

He turned and flung a measuring glance at the sun poised above him in the azure of the cloudless sky. Then he went down the canyon, following the line of shovel-holes he had made in filling the pans. He crossed the stream below the pool and disappeared through the green screen. There was little opportunity for the spirit of the place to return with its quietude and repose, for the man's voice, raised in ragtime song, still dominated the canyon with possession.

After a time, with a greater clashing of steel-shod feet on rock, he returned. The green screen was tremendously agitated. It surged back and forth in the throes of a struggle. There was a loud grating and clanging of metal. The man's voice leaped to a higher pitch and was sharp with imperativeness. A large body plunged and panted. There was a snapping and ripping and rending, and amid a shower of falling leaves a horse burst through the screen. On its back was a pack, and from this trailed broken vines and torn creepers. The animal gazed with astonished eyes at the scene into which it had been precipitated, then dropped its head to the grass and began contentedly to graze. A second horse scrambled into view, slipping once on the mossy rocks and regaining equilibrium when its hoofs sank into the yielding surface of the meadow. It was riderless, though on its back was a high-horned Mexican saddle, scarred and discolored by long usage.

The man brought up the rear. He threw off pack and saddle, with an eye to camp location, and gave the animals their free-

dom to graze. He unpacked his food and got out frying-pan
and coffee-pot. He gathered an armful of dry wood, and with a
few stones made a place for his fire.

"My!" he said, "but I've got an appetite. I could scoff iron-
filings an' horseshoe nails an' thank you kindly, ma'am, for a
second helpin'."

He straightened up, and, while he reached for matches in the
pocket of his overalls, his eyes traveled across the pool to the
side-hill. His fingers had clutched the match-box, but they
relaxed their hold and the hand came out empty. The man
wavered perceptibly. He looked at his preparations for cooking
and he looked at the hill.

"Guess I'll take another whack at her," he concluded, starting
to cross the stream.

"They ain't no sense in it, I know," he mumbled apologet-
ically. "But keepin' grub back an hour ain't goin' to hurt none, I
reckon."

A few feet back from his first of test-pans he started a second
line. The sun dropped down the western sky, the shadows
lengthened, but the man worked on. He began a third line of
test-pans. He was cross-cutting the hillside, line by line, as he
ascended. The center of each line produced the richest pans,
while the ends came where no colors showed in the pan. And as
he ascended the hillside the lines grew perceptibly shorter. The
regularity with which their length diminished served to indicate that somewhere up the slope the last line would be so short
as to have scarcely length at all, and that beyond could come
only a point. The design was growing into an inverted "V."
The converging sides of this "V" marked the boundaries of the
gold-bearing dirt.

The apex of the "V" was evidently the man's goal. Often he
ran his eye along the converging sides and on up the hill, trying
to divine the apex, the point where the gold-bearing dirt must
cease. Here resided "Mr. Pocket"—for so the man familiarly
addressed the imaginary point above him on the slope, crying
out:

"Come down out o' that, Mr. Pocket! Be right smart an'
agreeable, an' come down!"

"All right," he would add later, in a voice resigned to determination. "All right, Mr. Pocket. It's plain to me I got to come right up an' snatch you out bald-headed. An' I'll do it! I'll do it!" he would threaten still later.

Each pan he carried down to the water to wash, and as he went higher up the hill the pans grew richer, until he began to save the gold in an empty baking powder can which he carried carelessly in his hip-pocket. So engrossed was he in his toil that he did not notice the long twilight of oncoming night. It was not until he tried vainly to see the gold colors in the bottom of the pan that he realized the passage of time. He straightened up abruptly. An expression of whimsical wonderment and awe overspread his face as he drawled:

"Gosh darn my buttons! if I didn't plumb forget dinner!"

He stumbled across the stream in the darkness and lighted his long-delayed fire. Flapjacks and bacon and warmed-over beans constituted his supper. Then he smoked a pipe by the smouldering coals, listening to the night noises and watching the moonlight stream through the canyon. After that he unrolled his bed, took off his heavy shoes, and pulled the blankets up to his chin. His face showed white in the moonlight, like the face of a corpse. But it was a corpse that knew its resurrection, for the man rose suddenly on one elbow and gazed across at his hillside.

"Good night, Mr. Pocket," he called sleepily. "Good night."

He slept through the early gray of morning until the direct rays of the sun smote his closed eyelids, when he awoke with a start and looked about him until he had established the continuity of his existence and identified his present self with the days previously lived.

To dress, he had merely to buckle on his shoes. He glanced at his fireplace and at his hillside, wavered, but fought down the temptation and started the fire.

"Keep yer shirt on, Bill; keep yer shirt on," he admonished himself. "What's the good of rushin'? No use in gettin' all het up an' sweaty. Mr. Pocket'll wait for you. He ain't a-runnin' away before you can get your breakfast. Now, what you want, Bill, is something fresh in yer bill o' fare. So it's up to you to go an' get it."

He cut a short pole at the water's edge and drew from one of his pockets a bit of line and a draggled fly that had once been a royal coachman.

"Mebbe they'll bite in the early morning," he muttered, as he made his first cast into the pool. And a moment later he was gleefully crying: "What'd I tell you, eh? What'd I tell you?"

He had no reel, nor any inclination to waste time, and by main strength, and swiftly, he drew out of the water a flashing ten-inch trout. Three more, caught in rapid succession, furnished his breakfast. When he came to the stepping-stones on his way to his hillside, he was struck by a sudden thought, and paused.

"I'd just better take a hike down-stream a ways," he said. "There's no tellin' who may be snoopin' around."

But he crossed over on the stones, and with a "I really oughter take that hike," the need of the precaution passed out of his mind and he fell to work.

At nightfall he straightened up. The small of his back was stiff from stooping toil, and as he put his hand behind him to soothe the protesting muscles, he said:

"Now what d'ye think of that? I clean forgot my dinner again! If I don't watch out, I'll sure be degeneratin' into a two-meal-a-day crank.

"Pockets is the hangedest things I ever see for makin' a man absent-minded," he communed that night, as he crawled into his blankets. Nor did he forget to call up the hillside, "Good night, Mr. Pocket! Good night!"

Rising with the sun, and snatching a hasty breakfast, he was early at work. A fever seemed to be growing in him, nor did the increasing richness of the test-pans allay this fever. There was a flush in his cheek other than that made by the heat of the sun, and he was oblivious to fatigue and the passage of time. When he filled a pan with dirt, he ran down the hill to wash it; nor could he forbear running up the hill again, panting and stumbling profanely, to refill the pan.

He was now a hundred yards from the water, and the inverted "V" was assuming definite proportions. The width of the paydirt steadily decreased, and the man extended in his mind's eye the sides of the "V" to their meeting place far up the hill. This was his goal, the apex of the "V," and he panned many times to locate it.

"Just about two yards above that manzanita bush an' a yard to the right," he finally concluded.

Then the temptation seized him. "As plain as the nose on your face," he said, as he abandoned his laborious cross-cutting and climbed to the indicated apex. He filled a pan and carried it down the hill to wash. It contained no trace of gold. He dug deep, and he dug shallow, filling and washing a dozen pans, and was unrewarded even by the tiniest golden speck. He was enraged at having yielded to the temptation, and berated himself blasphemously and pridelessly. Then he went down the hill and took up the cross-cutting.

"Slow an' certain, Bill; slow an' certain," he crooned. "Short-cuts to fortune ain't in your line, an' it's about time you know it. Get wise, Bill; get wise. Slow an' certain's the only hand you can play; so get to it, an' keep to it, too."

As the cross-cuts decreased, showing that the sides of the "V" were converging, the depth of the "V" increased. The gold-trace was dipping into the hill. It was only at thirty inches beneath the surface that he could get colors in his pan. The dirt he found at twenty-five inches from the surface, and at thirty-five inches yielded barren pans. At the base of the "V," by the water's edge, he had found the gold colors at the grass roots. The higher he went up the hill, the deeper the gold dipped. To dig a hole three feet deep in order to get one test-pan was a task of no mean magnitude; while between the man and the apex intervened an untold number of such holes to be dug. "An' there's no tellin' how much deeper it'll pitch," he sighed, in a moment's pause, while his fingers soothed his aching back.

Feverish with desire, with aching back and stiffening muscles, with pick and shovel gouging and mauling the soft brown earth, the man toiled up the hill. Before him was the smooth slope, spangled with flowers and made sweet with their breath. Behind him was devastation. It looked like some terrible eruption breaking out on the smooth skin of the hill. His slow progress was like that of a slug, befouling beauty with a monstrous trail.

Though the dipping gold-trace increased the man's work, he found consolation in the increasing richness of the pans. Twenty cents, thirty cents, fifty cents, sixty cents, were the values of the gold found in the pans, and at nightfall he washed his banner pan, which gave him a dollar's worth of gold-dust from a shovelful of dirt.

"I'll just bet it's my luck to have some inquisitive one come buttin' in here on my pasture," he mumbled sleepily that night as he pulled the blankets up to his chin.

Suddenly he sat upright. "Bill!" he called sharply. "Now, listen to me, Bill; d'ye hear! It's up to you, to-morrow mornin', to mosey round an' see what you can see. Understand? To-morrow morning, an' don't you forget it!"

He yawned and glanced across at his side-hill. "Good night, Mr. Pocket," he called.

In the morning he stole a march on the sun, for he had finished breakfast when its first rays caught him, and he was climbing the wall of the canyon where it crumbled away and gave footing. From the outlook at the top he found himself in the midst of loneliness. As far as he could see, chain after chain of mountains heaved themselves into his vision. To the east his eyes, leaping the miles between range and range and between many ranges, brought up at last against the white-peaked Sierras—the main crest, where the backbone of the Western world reared itself against the sky. To the north and south he could see more distinctly the cross-systems that broke through the main trend of the sea of mountains. To the west the ranges fell away, one behind the other, diminishing and fading into the gentle foothills that, in turn, descended into the great valley which he could not see.

And in all that mighty sweep of earth he saw no sign of man nor of the handiwork of man—save only the torn bosom of the hillside at his feet. The man looked long and carefully. Once, far down his own canyon, he thought he saw in the air a faint hint of smoke. He looked again and decided that it was the purple haze of the hills made dark by a convolution of the canyon wall at its back.

"Hey, you, Mr. Pocket!" he called down into the canyon.

"Stand out from under! I'm a-comin', Mr. Pocket! I'm a-comin'!"

The heavy brogans on the man's feet made him appear clumsy-footed, but he swung down from the giddy height as lightly and airily as a mountain goat. A rock, turning under his foot on the edge of the precipice, did not disconcert him. He seemed to know the precise time required for the turn to culminate in disaster, and in the meantime he utilized the false footing itself for the momentary earth-contact necessary to carry him on into safety. Where the earth sloped so steeply that it was impossible to stand for a second upright, the man did not hesitate. His foot pressed the impossible surface for but a fraction of the fatal second and gave him the bound that carried him onward. Again, where even the fraction of a second's footing was out of the question, he would swing his body past by a moment's hand-grip on a jutting knob of rock, a crevice, or a precariously rooted shrub. At last, with a wild leap and yell, he exchanged the face of the wall for an earthslide and finished the descent in the midst of several tons of sliding earth and gravel.

His first pan of the morning washed out over two dollars in coarse gold. It was from the centre of the "V." To either side the diminution in the values of the pans was swift. His lines of cross-cutting holes were growing very short. The converging sides of the inverted "V" were only a few yards apart. Their meeting-point was only a few yards above him. But the pay-streak was dipping deeper and deeper into the earth. By early afternoon he was sinking the test-holes five feet before the pans could show the gold-trace.

For that matter, the gold-trace had become something more than a trace; it was a placer mine in itself, and the man resolved to come back after he had found the pocket and work over the ground. But the increasing richness of the pans began to worry him. By late afternoon the worth of the pans had grown to three and four dollars. The man scratched his head perplexedly and looked a few feet up the hill at the manzanita bush that marked approximately the apex of the "V." He nodded his head and said oracularly:

"It's one o' two things, Bill: one o' two things. Either Mr.

Pocket's spilled himself all out an' down the hill, or else Mr. Pocket's so rich you maybe won't be able to carry him all away with you. And that 'd be an awful shame, wouldn't it, now?" He chuckled at contemplation of so pleasant a dilemma.

Nightfall found him by the edge of the stream, his eyes wrestling with the gathering darkness over the washing of a five-dollar pan.

"Wisht I had an electric light to go on working," he said.

He found sleep difficult that night. Many times he composed himself and closed his eyes for slumber to overtake him; but his blood pounded with too strong desire, and as many times his eyes opened and he murmured wearily, "Wisht it was sun-up."

Sleep came to him in the end, but his eyes were open with the first paling of the stars, and the gray of dawn caught him with breakfast finished and climbing the hillside in the direction of the secret abiding-place of Mr. Pocket.

The first cross-cut the man made, there was space for only three holes, so narrow had become the pay-streak and so close was he to the fountainhead of the golden stream he had been following for four days.

"Be ca'm, Bill; be ca'm," he admonished himself, as he broke ground for the final hole where the sides of the "V" had at last come together in a point.

"I've got the almighty cinch on you, Mr. Pocket, an' you can't lose me," he said many times as he sank the hole deeper and deeper.

Four feet, five feet, six feet, he dug his way down into the earth. The digging grew harder. His pick grated on broken rock. He examined the rock. "Rotten quartz," was his conclusion as, with the shovel, he cleared the bottom of the hole of loose dirt. He attacked the crumbling quartz with the pick, bursting the disintegrating rock asunder with every stroke.

He thrust his shovel into the loose mass. His eye caught a gleam of yellow. He dropped the shovel and squatted suddenly on his heels. As a farmer rubs the clinging earth from fresh-dug potatoes, so the man, a piece of rotten quartz held in both hands, rubbed the dirt away.

"Sufferin' Sardanopolis!" he cried. "Lumps an' chunks of it! Lumps an' chunks of it!"

It was only half rock he held in his hand. The other half was virgin gold. He dropped it into his pan and examined another piece. Little yellow was to be seen, but with his strong fingers he crumbled the quartz away till both hands were filled with glowing yellow. He rubbed the dirt away from fragment after fragment, tossing them into the gold-pan. It was a treasure-hole. So much had the quartz rotted away that there was less of it than there was of gold. Now and again he found a piece to which no rock clung—a piece that was all gold. A chunk, where the pick had laid open the heart of the gold, glittered like a handful of yellow jewels, and he cocked his head at it and slowly turned it around and over to observe the rich play of the light upon it.

"Talk about yer Too Much Gold diggin's!" the man snorted contemptuously. "Why, this diggin' 'd make it look like thirty cents. This diggin' is All Gold. An' right here an' now I name this yere canyon 'All Gold Canyon,' b' gosh!"

Still squatting on his heels, he continued examining the fragments and tossing them into the pan. Suddenly there came to him a premonition of danger. It seemed a shadow had fallen upon him. But there was no shadow. His heart had given a great jump up into his throat and was choking him. Then his blood slowly chilled and he felt the sweat of his shirt cold against his flesh.

He did not spring up nor look around. He did not move. He was considering the nature of the premonition he had received, trying to locate the source of the mysterious force that had warned him, striving to sense the imperative presence of the unseen thing that threatened him. There is an aura of things hostile, made manifest by messengers too refined for the senses to know; and this aura he felt, but knew not how he felt it. His was the feeling as when a cloud passes over the sun. It seemed that between him and life had passed something dark and smothering and menacing; a gloom, as it were, that swallowed up life and made for death—his death.

Every force of his being impelled him to spring up and confront the unseen danger, but his soul dominated the panic, and he remained squatting on his heels, in his hands a chunk of gold. He did not dare to look around, but he knew by now that there was something behind him and above him. He made believe to be interested in the gold in his hand. He examined it critically, turned it over and over, and rubbed the dirt from it. And all the time he knew that something behind him was looking at the gold over his shoulder.

Still feigning interest in the chunk of gold in his hand, he listened intently and he heard the breathing of the thing behind him. His eyes searched the ground in front of him for a weapon, but they saw only the uprooted gold, worthless to him now in his extremity. There was the pick, a handy weapon on occasion; but this was not such an occasion. The man realized his predicament. He was in a narrow hole that was seven feet deep. His head did not come to the surface of the ground. He was in a trap.

He remained squatting on his heels. He was quite cool and collected; but his mind, considering every factor, showed him only his helplessness. He continued rubbing the dirt from the quartz fragments and throwing the gold into the pan. There was nothing else for him to do. Yet he knew that he would have to rise up, sooner or later, and face the danger that breathed at his back. The minutes passed, and with the passage of each minute he knew that by so much he was nearer the time when he must stand up, or else—and his wet shirt went cold against his flesh again at the thought—or else he might receive death as he stooped there over his treasure.

Still he squatted on his heels, rubbing dirt from gold and debating in just what manner he should rise up. He might rise up with a rush and claw his way out of the hole to meet whatever threatened on the even footing above ground. Or he might rise up slowly and carelessly, and feign casually to discover the thing that breathed at his back. His instinct and every fighting fibre of his body favored the mad, clawing rush to the surface. His intellect, and the craft thereof, favored the slow and cautious meeting with the thing that menaced and which he could not see. And while he debated, a loud, crashing noise burst on his ear. At the same instant he received a stunning blow on the left side of his back, and from the point of impact felt a rush of flame through his flesh. He sprang up in the air, but halfway to his feet collapsed. His body crumpled in like a leaf withered in sudden heat, and he came down, his chest across his pan of gold, his face in the dirt and rock, his legs tangled and twisted because of the restricted space at the bottom of the hole. His legs twitched convulsively several times. His body was shaken with a mighty ague. There was a slow expansion of the lungs, accompanied by a deep sigh. Then the air was slowly, very slowly, exhaled, and his body as slowly flattened itself down into inertness.

Above, revolver in hand, a man was peering down over the edge of the hole. He peered for a long time at the prone and motionless body beneath him. After a while the stranger sat down on the edge of the hole so that he could see into it, and rested the revolver on his knee. Reaching his hand into a pocket, he drew out a wisp of brown paper. Into this he dropped a few crumbs of tobacco. The combination became a cigarette, brown and squat, with the ends turned in. Not once did he take his eyes from the body at the bottom of the hole. He lighted the cigarette and drew its smoke into his lungs with a caressing intake of the breath. He smoked slowly. Once the cigarette went out and he relighted it. And all the while he studied the body beneath him.

In the end he tossed the cigarette stub away and rose to his feet. He moved to the edge of the hole. Spanning it, a hand resting on each edge, and with the revolver still in the right hand, he muscled his body down into the hole. While his feet were yet a yard from the bottom he released his hands and dropped down.

At the instant his feet struck bottom he saw the pocketminer's arm leap out, and his own legs knew a swift, jerking grip that overthrew him. In the nature of the jump his revolverhand was above his head. Swiftly as the grip had flashed about his legs, just as swiftly he brought the revolver down. He was still in the air, his fall in process of completion, when he pulled the trigger. The explosion was deafening in the confined space. The smoke filled the hole so that he could see nothing. He struck the bottom on his back, and like a cat's the pocketminer's body was on top of him. Even as the miner's body passed on top, the stranger crooked in his right arm to fire; and even in that instant the miner, with a quick thrust of elbow, struck his wrist. The muzzle was thrown up and the bullet thudded into the dirt of the side of the hole.

The next instant the stranger felt the miner's hand grip his wrist. The struggle was now for the revolver. Each man strove to turn it against the other's body. The smoke in the hole was clearing. The stranger, lying on his back, was beginning to see dimly. But suddenly he was blinded by a handful of dirt deliberately flung into his eyes by his antagonist. In that moment of shock his grip on the revolver was broken. In the next moment he felt a smashing darkness descend upon his brain, and in the midst of the darkness even the darkness ceased.

But the pocket-miner fired again and again, until the revolver was empty. Then he tossed it from him and, breathing heavily, sat down on the dead man's legs.

The miner was sobbing and struggling for breath. "Measly skunk!" he panted; "a-campin' on my trail an' lettin' me do the work, an' then shootin' me in the back!"

He was half crying from anger and exhaustion. He peered at the face of the dead man. It was sprinkled with loose dirt and gravel, and it was difficult to distinguish the features.

"Never laid eyes on him before," the miner concluded his scrutiny. "Just a common an' ordinary thief, hang him! An' he shot me in the back! He shot me in the back!"

He opened his shirt and felt himself, front and back, on his left side.

"Went clean through, and no harm done!" he cried jubilantly. "I'll bet he aimed all right all right; but he drew the gun over when he pulled the trigger—the cur! But I fixed 'm! Oh, I fixed 'm!"

His fingers were investigating the bullet-hole in his side, and a shade of regret passed over his face. "It's goin' to be stiffer'n hell," he said. "An' it's up to me to get mended an' get out o' here."

He crawled out of the hole and went down the hill to his camp. Half an hour later he returned, leading his pack-horse. His open shirt disclosed the rude bandages with which he had dressed his wound. He was slow and awkward with his left-hand movements, but that did not prevent his using the arm.

The bight of the pack-rope under the dead man's shoulders

enabled him to heave the body out of the hole. Then he set to work gathering up his gold. He worked steadily for several hours, pausing often to rest his stiffening shoulder and to exclaim:

"He shot me in the back, the measly skunk! He shot me in the back!"

When his treasure was quite cleaned up and wrapped securely into a number of blanket-covered parcels, he made an estimate of its value.

"Four hundred pounds, or I'm a Hottentot," he concluded. "Say two hundred in quartz an' dirt—that leaves two hundred pounds of gold. Bill! Wake up! Two hundred pounds of gold! Forty thousand dollars! An' it's yourn—all yourn!"

He scratched his head delightedly and his fingers blundered into an unfamiliar groove. They quested along it for several inches. It was a crease through his scalp where the second bullet had ploughed.

He walked angrily over to the dead man.

"You would, would you?" he bullied. "You would, eh? Well, I fixed you good an' plenty, an' I'll give you a decent burial, too. That's more'n you'd have done for me."

He dragged the body to the edge of the hole and toppled it in. It struck the bottom with a dull crash, on its side, the face twisted up to the light. The miner peered down at it.

"An' you shot me in the back!" he said accusingly.

With pick and shovel he filled the hole. Then he loaded the gold on his horse. It was too great a load for the animal, and when he had gained his camp he transferred part of it to his saddle-horse. Even so, he was compelled to abandon a portion of his outfit—pick and shovel and gold-pan, extra food and cooking utensils, and divers odds and ends.

The sun was at the zenith when the man forced the horses at the screen of vines and creepers. To climb the huge boulders the animals were compelled to uprear and struggle blindly through the tangled mass of vegetation. Once the saddle-horse fell heavily and the man removed the pack to get the animal on its feet. After it started on its way again the man thrust his head out from among the leaves and peered up at the hillside.

"The measly skunk!" he said, and disappeared.

There was a ripping and tearing of vines and boughs. The trees surged back and forth, marking the passage of the animals through the midst of them. There was a clashing of steel-shod hoofs on stone, and now and again a sharp cry of command. Then the voice of the man was raised in song:—

> "Tu'n around an' tu'n yo' face
> Untoe them sweet hills of grace
> (D' pow'rs of sin yo' am scornin'!).
> Look about an' look aroun'
> Fling yo' sin-pack on d' groun'
> (Yo' will meet wid d' Lord in d' mornin'!)."

The song grew faint and fainter, and through the silence crept back the spirit of the place. The stream once more drowsed and whispered; the hum of the mountain bees rose sleepily. Down through the perfume-weighted air fluttered the snowy fluffs of the cottonwoods. The butterflies drifted in and out among the trees, and over all blazed the quiet sunshine. Only remained the hoof-marks in the meadow and the torn hillside to mark the boisterous trail of the life that had broken the peace of the place and passed on.

EDWIN CORLE

The Ghost of Billy the Kid

A writer who devoted himself to dramatizing the deserts of the South-west and the people who dwelt there was Edwin Corle (1906–56). In a happy-go-lucky style, devoid of sentimentality, he told of the beauties and perils of those empty regions.

Born in Wildwood, New Jersey, Corle obtained a bachelor's degree from the University of California at Los Angeles and attended Yale University. He began writing for radio. His first story was published in the Atlantic Monthly. *"The Ghost of Billy the Kid," an account of a legendary figure of the Panamint Range west of Death Valley, is taken from Corle's first book,* Mojave: A Book of Stories *(1934). Other works by Corle include* Fig Tree John *(1935),* People of the Earth *(1937),* Desert Country *(1941),* In Winter Light *(1949),* The Gila, River of the Southwest *(1951), and a fictionalized life,* Billy the Kid *(1953).*

The Ghost of Billy the Kid haunts the Panamint country north of the Slate Range. Of course it is all nonsense because nobody believes in ghosts and Billy the Kid was never in California. But the rumor started and it continues to persist as rumors will.

Billy the Kid, since his death at the age of twenty-one, and his record of chivalry and deadliness (twenty-one men sent to eternity by this youth not counting Mexicans and Indians) has become the Robin Hood of New Mexico. The boy must have had charm and generosity and loyalty, for he has become something of a folk-hero in the half century since his death at the hand of Sheriff Pat Garrett in the Maxwell House at Old Fort Sumner in the early eighteen-eighties. But he also had a cold eye and a lightning trigger finger that allowed him to empty with accuracy a six-shooter a split second sooner than any other man in the southwest. . . .

After the Kid's death there were several absurd rumors to the effect that he had escaped to Mexico, that he was living in disguise in the Pecos Valley, and that he had fled to Arizona. All of these were absolutely groundless and it is an established fact that Billy the Kid is buried at the abandoned military burying ground at old Fort Sumner. The old military post was trail's end for Billy, and any further account of his life is sheer fiction and the embroidery of imaginative minds. What, then, of this ghost of Billy the Kid who lives in the Panamint Valley? Is it all a wild yarn with no truth to back it up? Yes, it's a wild yarn, but yet . . . ?

In one of the half deserted mining towns lives an old man whose only name seems to be "The Kid," but whose initials are W.B. And as every one knows who has been interested in the real Billy, his legitimate name was William Bonney.

This old man is close to eighty and his mind is not as co-herent as it might be. His speech rambles. He has a white beard and blue eyes. He is only about five feet eight inches tall and he has very small hands. Those hands are no longer steady, but in spite of that fact he can whip out a six-shooter and put six bullets in a target with astounding speed and accuracy. He won't tell any one his name, but insists that he has been "The Kid" for eighty years, and "The Kid" he intends to remain. He never mentions Billy the Kid, and never plays upon the idea that he was ever William Bonney. When asked if he has ever visited New Mexico, he says yes, but as it was almost sixty years ago, it seems like another life to him.

When asked what he did in New Mexico, The Kid replies that he roamed around, and punched cattle, and worked for some of the big cattle men of the time. And he always adds, "And I learned how to handle a gun." But at the mention of the Lincoln County War, and Murphy and McSween and Gover-nor Lew Wallace, he says nothing.

It is possible, however, to get this old man to admit that he has been outside the law several times in his life. But he will never be specific about it, and the most he ever says about New Mexico is that "life was pretty fast there in the old days."

Only a few people have associated this Panamint Valley Kid with Billy the Kid, and one of the more curious deliberately mentioned the name of Bob Ollinger to him. Now Bob Ollinger was a bad man of the eighteen-eighties and he wanted everybody to know it. He wasn't in trouble with the law, but he went around with the proverbial chip way out on the edge of his shoulder. He liked to be considered dangerous. Of course such a man was naive and even childish. Billy the Kid had none of the theatrical desperado about him. He had nothing but scorn for Ollinger. And it so happened that when Billy the Kid was in jail in Lincoln under sentence to be hung, Ollinger, and a man named Bell, were his guards. Bell was a decent sort, but Ollinger, who hated The Kid because he was jealous of his reputation, loved to irritate him and to talk about the approaching hanging. Ollinger must have had a sadistic streak, for he kept rubbing it into The Kid about his imminent death on the gallows, and how few days of life were remaining to him, and how he would dance in the air, and how the rope would choke the rotten life out of him, and how his body would stiffen, and how he himself would put a load of buckshot into the remains of The Kid if he had half a chance.

All that sort of thing must have made Billy writhe, but he said little or nothing in reply. But if he said nothing, he did plenty. A few days before the date of the hanging Ollinger was eating his dinner across the street from the jail in Lincoln. That left The Kid with the remaining guard, Bell. There has been much speculation as to how it was done, and some authorities romantically visualize it as over a card game, but by whatever means possible, Billy managed to get Bell's revolver. That was a costly mistake for Bell, and not being shrewd enough to placate The Kid, who bore him no particular malice, he tried to dash out of the room. The Kid, naturally enough, shot him through the heart.

Ollinger, finishing his meal across the street, gulped the remains of a cup of coffee, and went running back to the jail. The room in which The Kid had been confined was the second story of the old court house. And as Ollinger came lumbering across the street, a quiet, "Hello, Bob," stopped him in his tracks. He looked up ⸗i the second story window and saw The Kid smiling down at him with a smile that had little good humor in it. And that's the last thing he ever saw.

Every one in Lincoln knew the desperado was loose, and no one dared do anything about it. Billy the Kid took the county clerk's horse and rode out of town never to return. The entire episode was perhaps the most sensational jail break in the history of New Mexico, and certainly a high spot in the vivid escapades of The Kid.

Now if this old man living alone in the Panamint country were the real Billy, the entire Ollinger episode must have remained forever in his memory. So, of course, must his experiences with Sheriff Pat Garrett. But whenever Garrett's name is mentioned the old man fails to express any kind of an emotion or even recognition of the name. It is a discouraging test for any one who romantically hopes that he has stumbled upon the ghost of a bad man, or who wants to believe that this old man may have been Billy the Kid. And that is just as it should be. For he cannot be the real Billy if the real Billy died over fifty years ago at old Fort Sumner.

But to return to the incident of Bob Ollinger. Apparently, only one man ever mentioned Ollinger to this Panamint Valley Kid, and he got a reaction. The old man was sitting in the shade of his little shack which was on a slight rise of ground overlooking a dry wash. He and the stranger were making small talk of sidewinders and gila monsters. Leading the conversation to reptiles in general, the stranger casually said:

"I knew a rattlesnake once whose name was Bob Ollinger. Ever hear of him?"

The old man stared at the distant mountains, and very slowly began to smile. It was a cool and deliberate and extremely satisfied smile. He picked up a revolver that he had been toying with in his lap.

"Now he comes out of the hotel onto the porch," he remarked. "He's lookin' around to see where that first shot came from. He's wipin' the coffee off his mouth with one hand, and he trots across the street toward the jail. Now he's half way. Now he's right there where that tin can is settin'."

The stranger didn't say a word. He held his breath while the old man leveled the revolver at a tin can twenty feet away. The old man's hand was steady and his face had a cold, mirthless smile.

"Hello, Bob," he said softly with a slight drawl.

Then he fired and the tin gave six spasmodic jumps along the ground as six bullets went through it.

"And take that to hell with you," he said, and he put the revolver down beside him.

Then both men were quiet, and the stranger didn't know what to say. But presently the old man scratched the back of his neck.

"Ollinger, did you say?" He was looking blank and the smile was gone. "Ollinger, eh? Nope. Don't recollect that I ever heard of him."

IDWAL JONES

China Boy

Born in Wales, Idwal Jones (1887–1964) was brought to the eastern
United States as a child by his father, a quarryman. Although the boy
was partially deaf, he compensated with visual acuity and intuition
and so was able to make a living as a journalist (in fact, he was once
drama and music critic of the San Francisco Examiner). His father,
however, had decided that Idwal must be a laborer and put him to slave
in an upstate New York steel mill, where he contracted tuberculosis.
After recuperating in a sanatorium, Jones went to California in 1911 in
search of improved health. He acknowledged as the chief influence on
his writing the stories of Bret Harte. He is a laureate of the Mother
Lode as well as of the Napa Valley, scene of his masterwork, the novel
The Vineyard (1942).

Publication in 1926 of his first book enabled Jones to take his wife
and small daughter abroad for several years, but the depression caused
his return to the United States and until 1933 he was a reviewer,
columnist, and feature writer on the New York American. Thereafter he lived in San Francisco and, later, Los Angeles, as a Hollywood
publicity writer and free-lance author of articles and books.

China Boy and Other Stories, *from which "China Boy" is
taken, was published in 1936 by Primavera Press, the imprint of the
bookshop owner and poet Jake Zeitlin, whose place was a rendezvous
for Los Angeles bohemians and artists. The collection, drawing on the
author's adventures on the Mother Lode and the Sacramento–San
Joaquin deltas and in San Francisco, can be placed alongside Bret
Harte's best. The following selection is a straight-faced account of a
laboring Chinese immigrant perhaps not much more remarkable than*

many of his countrymen who came to labor on the railroads or in the fields of the promised land of America.

I first beheld Pon Look twelve years ago, and even then he was the oldest human creature in Fiddle Creek township. It was on top of Confidence Hill one August day, when the pines were withering in the terrific heat and the road was a foot deep in white dust. Pon Look came over the brow of the hill, from below.

He waddled like a crab, leaning on a staff, and extreme age had bent his body at a right angle to his stunted legs. His physiognomy was fearsome, like a Chinese actor's in a print. His head was sunk forward, so that his ears were in line with his shoulders, and the protuberant chin was adorned with sparse, silvery hairs. For all he had the aspect of a crippled galley-slave, he progressed smartly, slewing that head continually from side to side with a strange grace. He seemed to be propelling himself through the heat waves with that sculling movement. He had something alive, which he held in check with a rope. It was a large, feline animal, with a bobbed tail and a funny wicker hat fitting over its head, like a muzzle. At intervals this beast leaped into the air, and, uttering frantic cries, tore furiously at the muzzle with its forefeet. It had eyes as glittering as topazes. It was a superb catamount. Pon Look no more minded its antics than if they were the antics of a mosquito.

I offered Pon Look a cigar. His face wreathed instantly with smiles, and he took it shyly. Laughter wrinkles creased his smooth high forehead.

"You are taking your pet out for a breath of air?"

"Pet?" he queried. Meanwhile the catamount was whirring insanely in the dust, at taut rope, with the velocity of a squirrel in a cage. "Pet?—oh, no—I jus' catch heem now in the canyon."

"What are you going to do with him?"

Pon Look gave a fierce yank at the rope. "Oh—I tame him first. Then in two weeks, if not fliendly, I kill him." . . .

Across from the Flat was a narrow pass in a long mountain of black, igneous rock. The mountain was in a semi-circle, and encompassed many square miles of the only green land in the countryside. It was moist from hidden springs, and the virgin soil, overlaid with a humus of centuries, was phenomenal in its richness. Old Man Summerfield owned it. He was a hard-scrabble Vermont farmer who lived in a good house with his haggard wife. He waylaid cattle from the ox-trains, and de-coyed them into the enclosure. They bred calves, and he grew passably rich. He dwelt in antipathy with his neighbors, who at night frequently took potshots at him. It was on the domains of this ogre that Pon Look trespassed. The owner came riding out with a rifle.

"What do you want here, you yellow limb? Get off my place!"

"A job," responded Pon Look.

After some reflection, the farmer manoeuvred Pon Look, as if he were a stray ox, and drove him to the cow-house.

"Live there," he snarled. "You'll find some sacks to sleep on."

Pon Look entered upon his duties, and became known as Summerfield's China Boy. There were twenty-five head of cattle, and it was his function to ride about on horseback and keep a wary eye on them, and if they showed symptoms of bursting, to dismount and stab them in the belly with a trochar. Because of the succulence of the grass they would overeat and suffer from bloat.

He acquired a sympathy with these animals, and in his solici-tude would keep them moving incessantly, and try to retain them where the grass was somewhat less luxuriant. One night a handsome black bull escaped through the pass and vanished. Probably it got carved into steaks by unscrupulous neighbors. Old Man Summerfield frothed through his beard. He raged at Pon Look.

"What am I paying you board for, hey? To lose cattle for me? If that happens again—you get kicked out!"

The boy was aghast. There was every likelihood that it would happen again. It was then that he conceived the idea of building a wall around the ranch. It was a felicitous idea. Along one side of the low cliff was a talus of lava boulders; material right to hand. The stuff was in every size, from pebbles to bigness of a fist to rocks the size of a huge hog, and all rounded by aeons of time. The most of them resembled footballs, and were known locally as nigger-heads.

He built a stone-boat, trained a cadgy old ox to haul it, and began to close the pass. He built a wall six feet high, and three and a half wide, with a wooden gate in the middle. The quarry was a quarter mile distant, and his tools were a crowbar and an end of plank. The job was finished after a year of back-breaking toil and the cost of Pon Look's right toe. Old Man Summerfield was so proud of this entrance that he spent hours sitting on the gate so people could see him as they drove by.

It was a notably fine gate, portentous and eye-taking. It was a gate that connoted landed respectability, and its psychological effect was curious. Old Man Summerfield swelled with self-esteem. He loafed at the saloons in the camp, and leading talk to the job, arrogated to himself all the credit for its design and building.

"It's all in handling the ma-terial," he would say. "You got to know how to lay them boulders and lock 'em so they won't roll off like balloons. They's nothing like a good gate to keep the cattle in."

"A better gate 'ud be one that kept other folks' cattle out," some neighbor would remark, after Old Man Summerfield had left.

The China Boy's task was only just started. He now began to haul boulders to close in the southern and open arc of the circle. He lived on a diet of boiled beef and rice, which he cooked at his end of the cow-house, where he also slept. He arose before dawn, ate breakfast, then hitched the ox and boated a load of nigger-heads to the scene of operations. These he laid down before he returned to do the chores and attend to the milch cows. Not even after the rainy season was past was danger to the cattle over, and he had to be vigilant against the bloat. His masonry plan was to lay down the bottom tier, for the space of four miles, large boulders that required a trip apiece; then to superimpose smaller boulders, then loads upon loads of nigger-heads, until the wall was complete.

Progress was slow. The stone-boat ox would cough, then die

very soon, and Pon Look had to train another one; or the
vehicle would wear out, and he had to build another. Old Man
Summerfield's wife, who had kept within the house and was
wont to shout loud at night, gave up the ghost, so the master
went to San Francisco to do some wooing, and being, as he
said, "a particular man to please," it was three months before he
returned with her successor. The boy did the work of two men
in the meanwhile, but had to suspend work on the wall.

The new mistress was a fat shrew of a body, with a clacking
tongue, and much displeased Pon Look by her interference. She
made him beat carpets, trudge about the country to buy laying
hens, and dig a garden. He submitted to it all, and arose an hour
earlier, making a return trip with the stone-boat before sun-up.
On one occasion, as he was passing by the house, she called to
him to come in and wash the dishes. He said no. Whereupon
she rushed at him with a broom and smote him violently as he
stood in the yard. Pon Look took the blows without a murmur,
and remained like a statue, with hands folded, while his mistress, still plying the broom, waxed hysterical.

There was no budging Pon Look. She spun round to beat at
his face. It was serene, but pallid. The lips bespoke an obstinate
resolve, but the eyes gleamed mistly at her with pity and for-
giveness. Mrs. Summerfield's arms dropped, then she clutched
at her throat, and staring at him walked backward into the
house.

When Pon Look returned to the cow-house that night, he
found on his table a hot raisin pie. On the window-sill the next
morning, Mrs. Summerfield found the pie plate, scrubbed
with the sand so bright that it reflected the sun like a mirror,
and upon it a handful of the white daisies that grew nowhere
except near the bog a mile distant. Pon Look had dined that
night, as usual, on rice and beef. The mystified hens, before
going to roost, had filled their craws with pastry and raisins.

Thenceforward, Mrs. Summerfield treated Pon Look with a
respect that was a compound of both affection and fear. On no
pretext could he be induced to enter her house. She did not
know what to make of him, so she left him alone. She ran the
domestic establishment, but Pon Look, since the old man spent
all day and half the night in the camp saloon, saw to the running

of the ranch, the sale of the cattle, and of course, the con-
struction of the wall.

"You don't have ter build that wall entire of rocks, China
Boy," she said one evening, when the indomitable mason,
scrubbed, and in his fresh alpaca coat, stood surveying in the
dusk the lengthening boundary of the ranch. "Wire's just as
good, and fence-stakes is cheaper than they was."

Pon Look gave a smile so expansive that his eyes disappeared
in the creases. "Make 'um all stone, Mis' Sommyfeel'—begin
'um stone, and finish 'um stone, allee same niggy haid."

She plucked timorously at her alpaca apron. "Oh, well, it's
you're doing it, not us."

Yet she took a pride in the fabulous immensity of the task.
The editor of the county-town paper drove over one day and
watched China Boy wrestling with the boulders. The next
week he published a page story on the Summerfields' stone
wall. It was a monument to Mr. Summerfield's enterprise
and vision, he said; a testimony to the will, the perseverance
and crag-like virtues that made New England great, etc. He
dragged in quotations from the Latin poets. This story attracted a surprising lot of attention. Old Man Summerfield
bought several copies, and wore them to rags in making a
boozy tour of all the saloons in the county. People came to see,
and amongst them were women who owned family coaches.
Mrs. Summerfield made social contacts in this way, and finally
joined the Ladies' Aid Society, and bought a bombazine dress
and a landaulette so she could ride over to the meetings. Her
period of ostracism was over.

The year 1879 was memorable in the annals of the family.
Pon Look had completed the southern wall after the unremit-
ting labors of twenty-seven years. Death enfolded Mrs. Summerfield that Autumn, while she was pruning a rose-bush in
her garden. Pon Look worked by lantern-light in the barn and
built an enormous hexagonal coffin to house her frail body. It
was so heavy that eight men buckled under the weight as they
carried it to the hearse. Old Man Summerfield bought a new
silk hat for the occasion, and was very proud of it. The minister
held a service in the parlor, with no less than six families in
attendance; and all throughout the widower nursed the hat on

his knees, in full view of the admiring assemblage. Pon Look
participated by looking in through the open window. He did
not attend the funeral at the Odd Fellows' Cemetery, for there
was much to do.

He trudged all over the ground with a tape-measure, and
made mental calculations. He returned very late, and sat on the
veranda to smoke a pipe in the moonlight. The old lady had
latterly been quiet, and his thoughts were tinged with regret
that she had gone. He was gratified that the master had taken
things sensibly. A wind arose, and because it was cool, and he
was afraid of the moon shining on his temples and making him
mad, he got up to retire to the cow-shed. Between the lower
bars of the gate something white caught his eye. He thought it
one of the fluffy pom-poms that had been blown thither from
the garden where the old lady had planted a clump of Holy
Thistles. He drew nearer, picked up wonderingly a new silk
hat, and found that the object was Old Man Summerfield's
snowy head. Whiskey and grief had done for him.

There was some wearisome business with the coroner. Pon
Look wanted to attend the funeral, but could not, for some
excitable men detained him for a week in a stone room with
bars at the window. He was released with palliative back-
slappings and a handful of cigars after the inquest. He had been
put to a great inconvenience, for the rains were now on, coming down like firm and slanting spears without let-up for days
and days. He had to slosh around in the bog to lay a timber road
across which to sled his rock. The Summerfield heir, an elderly
nephew, took over the place a month afterwards. He was a
city man, with a waxed moustache and a square-cut derby.
He drank somewhat, and was inclined to be companionable.
China Boy avoided him, looking rigidly ahead every time they
passed.

"How much longer that job, John?" he asked one day.

"No can say."

"Well, then, how long did it take to build all that wall?"

"Oh—thirty—thirty-five year."

"Good God!" murmured the heir.

He sat under the trees dismally, like a strange bird. Then he
panned for gold in various corners of the ranch, and did other

foolish things. He would sit hunched on the sacred gate, mope about whistling with a dirge-like note, or keep to the house and drink. He was a lonely and wistful interloper. All his actions lowered himself in China Boy's esteem, and he knew it. China Boy strutted about with aloof and cold arrogance, and the heir's morale ebbed. Finally he accosted the mason and came to an understanding. China Boy was to keep an eye on the place, market the stock and keep a percentage for himself. Then he packed up his things in a wicker suit-case, and went away forever.

The Chinaman had the place to himself now, and sold off most of the heifers so they wouldn't breed and rob him of time he could apply to building. The wall progressed handsomely. He had stretched barbed wire across the northerly side of the farm until the work should be finished. When that was done the place would be a paradise for cattle. They could cram themselves with lush grass in one part of the ranch, then chew the cud in the cropped field adjoining. That would be the end of bloat. China Boy worked incessantly, visited by no one except the banker who came along every quarter to represent the routed heir. In time the wall got itself done. It undulated for miles over uneven ground, but plumb, as straight as a furrow, without a single bend. The job had taken China Boy forty years to complete. By this time he was doubled with age, his pigtail white, and his hands rock-hard and stumpy.

It was in August, when China Boy went up to ring the nose of the little black bull, that he saw the ground was parched. Down he went on his knees in the middle of the field and pulled up a handful of soil. It was as dry as ashes. The cattle came around with their tongues, leathery and swollen, hanging out. Palsied with terror, China Boy arose, and shading his myopic eyes, turned around and round like a weather cock, and stared for a glimpse of green. The entire ranch was as brown as a brick. Drouth had laid waste the ground as if with torches.

He saddled a pony and galloped, pigtail a-flying, to the bank. The banker, when he heard the plaint, grumbled:

"I knew there was a hoodoo on the damned place. It's cooking hot, but I'll come down and see."

Together they rode back. The banker drew up in the buggy

before a new mine in the field adjoining the Summerfield ranch. Here were a tall gallows-hoist, with sheaves whirring, a mill from which poundings emanated, and an engine house with a high stick. The ditch alongside the road was filled with a roaring flood of water.

"Ye-ah," he grunted, pointing at the ditch with his whip. "That's what I expected. The shaft has tapped the springs underlying the Summerfield flat. Might as well sell off the cattle, the place will be as dry as a volcano from now on." Then he scratched his head. "I'll have to send down some goats, Angora goats. Mebbe they'll pay off the taxes. Guess we can cut down some timber, too. I'll have a look at it."

China Boy got out and walked in a daze to the grove. The banker followed afoot, then paused when his guide appeared at the door of his cabin with a musket in his hands.

"Cattle can go," China boy informed him, "but these trees they stay up, I watch 'um."

And up they stayed. The story got about, for the banker, who had been taken by the handsomeness of the grove, told it on himself. "An arbor-maniac, that's what he is. He made that wall business a life-long job, so he could live right there among those trees. Poor old chap, I'll have him pensioned off."

The banker kept his word, but China Boy drove a hard bargain. His terms for being superannuated were the weekly dole of five pounds of corn flour, a piece of bacon, six cartridges and a quart of whiskey, all to be delivered at the cabin.

Thereafter China Boy lived in the grove. Two hundred trees! Lordly sugar-pines, gold traced with black, like Porto-Venere marble. Five sequoias, so colossal that only after staring at them for twenty minutes did their size dawn upon you, and then with a finality that took you in the pit of the stomach like a blow. Wine-stemmed manzanitas, gnarled chaparral. The rest were all redwoods, with high fluted columns; and through their branches interlaced overhead the sunlight streamed in lines and cast disks of silver upon the dark trunks and the ochre ground twinkling with ants. It was something like the inside of a church.

There was a wood for you! Visitors came rarely. Bearded blanket-stiffs, homeless men, tarried for a night on their way to the Middle Fork of the Stanislaus. An occasional prospector, reverent among trees, stayed sometimes two days. China Boy was their invisible host. He peered at them through the foliage, as if he were a bird, but never spoke to them, unless he perceived their shoes needed cobbling and he felt sure they could pay for the job, nothing less than a dollar, for even a philosopher must live. Aloof, and wrapped in an old army overcoat, he sometimes watched them all night, being afraid they would be careless with their pipes or forget to stamp out the embers of their camp fires.

His house, hidden away in the trees, was rather a nice one, of a single large room, very high, and built of brick. Decades before, he had come across an abandoned express office, and had carried it thither, piecemeal, a bushel of brick at a time, and set it up exactly as it was before, even to the legend board above the doorway: "Wells-Fargo Express."

It was a forest lover's house, with blackberry bushes climbing into the window, hedgehogs and gray squirrels sunning themselves on the step, and pine cones dropping like cannonballs on the roof. It held a cot, a stove, a shoe-last, and a library that consisted in a wisdom-banner that hung on the wall. If he found you, after years of acquaintance, worthy enough, he would translate the wiggly ideographs thus:

"It is shame to be ignorant at sixty, for time flies like a mountain stream."

Here in this tree sanctuary that was of hoary age long before the Sung dynasty had started, China Boy had gone to school. He listened to the wind wrestling with the tree tops, to the language of the birds, the cries of the coyotes and owls, and other sounds that made the air articulate and vibrant. He loved to sit in the middle of his grove at night, still and pensive amid the falling leaves, like a rheumy-eyed hamadryad.

At intervals he straggled afoot to Sonora, with shirt-tail out and the sun warded off by an umbrella: quite the gentleman of leisure. But these excursions bored him finally, and he desisted, except when he had to call at the bank to complain about the quality of the whiskey. It was surprising what an educated palate he had. He wouldn't let the grocer's boy depart until he had first sampled the liquor ration.

Two years ago he trapped a pair of fine wildcats, and carted them off to town, and tarried overlong. Some campers came to the grove and were careless with their fire. China Boy's woods made a gorgeous blaze, singing and burning for ten hours, with the gray squirrels plumping down roasted, and the philosopher's house turning to a black lump like fused glass.

The story made five lines in the county paper. The forest ranger said afterwards that he had seen the Old-Man-Mad-About-Trees pull up to the ruins in his buckboard, look on a few minutes, then drive away.

The banker was dubious. "Must have checked out through old age in the city," he said, "else he would have come up to the bank. He drove an awful hard bargain over that whiskey. He had me paying eleven dollars a bottle for the stuff I used to get for him at two before Prohibition. If anybody's ahead of the game, it's me."

JOHN STEINBECK

The Leader of the People

The great San Joaquin Valley and the Monterey Peninsula are the settings of John Ernst Steinbeck's best books and stories. The region is now known as "Steinbeck Country," and the shoreside street of Monterey has been renamed "Cannery Row" after one of the author's novels about the region.

Steinbeck (1902–68) was born in the valley town of Salinas. After graduating from the local high school, the young man entered Stanford University and spent several years there, learning to write and meeting other writers, although he never sought a degree. He then worked at various jobs—as a farm laborer, hod carrier, reporter, surveyor, fisherman, and fruit picker. For many years he was close to poverty; not until the publication of his fourth book, Tortilla Flat (1935), did he achieve popular success. His tenth book, The Grapes of Wrath (1939), a saga of refugees from the midwestern dust bowl, became an international best-seller that remains a classic of proletarian novels. Previously his story of two drifters on a ranch, Of Mice and Men (1938), had been a success as a stage play. Several other books were made into Broadway shows, and no fewer than a dozen have been made into films.

Steinbeck was an amazingly versatile writer. A correspondent during World War II, he also succeeded as a playwright, film script writer, and short-story artist of high craftsmanship and feeling. However, the farther he traveled from his native-son roots in the San Joaquin Valley and on the nearby Pacific Coast, the less enduring became his later books. In 1962 he was awarded the prestigious Nobel Prize in literature for his lifetime achievements.

"The Leader of the People" first appeared in The Long Valley

(1938). Told from the point of view of a farm boy—who sees his grandfather, formerly the leader of westering people seeking new lands in America, as an unappreciated hero—this story shows the details of ranch life as well as compassion for a generation that has vanished from the national scene.

On Saturday afternoon Billy Buck, the ranch-hand, raked together the last of the old year's haystack and pitched small forkfuls over the wire fence to a few mildly interested cattle. High in the air small clouds like puffs of cannon smoke were driven eastward by the March wind. The wind could be heard whishing in the brush on the ridge crests, but no breath of it penetrated down into the ranch-cup.

The little boy, Jody, emerged from the house eating a thick piece of buttered bread. He saw Billy working on the last of the haystack. Jody tramped down scuffing his shoes in a way he had been told was destructive to good shoe-leather. A flock of white pigeons flew out of the black cypress tree as Jody passed, and circled the tree and landed again. A half-grown tortoise-shell cat leaped from the bunkhouse porch, galloped on stiff legs across the road, whirled and galloped back again. Jody picked up a stone to help the game along, but he was too late, for the cat was under the porch before the stone could be discharged. He threw the stone into the cypress tree and started the white pigeons on another whirling flight.

Arriving at the used-up haystack, the boy leaned against the barbed wire fence. "Will that be all of it, do you think?" he asked.

The middle-aged ranch-hand stopped his careful raking and stuck his fork into the ground. He took off his black hat and smoothed down his hair. "Nothing left of it that isn't soggy from ground moisture," he said. He replaced his hat and rubbed his dry leathery hands together.

"Ought to be plenty mice," Jody suggested.

"Lousy with them," said Billy. "Just crawling with mice."

"Well, maybe, when you get all through, I could call the dogs and hunt the mice."

"Sure, I guess you could," said Billy Buck. He lifted a forkful of the damp ground-hay and threw it into the air. Instantly three mice leaped out and burrowed frantically under the hay again.

Jody sighed with satisfaction. Those plump, sleek, arrogant mice were doomed. For eight months they had lived and multiplied in the haystack. They had been immune from cats, from traps, from poison and from Jody. They had grown smug in their security, overbearing and fat. Now the time of disaster had come; they would not survive another day.

Billy looked up at the top of the hills that surrounded the ranch. "Maybe you better ask your father before you do it," he suggested.

"Well, where is he? I'll ask him now."

"He rode up to the ridge ranch after dinner. He'll be back pretty soon."

Jody slumped against the fence post. "I don't think he'd care."

As Billy went back to his work he said ominously, "You'd better ask him anyway. You know how he is."

Jody did know. His father, Carl Tiflin, insisted upon giving permission for anything that was done on the ranch, whether it was important or not. Jody sagged farther against the post until he was sitting on the ground. He looked up at the little puffs of wind-driven cloud. "Is it like to rain, Billy?"

"It might. The wind's good for it, but not strong enough."

"Well, I hope it don't rain until after I kill those damn mice." He looked over his shoulder to see whether Billy had noticed the mature profanity. Billy worked on without comment.

Jody turned back and looked at the side-hill where the road from the outside world came down. The hill was washed with lean March sunshine. Silver thistles, blue lupins and a few poppies bloomed among the sage bushes. Halfway up the hill Jody could see Doubletree Mutt, the black dog, digging in a squirrel hole. He paddled for a while and then paused to kick bursts of dirt out between his hind legs, and he dug with an earnestness which belied the knowledge he must have had that no dog had ever caught a squirrel by digging in a hole.

Suddenly, while Jody watched, the black dog stiffened, and backed out of the hole and looked up the hill toward the cleft in the ridge where the road came through. Jody looked up too. For a moment Carl Tiflin on horseback stood out against the pale sky and then he moved down the road toward the house. He carried something white in his hand.

The boy started to his feet. "He's got a letter," Jody cried. He trotted away toward the ranch house, for the letter would probably be read aloud and he wanted to be there. He reached the house before his father did, and ran in. He heard Carl dismount from his creaking saddle and slap the horse on the side to send it to the barn where Billy would unsaddle it and turn it out.

Jody ran into the kitchen. "We got a letter!" he cried.

His mother looked up from a pan of beans. "Who has?"

"Father has. I saw it in his hand."

Carl strode into the kitchen then, and Jody's mother asked, "Who's the letter from, Carl?"

He frowned quickly. "How did you know there was a letter?"

She nodded her head in the boy's direction. "Big-Britches Jody told me."

Jody was embarrassed.

His father looked down at him contemptuously. "He is getting to be a Big-Britches," Carl said. "He's minding everybody's business but his own. Got his big nose into everything."

Mrs. Tiflin relented a little. "Well, he hasn't enough to keep him busy. Who's the letter from?"

Carl still frowned on Jody. "I'll keep him busy if he isn't careful." He held out a sealed letter. "I guess it's from your father."

Mrs. Tiflin took a hairpin from her head and slit open the flap. Her lips pursed judiciously. Jody saw her eyes snap back and forth over the lines. "He says," she translated, "he says he's going to drive out Saturday to stay for a little while. Why, this is Saturday. The letter must have been delayed." She looked at the postmark. "This was mailed day before yesterday. It should have been here yesterday." She looked up questioningly at her husband, and then her face darkened angrily. "Now what have you got that look on you for? He doesn't come often."

Carl turned his eyes away from her anger. He could be stern

with her most of the time, but when occasionally her temper arose, he could not combat it.

"What's the matter with you?" she demanded again.

In his explanation there was a tone of apology Jody himself might have used. "It's just that he talks," Carl said lamely. "Just talks."

"Well, what of it? You talk yourself."

"Sure I do. But your father only talks about one thing."

"Indians!" Jody broke in excitedly. "Indians and crossing the plains!"

Carl turned fiercely on him. "You get out, Mr. Big-Britches! Go on, now! Get out!"

Jody went miserably out the back door and closed the screen with elaborate quietness. Under the kitchen window his shamed, downcast eyes fell upon a curiously shaped stone, a stone of such fascination that he squatted down and picked it up and turned it over in his hands.

The voices came clearly to him through the open kitchen window. "Jody's damn well right," he heard his father say. "Just Indians and crossing the plains. I've heard that story about how the horses got driven off about a thousand times. He just goes on and on, and he never changes a word in the things he tells."

When Mrs. Tiflin answered her tone was so changed that Jody, outside the window, looked up from his study of the stone. Her voice had become soft and explanatory. Jody knew how her face would have changed to match the tone. She said quietly, "Look at it this way, Carl. That was the big thing in my father's life. He led a wagon train clear across the plains to the coast, and when it was finished, his life was done. It was a big thing to do, but it didn't last long enough. Look!" she continued, "it's as though he was born to do that, and after he finished it, there wasn't anything more for him to do but think about it and talk about it. If there'd been any farther west to go, he'd have gone. He's told me so himself. But at last there was the ocean. He lives right by the ocean where he had to stop."

She had caught Carl, caught him and entangled him in her soft tone.

"I've seen him," he agreed quietly. "He goes down and stares off west over the ocean." His voice sharpened a little. "And then he goes up to the Horseshoe Club in Pacific Grove, and he tells people how the Indians drove off the horses."

She tried to catch him again. "Well, it's everything to him. You might be patient with him and pretend to listen."

Carl turned impatiently away. "Well, if it gets too bad, I can always go down to the bunkhouse and sit with Billy," he said irritably. He walked through the house and slammed the front door after him.

Jody ran to his chores. He dumped the grain to the chickens without chasing any of them. He gathered the eggs from the nests. He trotted into the house with the wood and interlaced it so carefully in the wood-box that two armloads seemed to fill it to overflowing.

His mother had finished the beans by now. She stirred up the fire and brushed off the stove-top with a turkey wing. Jody peered cautiously at her to see whether any rancor toward him remained. "Is he coming today?" Jody asked.

"That's what his letter said."

"Maybe I better walk up the road to meet him."

Mrs. Tiflin clanged the stove-lid shut. "That would be nice," she said. "He'd probably like to be met."

"I guess I'll just do it then."

Outside, Jody whistled shrilly to the dogs. "Come on up the hill," he commanded. The two dogs waved their tails and ran ahead. Along the roadside the sage had tender new tips. Jody tore off some pieces and rubbed them on his hands until the air was filled with the sharp wild smell. With a rush the dogs leaped from the road and yapped into the brush after a rabbit. That was the last Jody saw of them, for when they failed to catch the rabbit, they went back home.

Jody plodded on up the hill toward the ridge top. When he reached the little cleft where the road came through, the afternoon wind struck him and blew up his hair and ruffled his shirt. He looked down on the little hills and ridges below and then out at the huge green Salinas Valley. He could see the white town of Salinas far out in the flat and the flash of its windows under the waning sun. Directly below him, in an oak tree, a crow congress had convened. The tree was black with crows all cawing at once.

Then Jody's eyes followed the wagon road down from the ridge where he stood, and lost it behind a hill, and picked it up again on the other side. On that distant stretch he saw a cart slowly pulled by a bay horse. It disappeared behind the hill. Jody sat down on the ground and watched the place where the cart would reappear again. The wind sang on the hilltops and the puff-ball clouds hurried eastward.

Then the cart came into sight and stopped. A man dressed in black dismounted from the seat and walked to the horse's head. Although it was so far away, Jody knew he had unhooked the check-rein, for the horse's head dropped forward. The horse moved on, and the man walked slowly up the hill beside it. Jody gave a glad cry and ran down the road toward them. The squirrels bumped along off the road, and a road-runner flirted its tail and raced over the edge of the hill and sailed out like a glider.

Jody tried to leap into the middle of his shadow at every step. A stone rolled under his foot and he went down. Around a little bend he raced, and there, a short distance ahead, were his grandfather and the cart. The boy dropped from his unseemly running and approached at a dignified walk.

The horse plodded stumble-footedly up the hill and the old man walked beside it. In the lowering sun their giant shadows flickered darkly behind them. The grandfather was dressed in a black broadcloth suit and he wore kid congress gaiters and a black tie on a short, hard collar. He carried his black slouch hat in his hand. His white beard was cropped close and his white eyebrows overhung his eyes like moustaches. The blue eyes were sternly merry. About the whole face and figure there was a granite dignity, so that every motion seemed an impossible thing. Once at rest, it seemed the old man would be stone, would never move again. His steps were slow and certain. Once made, no step could ever be retraced; once headed in a direction, the path would never bend nor the pace increase nor slow.

When Jody appeared around the bend, Grandfather waved

his hat slowly in welcome, and he called, "Why, Jody! Come down to meet me, have you?"

Jody sidled near and turned and matched his step to the old man's step and stiffened his body and dragged his heels a little. "Yes, sir," he said. "We got your letter only today."

"Should have been here yesterday," said Grandfather. "It certainly should. How are all the folks?"

"They're fine, sir." He hesitated and then suggested shyly, "Would you like to come on a mouse hunt tomorrow, sir?"

"Mouse hunt, Jody?" Grandfather chuckled. "Have the people of this generation come down to hunting mice? They aren't very strong, the new people, but I hardly thought mice would be game for them."

"No, sir. It's just play. The haystack's gone. I'm going to drive out the mice to the dogs. And you can watch, or even beat the hay a little."

The stern, merry eyes turned down on him. "I see. You don't eat them, then. You haven't come to that yet."

Jody explained, "The dogs eat them, sir. It wouldn't be much like hunting Indians, I guess."

"No, not much—but then later, when the troops were hunting Indians and shooting children and burning tee-pees, it wasn't much different from your mouse hunt."

They topped the rise and started down into the ranch-cup, and they lost the sun from their shoulders. "You've grown," Grandfather said. "Nearly an inch, I should say."

"More," Jody boasted. "Where they mark me on the door, I'm up more than an inch since Thanksgiving even."

Grandfather's rich throaty voice said, "Maybe you're getting too much water and turning to pith and stalk. Wait until you head out, and then we'll see."

Jody looked quickly into the old man's face to see whether his feelings should be hurt, but there was no will to injure, no punishing nor putting-in-your-place light in the keen blue eyes. "We might kill a pig," Jody suggested.

"Oh, no! I couldn't let you do that. You're just humoring me. It isn't the time and you know it."

"You know Riley, the big boar, sir?"

"Yes. I remember Riley well."

"Well, Riley ate a hole into that same haystack, and it fell down on him and smothered him."

"Pigs do that when they can," said Grandfather.

"Riley was a nice pig, for a boar, sir. I rode him sometimes, and he didn't mind."

A door slammed at the house below them, and they saw Jody's mother standing on the porch waving her apron in welcome. And they saw Carl Tiflin walking up from the barn to be at the house for the arrival.

The sun had disappeared from the hills by now. The blue smoke from the house chimney hung in flat layers in the purpling ranch-cup. The puff-ball clouds, dropped by the falling wind, hung listlessly in the sky.

Billy Buck came out of the bunkhouse and flung a wash basin of soapy water on the ground. He had been shaving in midweek, for Billy held Grandfather in reverence, and Grandfather said that Billy was one of the few men of the new generation who had not gone soft. Although Billy was in middle age, Grandfather considered him a boy. Now Billy was hurrying toward the house too.

When Jody and Grandfather arrived, the three were waiting for them in front of the yard gate.

Carl said, "Hello, sir. We've been looking for you."

Mrs. Tiflin kissed Grandfather on the side of his beard, and stood still while his big hand patted her shoulder. Billy shook hands solemnly, grinning under his straw moustache. "I'll put up your horse," said Billy, and he led the rig away.

Grandfather watched him go, and then, turning back to the group, he said as he had said a hundred times before, "There's a good boy. I knew his father, old Mule-tail Buck. I never knew why they called him Mule-tail except he packed mules."

Mrs. Tiflin turned and led the way into the house. "How long are you going to stay, Father? Your letter didn't say."

"Well, I don't know. I thought I'd stay about two weeks. But I never stay as long as I think I'm going to."

In a short while they were sitting at the white oilcloth table eating their supper. The lamp with the tin reflector hung over the table. Outside the dining-room windows the big moths battered softly against the glass.

Grandfather cut his steak into tiny pieces and chewed slowly. "I'm hungry," he said. "Driving out here got my appetite up. It's like when we were crossing. We all got so hungry every night we could hardly wait to let the meat get done. I could eat about five pounds of buffalo meat every night."

"It's moving around does it," said Billy. "My father was a government packer. I helped him when I was a kid. Just the two of us could about clean up a deer's ham."

"I knew your father, Billy," said Grandfather. "A fine man he was. They called him Mule-tail Buck. I don't know why except he packed mules."

"That was it," Billy agreed. "He packed mules."

Grandfather put down his knife and fork and looked around the table. "I remember one time we ran out of meat—" His voice dropped to a curious low sing-song, dropped into a tonal groove the story had worn for itself. "There was no buffalo, no antelope, not even rabbits. The hunters couldn't even shoot a coyote. That was the time for the leader to be on the watch. I was the leader, and I kept my eyes open. Know why? Well, just the minute the people began to get hungry they'd start slaughtering the team oxen. Do you believe that? I've heard of parties that just ate up their draft cattle. Started from the middle and worked toward the ends. Finally they'd eat the lead pair, and then the wheelers. The leader of a party had to keep them from doing that."

In some manner a big moth got into the room and circled the hanging kerosene lamp. Billy got up and tried to clap it between his hands. Carl struck with a cupped palm and caught the moth and broke it. He walked to the window and dropped it out.

"As I was saying," Grandfather began again, but Carl interrupted him. "You'd better eat some more meat. All the rest of us are ready for our pudding."

Jody saw a flash of anger in his mother's eyes. Grandfather picked up his knife and fork. "I'm pretty hungry, all right," he said. "I'll tell you about that later."

When supper was over, when the family and Billy Buck sat in front of the fireplace in the other room, Jody anxiously watched Grandfather. He saw the signs he knew. The bearded head leaned forward; the eyes lost their sternness and looked wonderingly into the fire; the big lean fingers laced themselves on the black knees. "I wonder," he began, "I just wonder whether I ever told you how those thieving Piutes drove off thirty-five of our horses."

"I think you did," Carl interrupted. "Wasn't it just before you went up into the Tahoe country?"

Grandfather turned quickly toward his son-in-law. "That's right. I guess I must have told you that story."

"Lots of times," Carl said cruelly, and he avoided his wife's eyes. But he felt the angry eyes on him, and he said, " 'Course I'd like to hear it again."

Grandfather looked back at the fire. His fingers unlaced and laced again. Jody knew how he felt, how his insides were collapsed and empty. Hadn't Jody been called a Big-Britches that very afternoon? He arose to heroism and opened himself to the term Big-Britches again. "Tell about Indians," he said softly.

Grandfather's eyes grew stern again. "Boys always want to hear about Indians. It was a job for men, but boys want to hear about it. Well, let's see. Did I ever tell you how I wanted each wagon to carry a long iron plate?"

Everyone but Jody remained silent. Jody said, "No. You didn't."

"Well, when the Indians attacked, we always put the wagons in a circle and fought from between the wheels. I thought that if every wagon carried a long plate with rifle holes, the men could stand the plates on the outside of the wheels when the wagons were in the circle and they would be protected. It would save lives and that would make up for the extra weight of the iron. But of course the party wouldn't do it. No party had done it before and they couldn't see why they should go to the expense. They lived to regret it, too."

Jody looked at his mother, and knew from her expression that she was not listening at all. Carl picked at a callus on his thumb and Billy Buck watched a spider crawling up the wall.

Grandfather's tone dropped into its narrative groove again. Jody knew in advance exactly what words would fall. The story droned on, speeded up for the attack, grew sad over the wounds, struck a dirge at the burials on the great plains. Jody sat quietly watching Grandfather. The stern blue eyes were detached. He looked as though he were not very interested in the story himself.

When it was finished, when the pause had been politely respected as the frontier of the story, Billy Buck stood up and stretched and hitched his trousers. "I guess I'll turn in," he said. Then he faced Grandfather. "I've got an old powder horn and a cap and ball pistol down to the bunkhouse. Did I ever show them to you?"

Grandfather nodded slowly. "Yes, I think you did, Billy. Reminds me of a pistol I had when I was leading the people across." Billy stood politely until the little story was done, and then he said, "Good night," and went out of the house.

Carl Tiflin tried to turn the conversation then. "How's the country between here and Monterey? I've heard it's pretty dry."

"It is dry," said Grandfather. "There's not a drop of water in the Laguna Seca. But it's a long pull from '87. The whole country was powder then, and in '61 I believe all the coyotes starved to death. We had fifteen inches of rain this year."

"Yes, but it all came too early. We could do with some now." Carl's eye fell on Jody. "Hadn't you better be getting to bed?"

Jody stood up obediently. "Can I kill the mice in the old haystack, sir?"

"Mice? Oh! Sure, kill them all off. Billy said there isn't any good hay left."

Jody exchanged a secret and satisfying look with Grandfather. "I'll kill every one tomorrow," he promised.

Jody lay in his bed and thought of the impossible world of Indians and buffaloes, a world that had ceased to be forever. He wished he could have been living in the heroic time, but he knew he was not of heroic timber. No one living now, save possibly Billy Buck, was worthy to do the things that had been done. A race of giants had lived then, fearless men, men of a staunchness unknown in this day. Jody thought of the wide plains and of the wagons moving across like centipedes. He thought of Grandfather on a huge white horse, marshaling the people. Across his mind marched the great phantoms, and they marched off the earth and they were gone.

He came back to the ranch for a moment, then. He heard the dull rushing sound that space and silence make. He heard one of the dogs, out in the doghouse, scratching a flea and bumping his elbow against the floor with every stroke. Then the wind arose again and the black cypress groaned and Jody went to sleep.

He was up half an hour before the triangle sounded for breakfast. His mother was rattling the stove to make the flames roar when Jody went through the kitchen. "You're up early," she said. "Where are you going?"

"Out to get a good stick. We're going to kill the mice today."

"Who is 'we'?"

"Why, Grandfather and I."

"So you've got him in it. You always like to have someone in with you in case there's blame to share."

"I'll be right back," said Jody. "I just want to have a good stick ready for after breakfast."

He closed the screen door after him and went out into the cool blue morning. The birds were noisy in the dawn and the ranch cats came down from the hill like blunt snakes. They had been hunting gophers in the dark, and although the four cats were full of gopher meat, they sat in a semi-circle at the back door and mewed piteously for milk. Doubletree Mutt and Smasher moved sniffing along the edge of the brush, performing the duty with rigid ceremony, but when Jody whistled, their heads jerked up and their tails waved. They plunged down to him, wriggling their skins and yawning. Jody patted their heads seriously, and moved on to the weathered scrap pile. He selected an old broom handle and a short piece of inch-square scrap wood. From his pocket he took a shoelace and tied the ends of the sticks loosely together to make a flail. He whistled his new weapon through the air and struck the ground experimentally, while the dogs leaped aside and whined with apprehension.

Jody turned and started down past the house toward the old haystack ground to look over the field of slaughter, but Billy Buck, sitting patiently on the back steps, called to him, "You better come back. It's only a couple of minutes till breakfast."

Jody changed his course and moved toward the house. He

leaned his flail against the steps. "That's to drive the mice out," he said. "I'll bet they're fat. I'll bet they don't know what's going to happen to them today."

"No, nor you either," Billy remarked philosophically, "nor me, nor anyone."

Jody was staggered by this thought. He knew it was true. His imagination twitched away from the mouse hunt. Then his mother came out on the back porch and struck the triangle, and all thoughts fell in a heap.

Grandfather hadn't appeared at the table when they sat down. Billy nodded at his empty chair. "He's all right? He isn't sick?"

"He takes a long time to dress," said Mrs. Tiflin. "He combs his whiskers and rubs up his shoes and brushes his clothes."

Carl scattered sugar on his mush. "A man that's led a wagon train across the plains has got to be pretty careful how he dresses."

Mrs. Tiflin turned on him. "Don't do that, Carl! Please don't!" There was more of threat than of request in her tone. And the threat irritated Carl.

"Well, how many times do I have to listen to the story of the iron plates, and the thirty-five horses? That time's done. Why can't he forget it, now it's done?" He grew angrier while he talked, and his voice rose. "Why does he have to tell them over and over? He came across the plains. All right! Now it's finished. Nobody wants to hear about it over and over."

The door into the kitchen closed softly. The four at the table sat frozen. Carl laid his mush spoon on the table and touched his chin with his fingers.

Then the kitchen door opened and Grandfather walked in. His mouth smiled tightly and his eyes were squinted. "Good morning," he said, and he sat down and looked at his mush dish.

Carl could not leave it there. "Did—did you hear what I said?"

Grandfather jerked a little nod.

"I don't know what got into me, sir. I didn't mean it. I was just being funny."

Jody glanced in shame at his mother, and he saw that she was looking at Carl, and that she wasn't breathing. It was an awful thing that he was doing. He was tearing himself to pieces to talk like that. It was a terrible thing to him to retract a word, but to retract it in shame was infinitely worse.

Grandfather looked sidewise. "I'm trying to get right side up," he said gently. "I'm not being mad. I don't mind what you said, but it might be true, and I would mind that."

"It isn't true," said Carl. "I'm not feeling well this morning. I'm sorry I said it."

"Don't be sorry, Carl. An old man doesn't see things sometimes. Maybe you're right. The crossing is finished. Maybe it should be forgotten, now it's done."

Carl got up from the table. "I've had enough to eat. I'm going to work. Take your time, Billy!" He walked quickly out of the dining-room. Billy gulped the rest of his food and followed soon after. But Jody could not leave his chair.

"Won't you tell any more stories?" Jody asked.

"Why, sure I'll tell them, but only when—I'm sure people want to hear them."

"I like to hear them, sir."

"Oh! Of course you do, but you're a little boy. It was a job for men, but only little boys like to hear about it."

Jody got up from his place. "I'll wait outside for you, sir. I've got a good stick for those mice."

He waited by the gate until the old man came out on the porch. "Let's go down and kill the mice now," Jody called.

"I think I'll just sit in the sun, Jody. You go kill the mice."

"You can use my stick if you like."

"No, I'll just sit here a while."

Jody turned disconsolately away, and walked down toward the old haystack. He tried to whip up his enthusiasm with thoughts of the fat juicy mice. He beat the ground with his flail. The dogs coaxed and whined about him, but he could not go. Back at the house he could see Grandfather sitting on the porch, looking small and thin and black.

Jody gave up and went to sit on the steps at the old man's feet.

"Back already? Did you kill the mice?"

"No, sir. I'll kill them some other day."

The morning flies buzzed close to the ground and the ants

dashed about in front of the steps. The heavy smell of sage slipped down the hill. The porch boards grew warm in the sunshine.

Jody hardly knew when Grandfather started to talk. "I shouldn't stay here, feeling the way I do." He examined his strong old hands. "I feel as though the crossing wasn't worth doing." His eyes moved up the side-hill and stopped on a motionless hawk perched on a dead limb. "I tell those old stories, but they're not what I want to tell. I only know how I want people to feel when I tell them.

"It wasn't Indians that were important, nor adventures, nor even getting out here. It was a whole bunch of people made into one big crawling beast. And I was the head. It was westering and westering. Every man wanted something for himself, but the big beast that was all of them wanted only westering. I was the leader, but if I hadn't been there, someone else would have been the head. The thing had to have a head.

"Under the little bushes the shadows were black at white noonday. When we saw the mountains at last, we cried—all of us. But it wasn't getting here that mattered, it was movement and westering.

"We carried life out here and set it down the way those ants carry eggs. And I was the leader. The westering was as big as God, and the slow steps that made the movement piled up and piled up until the continent was crossed.

"Then we came down to the sea, and it was done." He stopped and wiped his eyes until the rims were red. "That's what I should be telling instead of stories."

When Jody spoke, Grandfather started and looked down at him. "Maybe I could lead the people some day," Jody said.

The old man smiled. "There's no place to go. There's the ocean to stop you. There's a line of old men along the shore hating the ocean because it stopped them."

"In boats I might, sir."

"No place to go, Jody. Every place is taken. But that's not the worst—no, not the worst. Westering has died out of the people. Westering isn't a hunger any more. It's all done. Your father is right. It is finished." He laced his fingers on his knee and looked at them.

Jody felt very sad. "If you'd like a glass of lemonade I could make it for you."

Grandfather was about to refuse, and then he saw Jody's face. "That would be nice," he said. "Yes, it would be nice to drink a lemonade."

Jody ran into the kitchen where his mother was wiping the last of the breakfast dishes. "Can I have a lemon to make a lemonade for Grandfather?"

His mother mimicked—"And another lemon to make a lemonade for you."

"No, ma'am. I don't want one."

"Jody! You're sick!" Then she stopped suddenly. "Take a lemon out of the cooler," she said softly. "Here, I'll reach the squeezer down to you."

WALTER VAN TILBURG CLARK

Hook

Born in Maine, Walter Van Tilburg Clark (1909–71) died in Reno, Nevada, almost a full continent away from his beginning. As a writer he taught himself to use the familiar materials of the western saga— the cowboy and the immigrant, for example—to explore the human psyche and to raise deep philosophical issues.

Clark spent his boyhood in Reno, the background for his growing-up novel, The City of Trembling Leaves *(1945). His best-known work is* The Ox-Bow Incident *(1940), a novel about the lynching in 1885 of three innocent men. The film resulting from this story, directed by William Wellman in 1942 and starring Henry Fonda, was described by a critic as "realism that is as sharp and cold as a knife." The Track of the Cat (1949) embodies a moral parable in the hunting tale. The following selection, "Hook," is taken from Clark's collection* The Watchful Gods and Other Stories *(1950). Clark spent his later years as a teacher of creative writing at San Francisco State College.*

Unique is this life story of Hook, a predatory bird forced to survive in a drought-stricken land as a fledgling but in his prime a master of the skies. Seldom among the survivors in the California scene has the will to live been epitomized as in this short masterpiece. "Hook" first appeared in the Atlantic Monthly *in August, 1940.*

Hook, the hawks' child, was hatched in a dry spring among the oaks beside the seasonal river, and was struck from the nest early. In the drouth his single-willed parents had to extend their hunting ground by more than twice, for the ground creatures upon which they fed died and dried by the hundreds. The range became too great for them to wish to return and feed Hook, and when they had lost interest in each other they drove Hook down into the sand and brush and went back to solitary courses over the bleaching hills.

Unable to fly yet, Hook crept over the ground, challenging all large movements with recoiled head, erected, rudimentary wings, and the small rasp of his clattering beak. It was during this time of abysmal ignorance and continual fear that his eyes took on the first quality of a hawk, that of being wide, alert and challenging. He dwelt, because of his helplessness, among the rattling brush which grew between the oaks and the river. Even in his thickets and near the water, the white sun was the dominant presence. Except in the dawn, when the land wind stirred, or in the late afternoon, when the sea wind became strong enough to penetrate the half-mile inland to this turn in the river, the sun was the major force, and everything was dry and motionless under it. The brush, small plants and trees alike husbanded the little moisture at their hearts; the moving creatures waited for dark, when sometimes the sea fog came over and made a fine, soundless rain which relieved them.

The two spacious sounds of his life environed Hook at this time. One was the great rustle of the slopes of yellowed wild wheat, with over it the chattering rustle of the leaves of the California oaks, already as harsh and individually tremulous as in autumn. The other was the distant whisper of the foaming edge of the Pacific, punctuated by the hollow shoring of the waves. But these Hook did not yet hear, for he was attuned by fear and hunger to the small, spasmodic rustlings of live things. Dry, shrunken, and nearly starved, and with his plumage delayed, he snatched at beetles, dragging in the sand to catch them. When swifter and stronger birds and animals did not reach them first, which was seldom, he ate the small, silver fish left in the mud by the failing river. He watched, with nearly chattering beak, the quick, thin lizards pause, very alert, and raise and lower themselves, but could not catch them because he had to raise his wings to move rapidly, which startled them.

Only one sight and sound not of his world of microscopic necessity was forced upon Hook. That was the flight of the big gulls from the beaches, which sometimes, in quealing play, came spinning back over the foothills and the river bed. For some inherited reason, the big, ship-bodied birds did not frighten Hook, but angered him. Small and chewed-looking, with his wide, already yellowing eyes glaring up at them, he would stand in an open place on the sand in the sun and spread his shaping wings and clatter his bill like shaken dice. Hook was furious about the swift, easy passage of gulls.

His first opportunity to leave off living like a ground owl came accidentally. He was standing in the late afternoon in the red light under the thicket, his eyes half-filmed with drowse and the stupefaction of starvation, when suddenly something beside him moved, and he struck, and killed a field mouse driven out of the wheat by thirst. It was a poor mouse, shriveled and lice ridden, but in striking, Hook had tasted blood, which raised nest memories and restored his nature. With started neck plumage and shining eyes, he tore and fed. When the mouse was devoured, Hook had entered hoarse adolescence. He began to seek with a conscious appetite, and to move more readily out of shelter. Impelled by the blood appetite, so glorious after his long preservation upon the flaky and bitter stuff of bugs, he ventured even into the wheat in the open sun beyond the oaks, and discovered the small trails and holes among the roots. With his belly often partially filled with flesh, he grew rapidly in strength and will. His eyes were taking on their final change, their yellow growing deeper and more opaque, their stare more constant, their challenge less desperate. Once during this transformation, he surprised a ground squirrel, and although he was ripped and wing-bitten and could not hold his prey, he was not dismayed by the conflict, but exalted. Even while the wing was still drooping and the pinions not grown back, he was excited by other ground squirrels and pursued them futilely, and was angered by their dusty escapes. He realized that his world was a great arena for killing, and felt the magnificence of it.

The two major events of Hook's young life occurred in the same day. A little after dawn he made the customary essay and succeeded in flight. A little before sunset, he made his first sustained flight of over two hundred yards, and at its termination struck and slew a great buck squirrel whose thrashing and terrified gnawing and squealing gave him a wild delight. When he had gorged on the strong meat, Hook stood upright, and in his eyes was the stare of the hawk, never flagging in intensity but never swelling beyond containment. After that the stare had only to grow more deeply challenging and more sternly controlled as his range and deadliness increased. There was no change in kind. Hook had mastered the first of the three hungers which are fused into the single, flaming will of a hawk, and he had experienced the second.

The third and consummating hunger did not awaken in Hook until the following spring, when the exultation of space had grown slow and steady in him, so that he swept freely with the wind over the miles of coastal foothills, circling, and ever in sight of the sea, and used without struggle the warm currents lifting from the slopes, and no longer desired to scream at the range of his vision, but intently sailed above his shadow swiftly climbing to meet him on the hillsides, sinking away and rippling across the brush-grown canyons.

That spring the rains were long, and Hook sat for hours, hunched and angry under their pelting, glaring into the fogs of the river valley, and killed only small, drenched things flooded up from their tunnels. But when the rains had dissipated, and there were sun and sea wind again, the game ran plentiful, the hills were thick and shining green, and the new river flooded about the boulders where battered turtles climbed up to shrink and sleep. Hook then was scorched by the third hunger. Ranging farther, often forgetting to kill and eat, he sailed for days with growing rage, and woke at night clattering on his dead tree limb, and struck and struck and struck at the porous wood of the trunk, tearing it away. After days, in the draft of a coastal canyon miles below his own hills, he came upon the acrid taint he did not know but had expected, and sailing down it, felt his neck plumes rise and his wings quiver so that he swerved unsteadily. He saw the unmated female perched upon the tall and jagged stump of a tree that had been shorn by storm, and he stooped, as if upon game. But she was older than he, and wary

of the gripe of his importunity, and banked off screaming, and
he screamed also at the intolerable delay.

At the head of the canyon, the screaming pursuit was crossed
by another male with a great wing-spread, and the light golden
in the fringe of his plumage. But his more skillful opening
played him false against the ferocity of the twice-balked Hook.
His rising maneuver for position was cut short by Hook's wild,
upward swoop, and at the blow he raked desperately and tumbled off to the side. Dropping, Hook struck him again, strug-
gled to clutch, but only raked and could not hold, and, diving,
struck once more in passage, and then beat up, yelling triumph,
and saw the crippled antagonist side-slip away, half-tumble
once, as the ripped wing failed to balance, then steady and glide
obliquely into the cover of brush on the canyon side. Beating
hard and stationary in the wind above the bush that covered his
competitor, Hook waited an instant, but when the bush was
still, screamed again, and let himself go off with the current,
reseeking, infuriated by the burn of his own wounds, the thin
choke-thread of the acrid taint.

On a hilltop projection of stone two miles inland, he struck
her down, gripping her rustling body with his talons, beating
her wings down with his wings, belting her head when she
whimpered or thrashed, and at last clutching her neck with his
hook and, when her coy struggles had given way to stillness,
succeeded.

In the early summer, Hook drove the three young ones from
their nest, and went back to lone circling above his own range.
He was complete.

2

Throughout that summer and the cool, growthless weather of
the winter, when the gales blew in the river canyon and the
ocean piled upon the shore, Hook was master of the sky and the
hills of his range. His flight became a lovely and certain thing,
so that he played with the treacherous currents of the air with a
delicate ease surpassing that of the gulls. He could sail for
hours, searching the blanched grasses below him with tele-
scopic eyes, gaining height against the wind, descending in
mile-long, gently declining swoops when he curved and rode

back, and never beating either wing. At the swift passage of his shadow within their vision, gophers, ground squirrels and rabbits froze, or plunged gibbering into their tunnels beneath matted turf. Now, when he struck, he killed easily in one hard-knuckled blow. Occasionally, in sport, he soared up over the river and drove the heavy and weaponless gulls downstream again, until they would no longer venture inland.

There was nothing which Hook feared now, and his spirit was wholly belligerent, swift and sharp, like his gaze. Only the mixed smells and incomprehensible activities of the people at the Japanese farmer's home, inland of the coastwise highway and south of the bridge across Hook's river, troubled him. The smells were strong, unsatisfactory and never clear, and the people, though they behaved foolishly, constantly running in and out of their built-up holes, were large, and appeared capable, with fearless eyes looking up at him, so that he instinctively swerved aside from them. He cruised over their yard, their gardens, and their bean fields, but he would not alight close to their buildings.

But this one area of doubt did not interfere with his life. He ignored it, save to look upon it curiously as he crossed, his afternoon shadow sliding in an instant over the chicken-and-crate-cluttered yard, up the side of the unpainted barn, and then out again smoothly, just faintly, liquidly rippling over the furrows and then over the stubble of the grazing slopes. When the season was dry, and the dead earth blew on the fields, he extended his range to satisfy his great hunger, and again narrowed it when the fields were once more alive with the minute movements he could not only see but anticipate.

Four times that year he was challenged by other hawks blowing up from behind the coastal hills to scud down his slopes, but two of these he slew in mid-air, and saw hurtle down to thump on the ground and lie still while he circled, and a third, whose wing he tore, he followed closely to earth and beat to death in the grass, making the crimson jet out from its breast and neck into the pale wheat. The fourth was a strong flier and experienced fighter, and theirs was a long, running battle, with brief, rising flurries of striking and screaming, from which down and plumage soared off.

Here, for the first time, Hook felt doubts, and at moments wanted to drop away from the scoring, burning talons and the twisted hammer strokes of the strong beak, drop away shrieking, and take cover and be still. In the end, when Hook, having outmaneuvered his enemy and come above him, wholly in control, and going with the wind, tilted and plunged for the death rap, the other, in desperation, threw over on his back and struck up. Talons locked, beaks raking, they dived earthward. The earth grew and spread under them amazingly, and they were not fifty feet above it when Hook, feeling himself turning toward the underside, tore free and beat up again on heavy, wrenched wings. The other, stroking swiftly, and so close to down that he lost wing plumes to a bush, righted himself and planed up, but flew on lumberingly between the hills and did not return. Hook screamed the triumph, and made a brief pretense of pursuit, but was glad to return, slow and victorious, to his dead tree.

In all these encounters Hook was injured, but experienced only the fighter's pride and exultation from the sting of wounds received in successful combat. And in each of them he learned new skill. Each time the wounds healed quickly, and left him a more dangerous bird.

In the next spring, when the rains and the night chants of the little frogs were past, the third hunger returned upon Hook with a new violence. In this quest, he came into the taint of a young hen. Others too were drawn by the unnerving perfume, but only one of them, the same with which Hook had fought his great battle, was a worthy competitor. This hunter drove off two, while two others, game but neophytes, were glad enough that Hook's impatience would not permit him to follow and kill. Then the battle between the two champions fled inland, and was a tactical marvel, but Hook lodged the neck-breaking blow, and struck again as they dropped past the tree-tops. The blood had already begun to pool on the gray, fallen foliage as Hook flapped up between branches, too spent to cry his victory. Yet his hunger would not let him rest until, late in the second day, he drove the female to ground among the laurels of a strange river canyon.

When the two fledglings of this second brood had been

driven from the nest, and Hook had returned to his own range, he was not only complete, but supreme. He slept without concealment on his bare limb, and did not open his eyes when, in the night, the heavy-billed cranes coughed in the shallows below him.

3

The turning point of Hook's career came that autumn, when the brush in the canyons rustled dryly and the hills, mowed close by the cattle, smoked under the wind as if burning. One midafternoon, when the black clouds were torn on the rim of the sea and the surf flowered white and high on the rocks, raining in over the low cliffs, Hook rode the wind diagonally across the river mouth. His great eyes, focused for small things stirring in the dust and leaves, overlooked so large and slow a movement as that of the Japanese farmer rising from the brush and lifting the two black eyes of his shotgun. Too late Hook saw and, startled, swerved, but wrongly. The surf muffled the reports, and nearly without sound, Hook felt the minute whips of the first shot, and the astounding, breath-breaking blow of the second.

Beating his good wing, tasting the blood that quickly swelled into his beak, he tumbled off with the wind and struck into the thickets on the far side of the river mouth. The branches tore him. Wild with rage, he thrust up and clattered his beak, challenging, but when he had fallen over twice, he knew that the trailing wing would not carry, and then heard the boots of the hunter among the stones in the river bed and, seeing him loom at the edge of the bushes, crept back among the thickest brush and was still. When he saw the boots stand before him, he reared back, lifting his good wing and cocking his head for the serpent-like blow, his beak open but soundless, his great eyes hard and very shining. The boots passed on. The Japanese farmer, who believed that he had lost chickens, and who had cunningly observed Hook's flight for many afternoons, until he could plot it, did not greatly want a dead hawk.

When Hook could hear nothing but the surf and the wind in the thicket, he let the sickness and shock overcome him. The fine film of the inner lid dropped over his big eyes. His heart beat frantically, so that it made the plumage of his shot-aching breast throb. His own blood throttled his breathing. But these things were nothing compared to the lightning of pain in his left shoulder, where the shot had bunched, shattering the airy bones so the pinions trailed on the ground and could not be lifted. Yet, when a sparrow lit in the bush over him, Hook's eyes flew open again, hard and challenging, his good wing was lifted and his beak strained open. The startled sparrow darted piping out over the river.

Throughout that night, while the long clouds blew across the stars and the wind shook the bushes about him, and throughout the next day, while the clouds still blew and massed until there was no gleam of sunlight on the sand bar, Hook remained stationary, enduring his sickness. In the second evening, the rains began. First there was a long, running patter of drops upon the beach and over the dry trees and bushes. At dusk there came a heavier squall, which did not die entirely, but slacked off to a continual, spaced splashing of big drops, and then returned with the front of the storm. In long, misty curtains, gust by gust, the rain swept over the sea, beating down its heaving, and coursed up the beach. The little jets of dust ceased to rise about the drops in the fields, and the mud began to gleam. Among the boulders of the river bed, darkling pools grew slowly.

Still Hook stood behind his tree from the wind, only gentle drops reaching him, falling from the upper branches and then again from the brush. His eyes remained closed, and he could still taste his own blood in his mouth, though it had ceased to come up freshly. Out beyond him, he heard the storm changing. As rain conquered the sea, the heave of the surf became a hushed sound, often lost in the crying of the wind. Then gradually, as the night turned toward morning, the wind also was broken by the rain. The crying became fainter, the rain settled toward steadiness, and the creep of the waves could be heard again, quiet and regular upon the beach.

At dawn there was no wind and no sun, but everywhere the roaring of the vertical, relentless rain. Hook then crept among the rapid drippings of the bushes, dragging his torn sail, seeking better shelter. He stopped often and stood with the shutters of film drawn over his eyes. At midmorning he found a little cave under a ledge at the base of the sea cliff. Here, lost without branches and leaves about him, he settled to await improvement.

When, at midday of the third day, the rain stopped altogether, and the sky opened before a small, fresh wind, letting light through to glitter upon a tremulous sea, Hook was so weak that his good wing trailed also to prop him upright, and his open eyes were lusterless. But his wounds were hardened, and he felt the return of hunger. Beyond his shelter, he heard the gulls flying in great numbers and crying their joy at the cleared air. He could even hear, from the fringe of the river, the ecstatic and unstinted bubblings and chirpings of the small birds. The grassland, he felt, would be full of the stirring anew of the close-bound life, the undrowned insects clicking as they dried out, the snakes slithering down, heads half erect, into the grasses where the mice, gophers and ground squirrels ran and stopped and chewed and licked themselves smoother and drier.

With the aid of this hunger, and on the crutches of his wings, Hook came down to stand in the sun beside his cave, whence he could watch the beach. Before him, in ellipses on tilting planes, the gulls flew. The surf was rearing again, and beginning to shelve and hiss on the sand. Through the white foam-writing it left, the long-billed pipers twinkled in bevies, escaping each wave, then racing down after it to plunge their fine drills into the minute double holes where the sand crabs bubbled. In the third row of breakers two seals lifted sleek, streaming heads and barked, and over them, trailing his spider legs, a great crane flew south. Among the stones at the foot of the cliff, small red and green crabs made a little, continuous rattling and knocking. The cliff swallows glittered and twanged on aerial forays.

The afternoon began auspiciously for Hook also. One of the two gulls which came squabbling above him dropped a freshly caught fish to the sand. Quickly Hook was upon it. Gripping it, he raised his good wing and cocked his head with open beak at the many gulls which had circled and come down at once

toward the fall of the fish. The gulls sheered off, cursing rau-
cously. Left alone on the sand, Hook devoured the fish and,
after resting in the sun, withdrew again to his shelter.

4

In the succeeding days, between rains, he foraged on the beach.
He learned to kill and crack the small green crabs. Along the
edge of the river mouth, he found the drowned bodies of mice
and squirrels and even sparrows. Twice he managed to drive
feeding gulls from their catch, charging upon them with buf-
feting wing and clattering beak. He grew stronger slowly, but
the shot sail continued to drag. Often, at the choking thought
of soaring and striking and the good, hot-blood kill, he strove
to take off, but only the one wing came up, winnowing with a
hiss, and drove him over onto his side in the sand. After these
futile trials, he would rage and clatter. But gradually he learned
to believe that he could not fly, that his life must now be that of
the discharged nestling again. Denied the joy of space, without
which the joy of loneliness was lost, the joy of battle and
killing, the blood lust, became his whole concentration. It was
his hope, as he charged feeding gulls, that they would turn and
offer battle, but they never did. The sandpipers, at his approach, fled peeping, or, like a quiver of arrows shot together,
streamed out over the surf in a long curve. Once, pent beyond
bearing, he disgraced himself by shrieking challenge at the
businesslike heron which flew south every evening at the same
time. The heron did not even turn his head, but flapped and
glided on.

   Hook's shame and anger became such that he stood awake at
night. Hunger kept him awake also, for these little leavings of
the gulls could not sustain his great body in its renewed violence. He became aware that the gulls slept at night in flocks on
the sand, each with one leg tucked under him. He discovered
also that the curlews and the pipers, often mingling, likewise
slept, on the higher remnant of the bar. A sensation of evil
delight filled him in the consideration of protracted striking
among them.

   There was only half of a sick moon in a sky of running but

far-separated clouds on the night when he managed to stalk
into the center of the sleeping gulls. This was light enough, but
so great was his vengeful pleasure that there broke from him a
shrill scream of challenge as he first struck. Without the power
of flight behind it, the blow was not murderous, and this newly
discovered impotence made Hook crazy, so that he screamed
again and again as he struck and tore at the felled gull. He slew
the one, but was twice knocked over by its heavy flounderings,
and all the others rose above him, weaving and screaming,
protesting in the thin moonlight. Wakened by their clamor, the
wading birds also took wing, startled and plaintive. When the
beach was quiet again, the flocks had settled elsewhere, beyond
his pitiful range, and he was left alone beside the single kill. It
was a disappointing victory. He fed with lowering spirit.

Thereafter, he stalked silently. At sunset he would watch
where the gulls settled along the miles of beach, and after dark
he would come like a sharp shadow among them, and drive
with his hook on all sides of him, till the beatings of a poorly
struck victim sent the flock up. Then he would turn vindic-
tively upon the fallen and finish them. In his best night, he
killed five from one flock. But he ate only a little from one, for
the vigor resulting from occasional repletion strengthened only
his ire, which became so great at such a time that food revolted
him. It was not the joyous, swift, controlled hunting anger of a
sane hawk, but something quite different, which made him
dizzy if it continued too long, and left him unsatisfied with any
kill.

Then one day, when he had very nearly struck a gull while
driving it from a gasping yellowfin, the gull's wing rapped
against him as it broke for its running start, and, the trailing
wing failing to support him, he was knocked over. He flurried
awkwardly in the sand to regain his feet, but his mastery of the
beach was ended. Seeing him, in clear sunlight, struggling after
the chance blow, the gulls returned about him in a flashing cloud, circling and pecking on the wing. Hook's plumage
showed quick little jets of irregularity here and there. He reared
back, clattering and erecting the good wing, spreading the
great, rusty tail for balance. His eyes shone with a little of the
old pleasure. But it died, for he could reach none of them. He

was forced to turn and dance awkwardly on the sand, trying to clash bills with each tormentor. They banked up quealing and returned, weaving about him in concentric and overlapping circles. His scream was lost in their clamor, and he appeared merely to be hopping clumsily with his mouth open. Again he fell sideways. Before he could right himself, he was bowled over, and a second time, and lay on his side, twisting his neck to reach them and clappering in blind fury, and was struck three times by three successive gulls, shrieking their flock triumph.

Finally he managed to roll to his breast, and to crouch with his good wing spread wide and the other stretched nearly as far, so that he extended like a gigantic moth, only his snake head, with its now silent scimitar, erect. One great eye blazed under its level brow, but where the other had been was a shallow hole from which thin blood trickled to his russet gap.

In this crouch, by short stages, stopping repeatedly to turn and drive the gulls up, Hook dragged into the river canyon and under the stiff cover of the bitter-leafed laurel. There the gulls left him, soaring up with great clatter of their valor. Till nearly sunset Hook, broken spirited and enduring his hardening eye socket, heard them celebrating over the waves.

When his will was somewhat replenished, and his empty eye socket had stopped the twitching and vague aching which had forced him often to roll ignominiously to rub it in the dust, Hook ventured from the protective lacings of his thicket. He knew fear again, and the challenge of his remaining eye was once more strident, as in adolescence. He dared not return to the beaches, and with a new, weak hunger, the home hunger, enticing him, made his way by short hunting journeys back to the wild wheat slopes and the crisp oaks. There was in Hook an unwonted sensation now, that of the ever-neighboring possibility of death. This sensation was beginning, after his period as a mad bird on the beach, to solidify him into his last stage of life. When, during his slow homeward passage, the gulls wafted inland over him, watching the earth with curious, miserish eyes, he did not cower, but neither did he challenge, either by opened beak or by raised shoulder. He merely watched carefully, learning his first lessons in observing the world with one eye.

At first the familiar surroundings of the bend in the river and the tree with the dead limb to which he could not ascend, aggravated his humiliation, but in time, forced to live cunningly and half-starved, he lost much of his savage pride. At the first flight of a strange hawk over his realm, he was wild at his helplessness, and kept twisting his head like an owl, or spinning in the grass like a small and feathered dervish, to keep the hateful beauty of the wind-rider in sight. But in the succeeding weeks, as one after another coasted his beat, his resentment declined, and when one of the raiders, a haughty yearling, sighted his up-staring eye, and plunged and struck him dreadfully, and failed to kill him only because he dragged under a thicket in time, the second of his great hungers was gone. He had no longer the true lust to kill, no joy of battle, but only the poor desire to fill his belly.

Then truly he lived in the wheat and the brush like a ground owl, ridden with ground lice, dusty or muddy, ever half-starved, forced to sit for hours by small holes for petty and unsatisfying kills. Only once during the final months before his end did he make a kill where the breath of danger recalled his valor, and then the danger was such as a hawk with wings and eyes would scorn. Waiting beside a gopher hole, surrounded by the high, yellow grass, he saw the head emerge, and struck, and was amazed that there writhed in his clutch the neck and dusty coffin-skull of a rattlesnake. Holding his grip, Hook saw the great, thick body slither up after, the tip an erect, strident blur, and writhe on the dirt of the gopher's mound. The weight of the snake pushed Hook about, and once threw him down, and the rising and falling whine of the rattles made the moment terrible, but the vaulted mouth, gaping from the closeness of Hook's gripe, so that the pale, envenomed sabers stood out free, could not reach him. When Hook replaced the grip of his beak with the grip of his talons, and was free to strike again and again at the base of the head, the struggle was over. Hook tore and fed on the fine, watery flesh, and left the tattered armor and the long, jointed bone for the marching ants.

When the heavy rains returned, he ate well during the period of the first escapes from flooded burrows, and then well enough, in a vulture's way, on the drowned creatures. But as the rains lingered, and the burrows hung full of water, and there were no insects in the grass and no small birds sleeping in the thickets, he was constantly hungry, and finally unbearably hungry. His sodden and ground-broken plumage stood out raggedly about him, so that he looked fat, even bloated, but underneath it his skin clung to his bones. Save for his great talons and clappers, and the rain in his down, he would have been like a handful of air. He often stood for a long time under some bush or ledge, heedless of the drip, his one eye filmed over, his mind neither asleep or awake, but between. The gurgle and swirl of the brimming river, and the sound of chunks of the bank cut away to splash and dissolve in the already muddy flood, became familiar to him, and yet a torment, as if that great, ceaselessly working power of water ridiculed his frailty, within which only the faintest spark of valor still glimmered. The last two nights before the rain ended, he huddled under the floor of the bridge on the coastal highway, and heard the palpitant thunder of motors swell and roar over him. The trucks shook the bridge so that Hook, even in his famished lassitude, would sometimes open his one great eye wide and startled.

5

After the rains, when things became full again, bursting with growth and sound, the trees swelling, the thickets full of song and chatter, the fields, turning green in the sun, alive with rustling passages, and the moonlit nights strained with the song of the peepers all up and down the river and in the pools in the fields, Hook had to bear the return of the one hunger left him. At times this made him so wild that he forgot himself and screamed challenge from the open ground. The fretfulness of it spoiled his hunting, which was now entirely a matter of patience. Once he was in despair, and lashed himself through the grass and thickets, trying to rise when that virgin scent drifted for a few moments above the current of his own river. Then, breathless, his beak agape, he saw the strong suitor ride swiftly down on the wind over him, and heard afar the screaming fuss of the harsh wooing in the alders. For that moment even the battle heart beat in him again. The rim of his good eye was scarlet, and a little bead of new blood stood in the socket of the other. With beak and talon, he ripped at a fallen log, and made loam and leaves fly from about it.

But the season of love passed over to the nesting season, and Hook's love hunger, unused, shriveled in him with the others, and there remained in him only one stern quality befitting a hawk, and that the negative one, the remnant, the will to endure. He resumed his patient, plotted hunting, now along a field of the Japanese farmer, but ever within reach of the river thickets.

Growing tough and dry again as the summer advanced, inured to the family of the farmer, whom he saw daily, stooping and scraping with sticks in the ugly, open rows of their fields, where no lovely grass rustled and no life stirred save the shameless gulls, which walked at the heels of the workers, gobbling the worms and grubs they turned up, Hook became nearly content with his shard of life. The only longing or resentment to pierce him was that which he suffered occasionally when forced to hide at the edge of the mile-long bean field from the wafted cruising and the restive, down-bent gaze of one of his own kind. For the rest, he was without flame, a snappish, dust-colored creature, fading into the grasses he trailed through, and suited to his petty ways.

At the end of that summer, for the second time in his four years, Hook underwent a drouth. The equinoctial period passed without a rain. The laurel and the rabbit-brush dropped dry leaves. The foliage of the oaks shriveled and curled. Even the night fogs in the river canyon failed. The farmer's red cattle on the hillside lowed constantly, and could not feed on the dusty stubble. Grass fires broke out along the highway, and ate fast in the wind, filling the hollows with the smell of smoke, and died in the dirt of the shorn hills. The river made no sound. Scum grew on its vestigial pools, and turtles died and stank among the rocks. The dust rode before the wind, and ascended and flowered to nothing between the hills, and every sunset was red with the dust in the air. The people in the farmer's house quarreled, and even struck one another. Birds were silent, and only the hawks flew much. The animals lay breathing hard for very long spells, and ran and crept jerkily. Their flanks were fallen in, and their eyes were red.

At first Hook gorged at the fringe of the grass fires on the multitudes of tiny things that came running and squeaking. But thereafter there were the blackened strips on the hills, and little more in the thin, crackling grass. He found mice and rats, gophers and ground squirrels, and even rabbits, dead in the stubble and under the thickets, but so dry and fleshless that only a faint smell rose from them, even on the sunny days. He starved on them. By early December he had wearily stalked the length of the eastern foothills, hunting at night to escape the voracity of his own kind, resting often upon his wings. The queer trail of his short steps and great horned toes zigzagged in the dust and was erased by the wind at dawn. He was nearly dead, and could make no sound through the horn funnels of his clappers.

Then one night the dry wind brought him, with the familiar, lifeless dust, another familiar scent, troublesome, mingled and unclear. In his vision-dominated brain he remembered the swift circle of his flight a year past, crossing in one segment, his shadow beneath him, a yard cluttered with crates and chickens, a gray barn and then again the plowed land and the stubble. Traveling faster than he had for days, impatient of his shrunken sweep, Hook came down to the farm. In the dark wisps of cloud blown among the stars over him, but no moon, he stood outside the wire of the chicken run. The scent of fat and blooded birds reached him from the shelter, and also within the enclosure was water. At the breath of the water, Hook's gorge contracted, and his tongue quivered and clove in its groove of horn. But there was the wire. He stalked its perimeter and found no opening. He beat it with his good wing, and felt it cut but not give. He wrenched at it with his beak in many places, but could not tear it. Finally, in a fury which drove the thin blood through him, he leaped repeatedly against it, beating and clawing. He was thrown back from the last leap as from the first, but in it he had risen so high as to clutch with his beak at the top wire. While he lay on his breast on the ground, the significance of this came upon him.

Again he leapt, clawed up the wire, and, as he would have

fallen, made even the dead wing bear a little. He grasped the top
and tumbled within. There again he rested flat, searching the
dark with quick-turning head. There was no sound or motion
but the throb of his own body. First he drank at the chill metal
trough hung for the chickens. The water was cold, and loosened his tongue and his tight throat, but it also made him drunk
and dizzy, so that he had to rest again, his claws spread wide to
brace him. Then he walked stiffly, to stalk down the scent. He
trailed it up the runway. Then there was the stuffy, body-warm
air, acrid with droppings, full of soft rustlings as his talons
clicked on the board floor. The thick, white shapes showed
faintly in the darkness. Hook struck quickly, driving a hen to
the floor with one blow, its neck broken and stretched out
stringily. He leaped the still pulsing body, and tore it. The rich,
streaming blood was overpowering to his dried senses, his
starved, leathery body. After a few swallows, the flesh choked
him. In his rage, he struck down another hen. The urge to kill
took him again, as in those nights on the beach. He could let
nothing go. Balked of feeding, he was compelled to slaughter.
Clattering, he struck again and again. The henhouse was suddenly filled with the squawking and helpless rushing and buf-
feting of the terrified, brainless fowls.

Hook reveled in mastery. Here was game big enough to offer
weight against a strike, and yet unable to soar away from his
blows. Turning in the midst of the turmoil, cannily, his fury
caught at the perfect pitch, he struck unceasingly. When the
hens finally discovered the outlet, and streamed into the yard,
to run around the fence, beating and squawking, Hook followed them, scraping down the incline, clumsy and joyous. In
the yard, the cock, a bird as large as he, and much heavier,
found him out and gave valiant battle. In the dark, and both
earthbound, there was little skill, but blow upon blow, and
only chance parry. The still squawking hens pressed into one
corner of the yard. While the duel went on, a dog, excited by
the sustained scuffling, began to bark. He continued to bark,
running back and forth along the fence on one side. A light
flashed on in an uncurtained window of the farmhouse, and
streamed whitely over the crates littering the ground.

Enthralled by his old battle joy, Hook knew only the burly

cock before him. Now, in the farthest reach of the window light, they could see each other dimly. The Japanese farmer, with his gun and lantern, was already at the gate when the finish came. The great cock leapt to jab with his spurs and, toppling forward with extended neck as he fell, was struck and extinguished. Blood had loosened Hook's throat. Shrilly he cried his triumph. It was a thin and exhausted cry, but within him as good as when he shrilled in mid-air over the plummeting descent of a fine foe in his best spring.

The light from the lantern partially blinded Hook. He first turned and ran directly from it, into the corner where the hens were huddled. They fled apart before his charge. He essayed the fence, and on the second try, in his desperation, was out. But in the open dust, the dog was on him, circling, dashing in, snapping. The farmer, who at first had not fired because of the chickens, now did not fire because of the dog, and, when he saw that the hawk was unable to fly, relinquished the sport to the dog, holding the lantern up in order to see better. The light showed his own flat, broad, dark face as sunken also, the cheekbones very prominent, and showed the torn-off sleeves of his shirt and the holes in the knees of his overalls. His wife, in a stained wrapper, and barefooted, heavy black hair hanging around a young, passionless face, joined him hesitantly, but watched, fascinated and a little horrified. His son joined them too, encouraging the dog, but quickly grew silent. Courageous and cruel death, however it may afterward sicken the one who has watched it, is impossible to look away from.

In the circle of the light, Hook turned to keep the dog in front of him. His one eye gleamed with malevolence. The dog was an Airedale, and large. Each time he pounced, Hook stood ground, raising his good wing, the pinions newly torn by the fence, opening his beak soundlessly, and, at the closest approach, hissed furiously, and at once struck. Hit and ripped twice by the whetted horn, the dog recoiled more quickly from several subsequent jumps and, infuriated by his own cowardice, began to bark wildly. Hook maneuvered to watch him, keeping his head turned to avoid losing the foe on the blind side. When the dog paused, safely away, Hook watched him quietly, wing partially lowered, beak closed, but at the first move again lifted the wing and gaped. The dog whined, and the man spoke to him encouragingly. The awful sound of his voice made Hook for an instant twist his head to stare up at the immense figures behind the light. The dog again sallied, barking, and Hook's head spun back. His wing was bitten this time, and with a furious side-blow, he caught the dog's nose. The dog dropped him with a yelp, and then, smarting, came on more warily, as Hook propped himself up from the ground again between his wings. Hook's artificial strength was waning, but his heart still stood to the battle, sustained by a fear of such dimension as he had never known before, but only anticipated when the arrogant young hawk had driven him to cover. The dog, unable to find any point at which the merciless, unwinking eye was not watching him, the parted beak waiting, paused and whimpered again.

"Oh, kill the poor thing," the woman begged.

The man, though, encouraged the dog again, saying, "Sick him; sick him."

The dog rushed bodily. Unable to avoid him, Hook was bowled down, snapping and raking. He left long slashes, as from the blade of a knife, on the dog's flank, but before he could right himself and assume guard again, was caught by the good wing and dragged, clattering, and seeking to make a good stroke from his back. The man followed them to keep the light on them, and the boy went with him, wetting his lips with his tongue and keeping his fists closed tightly. The woman remained behind, but could not help watching the diminished conclusion.

In the little, palely shining arena, the dog repeated his successful maneuver three times, growling but not barking, and when Hook thrashed up from the third blow, both wings were trailing, and dark, shining streams crept on his black-fretted breast from the shoulders. The great eye flashed more furiously than it ever had in victorious battle, and the beak still gaped, but there was no more clatter. He faltered when turning to keep front; the broken wings played him false even as props. He could not rise to use his talons.

The man had tired of holding the lantern up, and put it down to rub his arm. In the low, horizontal light, the dog charged again, this time throwing the weight of his forepaws against Hook's shoulder, so that Hook was crushed as he struck. With his talons up, Hook raked at the dog's belly, but the dog conceived the finish, and furiously worried the feathered bulk. Hook's neck went limp, and between his gaping clappers came only a faint chittering, as from some small kill of his own in the grasses.

In this last conflict, however, there had been some minutes of the supreme fire of the hawk whose three hungers are perfectly fused in the one will; enough to burn off a year of shame.

Between the great sails the light body lay caved and perfectly still. The dog, smarting from his cuts, came to the master and was praised. The woman, joining them slowly, looked at the great wingspread, her husband raising the lantern that she might see it better.

"Oh, the brave bird," she said.

DASHIELL HAMMETT

The Gutting of Couffignal

Best known as the writer of mystery stories who took the detective out of the country house and into the sordid streets of San Francisco, Hammett is acknowledged as the creator of a frank and violent school of realistic, tough gumshoes that is still popular today.

Samuel Dashiell Hammett (1894–1961) was born in Maryland, left school at the age of thirteen, and worked at various odd jobs before spending eight years as an operative for the Pinkerton Agency in San Francisco. He volunteered for service in World War I and in camp contracted influenza that left him with a lifelong tendency toward tuberculosis. He began writing stories for the penny-a-word pulp magazines like Black Mask *and published two mystery novels before achieving a smashing success with* The Maltese Falcon *(1930). His private eye, Sam Spade, played by Humphrey Bogart in the 1931 film, set a fashion for many imitators.*

When he was thirty-six Hammett met his future lifetime companion, Lillian Hellman, who was to become a noted essayist and playwright. She was the inspiration for the character of Nora in Hammett's novel The Thin Man *(1932), which established a pattern for a series of films about a sophisticated, witty couple who solve mysteries during interludes of wisecracking conversation.*

Hammett served in the Aleutian Islands in World War II and was discharged with emphysema. In 1951, during the McCarthy era, he refused on principle to name contributors to the bail-bond fund of the Civil Rights Congress, of which he was a trustee, although he did not in fact know a single name. His six-month jail term did little to improve his health, impaired by heavy drinking. A few days after New Year's Eve, 1960, he died of lung cancer.

"The Gutting of Couffignal" is a good example of the "Continental Op" stories of Hammett's years when he was forging the narrative style for which he is famous. It is taken from a collection, The Big Knockover *(1966), with an introduction by Lillian Hellman.*

Wedge-shaped Couffignal is not a large island, and not far from the mainland, to which it is linked by a wooden bridge. Its western shore is a high, straight cliff that jumps abruptly up out of San Pablo Bay. From the top of this cliff the island slopes eastward, down to a smooth pebble beach that runs into the water again, where there are piers and a clubhouse and moored pleasure boats.

Couffignal's main street, paralleling the beach, has the usual bank, hotel, moving-picture theater, and stores. But it differs from most main streets of its size in that it is more carefully arranged and preserved. There are trees and hedges and strips of lawn on it, and no glaring signs. The buildings seem to belong beside one another, as if they had been designed by the same architect, and in the stores you will find goods of a quality to match the best city stores.

The intersecting streets—running between rows of neat cottages near the foot of the slope—become winding hedged roads as they climb toward the cliff. The higher these roads get, the farther apart and larger are the houses they lead to. The occupants of these higher houses are the owners and rulers of the island. Most of them are well-fed old gentlemen who, the profits they took from the world with both hands in their younger days now stowed away at safe percentages, have bought into the island colony so they may spend what is left of their lives nursing their livers and improving their golf among their kind. They admit to the island only as many storekeepers, working people, and similar riffraff as are needed to keep them comfortably served.

That is Couffignal.

It was some time after midnight. I was sitting in a second-story room in Couffignal's largest house, surrounded by wedding presents whose value would add up to something between fifty and a hundred thousand dollars.

Of all the work that comes to a private detective (except divorce work, which the Continental Detective Agency doesn't handle) I like weddings as little as any. Usually I manage to avoid them, but this time I hadn't been able to. Dick Foley, who had been slated for the job, had been handed a black eye by an unfriendly pickpocket the day before. That let Dick out and me in. I had come up to Couffignal—a two-hour ride from San Francisco by ferry and auto stage—that morning, and would return the next.

This had been neither better nor worse than the usual wedding detail. The ceremony had been performed in a little stone church down the hill. Then the house had begun to fill with reception guests. They had kept it filled to overflowing until some time after the bride and groom had sneaked off to their eastern train.

The world had been well represented. There had been an admiral and an earl or two from England; an ex-president of a South American country; a Danish baron; a tall young Russian princess surrounded by lesser titles, including a fat, bald, jovial and black-bearded Russian general, who had talked to me for a solid hour about prize fights, in which he had a lot of interest, but not so much knowledge as was possible; an ambassador from one of the Central European countries; a justice of the Supreme Court; and a mob of people whose prominence and near-prominence didn't carry labels.

In theory, a detective guarding wedding presents is supposed to make himself indistinguishable from the other guests. In practice, it never works out that way. He has to spend most of his time within sight of the booty, so he's easily spotted. Besides that, eight or ten people I recognized among the guests were clients or former clients of the Agency, and so knew me. However, being known doesn't make so much difference as you might think, and everything had gone off smoothly.

A couple of the groom's friends, warmed by wine and the necessity of maintaining their reputations as cutups, had tried to smuggle some of the gifts out of the room where they were displayed and hide them in the piano. But I had been expecting that familiar trick, and blocked it before it had gone far enough to embarrass anybody.

Shortly after dark a wind smelling of rain began to pile storm clouds up over the bay. Those guests who lived at a distance, especially those who had water to cross, hurried off for their homes. Those who lived on the island stayed until the first raindrops began to patter down. Then they left.

The Hendrixson house quieted down. Musicians and extra servants left. The weary house servants began to disappear in the direction of their bedrooms. I found some sandwiches, a couple of books and a comfortable armchair, and took them up to the room where the presents were now hidden under gray-white sheeting.

Keith Hendrixson, the bride's grandfather—she was an orphan—put his head in at the door. "Have you everything you need for your comfort?" he asked.

"Yes, thanks."

He said good night and went off to bed—a tall old man, slim as a boy.

The wind and the rain were hard at it when I went downstairs to give the lower windows and doors the up-and-down. Everything on the first floor was tight and secure, everything in the cellar. I went upstairs again.

Pulling my chair over by a floor lamp, I put sandwiches, books, ashtray, gun and flashlight on a small table beside it. Then I switched off the other lights, set fire to a Fatima, sat down, wriggled my spine comfortably into the chair's padding, picked up one of the books, and prepared to make a night of it.

The book was called *The Lord of the Sea,* and had to do with a strong, tough and violent fellow named Hogarth, whose modest plan was to hold the world in one hand. There were plots and counterplots, kidnapings, murders, prisonbreakings, forgeries and burglaries, diamonds large as hats and floating forts larger than Couffignal. It sounds dizzy here, but in the book it was as real as a dime.

Hogarth was still going strong when the lights went out.

In the dark, I got rid of the glowing end of my cigarette by grinding it in one of the sandwiches. Putting the book down, I picked up gun and flashlight, and moved away from the chair.

Listening for noises was no good. The storm was making hundreds of them. What I needed to know was why the lights had gone off. All the other lights in the house had been turned off some time ago. So the darkness of the hall told me nothing.

I waited. My job was to watch the presents. Nobody had touched them yet. There was nothing to get excited about.

Minutes went by, perhaps ten of them.

The floor swayed under my feet. The windows rattled with a violence beyond the strength of the storm. The dull boom of a heavy explosion blotted out the sounds of wind and falling water. The blast was not close at hand, but not far enough away to be off the island.

Crossing to the window, peering through the wet glass, I could see nothing. I should have seen a few misty lights far down the hill. Not being able to see them settled one point. The lights had gone out all over Couffignal, not only in the Hendrixson house.

That was better. The storm could have put the lighting system out of whack, could have been responsible for the explosion—maybe.

Staring through the black window, I had an impression of great excitement down the hill, of movement in the night. But all was too far away for me to have seen or heard even had there been lights, and all too vague to say what was moving. The impression was strong but worthless. It didn't lead anywhere. I told myself I was getting feeble-minded, and turned away from the window.

Another blast spun me back to it. This explosion sounded nearer than the first, maybe because it was stronger. Peering through the glass again, I still saw nothing. And still had the impression of things that were big moving down there.

Bare feet pattered in the hall. A voice was anxiously calling my name. Turning from the window again, I pocketed my gun and snapped on the flashlight. Keith Hendrixson, in pajamas and bathrobe, looking thinner and older than anybody could be, came into the room.

"Is it—"

"I don't think it's an earthquake," I said, since that is the first calamity your Californian thinks of. "The lights went off a little while ago. There have been a couple of explosions down the hill since the—"

I stopped. Three shots, close together, had sounded. Rifle-shots, but of the sort that only the heaviest of rifles could make. Then, sharp and small in the storm, came the report of a far-away pistol.

"What is it?" Hendrixson demanded.

"Shooting."

More feet were pattering in the halls, some bare, some shod. Excited voices whispered questions and exclamations. The butler, a solemn, solid block of a man, partly dressed and carrying a lighted five-pronged candlestick, came in.

"Very good, Brophy," Hendrixson said as the butler put the candlestick on the table beside my sandwiches. "Will you try to learn what is the matter?"

"I have tried, sir. The telephone seems to be out of order, sir. Shall I send Oliver down to the village?"

"No-o. I don't suppose it's that serious. Do you think it is anything serious?" he asked me.

I said I didn't think so, but I was paying more attention to the outside than to him. I had heard a thin screaming that could have come from a distant woman, and a volley of small-arms shots. The racket of the storm muffled these shots, but when the heavier firing we had heard before broke out again, it was clear enough.

To have opened the window would have been to let in gallons of water without helping us to hear much clearer. I stood with an ear tilted to the pane, trying to arrive at some idea of what was happening outside.

Another sound took my attention from the window—the ringing of the bell-pull at the front door. It rang loudly and persistently.

Hendrixson looked at me. I nodded. "See who it is, Bro-phy," he said.

The butler went solemnly away, and came back even more solemnly. "Princess Zhukovski," he announced.

She came running into the room—the tall Russian girl I had seen at the reception. Her eyes were wide and dark with excite-ment. Her face was very white and wet. Water ran in streams down her blue waterproof cape, the hood of which covered her dark hair.

"Oh, Mr. Hendrixson!" She had caught one of his hands in both of hers. Her voice, with nothing foreign in its accents, was the voice of one who is excited over a delightful surprise. "The bank is being robbed, and the—what do you call him?—marshal of police has been killed!"

"What's that?" the old man exclaimed, jumping awkwardly because water from her cape had dripped down on one of his bare feet. "Weegan killed? And the bank robbed?"

"Yes! Isn't it terrible?" She said it as if she were saying wonderful. "When the first explosion woke us, the general sent Ignati down to find out what was the matter, and he got down there just in time to see the bank blown up. Listen!"

We listened, and heard a wild outbreak of mixed gunfire.

"That will be the general arriving!" she said. "He'll enjoy himself most wonderfully. As soon as Ignati returned with the news, the general armed every male in the household from Aleksander Sergyeevich to Ivan the cook, and led them out happier than he's been since he took his division to East Prussia in 1914."

"And the duchess?" Hendrixson asked.

"He left her at home with me, of course, and I furtively crept out and away from her while she was trying for the first time in her life to put water in a samovar. This is not the night for one to stay at home!"

"H-m-m," Hendrixson said, his mind obviously not on her words. "And the bank!"

He looked at me. I said nothing. The racket of another volley came to us.

"Could you do anything down there?" he asked.

"Maybe, but—" I nodded at the presents under their covers.

"Oh, those!" the old man said. "I'm as much interested in the bank as in them; and besides, we will be here."

"All right!" I was willing enough to carry my curiosity down the hill. "I'll go down. You'd better have the butler stay in here, and plant the chauffeur inside the front door. Better give them guns if you have any. Is there a raincoat I can borrow? I brought only a light overcoat with me."

Brophy found a yellow slicker that fit me. I put it on, stowed gun and flashlight conveniently under it, and found my hat while Brophy was getting and loading an automatic pistol for himself and a rifle for Oliver, the mulatto chauffeur.

Hendrixson and the princess followed me downstairs. At the door I found she wasn't exactly following me—she was going with me.

"But, Sonya!" the old man protested.

"I'm not going to be foolish, though I'd like to," she promised him. "But I'm going back to my Irinia Androvna, who will perhaps have the samovar watered by now."

"That's a sensible girl!" Hendrixson said, and let us out into the rain and the wind.

It wasn't weather to talk in. In silence we turned downhill between two rows of hedging, with the storm driving at our backs. At the first break in the hedge I stopped, nodding toward the black blot a house made. "That is your—"

Her laugh cut me short. She caught my arm and began to urge me down the road again. "I only told Mr. Hendrixson that so he would not worry," she explained. "You do not think I am not going down to see the sights."

She was tall. I am short and thick. I had to look up to see her face—to see as much of it as the rain-gray night would let me see. "You'll be soaked to the hide, running around in this rain," I objected.

"What of that? I am dressed for it." She raised a foot to show me a heavy waterproof boot and a woolen-stockinged leg.

"There's no telling what we'll run into down there, and I've got work to do," I insisted. "I can't be looking out for you."

"I can look out for myself." She pushed her cape aside to show me a square automatic pistol in one hand.

"You'll be in my way."

"I will not," she retorted. "You'll probably find I can help you. I'm as strong as you, and quicker, and I can shoot."

The reports of scattered shooting had punctuated our argument, but now the sound of heavier firing silenced the dozen objections to her company that I could still think of. After all, I could slip away from her in the dark if she became too much of a nuisance.

"Have it your own way," I growled, "but don't expect anything from me."

"You're so kind," she murmured as we got under way again, hurrying now, with the wind at our backs speeding us along.

Occasionally dark figures moved on the road ahead of us, but too far away to be recognizable. Presently a man passed us, running uphill—a tall man whose nightshirt hung out of his trousers, down below his coat, identifying him as a resident.

"They've finished the bank and are at Medcraft's!" he yelled as he went by.

"Medcraft is the jeweler," the girl informed me.

The sloping under our feet grew less sharp. The houses—dark but with faces vaguely visible here and there at windows—came closer together. Below, the flash of a gun could be seen now and then—orange streaks in the rain.

Our road put us into the lower end of the main street just as a staccato rat-ta-tat broke out.

I pushed the girl into the nearest doorway, and jumped in after her.

Bullets ripped through walls with the sound of hail tapping on leaves.

That was the thing I had taken for an exceptionally heavy rifle—a machine gun.

The girl had fallen back in a corner, all tangled up with something. I helped her up. The something was a boy of seventeen or so, with one leg and a crutch.

"It's the boy who delivers papers," Princess Zhukovski said, "and you've hurt him with your clumsiness."

The boy shook his head, grinning as he got up. "No'm, I ain't hurt none, but you kind of scared me, jumping on me like that."

She had to stop and explain that she hadn't jumped on him, that she had been pushed into him by me, and that she was sorry and so was I.

"What's happening?" I asked the newsboy when I could get a word in.

"Everything," he boasted, as if some of the credit were his. "There must be a hundred of them, and they've blowed the bank wide open, and now some of 'em is in Medcraft's, and I

guess they'll blow that up, too. And they killed Tom Weegan.
They got a machine gun on a car in the middle of the street.
That's it shooting now."

"Where's everybody—all the merry villagers?"

"Most of 'em are up behind the Hall. They can't do nothing, though, because the machine gun won't let 'em get near
enough to see what they're shooting at, and that smart Bill
Vincent told me to clear out, 'cause I've only got one leg, as if I
couldn't shoot as good as the next one, if I only had something
to shoot with!"

"That wasn't right of them," I sympathized. "But you can
do something for me. You can stick here and keep your eye on
this end of the street, so I'll know if they leave in this direction."

"You're not just saying that so I'll stay here out of the way,
are you?"

"No," I lied. "I need somebody to watch. I was going to
leave the princess here, but you'll do better."

"Yes," she backed me up, catching the idea. "This gentleman
is a detective, and if you do what he asks you'll be helping more
than if you were up with the others."

The machine gun was still firing, but not in our direction
now.

"I'm going across the street," I told the girl. "If you—"

"Aren't you going to join the others?"

"No. If I can get around behind the bandits while they're
busy with the others, maybe I can turn a trick."

"Watch sharp now!" I ordered the boy, and the princess and I
made a dash for the opposite sidewalk.

We reached it without drawing lead, sidled along a building
for a few yards, and turned into an alley. From the alley's other
end came the smell and wash and the dull blackness of the bay.

While we moved down this alley I composed a scheme by
which I hoped to get rid of my companion, sending her off on a
safe wild-goose chase. But I didn't get a chance to try it out.

The big figure of a man loomed ahead of us.

Stepping in front of the girl, I went on toward him. Under
my slicker I held my gun on the middle of him.

He stood still. He was larger than he had looked at first. A
big, slope-shouldered, barrel-bodied husky. His hands were

empty. I spotted the flashlight on his face for a split second. A flat-cheeked, thick-featured face, with high cheekbones and a lot of ruggedness in it.

"Ignati!" the girl exclaimed over my shoulder.

He began to talk what I suppose was Russian to the girl. She laughed and replied. He shook his big head stubbornly, insisting on something. She stamped her foot and spoke sharply. He shook his head again and addressed me. "General Pleshskev, he tell me bring Princess Sonya to home."

His English was almost as hard to understand as his Russian. His tone puzzled me. It was as if he was explaining some absolutely necessary thing that he didn't want to be blamed for, but that nevertheless he was going to do.

While the girl was speaking to him again, I guessed the answer. This big Ignati had been sent out by the general to bring the girl home, and he was going to obey his orders if he had to carry her. He was trying to avoid trouble with me by explaining the situation.

"Take her," I said, stepping aside.

The girl scowled at me, laughed. "Very well, Ignati," she said in English, "I shall go home," and she turned on her heel and went back up the alley, the big man close behind her.

Glad to be alone, I wasted no time in moving in the opposite direction until the pebbles of the beach were under my feet. The pebbles ground harshly under my heels. I moved back to more silent ground and began to work my way as swiftly as I could up the shore toward the center of action. The machine gun barked on. Smaller guns snapped. Three concussions, close together—bombs, hand grenades, my ears and my memory told me.

The stormy sky glared pink over a roof ahead of me and to the left. The boom of the blast beat my eardrums. Fragments I couldn't see fell around me. That, I thought, would be the jeweler's safe blowing apart.

I crept on up the shore line. The machine gun went silent. Lighter guns snapped, snapped. Another grenade went off. A man's voice shrieked pure terror.

Risking the crunch of pebbles, I turned down to the water's edge again. I had seen no dark shape on the water that could

have been a boat. There had been boats moored along this
beach in the afternoon. With my feet in the water of the bay I
still saw no boat. The storm could have scattered them, but I
didn't think it had. The island's western height shielded this
shore. The wind was strong here, but not violent.

My feet sometimes on the edge of the pebbles, sometimes in
the water, I went on up the shore line. Now I saw a boat. A
gently bobbing black shape ahead. No light was on it. Nothing
I could see moved on it. It was the only boat on that shore. That
made it important.

Foot by foot, I approached.

A shadow moved between me and the dark rear of a building. I froze. The shadow, man-size, moved again, in the direction from which I was coming.

Waiting, I didn't know how nearly invisible, or how plain, I
might be against my background. I couldn't risk giving myself
away by trying to improve my position.

Twenty feet from me the shadow suddenly stopped.

I was seen. My gun was on the shadow.

"Come on," I called softly. "Keep coming. Let's see who you
are."

The shadow hesitated, left the shelter of the building, drew
nearer. I couldn't risk the flashlight. I made out dimly a handsome face, boyishly reckless, one cheek dark-stained.

"Oh, how d'you do?" the face's owner said in a musical
baritone voice. "You were at the reception this afternoon."

"Yes."

"Have you seen Princess Zhukovski? You know her?"

"She went home with Ignati ten minutes or so ago."

"Excellent!" He wiped his stained cheek with a stained handkerchief, and turned to look at the boat. "That's Hendrixson's
boat," he whispered. "They've got it and they've cast the
others off."

"That would mean they are going to leave by water."

"Yes," he agreed, "unless—Shall we have a try at it?"

"You mean jump it?"

"Why not?" he asked. "There can't be very many aboard.
God knows there are enough of them ashore. You're armed.
I've a pistol."

"We'll size it up first," I decided, "so we'll know what we're jumping."

"That is wisdom," he said, and led the way back to the shelter of the buildings.

Hugging the rear walls of the buildings, we stole toward the boat.

The boat grew clearer in the night. A craft perhaps forty-five feet long, its stern to the shore, rising and falling beside a small pier. Across the stern something protruded. Something I couldn't quite make out. Leather soles scuffled now and then on the wooden deck. Presently a dark head and shoulders showed over the puzzling thing in the stern.

The Russian lad's eyes were better than mine.

"Masked," he breathed in my ear. "Something like a stocking over his head and face."

The masked man was motionless where he stood. We were motionless where we stood.

"Could you hit him from here?" the lad asked.

"Maybe, but night and rain aren't a good combination for sharpshooting. Our best bet is to sneak as close as we can, and start shooting when he spots us."

"That is wisdom," he agreed.

Discovery came with our first step forward. The man in the boat grunted. The lad at my side jumped forward. I recognized the thing in the boat's stern just in time to throw out a leg and trip the young Russian. He tumbled down, all sprawled out on the pebbles. I dropped behind him.

The machine gun in the boat's stern poured metal over our heads.

"No good rushing that!" I said. "Roll out of it!"

I set the example by revolving toward the back of the building we had just left.

The man at the gun sprinkled the beach, but sprinkled it at random, his eyes no doubt spoiled for night-seeing by the flash of his gun.

Around the corner of the building, we sat up.

"You saved my life by tripping me," the lad said coolly.

"Yes. I wonder if they've moved the machine gun from the street, or if—"

The answer to that came immediately. The machine gun in the street mingled its vicious voice with the drumming of the one in the boat.

"A pair of them!" I complained. "Know anything about the layout?"

"I don't think there are more than ten or twelve of them," he said, "although it is not easy to count in the dark. The few I have seen are completely masked—like the man in the boat. They seem to have disconnected the telephone and light lines first and then to have destroyed the bridge. We attacked them while they were looting the bank, but in front they had a machine gun mounted in an automobile, and we were not equipped to combat on equal terms."

"Where are the islanders now?"

"Scattered, and most of them in hiding, I fancy, unless General Pleshskev has succeeded in rallying them again."

I frowned and beat my brains together. You can't fight machine guns and hand grenades with peaceful villagers and retired capitalists. No matter how well led and armed they are, you can't do anything with them. For that matter, how could anybody do much against a game of that toughness?

"Suppose you stick here and keep your eye on the boat," I suggested. "I'll scout around and see what's doing farther up, and if I can get a few good men together, I'll try to jump the boat again, probably from the other side. But we can't count on that. The get-away will be by boat. We can count on that, and try to block it. If you lie down you can watch the boat around the corner of the building without making much of a target yourself. I wouldn't do anything to attract attention until the break for the boat comes. Then you can do all the shooting you want."

"Excellent!" he said. "You'll probably find most of the islanders up behind the church. You can get to it by going straight up the hill until you come to an iron fence, and then follow that to the right."

"Right."

I moved off in the direction he had indicated.

At the main street I stopped to look around before venturing across. Everything was quiet there. The only man I could see was spread out face-down on the sidewalk near me.

On hands and knees I crawled to his side. He was dead. I didn't stop to examine him further, but sprang up and streaked for the other side of the street.

Nothing tried to stop me. In a doorway, flat against a wall, I peeped out. The wind had stopped. The rain was no longer a driving deluge, but a steady down-pouring of small drops. Couffignal's main street, to my senses, was a deserted street.

I wondered if the retreat to the boat had already started. On the sidewalk, walking swiftly toward the bank, I heard the answer to that guess.

High up on the slope, almost up to the edge of the cliff, by the sound, a machine gun began to hurl out its stream of bullets.

Mixed with the racket of the machine gun were the sounds of smaller arms, and a grenade or two.

At the first crossing, I left the main street and began to run up the hill. Men were running toward me. Two of them passed, paying no attention to my shouted, "What's up now?"

The third man stopped because I grabbed him—a fat man whose breath bubbled, and whose face was fish-belly white.

"They've moved the car with the machine gun on it up behind us," he gasped when I had shouted my question into his ear again.

"What are you doing without a gun?" I asked.

"I—I dropped it."

"Where's General Pleshskev?"

"Back there somewhere. He's trying to capture the car, but he'll never do it. It's suicide! Why don't help come?"

Other men had passed us, running downhill, as we talked. I let the white-faced man go, and stopped four men who weren't running so fast as the others.

"What's happening now?" I questioned them.

"They's going through the houses up the hill," a sharp-featured man with a small mustache and a rifle said.

"Has anybody got word off the island yet?" I asked.

"Can't," another informed me. "They blew up the bridge first thing."

"Can't anybody swim?"

"Not in that wind. Young Catlan tried it and was lucky to get out again with a couple of broken ribs."

"The wind's gone down," I pointed out.

The sharp-featured man gave his rifle to one of the others and took off his coat. "I'll try it," he promised.

"Good! Wake up the whole country, and get word through to the San Francisco police boat and to the Mare Island Navy Yard. They'll lend a hand if you tell 'em the bandits have machine guns. Tell 'em the bandits have an armed boat waiting to leave in. It's Hendrixson's."

The volunteer swimmer left.

"A boat?" two of the men asked together.

"Yes. With a machine gun on it. If we're going to do anything, it'll have to be now, while we're between them and their get-away. Get every man and every gun you can find down there. Tackle the boat from the roofs if you can. When the bandits' car comes down there, pour it into it. You'll do better from the buildings than from the street."

The three men went on downhill. I went uphill, toward the crackling of firearms ahead. The machine gun was working irregularly. It would pour out its rat-tat-tat for a second or so, and then stop for a couple of seconds. The answering fire was thin, ragged.

I met more men, learned from them the general, with less than a dozen men, was still fighting the car. I repeated the advice I had given the other men. My informants went down to join them. I went on up.

A hundred yards farther along, what was left of the general's dozen broke out of the night, around and past me, flying downhill, with bullets hailing after them.

The road was no place for mortal man. I stumbled over two bodies, scratched myself in a dozen places getting over a hedge. On soft, wet sod I continued my uphill journey.

The machine gun on the hill stopped its clattering. The one in the boat was still at work.

The one ahead opened again, firing too high for anything near at hand to be its target. It was helping its fellow below, spraying the main street.

Before I could get closer it had stopped. I heard the car's motor racing. The car moved toward me.

Rolling into the hedge, I lay there, straining my eyes through the spaces between the stems. I had six bullets in a gun that hadn't yet been fired on this night that had seen tons of powder burned.

When I saw wheels on the lighter face of the road, I emptied my gun, holding it low.

The car went on.

I sprang out of my hiding-place.

The car was suddenly gone from the empty road.

There was a grinding sound. A crash. The noise of metal folding on itself. The tinkle of glass.

I raced toward those sounds.

Out of a black pile where an engine sputtered, a black figure leaped—to dash off across the soggy lawn. I cut after it, hoping that the others in the wreck were down for keeps.

I was less than fifteen feet behind the fleeing man when he cleared a hedge. I'm no sprinter, but neither was he. The wet grass made slippery going.

He stumbled while I was vaulting the hedge. When we straightened out again I was not more than ten feet behind him.

Once I clicked my gun at him, forgetting I had emptied it. Six cartridges were wrapped in a piece of paper in my vest pocket, but this was no time for loading.

I was tempted to chuck the empty gun at his head. But that was too chancy.

A building loomed ahead. My fugitive bore off to the right, to clear the corner.

To the left a heavy shotgun went off.

The running man disappeared around the house-corner.

"Sweet God!" General Pleshskev's mellow voice complained. "That with a shotgun I should miss all of a man at the distance!"

"Go round the other way!" I yelled, plunging around the corner after my quarry.

His feet thudded ahead. I could not see him. The general puffed around from the other side of the house.

"You have him?"

"No."

In front of us was a stone-faced bank, on top of which ran a path. On either side of us was a high and solid hedge.

"But, my friend," the general protested. "How could he have—?"

A pale triangle showed on the path above—a triangle that could have been a bit of shirt showing above the opening of a vest.

"Stay here and talk!" I whispered to the general, and crept forward.

"It must be that he has gone the other way," the general carried out my instructions, rambling on as if I were standing beside him, "because if he had come my way I should have seen him, and if he had raised himself over either of the hedges or the embankment, one of us would surely have seen him against . . ."

He talked on and on while I gained the shelter of the bank on which the path sat, while I found places for my toes in the rough stone facing.

The man on the road, trying to make himself small with his back in a bush, was looking at the talking general. He saw me when I had my feet on the path.

He jumped, and one hand went up.

I jumped, with both hands out.

A stone, turning under my foot, threw me sidewise, twisting my ankle, but saving my head from the bullet he sent at it.

My outflung left arm caught his legs as I spilled down. He came over on top of me. I kicked him once, caught his gun-arm, and had just decided to bite it when the general puffed up over the edge of the path and prodded the man off me with the muzzle of the shotgun.

When it came my turn to stand up, I found it not so good. My twisted ankle didn't like to support its share of my hundred-and-eighty-some pounds. Putting most of my weight on the other leg, I turned my flashlight on the prisoner.

"Hello, Flippo!" I exclaimed.

"Hello!" he said without joy in the recognition.

He was a roly-poly Italian youth of twenty-three or -four. I had helped send him to San Quentin four years ago for his part in a payroll stick-up. He had been out on parole for several months now.

"The prison board isn't going to like this," I told him.

"You got me wrong," he pleaded. "I ain't been doing a thing. I was up here to see some friends. And when this thing busted loose I had to hide, because I got a record, and if I'm picked up I'll be railroaded for it. And now you got me, and you think I'm in on it!"

"You're a mind reader," I assured him, and asked the general, "Where can we pack this bird away for a while, under lock and key?"

"In my house there is a lumber-room with a strong door and not a window."

"That'll do it. March, Flippo!"

General Pleshskev collared the youth, while I limped along behind them, examining Flippo's gun, which was loaded except for the one shot he had fired at me, and reloading my own.

We had caught our prisoner on the Russian's grounds, so we didn't have far to go.

The general knocked on the door and called out something in his language. Bolts clicked and grated, and the door was swung open by a heavily mustached Russian servant. Behind him the princess and a stalwart older woman stood.

We went in while the general was telling his household about the capture, and took the captive up to the lumber-room. I frisked him for his pocketknife and matches—he had nothing else that could help him get out—locked him in and braced the door solidly with a length of board. Then we went downstairs again.

"You are injured!" the princess cried, seeing me limp across the floor.

"Only a twisted ankle," I said. "But it does bother me some. Is there any adhesive tape around?"

"Yes," and she spoke to the mustached servant, who went out of the room and presently returned, carrying rolls of gauze and tape and a basin of steaming water.

"If you'll sit down," the princess said, taking these things from the servant.

But I shook my head and reached for the adhesive tape.

"I want cold water, because I've got to go out in the wet again. If you'll show me the bathroom, I can fix myself up in no time."

We had to argue about that, but I finally got to the bathroom, where I ran cold water on my foot and ankle, and strapped it with adhesive tape, as tight as I could without stopping the circulation altogether. Getting my wet shoe on again was a job, but when I was through I had two firm legs under me, even if one of them did hurt some.

When I rejoined the others I noticed that sounds of firing no longer came up the hill, and that the patter of rain was lighter, and a gray streak of coming daylight showed under a drawn blind.

I was buttoning my slicker when the knocker rang on the front door. Russian words came through, and the young Russian I had met on the beach came in.

"Aleksander, you're—" The stalwart older woman screamed, when she saw the blood on his cheek, and fainted.

He paid no attention to her at all, as if he was used to having her faint.

"They've gone in the boat," he told me while the girl and two men servants gathered up the woman and laid her on an ottoman.

"How many?" I asked.

"I counted ten, and I don't think I missed more than one or two, if any."

"The men I sent down there couldn't stop them?"

He shrugged. "What would you? It takes a strong stomach to face a machine gun. Your men had been cleared out of the buildings almost before they arrived."

The woman who had fainted had revived by now and was pouring anxious questions in Russian at the lad. The princess was getting into her blue cape. The woman stopped questioning the lad and asked her something.

"It's all over," the princess said. "I am going to view the ruins."

That suggestion appealed to everybody. Five minutes later all of us, including the servants, were on our way downhill.

Behind us, around us, in front of us, were other people going downhill, hurrying along in the drizzle that was very gentle now, their faces tired and excited in the bleak morning light.

Halfway down, a woman ran out of a cross-path and began to tell me something. I recognized her as one of Hendrixson's maids.

I caught some of her words.

"Presents gone. . . . Mr. Brophy murdered . . . Oliver . . ."

"I'll be down later," I told the others, and set out after the maid.

She was running back to the Hendrixson house. I couldn't run, couldn't even walk fast. She and Hendrixson and more of his servants were standing on the front porch when I arrived.

"They killed Oliver and Brophy," the old man said.

"How?"

"We were in the back of the house, the rear second story, watching the flashes of the shooting down in the village. Oliver was down here, just inside the front door, and Brophy in the room with the presents. We heard a shot in there, and immediately a man appeared in the doorway of our room, threatening us with two pistols, making us stay there for perhaps ten minutes. Then he shut and locked the door and went away. We broke the door down—and found Brophy and Oliver dead."

"Let's look at them."

The chauffeur was just inside the front door. He lay on his back, with his brown throat cut straight across the front, almost back to the vertebrae. His rifle was under him. I pulled it out and examined it. It had not been fired.

Upstairs, the butler Brophy was huddled against a leg of one of the tables on which the presents had been spread. His gun was gone. I turned him over, straightened him out, and found a bullet-hole in his chest. Around the hole his coat was charred in a large area.

Most of the presents were still there. But the most valuable pieces were gone. The others were in disorder, lying around any which way, their covers pulled off.

"What did the one you saw look like?" I asked.

"I didn't see him very well," Hendrixson said. "There was no light in our room. He was simply a dark figure against the candle burning in the hall. A large man in a black rubber raincoat, with some sort of black mask that covered his whole head and face, with small eyeholes."

"No hat?"

"No, just the mask over his entire face and head."

As we went downstairs again I gave Hendrixson a brief account of what I had seen and heard and done since I had left him. There wasn't enough of it to make a long tale.

"Do you think you can get information about the others from the one you caught?" he asked, as I prepared to go out.

"No. But I expect to bag them just the same."

Couffignal's main street was jammed with people when I limped into it again. A detachment of Marines from Mare Island was there, and men from a San Francisco police boat. Excited citizens in all degrees of partial nakedness boiled around them. A hundred voices were talking at once, recounting their personal adventures and braveries and losses and what they had seen. Such words as machine gun, bomb, bandit, car, shot, dynamite, and killed sounded again and again, in every variety of voice and tone.

The bank had been completely wrecked by the charge that had blown the vault. The jewelry store was another ruin. A grocer's across the street was serving as a field hospital. Two doctors were toiling there, patching up damaged villagers.

I recognized a familiar face under a uniform cap—Sergeant Roche of the harbor police—and pushed through the crowd to him.

"Just get here?" he asked as we shook hands. "Or were you in on it?"

"In on it."

"What do you know?"

"Everything."

"Who ever heard of a private detective that didn't," he joshed as I led him out of the mob.

"Did you people run into an empty boat out in the bay?" I asked when we were away from audiences.

"Empty boats have been floating around the bay all night," he said.

I hadn't thought of that.

"Where's your boat now?" I asked him.

"Out trying to pick up the bandits. I stayed with a couple of men to lend a hand here."

"You're in luck," I told him. "Now sneak a look across the street. See the stout old boy with the black whiskers, standing in front of the druggist's?"

General Pleshskev stood there, with the woman who had fainted, the young Russian whose bloody cheek had made her faint, and a pale, plump man of forty-something who had been with them at the reception. A little to one side stood big Ignati, the two men-servants I had seen at the house, and another who was obviously one of them. They were chatting together and watching the excited antics of a red-faced property-owner who was telling a curt lieutenant of Marines that it was his own personal private automobile that the bandits had stolen to mount their machine gun on, and what he thought should be done about it.

"Yes," said Roche, "I see your fellow with the whiskers."

"Well, he's your meat. The woman and two men with him are also your meat. And those four Russians standing to the left are some more of it. There's another missing, but I'll take care of that one. Pass the word to the lieutenant, and you can round up those babies without giving them a chance to fight back. They think they're safe as angels."

"Sure, are you?" the sergeant asked.

"Don't be silly!" I growled, as if I had never made a mistake in my life.

I had been standing on my one good prop. When I put my weight on the other to turn away from the sergeant, it stung me all the way to the hip. I pushed my back teeth together and began to work painfully through the crowd to the other side of the street.

The princess didn't seem to be among those present. My idea was that, next to the general, she was the most important member of the push. If she was at their house, and not yet suspicious, I figured I could get close enough to yank her in without a riot.

Walking was hell. My temperature rose. Sweat rolled out on me.

"Mister, they didn't none of 'em come down that way."

The one-legged newsboy was standing at my elbow. I greeted him as if he were my pay-check.

"Come on with me," I said, taking his arm. "You did fine down there, and now I want you to do something else for me."

Half a block from the main street I led him up on the porch of a small yellow cottage. The front door stood open, left that way when the occupants ran down to welcome police and Marines, no doubt. Just inside the door, beside a hall rack, was a wicker porch chair. I committed unlawful entry to the extent of dragging that chair out on the porch.

"Sit down, son," I urged the boy.

He sat, looking up at me with puzzled freckled face. I took a firm grip on his crutch and pulled it out of his hand.

"Here's five bucks for rental," I said, "and if I lose it I'll buy you one of ivory and gold."

And I put the crutch under my arm and began to propel myself up the hill.

It was my first experience with a crutch. I didn't break any records. But it was a lot better than tottering along on an unassisted bum ankle.

The hill was longer and steeper than some mountains I've seen, but the gravel walk to the Russians' house was finally under my feet.

I was still some dozen feet from the porch when Princess Zhukovski opened the door.

"Oh!" she exclaimed, and then, recovering from her surprise, "your ankle is worse!" She ran down the steps to help me climb them. As she came I noticed that something heavy was sagging and swinging in the right-hand pocket of her gray flannel jacket.

With one hand under my elbow, the other arm across my back, she helped me up the steps and across the porch. That assured me she didn't think I had tumbled to the game. If she had, she wouldn't have trusted herself within reach of my hands. Why, I wondered, had she come back to the house after starting downhill with the others?

While I was wondering we went into the house, where she planted me in a large and soft leather chair.

"You must certainly be starving after your strenuous night," she said. "I will see if—"

"No, sit down." I nodded at a chair facing mine. "I want to talk to you."

She sat down, clasping her slender white hands in her lap. In neither face nor pose was there any sign of nervousness, not even of curiosity. And that was overdoing it.

"Where have you cached the plunder?" I asked.

The whiteness of her face was nothing to go by. It had been white as marble since I had first seen her. The darkness of her eyes was as natural. Nothing happened to her other features. Her voice was smoothly cool.

"I am sorry," she said. "The question doesn't convey anything to me."

"Here's the point," I explained. "I'm charging you with complicity in the gutting of Couffignal, and in the murders that went with it. And I'm asking you where the loot has been hidden."

Slowly she stood up, raised her chin, and looked at least a mile down at me.

"How dare you? How dare you speak so to me, a Zhukovski!"

"I don't care if you're one of the Smith Brothers!" Leaning forward, I had pushed my twisted ankle against a leg of the chair, and the resulting agony didn't improve my disposition. "For the purpose of this talk you are a thief and a murderer."

Her strong slender body became the body of a lean crouching animal. Her white face became the face of an enraged animal. One hand—claw now—swept to the heavy pocket of her jacket.

Then, before I could have batted an eye—though my life seemed to depend on my not batting it—the wild animal had vanished. Out of it—and now I know where the writers of the old fairy stories got their ideas—rose the princess again, cool and straight and tall.

She sat down, crossed her ankles, put an elbow on an arm of her chair, propped her chin on the back of that hand, and looked curiously into my face.

"How ever," she murmured, "did you chance to arrive at so strange and fanciful a theory?"

"It wasn't chance, and it's neither strange nor fanciful," I said. "Maybe it'll save time and trouble if I show you part of the score against you. Then you'll know how you stand and won't waste your brains pleading innocence."

"I shall be grateful," she smiled, "very!"

I tucked my crutch in between one knee and the arm of my chair, so my hands would be free to check off my points on my fingers.

"First—whoever planned the job knew the island—not fairly well, but every inch of it. There's no need to argue about that. Second—the car on which the machine gun was mounted was local property, stolen from the owner here. So was the boat in which the bandits were supposed to have escaped. Bandits from the outside would have needed a car or a boat to bring their machine guns, explosives, and grenades here, and there doesn't seem to be any reason why they shouldn't have used that car or boat instead of stealing a fresh one. Third—there wasn't the least of hint of the professional bandit touch on this job. If you ask me, it was a military job from beginning to end. And the worst safe-burglar in the world could have got into both the bank vault and the jeweler's safe without wrecking the buildings. Fourth—bandits from the outside wouldn't have destroyed the bridge. They might have blocked it, but they wouldn't have destroyed it. They'd have saved it in case they had to make their get-away in that direction. Fifth—bandits figuring on a get-away by boat would have cut the job short, wouldn't have spread it over the whole night. Enough racket was made here to wake up California all the way from Sacramento to Los Angeles. What you people did was to send one man out in the boat, shooting, and he didn't go far. As soon as he was at a safe distance, he went overboard, and swam back to the island. Big Ignati could have done it without turning a hair."

That exhausted my right hand. I switched over, counting on my left.

"Sixth—I met one of your party, the lad, down on the beach, and he was coming from the boat. He suggested that we jump it. We were shot at, but the man behind the gun was playing with us. He could have wiped us out in a second if he had been in earnest, but he shot over our heads. Seventh—that same lad is the only man on the island, so far as I know, who saw the departing bandits. Eighth—all of your people that I ran into were especially nice to me, the general even spending an hour talking to me at the reception this afternoon. That's a distinctive amateur crook trait. Ninth—after the machine gun car had been wrecked I chased its occupant. I lost him around this house. The Italian boy I picked up wasn't him. He couldn't have climbed up on the path without my seeing him. But he could have run around to the general's side of the house and vanished indoors there. The general liked him, and would have helped him. I know that, because the general performed a downright miracle by missing him at some six feet with a shotgun. Tenth—you called at Hendrixson's house for no other purpose than to get me away from there."

That finished the left hand. I went back to the right.

"Eleventh—Hendrixson's two servants were killed by someone they knew and trusted. Both were killed at close quarters and without firing a shot. I'd say you got Oliver to let you into the house, and were talking to him when one of your men cut his throat from behind. Then you went upstairs and probably shot the unsuspecting Brophy yourself. He wouldn't have been on his guard against you. Twelfth—but that ought to be enough, and I'm getting a sore throat from listing them."

She took her chin off her hand, took a fat white cigarette out of a thin black case, and held it in her mouth while I put a match to the end of it. She took a long pull at it—a draw that accounted for a third of its length—and blew the smoke down at her knees.

"That would be enough," she said when all these things had been done, "if it were not that you yourself know it was impossible for us to have been so engaged. Did you not see us—did not everyone see us—time and time again?"

"That's easy!" I argued. "With a couple of machine guns, a trunkful of grenades, knowing the island from top to bottom, in the darkness and in a storm, against bewildered civilians—it was duck soup. There are nine of you that I know of, including two women. Any five of you could have carried on the work, once it was started, while the others took turns appearing here and there, establishing alibis. And that is what you did. You took turns slipping out to alibi yourselves. Everywhere I went I ran into one of you. And the general! That whiskered old joker running around leading the simple citizens to battle! I'll bet he led 'em plenty! They're lucky there are any of 'em alive this morning!"

She finished her cigarette with another inhalation, dropped the stub on the rug, ground out the light with one foot, sighed wearily, put her hands on her hips, and asked, "And now what?"

"Now I want to know where you have stowed the plunder."

The readiness of her answer surprised me.

"Under the garage, in a cellar we secretly dug there some months ago."

I didn't believe that, of course, but it turned out to be the truth.

I didn't have anything else to say. When I fumbled with my borrowed crutch, preparing to get up, she raised a hand and spoke gently. "Wait a moment, please. I have something to suggest."

Half standing, I leaned toward her, stretching out one hand until it was close to her side.

"I want the gun," I said.

She nodded, and sat still while I plucked it from her pocket, put it in one of my own, and sat down again.

"You said a little while ago that you didn't care who I was," she began immediately. "But I want you to know. There are so many of us Russians who once were somebodies and who now are nobodies that I won't bore you with the repetition of a tale the world has grown tired of hearing. But you must remember that this weary tale is real to us who are its subjects. However, we fled from Russia with what we could carry of our property, which fortunately was enough to keep us in bearable comfort for a few years.

"In London we opened a Russian restaurant, but London was suddenly full of Russian restaurants, and ours became, instead of a means of livelihood, a source of loss. We tried teaching music and languages, and so on. In short, we hit on all the means of earning our living that other Russian exiles hit upon, and so always found ourselves in overcrowded, and thus un-profitable, fields. But what else did we know—could we do?

"I promised not to bore you. Well, always our capital shrank, and always the day approached on which we should be shabby and hungry, the day when we should become familiar to read-ers of your Sunday papers—charwomen who had been prin-cesses, dukes who now were butlers. There was no place for us in the world. Outcasts easily become outlaws. Why not? Could it be said that we owed the world any fealty? Had not the world sat idly by and seen us despoiled of place and property and country?

"We planned it before we had heard of Couffignal. We could find a small settlement of the wealthy, sufficiently isolated, and, after establishing ourselves there, we would plunder it. Couf-fignal, when we found it, seemed to be the ideal place. We leased this house for six months, having just enough capital remaining to do that and to live properly here while our plans matured. Here we spent four months establishing ourselves, collecting our arms and our explosives, mapping our offensive, waiting for a favorable night. Last night seemed to be that night, and we had provided, we thought, against every even-tuality. But we had not, of course, provided against your pres-ence and your genius. They were simply others of the unfore-seen misfortunes to which we seem eternally condemned."

She stopped, and fell to studying me with mournful large eyes that made me feel like fidgeting.

"It's no good calling me a genius," I objected. "The truth is you people botched your job from beginning to end. Your general would get a big laugh out of a man without military training who tried to lead an army. But here are you people with absolutely no criminal experience trying to swing a trick that needed the highest sort of criminal skill. Look at how you all played around with me! Amateur stuff! A professional crook with any intelligence would have either let me alone or knocked me off. No wonder you flopped! As for the rest of it—your troubles—I can't do anything about them."

"Why?" very softly. "Why can't you?"

"Why should I?" I made it blunt.

"No one else knows what you know." She bent forward to

put a white hand on my knee. "There is wealth in that cellar beneath the garage. You may have whatever you ask."

I shook my head.

"You aren't a fool!" she protested. "You know——"

"Let me straighten this out for you," I interrupted. "We'll disregard whatever honesty I happen to have, sense of loyalty to employers, and so on. You might doubt them, so we'll throw them out. Now I'm a detective because I happen to like the work. It pays me a fair salary, but I could find other jobs that would pay more. Even a hundred dollars more a month would be twelve hundred a year. Say twenty-five or thirty thousand dollars in the years between now and my sixtieth birthday.

"Now I pass up about twenty-five or thirty thousand of honest gain because I like being a detective, like the work. And liking work makes you want to do it as well as you can. Otherwise there'd be no sense to it. That's the fix I am in. I don't know anything else, don't enjoy anything else, don't want to know or enjoy anything else. You can't weigh that against any sum of money. Money is good stuff. I haven't anything against it. But in the past eighteen years I've been getting my fun out of chasing crooks and tackling puzzles, my satisfaction out of catching crooks and solving riddles. It's the only kind of sport I know anything about, and I can't imagine a pleasanter future than twenty-some years more of it. I'm not going to blow that up!"

She shook her head slowly, lowering it, so that now her dark eyes looked up at me under the thin arcs of her brows.

"You speak only of money," she said. "I said you may have whatever you ask."

That was out. I don't know where these women get their ideas.

"You're still all twisted up," I said brusquely, standing now and adjusting my borrowed crutch. "You think I'm a man and you're a woman. That's wrong. I'm a manhunter and you're something that has been running in front of me. There's nothing human about it. You might just as well expect a hound to play tiddly-winks with the fox he's caught. We're wasting time anyway. I've been thinking the police or Marines might come up here and save me a walk. You've been waiting for your mob to come back and grab me. I could have told you they were being arrested when I left them."

That shook her. She had stood up. Now she fell back a step, putting a hand behind her for steadiness, on her chair. An exclamation I didn't understand popped out of her mouth. Russian, I thought, but the next moment I knew it had been Italian.

"Put your hands up." It was Flippo's husky voice. Flippo stood in the doorway, holding an automatic.

I raised my hands as high as I could without dropping my supporting crutch, meanwhile cursing myself for having been too careless, or too vain, to keep a gun in my hand while I talked to the girl.

So this was why she had come back to the house. If she freed the Italian, she had thought, we would have no reason for suspecting that he hadn't been in on the robbery, and so we would look for the bandits among his friends. A prisoner, of course, he might have persuaded us of his innocence. She had given him the gun so he could either shoot his way clear, or, what would help her as much, get himself killed trying.

While I was arranging these thoughts in my head, Flippo had come up behind me. His empty hand passed over my body, taking away my own gun, his, and the one I had taken from the girl.

"A bargain, Flippo," I said when he had moved away from me, a little to one side, where he made one corner of a triangle whose other corners were the girl and I. "You're out on parole, with some years still to be served. I picked you up with a gun on you. That's plenty to send you back to the big house. I know you weren't in on this job. My idea is that you were up here on a smaller one of your own, but I can't prove that and don't want to. Walk out of here, alone and neutral, and I'll forget I saw you."

Little thoughtful lines grooved the boy's round, dark face.

The princess took a step toward him.

"You heard the offer I just now made him?" she asked. "Well, I make that offer to you, if you will kill him."

The thoughtful lines in the boy's face deepened.

"There's your choice, Flippo," I summed up for him. "All I can give you is freedom from San Quentin. The princess can give you a fat cut of the profits in a busted caper, with a good chance to get yourself hanged."

The girl, remembering her advantage over me, went at him hot and heavy in Italian, a language in which I know only four words. Two of them are profane and the other two obscene. I said all four.

The boy was weakening. If he had been ten years older, he'd have taken my offer and thanked me for it. But he was young and she—now that I thought of it—was beautiful. The answer wasn't hard to guess.

"But not to bump him off," he said to her in English, for my benefit. "We'll lock him up in there where I was at."

I suspected Flippo hadn't any great prejudice against murder. It was just that he thought this one unnecessary, unless he was kidding me to make the killing easier.

The girl wasn't satisfied with his suggestion. She poured more hot Italian at him. Her game looked surefire, but it had a flaw. She couldn't persuade him that his chances of getting any of the loot away were good. She had to depend on her charms to swing him. And that meant she had to hold his eye.

He wasn't far from me.

She came close to him. She was singing, chanting, crooning Italian syllables into his round face.

She had him.

He shrugged. His whole face said yes. He turned—

I knocked him on the noodle with my borrowed crutch.

The crutch splintered apart. Flippo's knees bent. He stretched up to his full height. He fell on his face on the floor. He lay there, dead-still, except for a thin worm of blood that crawled out of his hair to the rug.

A step, a tumble, a foot or so of hand-and-knee scrambling put me within reach of Flippo's gun.

The girl, jumping out of my path, was halfway to the door when I sat up with the gun in my hand.

"Stop!" I ordered.

"I shan't," she said, but she did, for the time at least. "I am going out."

"You are going out when I take you."

She laughed, a pleasant laugh, low and confident.

"I'm going out before that," she insisted good-naturedly. I shook my head.

"How do you purpose stopping me?" she asked.

"I don't think I'll have to," I told her. "You've got too much sense to try to run while I'm holding a gun on you."

She laughed again, an amused ripple.

"I've got too much sense to stay," she corrected me. "Your crutch is broken, and you're lame. You can't catch me by running after me, then. You pretend you'll shoot me, but I don't believe you. You'd shoot me if I attacked you, of course, but I shan't do that. I shall simply walk out, and you know you won't shoot me for that. You'll wish you could, but you won't. You'll see."

Her face turned over her shoulder, her dark eyes twinkling at me, she took a step toward the door.

"Better not count on that!" I threatened.

For answer to that she gave me a cooing laugh. And took another step.

"Stop, you idiot!" I bawled at her.

Her face laughed over her shoulder at me. She walked without haste to the door, her short skirt of gray flannel shaping itself to the calf of each gray wool-stockinged leg as its mate stepped forward.

Sweat greased the gun in my hand.

When her right foot was on the doorsill, a little chuckling sound came from her throat.

"Adieu!" she said softly.

And I put a bullet in the calf of her left leg.

She sat down—plump! Utter surprise stretched her white face. It was too soon for pain.

I had never shot a woman before. I felt queer about it.

"You ought to have known I'd do it!" My voice sounded harsh and savage and like a stranger's in my ears. "Didn't I steal a crutch from a cripple?"

RAYMOND CHANDLER

I'll Be Waiting

Raymond Chandler (1888–1959) was Southern California's answer to Dashiell Hammett. Like Hammett, Chandler was a screenwriter and author of detective thrillers filmed with stars like Humphrey Bogart. His favorite eye, Philip Marlowe, roamed the back streets of Los Angeles as well as the canyons and beaches of the southland of the 1940s and solved crimes in volumes still reprinted today.

Born in Chicago, Raymond Thornton Chandler lived in England from 1896 to 1912 with his mother, a British subject native to Ireland. Although he was a California resident and an American citizen in 1914, Chandler enlisted in the Canadian Army and then served in the Royal Flying Corps. He returned to California in 1919 and was a successful business executive until the Depression prompted him to turn to writing for the pulp fiction magazines. His first story, "Black-mailers Don't Shoot," appeared in Black Mask *in 1933. His best-known novels are* The Big Sleep *(1939),* Farewell, My Lovely *(1940), and* The Long Goodbye *(1954).*

From 1943 Chandler wrote scripts for such films as "Double Indemnity" and "Strangers on a Train." Of the seven novels featuring his tough-guy gumshoe Marlowe, several were made into films. The best of these, "The Big Sleep" (1946), on whose script William Faulkner collaborated, was acclaimed some thirty years later as "harder, faster, tougher, funnier, and more laconic than any thriller since." The cynical but incorruptible Marlowe was featured in a television series in 1959. "I'll Be Waiting" first appeared in the Saturday Evening Post *in 1939.*

At one o'clock in the morning, Carl, the night porter, turned down the last of three table lamps in the main lobby of the Windermere Hotel. The blue carpet darkened a shade or two and the walls drew back into remoteness. The chairs filled with shadowy loungers. In the corners were memories like cobwebs.

Tony Reseck yawned. He put his head on one side and listened to the frail, twittery music from the radio room beyond a dim arch at the far side of the lobby. He frowned. That should be his radio room after one a.m. Nobody should be in it. That red-haired girl was spoiling his nights.

The frown passed and a miniature of a smile quirked at the corners of his lips. He sat relaxed, a short, pale, paunchy, middle-aged man with long, delicate fingers clasped on the elk's tooth on his watch chain; the long delicate fingers of a sleight-of-hand artist, fingers with shiny, moulded nails and tapering first joints, fingers a little spatulate at the ends. Handsome fingers. Tony Reseck rubbed them gently together and there was peace in his quiet sea-grey eyes.

The frown came back on his face. The music annoyed him. He got up with a curious litheness, all in one piece, without moving his clasped hands from the watch chain. At one moment he was leaning back relaxed, and the next he was standing balanced on his feet, perfectly still, so that the movement of rising seemed to be a thing imperfectly perceived, an error of vision.

He walked with small, polished shoes delicately across the blue carpet and under the arch. The music was louder. It contained the hot, acid blare, the frenetic, jittering runs of a jam session. It was too loud. The red-haired girl sat there and stared silently at the fretted part of the big radio cabinet as though she could see the band with its fixed professional grin and the sweat running down its back. She was curled up with her feet under her on a davenport which seemed to contain most of the cushions in the room. She was tucked among them carefully, like a corsage in the florist's tissue paper.

She didn't turn her head. She leaned there, one hand in a small fist on her peach-coloured knee. She was wearing lounging pyjamas of heavy ribbed silk embroidered with black lotus buds.

'You like Goodman, Miss Cressy?' Tony Reseck asked.

The girl moved her eyes slowly. The light in there was dim, but the violet of her eyes almost hurt. They were large, deep eyes without a trace of thought in them. Her face was classical and without expression.

She said nothing.

Tony smiled and moved his fingers at his sides, one by one, feeling them move. 'You like Goodman, Miss Cressy?' he repeated gently.

'Not to cry over,' the girl said tonelessly.

Tony rocked back on his heels and looked at her eyes. Large, deep, empty eyes. Or were they? He reached down and muted the radio.

'Don't get me wrong,' the girl said. 'Goodman makes money, and a lad that makes legitimate money these days is a lad you have to respect. But this jitterbug music gives me the backdrop of a beer flat. I like something with roses in it.'

'Maybe you like Mozart,' Tony said.

'Go on, kid me,' the girl said.

'I wasn't kidding you, Miss Cressy. I think Mozart was the greatest man that ever lived—and Toscanini is his prophet.'

'I thought you were the house dick.' She put her head back on a pillow and stared at him through her lashes. 'Make me some of that Mozart,' she added.

'It's too late,' Tony sighed. 'You can't get it now.'

She gave him another long lucid glance. 'Got the eye on me, haven't you, flatfoot?' She laughed a little, almost under her breath. 'What did I do wrong?'

Tony smiled his toy smile. 'Nothing, Miss Cressy. Nothing at all. But you need some fresh air. You've been five days in this hotel and you haven't been outdoors. And you have a tower room.'

She laughed again. 'Make me a story about it. I'm bored.'

'There was a girl here once had your suite. She stayed in the hotel a whole week, like you. Without going out at all, I mean. She didn't speak to anybody hardly. What do you think she did then?'

The girl eyed him gravely. 'She jumped her bill.'

He put his long delicate hand out and turned it slowly, fluttering the fingers, with an effect almost like a lazy wave breaking. 'Uh-huh. She sent down for her bill and paid it. Then she told the hop to be back in half an hour for her suitcases. Then she went out on her balcony.'

The girl leaned forward a little, her eyes still grave, one hand capping her peach-coloured knee. 'What did you say your name was?'

'Tony Reseck.'

'Sounds like a hunky.'

'Yeah,' Tony said. 'Polish.'

'Go on, Tony.'

'All the tower suites have private balconies, Miss Cressy. The walls of them are too low for fourteen storeys above the street. It was a dark night, that night, high clouds.' He dropped his hand with a final gesture, a farewell gesture. 'Nobody saw her jump. But when she hit, it was like a big gun going off.'

'You're making it up, Tony.' Her voice was a clean dry whisper of sound.

He smiled his toy smile. His quiet sea-grey eyes seemed almost to be smoothing the long waves of her hair. 'Eve Cressy,' he said musingly. 'A name waiting for lights to be in.'

'Waiting for a tall dark guy that's no good, Tony. You wouldn't care why. I was married to him once. I might be married to him again. You can make a lot of mistakes in just one lifetime.' The hand on her knee opened slowly until the fingers were strained back as far as they would go. Then they closed quickly and tightly, and even in that dim light the knuckles shone like the little polished bones. 'I played him a low trick once. I put him in a bad place—without meaning to. You wouldn't care about that either. It's just that I owe him something.'

He leaned over softly and turned the knob on the radio. A waltz formed itself dimly on the air. A tinsel waltz, but a waltz. He turned the volume up. The music gushed from the loudspeaker in a swirl of shadowed melody. Since Vienna died, all waltzes are shadowed.

The girl put her head on one side and hummed three or four bars and stopped with a sudden tightening of her mouth.

'Eve Cressy,' she said. 'It was in lights once. At a bum night club. A dive. They raided it and the lights went out.'

He smiled at her almost mockingly. 'It was no dive while you were there, Miss Cressy . . . That's the waltz the orchestra always played when the old porter walked up and down in front of the hotel entrance, all swelled up with his medals on his chest. *The Last Laugh*. Emil Jannings. You wouldn't remember that one, Miss Cressy.'

'Spring, Beautiful Spring,' she said. 'No, I never saw it.'

He walked three steps away from her and turned. 'I have to go upstairs and palm doorknobs. I hope I didn't bother you. You ought to go to bed now. It's pretty late.'

The tinsel waltz stopped and a voice began to talk. The girl spoke through the voice. 'You really thought something like that—about the balcony?'

He nodded. 'I might have,' he said softly. 'I don't any more.'

'No chance, Tony.' Her smile was a dim lost leaf. 'Come and talk to me some more. Redheads don't jump, Tony. They hang on—and wither.'

He looked at her gravely for a moment and then moved away over the carpet. The porter was standing in the archway that led to the main lobby. Tony hadn't looked that way yet, but he knew somebody was there. He always knew if anybody was close to him. He could hear the grass grow, like the donkey in *The Blue Bird*.

The porter jerked his chin at him urgently. His broad face above the uniform collar looked sweaty and excited. Tony stepped up close to him and they went together through the arch and out to the middle of the dim lobby.

'Trouble?' Tony asked wearily.

'There's a guy outside to see you, Tony. He won't come in. I'm doing a wipe-off on the plate glass of the doors and he comes up beside me, a tall guy. "Get Tony," he says, out of the side of his mouth.'

Tony said: 'Uh-huh,' and looked at the porter's pale blue eyes. 'Who was it?'

'Al, he said to say he was.'

Tony's face became as expressionless as dough. 'Okay.' He started to move off.

The porter caught his sleeve. 'Listen, Tony. You got any enemies?'

Tony laughed politely, his face still like dough.

'Listen, Tony.' The porter held his sleeve tightly. 'There's a big black car down the block, the other way from the hacks. There's a guy standing beside it with his foot on the running board. This guy that spoke to me, he wears a dark-coloured, wrap-around overcoat with a high collar turned up against his ears. His hat's way low. You can't hardly see his face. He says, "Get Tony," out of the side of his mouth. You ain't got any enemies, have you, Tony?'

'Only the finance company,' Tony said. 'Beat it.'

He walked slowly and a little stiffly across the blue carpet, up the three shallow steps to the entrance lobby with the three elevators on one side and the desk on the other. Only one elevator was working. Beside the open doors, his arms folded, the night operator stood silent in a neat blue uniform with silver facings. A lean, dark Mexican named Gomez. A new boy, breaking in on the night shift.

The other side was the desk, rose marble, with the night clerk leaning on it delicately. A small neat man with a wispy reddish moustache and cheeks so rosy they looked rouged. He stared at Tony and poked a nail at his moustache.

Tony pointed a stiff index finger at him, folded the other three fingers tight to his palm, and flicked his thumb up and down on the stiff finger. The clerk touched the other side of his moustache and looked bored.

Tony went on past the closed and darkened news-stand and the side entrance to the drugstore, out to the brass-bound plate-glass doors. He stopped just inside them and took a deep, hard breath. He squared his shoulders, pushed the doors open and stepped out into the cold, damp night air.

The street was dark, silent. The rumble of traffic on Wilshire, two blocks away, had no body, no meaning. To the left were two taxis. Their drivers leaned against a fender, side by side, smoking. Tony walked the other way. The big dark car was a third of a block from the hotel entrance. Its lights were dimmed and it was only when he was almost up to it that he heard the gentle sound of its engine turning over.

A tall figure detached itself from the body of the car and strolled towards him, both hands in the pockets of the dark overcoat with the high collar. From the man's mouth a cigarette tip glowed faintly, a rusty pearl.

They stopped two feet from each other.

The tall man said: 'Hi, Tony. Long time no see.'

'Hello, Al. How's it going?'

'Can't complain.' The tall man started to take his right hand out of his overcoat pocket, then stopped and laughed quietly. 'I forgot. Guess you don't want to shake hands.'

'That don't mean anything,' Tony said. 'Shaking hands. Monkeys can shake hands. What's on your mind, Al?'

'Still the funny little fat guy, eh, Tony?'

'I guess,' Tony winked his eyes tight. His throat felt tight.

'You like your job back there?'

'It's a job.'

Al laughed his quiet laugh again. 'You take it slow, Tony. I'll take it fast. So it's a job and you want to hold it. Oke. There's a girl named Eve Cressy flopping in your quiet hotel. Get her out. Fast and right now.'

'What's the trouble?'

The tall man looked up and down the street. A man behind in the car coughed lightly. 'She's hooked with a wrong number. Nothing against her personal, but she'll lead trouble to you. Get her out, Tony. You got maybe an hour.'

'Sure,' Tony said aimlessly, without meaning.

Al took his hand out of his pocket and stretched it against Tony's chest. He gave him a light, lazy push. 'I wouldn't be telling you just for the hell of it, little fat brother. Get her out of there.'

'Okay,' Tony said, without any tone in his voice.

The tall man took back his hand and reached for the car door. He opened it and started to slip in like a lean black shadow.

Then he stopped and said something to the men in the car and got out again. He came back to where Tony stood silent, his pale eyes catching a little dim light from the street.

'Listen, Tony. You always kept your nose clean. You're a good brother, Tony.'

Tony didn't speak.

Al leaned towards him, a long urgent shadow, the high collar almost touching his ears. 'It's trouble business, Tony. The boys won't like it, but I'm telling you just the same. This Cressy was married to a lad named Johnny Ralls. Ralls is out of Quentin two, three days, or a week. He did a three-spot for manslaughter. The girl put him there. He ran down an old man one night when he was drunk, and she was with him. He wouldn't stop. She told him to go in and tell it, or else. He didn't go in. So the Johns come for him.'

Tony said, 'That's too bad.'

'It's kosher, kid. It's my business to know. This Ralls flapped his mouth in stir about how the girl would be waiting for him when he got out, all set to forgive and forget, and he was going straight to her.'

Tony said: 'What's he to you?' His voice had a dry, stiff crackle, like thick paper.

Al laughed. 'The trouble boys want to see him. He ran a table at a spot on the Strip and figured out a scheme. He and another guy took the house for fifty grand. The other lad coughed up, but we still need Johnny's twenty-five. The trouble boys don't get paid to forget.'

Tony looked up and down the dark street. One of the taxi drivers flicked a cigarette stub in a long arc over the top of one of the cabs. Tony watched it fall and spark on the pavement. He listened to the quiet sound of the big car's motor.

'I don't want any part of it,' he said. 'I'll get her out.'

Al backed away from him, nodding. 'Wise kid. How's mom these days?'

'Okay,' Tony said.

'Tell her I was asking for her.'

'Asking for her isn't anything,' Tony said.

Al turned quickly and got into the car. The car curved lazily in the middle of the block and drifted back toward the corner. Its lights went up and sprayed on a wall. It turned a corner and was gone. The lingering smell of its exhaust drifted past Tony's nose. He turned and walked back to the hotel, and into it. He went along to the radio room.

The radio still muttered, but the girl was gone from the davenport in front of it. The pressed cushions were hollowed out by her body. Tony reached down and touched them. He thought they were still warm. He turned the radio off and stood there, turning a thumb slowly in front of his body, his hand flat against his stomach. Then he went back through the lobby toward the elevator bank and stood beside a majolica jar of white sand. The clerk fussed behind a pebbled-glass screen at one end of the desk. The air was dead.

The elevator bank was dark. Tony looked at the indicator of the middle car and saw that it was at 14.

'Gone to bed,' he said under his breath.

The door of the porter's room beside the elevators opened and the little Mexican night operator came out in street clothes. He looked at Tony with a quiet sidewise look out of eyes the colour of dried-out chestnuts.

'Good night, boss.'

'Yeah,' Tony said absently.

He took a thin dappled cigar out of his vest pocket and smelled it. He examined it slowly, turning it around in his neat fingers. There was a small tear along the side. He frowned at that and put the cigar away.

There was a distant sound and the hand on the indicator began to steal around the bronze dial. Light glittered up in the shaft and the straight line of the car floor dissolved the darkness below. The car stopped and the doors opened, and Carl came out of it.

His eyes caught Tony's with a kind of jump and he walked over to him, his head on one side, a thin shine along his pink upper lip.

'Listen, Tony.'

Tony took his arm in a hard swift hand and turned him. He pushed him quickly, yet somehow casually, down the steps to the dim main lobby and steered him into a corner. He let go of the arm. His throat tightened again, for no reason he could think of.

'Well?' he said darkly. 'Listen to what?'

The porter reached into a pocket and hauled out a dollar bill. 'He gimme this,' he said loosely. His glittering eyes looked past

Tony's shoulder at nothing. They winked rapidly. 'Ice and ginger ale.'

'Don't stall,' Tony growled.

'Guy in 14B,' the porter said.

'Lemme smell your breath.'

The porter leaned toward him obediently.

'Liquor,' Tony said harshly.

'He gimme a drink.'

Tony looked down at the dollar bill. 'Nobody's in 14B. Not on my list,' he said.

'Yeah. There is.' The porter licked his lips and his eyes opened and shut several times. 'Tall dark guy.'

'All right,' Tony said crossly. 'All right. There's a tall dark guy in 14B and he gave you a buck and a drink. Then what?'

'Gat under his arm,' Carl said, and blinked.

Tony smiled, but his eyes had taken on the lifeless glitter of thick ice. 'You take Miss Cressy up to her room?'

Carl shook his head. 'Gomez. I saw her go up.'

'Get away from me,' Tony said between his teeth. 'And don't accept any more drinks from the guests.'

He didn't move until Carl had gone back into his cubby-hole by the elevators and shut the door. Then he moved silently up the three steps and stood in front of the desk, looking at the veined rose marble, the onyx pen set, the fresh registration card in its leather frame. He lifted a hand and smacked it down hard on the marble. The clerk popped out from behind the glass screen like a chipmunk coming out of its hole.

Tony took a flimsy out of his breast pocket and spread it on the desk. 'No 14B on this,' he said in a bitter voice.

The clerk wisped politely at his moustache. 'So sorry. You must have been out to supper when he checked in.'

'Who?'

'Registered as James Watterson, San Diego.' The clerk yawned.

'Ask for anybody?'

The clerk stopped in the middle of the yawn and looked at the top of Tony's head. 'Why, yes. He asked for a swing band. Why?'

'Smart, fast and funny,' Tony said. 'If you like 'em that way.'

He wrote on his flimsy and stuffed it back into his pocket. 'I'm going upstairs and palm doorknobs. There's four tower rooms you ain't rented yet. Get up on your toes, son. You're slipping.'

'I make out,' the clerk drawled, and completed his yawn. 'Hurry back, pop. I don't know how I'll get through the time.'

'You could shave that pink fuzz off your lip,' Tony said, and went across to the elevators.

He opened up a dark one and lit the dome light and shot the car up to fourteen. He darkened it again, stepped out and closed the doors. This lobby was smaller than any other, except the one immediately below it. It had a single blue-panelled door in each of the walls other than the elevator wall. On each door was a gold number and letter with a gold wreath around it. Tony walked over to 14A and put his ear to the panel.

He heard nothing. Eve Cressy might be in bed asleep, or in the bathroom, or out on the balcony. Or she might be sitting there in the room, a few feet from the door, looking at the wall. Well, he wouldn't expect to be able to hear her sit and look at the wall. He went over to 14B and put his ear to that panel. This was different. There was a sound in there. A man coughed. It sounded somehow like a solitary cough. There were no voices. Tony pressed the small nacre button beside the door.

Steps came without hurry. A thickened voice spoke through the panel. Tony made no answer, no sound. The thickened voice repeated the question. Lightly, maliciously, Tony pressed the bell again.

Mr. James Watterson, of San Diego, should now open the door and give forth noise. He didn't. A silence fell beyond that door that was like the silence of a glacier. Once more Tony put his ear to the wood. Silence utterly.

He got out a master key on a chain and pushed it delicately into the lock of the door. He turned it, pushed the door inward three inches and withdrew the key. Then he waited.

'All right,' the voice said harshly. 'Come in and get it.'

Tony pushed the door wide and stood there, framed against the light from the lobby. The man was tall, black-haired, angular and white-faced. He held a gun. He held it as though he knew about guns.

'Step right in,' he drawled.

Tony went in through the door and pushed it shut with his shoulder. He kept his hands a little out from his sides, the clever fingers curled and slack. He smiled his quiet little smile.

'Mr. Watterson?'

'And after that what?'

'I'm the house detective here.'

'It slays me.'

The tall, white-faced, somehow handsome and somehow not handsome man backed slowly into the room. It was a large room with a low balcony around two sides of it. French doors opened out on the little, private, open-air balcony that each of the tower rooms had. There was a grate set for a log fire behind a panelled screen in front of a cheerful davenport. A tall misted glass stood on a hotel tray beside a deep, easy chair. The man backed toward this and stood in front of it. The large, glistening gun drooped and pointed at the floor.

'It slays me,' he said. 'I'm in the dump an hour and the house copper gives me the buzz. Okay, sweetheart, look in the closet and bathroom. But she just left.'

'You didn't see her yet,' Tony said.

The man's bleached face filled with unexpected lines. His thickened voice edged toward a snarl. 'Yeah? Who didn't I see yet?'

'A girl named Eve Cressy.'

The man swallowed. He put his gun down on the table beside the tray. He let himself down into the chair backwards, stiffly, like a man with a touch of lumbago. Then he leaned forward and put his hands on his kneecaps and smiled brightly between his teeth. 'So she got here, huh? I didn't ask about her yet. I'm a careful guy. I didn't ask yet.'

'She's been here five days,' Tony said. 'Waiting for you. She hasn't left the hotel a minute.'

The man's mouth worked a little. His smile had a knowing tilt to it. 'I got delayed a little up north,' he said smoothly. 'You know how it is. Visiting old friends. You seem to know a lot about my business, copper.'

'That's right, Mr. Ralls.'

The man lunged to his feet and his hand snapped at the gun. He stood leaning over, holding it on the table, staring. 'Dames talk too much,' he said with a muffled sound in his voice, as though he held something soft between his teeth and talked through it.

'Not dames, Mr. Ralls.'

'Huh?' The gun slithered on the hard wood of the table. 'Talk it up, copper. My mind reader just quit.'

'Not dames. Guys. Guys with guns.'

The glacier silence fell between them again. The man straightened his body slowly. His face was washed clean of expression, but his eyes were haunted. Tony leaned in front of him, a shortish plump man with quiet, pale, friendly face and eyes as simple as forest water.

'They never run out of gas—those boys,' Johnny Ralls said, and licked at his lip. 'Early and late, they work. The old firm never sleeps.'

'You know who they are?' Tony said softly.

'I could maybe give nine guesses. And twelve of them would be right.'

'The trouble boys,' Tony said, and smiled a brittle smile.

'Where is she?' Johnny Ralls asked harshly.

'Right next door to you.'

The man walked to the wall and left his gun lying on the table. He stood in front of the wall, studying it. He reached up and gripped the grillwork of the balcony railing. When he dropped his hand and turned, his face had lost some of its lines. His eyes had a quieter glint. He moved back to Tony and stood over him.

'I've got a stake,' he said. 'Eve sent me some dough and I built it up with a touch I made up north. Case dough, what I mean. The trouble boys talk about twenty-five grand.' He smiled crookedly. 'Five C's I can count. I'd have a lot of fun making them believe that, I would.'

'What did you do with it?' Tony asked indifferently.

'I never had it, copper. Leave that lay. I'm the only guy in the world that believes it. It was a little deal I got suckered on.'

'I'll believe it,' Tony said.

'They don't kill often. But they can be awful tough.'

'Mugs,' Tony said with a sudden bitter contempt. 'Guys with guns. Just mugs.'

Johnny Ralls reached for his glass and drained it empty. The ice cubes tinkled softly as he put it down. He picked his gun up, danced it on his palm, then tucked it, nose down, into an inner breast pocket. He stared at the carpet.

'How come you're telling me this, copper?'

'I thought maybe you'd give her a break.'

'And if I wouldn't?'

'I kind of think you will,' Tony said.

Johnny Ralls nodded quietly. 'Can I get out of here?'

'You could take the service elevator to the garage. You could rent a car. I can give you a card to the garage-man.'

'You're a funny little guy,' Johnny Ralls said.

Tony took out a worn ostrich-skin billfold and scribbled on a printed card. Johnny Ralls read it, and stood holding it, tapping it against a thumbnail.

'I could take her with me,' he said, his eyes narrow.

'You could take a ride in a basket too,' Tony said. 'She's been here five days, I told you. She's been spotted. A guy I know called me up and told me to get her out of here. Told me what it was all about. So I'm getting you out instead.'

'They'll love that,' Johnny Ralls said. 'They'll send you violets.'

'I'll weep about it on my day off.'

Johnny Ralls turned his hand over and stared at the palm. 'I could see her, anyway. Before I blow. Next door to here, you said?'

Tony turned on his heel and started for the door. He said over his shoulder, 'Don't waste a lot of time, handsome. I might change my mind.'

The man said, almost gently: 'You might be spotting me right now, for all I know.'

Tony didn't turn his head. 'That's a chance you have to take.'

He went on to the door and passed out of the room. He shut it carefully, silently, looked once at the door of 14A and got into his dark elevator. He rode it down to the linen-room floor and got out to remove the basket that held the service elevator open at that floor. The door slid quietly shut. He held it so that it made no noise. Down the corridor, light came from the open door of the housekeeper's office. Tony got back into his elevator and went on down to the lobby.

The little clerk was out of sight behind his pebbled-glass screen, auditing accounts. Tony went through the main lobby and turned into the radio room. The radio was on again, soft. She was there, curled on the davenport again. The speaker hummed to her, a vague sound so low that what it said was as wordless as the murmur of trees. She turned her head slowly and smiled at him.

'Finished palming doorknobs? I couldn't sleep worth a nickel. So I came down again. Okay?'

He smiled and nodded. He sat down in a green chair and patted the plump brocade arms of it. 'Sure, Miss Cressy.'

'Waiting is the hardest kind of work, isn't it? I wish you'd talk to that radio. It sounds like a pretzel being bent.'

Tony fiddled with it, got nothing he liked, set it back where it had been.

'Beer-parlour drunks are all the customers now.'

She smiled at him again.

'I don't bother you being here, Miss Cressy?'

'I like it. You're a sweet little guy, Tony.'

He looked stiffly at the floor and a ripple touched his spine. He waited for it to go away. It went slowly. Then he sat back, relaxed again, his neat fingers clasped on his elk's tooth. He listened. Not to the radio—to far-off, uncertain things, menacing things. And perhaps to just the safe whir of wheels going away into a strange night.

'Nobody's all bad,' he said out loud.

The girl looked at him lazily. 'I've met two or three I was wrong on, then.'

He nodded. 'Yeah,' he admitted judiciously. 'I guess there's some that are.'

The girl yawned and her deep violet eyes half closed. She nestled back into the cushions. 'Sit there a while, Tony. Maybe I could nap.'

'Sure. Not a thing for me to do. Don't know why they pay me.'

She slept quickly and with complete stillness, like a child. Tony hardly breathed for ten minutes. He just watched her, his mouth a little open. There was a quiet fascination in his limpid eyes, as if he was looking at an altar.

Then he stood up with infinite care and padded away under the arch to the entrance lobby and the desk. He stood at the desk listening for a little while. He heard a pen rustling out of sight. He went around the corner to the row of house phones in little glass cubbyholes. He lifted one and asked the night operator for the garage.

It rang three or four times and then a boyish voice answered: 'Windermere Hotel. Garage speaking.'

'This is Tony Reseck. That guy Watterson I gave a card to. He leave?'

'Sure, Tony. Half an hour almost. Is it your charge?'

'Yeah,' Tony said. 'My party. Thanks. Be seein' you.'

He hung up and scratched his neck. He went back to the desk and slapped a hand on it. The clerk wafted himself around the screen with his greeter's smile in place. It dropped when he saw Tony.

'Can't a guy catch up on his work?' he grumbled.

'What's the professional rate on 14B?'

The clerk stared morosely. 'There's no professional rate in the tower.'

'Make one. The fellow left already. Was there only an hour.'

'Well, well,' the clerk said airily. 'So the personality didn't click tonight. We get a skip-out.'

'Will five bucks satisfy you?'

'Friend of yours?'

'No. Just a drunk with delusions of grandeur and no dough.'

'Guess we'll have to let it ride, Tony. How did he get out?'

'I took him down the service elevator. You was asleep. Will five bucks satisfy you?'

'Why?'

The worn ostrich-skin wallet came out and a weedy five slipped across the marble. 'All I could shake him for,' Tony said loosely.

The clerk took the five and looked puzzled. 'You're the

boss,' he said, and shrugged. The phone shrilled on the desk and he reached for it. He listened and then pushed it toward Tony. 'For you.'

Tony took the phone and cuddled it close to his chest. He put his mouth close to the transmitter. The voice was strange to him. It had a metallic sound. Its syllables were meticulously anonymous.

'Tony? Tony Reseck?'

'Talking.'

'A message from Al. Shoot?'

Tony looked at the clerk. 'Be a pal,' he said over the mouthpiece. The clerk flicked a narrow smile at him and went away. 'Shoot,' Tony said into the phone.

'We had a little business with a guy in your place. Picked him up scramming. Al had a hunch you'd run him out. Tailed him and took him to the kerb. Not so good. Backfire.'

Tony held the phone very tight and his temples chilled with the evaporation of moisture. 'Go on,' he said. 'I guess there's more.'

'A little. The guy stopped the big one. Cold. Al—Al said to tell you good-bye.'

Tony leaned hard against the desk. His mouth made a sound that was not speech.

'Get it?' The metallic voice sounded impatient, a little bored. 'This guy had him a rod. He used it. Al won't be phoning anybody any more.'

Tony lurched at the phone, and the base of it shook on the rose marble. His mouth was a hard dry knot.

The voice said: 'That's as far as we go, bud. G'night.' The phone clicked dryly, like a pebble hitting a wall.

Tony put the phone down in its cradle very carefully, so as not to make any sound. He looked at the clenched palm of his left hand. He took a handkerchief out and rubbed the palm softly and straightened the fingers out with his other hand. Then he wiped his forehead. The clerk came around the screen again and looked at him with glinting eyes.

'I'm off Friday. How about lending me that phone number?'

Tony nodded at the clerk and smiled a minute frail smile. He put his handkerchief away and patted the pocket he had put it in. He turned and walked away from the desk, across the entrance lobby, down the three shallow steps, along the shadowy reaches of the main lobby, and so in through the arch to the radio room once more. He walked softly, like a man moving in a room where somebody is very sick. He reached the chair he had sat in before and lowered himself into it inch by inch. The girl slept on, motionless, in that curled-up looseness achieved by some women and all cats. Her breath made no slightest sound against the vague murmur of the radio.

Tony Reseck leaned back in the chair and clasped his hands on his elk's tooth and quietly closed his eyes.

EVELYN WAUGH

Whispering Glades

Over the decades, the motion picture industry brought dozens of talented writers to Southern California. Like William Faulkner, F. Scott Fitzgerald, and many another novelist, Evelyn Waugh was attracted by the flame of Hollywood.

Evelyn Arthur St. John Waugh (1903–66), English by birth and sojourner in California, has been called the most brilliant satirical novelist of his day. After an education at Oxford, he converted to Catholicism in 1930. Beginning in 1928 with Decline and Fall, *he issued novels that bitingly ridiculed the manners of upper-class British "bright young things" between the world wars. During the second of those wars he served as an officer in the Royal Marines. Later in life he wrote a trilogy stressing the conflict between culture and barbarism in the military. Perhaps his best-known novel, however, is* Brideshead Revisited *(1945, revised 1960), which follows the vicissitudes of a landed Catholic family. Waugh also wrote notable travel books and biographies.*

Waugh was fascinated by the Hollywood colony's obsession with fashionable funerals. In "Whispering Glades," the reader is given a taste of his satirical wit. Upon the young Englishman Dennis Barlow, whose titled employer he had that morning discovered as a suicide victim, devolves the task of arranging a stylish interment. The selection is drawn from Waugh's celebrated novel The Loved One: An Anglo-American Tragedy *(1948).*

Dennis was a young man of sensibility rather than of sentiment. He had lived his twenty–eight years at arm's length from violence, but he came of a generation which enjoys a vicarious intimacy with death. Never, it so happened, had he seen a human corpse until that morning when, returning tired from night duty, he found his host strung to the rafters. The spectacle had been rude and momentarily unnerving; perhaps it had left a scar somewhere out of sight in his subconscious mind. But his reason accepted the event as part of the established order. Others in gentler ages had had their lives changed by such a revelation; to Dennis it was the kind of thing to be expected in the world he knew and, as he drove to Whispering Glades, his conscious mind was pleasantly exhilarated and full of curiosity.

Times without number since he first came to Hollywood he had heard the name of that great necropolis on the lips of others; he had read it in the local news-sheets when some more than usually illustrious body was given more than usually splendid honours or some new acquisition was made to its collected masterpieces of contemporary art. Of recent weeks his interest had been livelier and more technical for it was in humble emulation of its great neighbour that the Happier Hunting Ground was planned. The language he daily spoke in his new trade was a *patois* derived from that high pure source. More than once Mr. Schultz had exultantly exclaimed after one of his performances: "It was worthy of Whispering Glades." As a missionary priest making his first pilgrimage to the Vatican, as a paramount chief of equatorial Africa mounting the Eiffel Tower, Dennis Barlow, poet and pets' mortician, drove through the Golden Gates.

They were vast, the largest in the world, and freshly regilt. A notice proclaimed the inferior dimensions of their Old World rivals. Beyond them lay a semi-circle of golden yew, a wide gravel roadway and an island of mown turf on which stood a singular and massive wall of marble sculptured in the form of an open book. Here, in letters a foot high, was incised:

THE DREAM
   BEHOLD I DREAMED A DREAM AND I SAW A NEW EARTH
SACRED TO HAPPINESS. THERE AMID ALL THAT NATURE
AND ART COULD OFFER TO ELEVATE THE SOUL OF MAN I SAW

THE HAPPY RESTING PLACE OF COUNTLESS LOVED ONES.
AND I SAW THE WAITING ONES WHO STILL STOOD AT THE
BRINK OF THAT NARROW STREAM THAT NOW SEPARATED
THEM FROM THOSE WHO HAD GONE BEFORE. YOUNG AND
OLD, THEY WERE HAPPY TOO. HAPPY IN BEAUTY, HAPPY IN
THE CERTAIN KNOWLEDGE THAT THEIR LOVED ONES WERE
VERY NEAR, IN BEAUTY AND HAPPINESS SUCH AS THE EARTH
CANNOT GIVE.

I HEARD A VOICE SAY: "DO THIS."

AND BEHOLD I AWOKE AND IN THE LIGHT AND PROMISE OF
MY DREAM I MADE WHISPERING GLADES.

ENTER STRANGER AND BE HAPPY.

And below, in vast cursive facsimile, the signature:

Wilbur Kenworthy, The Dreamer.

A modest wooden signboard beside it read: Prices on enqui-
ry at Administrative Building. Drive straight on.

Dennis drove on through green parkland and presently came
in sight of what in England he would have taken for the country seat of an Edwardian financier. It was black and white, tim-
bered and gabled, with twisting brick chimneys and wrought
iron windvanes. He left his car among a dozen others and proceeded on foot through a box walk, past a sunken herb garden,
a sun-dial, a birdbath and fountain, a rustic seat and a pigeon-
cote. Music rose softly all round him, the subdued notes of the
"Hindu Love-song" relayed from an organ through countless
amplifiers concealed about the garden.

When as a newcomer to the Megalopolitan Studios he first
toured the lots, it had taxed his imagination to realize that those
solid-seeming streets and squares of every period and climate
were in fact plaster facades whose backs revealed the structure
of bill-boardings. Here the illusion was quite otherwise. Only
with an effort could Dennis believe that the building before him
was three-dimensional and permanent; but here, as everywhere
in Whispering Glades, failing credulity was fortified by the
painted word.

This perfect replica of an Old English Manor, a notice said, *like
all the buildings of Whispering Glades, is constructed throughout of*

Grade A steel and concrete with foundations extending into solid rock.
It is certified proof against fire, earthquake and   . Their name
liveth for evermore who record it in Whispering Glades.

At the blank patch a signwriter was even then at work and
Dennis, pausing to study it, discerned the ghost of the words
"high explosive" freshly obliterated and the outlines of "nu-
clear fission" about to be filled in as substitute.

Followed by music he stepped as it were from garden to
garden for the approach to the offices lay through a florist's
shop. Here one young lady was spraying scent over a stall of
lilac while a second was talking on the telephone: ". . . Oh,
Mrs. Bogolov, I'm really sorry but it's just one of the things
that Whispering Glades does not do. The Dreamer does not
approve of wreaths or crosses. We just arrange the flowers in
their own natural beauty. It's one of the Dreamer's own ideas.
I'm sure Mr. Bogolov would prefer it himself. Won't you just
leave it to us, Mrs. Bogolov? You tell us what you want to
spend and we will do the rest. I'm sure you will be more than
satisfied. Thank you, Mrs. Bogolov, it's a pleasure. . . ."

Dennis passed through and opening the door marked *En-
quiries* found himself in a raftered banqueting hall. The "Hindu
Love-song" was here also, gently discoursed from the dark oak
panelling. A young lady rose from a group of her fellows to
welcome him, one of that new race of exquisite, amiable,
efficient young ladies whom he had met everywhere in the
United States. She wore a white smock and over her sharply
supported left breast was embroidered the words, *Mortuary
Hostess*.

"Can I help you in any way?"

"I came to arrange about a funeral."

"Is it for yourself?"

"Certainly not. Do I look so moribund?"

"Pardon me?"

"Do I look as if I were about to die?"

"Why, no. Only many of our friends like to make Before
Need Arrangements. Will you come this way?"

She led him from the hall into a soft passage. The decor here
was Georgian. The "Hindu Love-song" came to its end and
was succeeded by the voice of a nightingale. In a little chintzy

parlour he and his hostess sat down to make their arrangements.

"I must first record the Essential Data."

He told her his name and Sir Francis's.

"Now, Mr. Barlow, what had you in mind? Embalmment of course, and after that incineration or not, according to taste. Our crematory is on scientific principles, the heat is so intense that all inessentials are volatilized. Some people did not like the thought that ashes of the casket and clothing were mixed with the Loved One's. Normal disposal is by inhumement, entombment, inurnment, or immurement, but many people just lately prefer insarcophagusment. That is *very* individual. The casket is placed inside a sealed sarcophagus, marble or bronze, and rests permanently above ground in a niche in the mausoleum, with or without a personal stained-glass window above. That, of course, is for those with whom price is not a primary consideration."

"We want my friend buried."

"This is not your first visit to Whispering Glades?"

"Yes."

"Then let me explain the Dream. The Park is zoned. Each zone has its own name and appropriate Work of Art. Zones of course vary in price and within the zones the prices vary according to their proximity to the Work of Art. We have single sites as low as fifty dollars. That is in Pilgrims' Rest, a zone we are just developing behind the Crematory fuel dump. The most costly are those on Lake Isle. They range about a thousand dollars. Then there is Lovers' Nest, zoned about a very, very beautiful marble replica of Rodin's famous statue, the Kiss. We have double plots there at seven hundred and fifty dollars the pair. Was your Loved One married?"

"No."

"What was his business?"

"He was a writer."

"Ah, then Poets' Corner would be the place for him. We have many of our foremost literary names there, either in person or as Before Need reservations. You are no doubt acquainted with the works of Amelia Bergson?"

"I know of them."

"We sold Miss Bergson a Before Need reservation only yesterday, under the statue of the prominent Greek poet Homer. I could put your friend right next to her. But perhaps you would like to see the zone before deciding?"

"I want to see everything."

"There certainly is plenty to see. I'll have one of our guides take you round just as soon as we have all the Essential Data, Mr. Barlow. Was your Loved One of any special religion?"

"An Agnostic."

"We have two non-sectarian churches in the Park and a number of non-sectarian pastors. Jews and Catholics seem to prefer to make their own arrangements."

"I believe Sir Ambrose Abercrombie is planning a special service."

"Oh, was your Loved One in films, Mr. Barlow? In that case he ought to be in Shadowland."

"I think he would prefer to be with Homer and Miss Bergson."

"Then the University Church would be most convenient. We like to save the Waiting Ones a long procession. I presume the Loved One was Caucasian?"

"No, why did you think that? He was purely English."

"English are purely Caucasian, Mr. Barlow. This is a restricted park. The Dreamer has made that rule for the sake of the Waiting Ones. In their time of trial they prefer to be with their own people."

"I think I understand. Well, let me assure you Sir Francis was quite white."

EUGENE BURDICK

A Simple Genius

*Born in Iowa, Eugene Burdick (1918–65) went as a child to Califor-
nia. After high school he worked as a clerk, ditchdigger, and truck
driver until he had saved $150, enough to enable him to enter Stanford
University. He graduated in 1941. Soon thereafter he married, was
taken into the Navy, and was sent to Guadalcanal. He spent twenty-
six months in the Pacific as a gunnery officer.*

*Burdick returned to Stanford to take Wallace Stegner's writing
course and then earned a Ph.D. degree at Oxford as a Rhodes scholar.
While a professor of political science at the University of California,
Berkeley, he published his first novel,* The Ninth Wave *(1956).
Thereafter he gained celebrity as coauthor of* The Ugly American
with William Lederer (1958) and Fail-Safe *with Harvey Wheeler
(1962). The* Blue of Capricorn *(1961) is a classic collection of his
essays and stories about the Pacific region.*

*"A Simple Genius," a tale of carefree college days and innocent
love, shows what could happen when, in the early stages of the
computer revolution, a football season for a small college made athletic
history. The story was collected in* A Role in Manila *(1966).*

His eyes, his deep blue and perfectly round eyes, told almost
everything about Andy Black. His eyes were intelligent
and they were simple. Everyone at Berkeley College was prepared for the intelligence: he was the son of Grotius Black.
Grotius Black had graduated from Stanford in classics when he
was twenty-two. When he was twenty-five he had a Ph.D. in
physics from MIT. At twenty-seven he had a D.Phil. from

Oxford in mathematics and at thirty he had won a Nobel Prize. Sometime during World War II he had made a critical calculation that led to "implosion," a method for triggering the atomic bomb.

So no one was surprised that Grotius Black's son was brilliant.

But no one was prepared for Andy's simplicity. Not that Berkeley College is a sophisticated place, because it isn't. Today, since the Big Season, everyone knows something about Berkeley College. Actually it's a very excellent and very small liberal arts college, tucked in the hills across the bay from San Francisco. It's a tough college and the students tend to be brainy and classical. Also they tend toward practical jokes.

The first week Andy Black was there they took him on a "snipe hunt" and were astounded when he spent the whole night in the field, patiently holding the bag, waiting for the snipes to run in. Another time they had him serenade under a window and the horse-faced Dean of Women opened it and frowned sourly down on him and he kept right on serenading. The jokes were endless and Andy never anticipated them. And that surprised people because they had not expected him to be so simple.

However, no one rode Andy very hard. He took jokes so well. He would stare at a person for a moment, then his fine blue eyes would light up. Then he would laugh, a soft laugh with no harshness in it. The other students sensed that Grotius Black and the very serious adults at Los Alamos and Oak Ridge and MIT had never taught Andy how to play.

The first year Andy made a straight *A* record, read a lot, drank his first quart of beer. He learned to play a fair game of tennis. And he became aware of Georgia Ryan.

Georgia was a sophomore and she was working her way through school hashing at tables. Her father was a chief bosun in the Navy. Georgia was very Irish and she had green eyes, a firm small body, a gay face and a very pure complexion.

The first time he took her out Andy did not date her. He didn't know how. He just waited around in the Commons until she was finished hashing and walked outside with her. She looked at him once curiously, smiled, and began talking. They walked through the grove of California live oaks and at once the sun became soft and mellowed, tattered by the green leaves. When they came out of the grove they saw the red soaring towers of the Golden Gate Bridge just disappearing into the billowing masses of spring fog.

They walked through the clear sunlight to the edge of Football Arroyo. They looked down and saw the diminished figures of the players running back and forth. The solid chunking sound of a punted ball, the smack of shoulders hitting tackle dummies, the trill of a whistle came to their ears.

Andy looked at Georgia's strong chin, her crisp black hair, the sprinkle of freckles across her nose. He wanted her to stay there talking to him and his mind frantically searched for things to say.

"That's Professor Deever over there," Georgia said. "The one with the whistle and the tweed suit. He doubles as football coach. Football and Greek. But he only gets paid for the Greek."

"Why does he do it?" Andy asked. "He doesn't have to coach."

"For fun, I guess," Georgia said. "Or maybe it's because he's Irish like me. We'd both like to see Berkeley win a game instead of always winding up a season in the cellar. Or maybe after Greek grammar football seems nice and chaotic and unsystematic."

"I don't think football's chaotic or unsystematic," he said. He did not know anything about it, but he had to keep the conversation going or Georgia would leave. He knew nothing about Irishmen so he said something about systems. "I heard Ludwig von Bertelannffy and Dad talking once about General Systems Theory. They agreed that everything, at base, is systematic. Even very complex social phenomena. And that's all football is . . . a sort of social phenomenon."

"It's plenty complex," Georgia said. "But it's not systematic. It's a game. A game where the big tough boys lick the little tough boys. And the big tough boys go to Cal or Stanford or UCLA. So we lose."

In the next few seconds the Big Season was born. And it was all by accident. Andy only wanted to keep Georgia there, to stand at the edge of the arroyo and smell the spring smells and hear the dim fine sounds of spring practice . . . and look at Georgia.

"I don't think success in football has anything to do with size," Andy said. "Remember when Galileo dropped the iron balls from the Tower of Pisa the little balls fell just as fast as the big ones? It's all a question of inertia. There are natural laws."

"But football isn't iron balls dropped from a tower," Georgia said. "It's twenty-two boys doing something very difficult."

Her voice was sharp. She thought Andy was being condescending. Unfortunately, intelligence when combined with simplicity often gives the impression of a languid superiority. Georgia's back stiffened. She could not know that Andy's mind was working with a white-hot intensity merely to find something to keep her there.

"But you could work it out," Andy said. He glanced down at the black antlike figures of the players. "Set it up like a regular experiment. Look for regularities, analyze them statistically. . . ."

"All right, Andy Black, you work it out," Georgia said and her voice shook slightly. Arrogant son of a famous man, she thought. Acting so smart. "You work it out and I'll invite you down to San Diego for Christmas vacation. My dad will show you how to rig a breeches buoy and drink beer and shoot craps with sailors."

But the sarcasm was wasted on Andy. He heard only the words and as he turned them over in his mind they seemed wonderful and full of promise.

Andy did not see much of Georgia that spring. He spent most of his time in a seminar room running off the movies of past Berkeley games. He sat with a stop watch in his hand, a slide rule on the table and an absorbed happy look on his face.

That summer vacation Georgia went to Yosemite to hash at the Awahnee Lodge. She received one letter a week from Andy. She learned that he had gone to Cambridge to a cybernetics seminar with his father, then to a MIT seminar on mathematical models and then to New York to a week-long meeting with Professor Lazarsfeld on latent structure analysis. In one letter he mentioned that his father had allowed him to use the enormously complicated and expensive electronic brains at MIT for six hours.

The first day of the fall semester Andy was waiting for Georgia as she came out of Commons. He stared at her new cashmere sweater and her new short haircut and if any other boy had done it Georgia would have been offended. But when Andy said "Hello" in a dazed voice and shook hands with her it was different. He picked up a heavy briefcase and they walked to the edge of the arroyo. They walked down the path and out on the playing field.

They found Professor Deever on the sidelines and stood behind him while he shouted some instructions. Professor Deever had round cheeks and a bald head, a slightly potted belly and a great consuming interest in football. His squad was small and made up of light fast boys. He had no expectation of winning, but he still liked football.

"Professor Deever, I'd like to show you something I worked up during the summer," Andy said.

He put down his briefcase and took out what looked like a roll from one of those old player pianos. He spread it out on the turf.

"What have you got, Andy?" Professor Deever asked. He was watching the boys doing high-low blocks. They were not very good.

"It's a sort of football system," Andy said. "A sort of guide to win football games."

Professor Deever glanced at Andy, then at Georgia, and then down at the long roll of paper. It was really a very complex graph. Thousands of spider-web lines rose and fell, crisscrossed the paper. Occasionally the lines, as fine as hairs, flowed together in a knot and these had been marked with a red pencil. At the bottom of the graph it said: "General Systems Model for Football. Based on 13,466 plays."

Professor Deever almost laughed, but not quite. For he thought of two things. When he saw Andy look from the piano roll to Georgia he knew that Andy loved the girl. And then he remembered that Andy was the son of Grotius Black. Professor Deever was Irish enough to believe that under the pressure of love a good intelligence can do remarkable things. So he knelt down beside Andy.

"Explain it to me," he said.

"It's not a science of football or anything like that," Andy said. "It's really just a graph of all of the uniformities in football. First, I watched a lot of football movies. It was amazing the number of uniformities I found. For example, almost all players run 8.3 yards per second at their full speed. Most of them weigh between 165 and 200 pounds. Light backs tend to run toward the sidelines when they have the choice and heavy backs tend to run toward the center of the field."

"Why?" Professor Deever asked suddenly.

"I don't know," Andy said. "I didn't study the cause . . . I just studied the effect. And I found dozens of uniform effects. Like almost everyone tackles with his right shoulder and defensive fullbacks always tend to guess the play is a running play if a pass isn't made in three seconds. There were really hundreds of things like that."

"What did you do after you found the uniformities?" Professor Deever said.

"Well, I had to wait until I got to the electronic brains at MIT. It would have taken forty men almost twenty years to make the calculations, but the brains did them in six hours. Then Professor Weiner and Dad helped me put them on this graph."

"What does the graph mean?" Professor Deever asked.

"The red pencil marks indicate the plays which have the greatest number of uniformities," Andy said. He pointed at one cluster. "Now that's the kickoff play. It's got a lot of uniformities because one team is moving straight down the field and the other is moving in the opposite direction, but no one is running across the field. Also, everyone is running at top speed. And everyone is equally fresh. Gee, the kickoff is just a lot of uniformities."

"Look, Andy, you said this would help to win games," Professor Deever said. "How does it help?"

"It's simple. You take the plays in which there is a lot of uniformity and you do just a few things differently."

"Differently?" Georgia asked.

"Just a bit differently. What the graph indicates is that some plays are done almost the same by every football team. So by doing a few things differently in one of those plays you have an advantage, you can control the situation."

Professor Deever thought of a thousand objections. He looked at Georgia, however, and for one of those sharp blinding moments there was communication between an older and a younger person. He sensed perfectly that she loved Andy and that she wanted him to have a chance and that she was trying to tell him this. So he did not ask a single question. He got to his feet and blew his whistle and called to the first string to put on red jerseys and the second string to put on black and there would be a scrimmage. The boys went yelling over to the sidelines and scrambled into the shirts.

"All right, Andy, we'll try it," Professor Deever said. "You tell the Blacks how to run back a kickoff and we'll see how they do."

"Swell. I'd like to," Andy said. He stood up with the roll of paper in his hands. Georgia watched him with her mouth slightly open, astounded at his confidence.

Andy pulled the quarterback, the two halfbacks and the ends aside and for five minutes he coached them. They were surprised by what he said, but they nodded agreement.

Andy and Georgia stood beside Professor Deever as the Reds swept forward. The kickoff was high and graceful and it went to Jacobson, the first string quarterback, on his one-yard line. When Jacobson reached the twenty-yard line the first Red was within a few feet of him, charging fast and lowering for the tackle. Jacobson turned away and threw the ball straight up into the air and behind him. At the same time the Blacks started to run at full speed. The Red tackler tried to stop, but he couldn't and he crashed into Jacobson.

The ball went slowly up into the air, and no one was within twenty feet of it. It reached its peak and started to fall. Suddenly, just as the ball was chest-high, little Bobbie Grey the fullback came running under it, counting steps under his breath. He opened his arms, gathered the ball in and ran toward the sidelines . . . instead of toward the Red goal. A knot of Red tacklers plunged through the empty air he would have occupied if he *had* run toward the Red goal.

"I think they do that because they have a conditioned reflex always to keep themselves between the man with the ball and their own goal," Andy muttered as if he were watching a laboratory experiment. "It's a protective instinct."

Just as Grey reached the sideline he turned and as smartly as a platoon falling in there were four Black blockers in front of him. They swept off down the field. One of the blockers took out the first Red back who came running up. Then there was only one more Red between Grey and the goal. The three Black blockers launched themselves at him. They brought him down. Grey ran, in lonely splendor, to the goal line.

"The Reds were going so fast in one direction that they couldn't check their forward speed," Andy said. "The Black backs were only going half speed so they could reverse direction more quickly and that gave them the advantage."

Professor Deever, along with all the players, was staring at Grey. Then he turned and looked at Andy. There was a sparkle in his eye. He did an elaborate fast little jig on the turf. "Oh, Andy boy, we'll show 'em this year." And he shook his fist at the sky.

The first game of the season was with Stanford. It had always been a warm-up for Stanford. Berkeley had never yet won. On the day of the game Andy and Georgia were invited by Professor Deever to sit on the bench with the team. It was a warm and very clear fall day.

"Maybe we'd better use those modifications you made for hot weather, Andy?" Professor Deever asked.

"Sure. Let's play it as hot weather," Andy said. He took out a file of papers and made some quick changes on the piano roll.

The kickoff was a long low ball that Jacobson picked up on the ten-yard line. He held it gingerly for a moment and then he started forward and the Big Season had begun. It was a slaughter. The Stanford team did not even come close to stopping Berkeley on the kickoff. The Berkeley men trotted slowly about the field, cutting sideways, throwing laterals and then regrouping. It was like watching a clumsy bull facing the best of matadors. The Berkeley men were no better or stronger than they used to be, but the Stanford men always seemed to be a yard or two out of position, standing still when they should be running, running when they should be turning, turning when they should be going ahead. When Jacobson crossed the goal no one was within thirty yards of him.

The stadium was utterly quiet. The officials stood like marble statues. The players stared down the field.

"It works," Professor Deever whispered and he slapped his thigh. The sound carried over the field. The umpire blew his whistle and everyone came to life again.

"Oh, Andy, you've done it," Georgia said. She gripped his arm and laughed with pure pleasure. "It's working. But what happens when they get the ball?"

"Wait and see," Andy said. He smiled.

The Stanford team waited for the kickoff with savage impatience. They smacked their fists, grimaced, jumped up and down, shouted down the field. The kickoff was short and wobbly. Wilson, the Stanford full, picked it up. At once a huge wedge of Stanford men formed in front of him and began sweeping down the field.

"That's bad. They shouldn't do that," Andy said in a deliberate voice. "It's too anticipatory."

Georgia was not sure what he meant, but she felt a quick second of doubt. The Stanford men looked huge and fast. She watched as Bobbie Grey came running up toward the point of the Stanford wedge. Wilson was almost invisible behind his interference. When he was about ten yards away Grey suddenly tucked his arm up as if he had a ball and danced away from the wedge, throwing his hand out as if he were giving them a straight-arm.

Instantly the wedge quivered, hesitated, seemed to flaw. Then two of the Stanford men shot out of the wedge and flew after Grey. The wedge crashed in a heap as someone stumbled. Wilson ran into his interference and fell.

"The interference was thrown off when they saw Grey do that break-away motion," Andy said. "Instinctively they thought he had the ball and all their defensive reflexes came into play and they went after him. You see, the better trained a team is the more they are the victims of their training. If their opponents don't act exactly as they should the well-trained player doesn't know what to do. The better trained he is the more he acts on reflex. So the trick is to trigger off the kind of reflex you want. And that's what we do."

At half time Berkeley was leading 115 to 0.

During the second half Berkeley continued to widen its lead. But Andy hardly watched the game; he was more interested in Georgia. In fact he did not care for football very much. But he cared for Georgia very much. And something that happened in the second half disturbed him. Georgia yawned. Just as Jacobson was going over for his fourteenth touchdown of the day she yawned.

Andy looked out over the field. He noticed that in the huddle a few of the Berkeley boys were yawning too.

The San Francisco *Chronicle* the next morning had a headline in the sports section: THE BIG SEASON FOR BERKELEY; THEY BEAT CARDINALS 217 TO 0.

That is how the Big Season got its name. The name was picked up by the AP and the UP and put on the wire services as a curiosity. COW COLLEGE HAVING BIG SEASON, EXPERTS CONFUSED BY RECORD SCORE OF BIG SEASON. At Berkeley College excitement began to soar, although, curiously, there was very little discussion of the Stanford game. Everyone was excited about the huge score.

But it remained a sort of curiosity until the game the next week with San Jose State. The final score was Berkeley 282, San Jose 0. That did it. Bigtime sports writers descended on Berkeley; the score made headlines clear across the country; Edward R. Murrow did a *See It Now* program from the campus and the professional football scouts began quietly to nose around.

When the game with Texas Christian came up it was moved to Kezar Stadium in San Francisco. Seventy thousand people had to be turned away. You probably remember the famous picture that appeared in *Life* of the big Texas Christian end biting the turf as a little Berkeley back scoots past him for a touchdown. Someone wrote a song called "The Big Season" and it was a best-seller in three weeks.

Professor Deever told no one about the piano roll or about

Andy Black's role in the whole thing. Andy had asked him not to. For Andy was not happy.

Andy was not happy because of something that happened during the Texas Christian game. It was in the third quarter when Berkeley was leading 185 to 0. Georgia yawned and then looked sharply over at Andy.

"I can't help it, Andy," she said. "It's kind of boring. Really it's kind of unfair, as if we're taking advantage of them or something."

"But we're winning," Andy said. "I thought you wanted to win."

He smiled very tentatively for he did not want to make Georgia angry. But his expression was so simple that Georgia could only believe he was being ironic. Her shoulders drew tight.

"I did want to win, but not this way. Not like this . . . ," and she moved her hands to take in the football field and the players. "It's just not very much fun. I thought it would be different."

Andy looked out over the field. He could not understand her. After all, he thought, football is football. One game did not look much different than another to him. He was a bit worried by the fact that two of the Berkeley players had fallen asleep during the half and had had to be shaken awake. He was dimly aware that the crowd in the stands was held there by a sense of curiosity rather than by excitement, but he couldn't understand that either. "You wanted to win," he said again.

Georgia slapped him.

In October the incredible happened. Notre Dame agreed to play Berkeley at Soldier's Field in Chicago on November 15. Look back at the old newspapers and it will all come back to you. 50,000 WAIT ALL NIGHT TO BUY FOOTBALL CLASSIC TICKETS, COACH DEEVER SAYS HE WILL NOT SCOUT NOTRE DAME were only two of the headlines. The phrase *the Big Season* was on everyone's lips.

The competition for tickets was enormous. The American Legion passed a resolution urging that veterans be given priority. The Chamber of Commerce proposed that the entire sale of the tickets be put "in the hands of a recognized businessman of high integrity" and suggested Bernard Baruch. A Southern Senator demanded that the game be termed an interstate enterprise so that the ICC could regulate the sale of tickets. He was hooted down when it was discovered that in the small print of the bill he had provided that forty-five Senators be given free tickets on the fifty-yard line to "serve as Congressional observers." The FBI broke up seven different rings that were printing counterfeit tickets.

Professor Deever insisted that Andy and Georgia go to Chicago with the Berkeley team. Andy was miserable. When he managed to see Georgia she looked at him coldly. All during the welcoming ceremonies she avoided him and once he thought she had been crying.

Soldier's Field was full at eight o'clock the morning of the game. One hundred seven thousand people had seats and fifty thousand fans milled around outside the gates. Seats were scalped at two hundred fifty dollars each in the morning, but by game time it was rumored that one scalper had made a fortune on a set of four tickets.

When Berkeley trotted out on the field the roar that went up was solid, sustained, and enormous. The Berkeley players looked up nervously at the huge crowd, but in a few minutes their nervousness passed as they threw the ball around and did some wind-sprints.

Then the Notre Dame squad poured out. There were eighty-five of them. They had round powerful calves, crew-cut bullet-like heads, strong backs, and they were fast. Their warm-up plays peeled off like simple, powerful perfection. The Berkeley boys stared and then as it slowly dawned on them that they were actually playing Notre Dame they became tense. Most of them were pale when the game started.

The field was cleared, the two teams lined up. The Notre Dame captain raised his hand, the Berkeley captain raised his hand. A whistle shrilled and it was the only sound in the stadium. The Notre Dame team swept forward and kicked off. The kick was high, savage and long. Jacobson caught it with his foot on the end-zone line.

He started straight down the middle of the field at three-quarters speed. The Notre Dame team moved down quickly, but cautiously, waiting for a surprise. As Jacobson reached the twenty-yard line he stopped, counted three, and turned. He threw the ball in a great soaring lateral toward the far corner of the end zone . . . and the end zone was empty! Notre Dame froze, moved warily like lions who had become wise. Just as the ball came down Grey trotted under it, scooped it into his arms and ran parallel to the end-zone line, behind the goal. It was too much for Notre Dame. In a collective, unleashed and concerted movement they ripped toward Grey. He ran to the end of the end zone, turned, trotted to the goal-line and paused. When the first Notre Dame man was three yards away he turned and threw the ball in a hard, flat, fast lateral to the opposite corner. And standing there, waiting, was Jacobson.

The Notre Dame team knew they had been tricked. They fell on Grey in a great swarming angry mass even as Jacobson started to streak down the sidelines toward the goal 109 yards away. It was one of the most lonely touchdowns in history.

There was a vast slow exhalation of breath from the crowd. A stunned, unbelieving sound.

"Listen," Georgia said. "It's like a moan." They were the first words she had spoken to Andy.

"They must be Notre Dame fans," Andy said dully. He looked up at the curiously silent crowd, at the thousands of eyes.

"No. They're surprised and they're shocked," Georgia said. Andy looked at her. "Andy, don't you see what's happened? This isn't football anymore. It's . . . it's . . . it's like a mathematics problem. Or something. But not football."

"But we're winning," Andy said stubbornly. His face was confused. "I thought that's what you wanted. You said so."

She stared at him and then she shook her head in misery. Her eyes brimmed with tears.

"Andy, Andy, don't you understand?" she asked. "Not even a little?"

They sat quietly watching the game unfold. It was like every other game of the Big Season. Berkeley made touchdown after touchdown and Notre Dame could not do a thing. The Berkeley players oozed around and through and over the big swift Notre Dame players and it was very dull to watch.

Just before the half ended Andy turned to Georgia. His eyes were sparkling and the simple intelligent look had been replaced by excitement.

"Look, Georgia, I know what's wrong," he said. "It can't be a game and a science at the same time. A game is like politics; it's got to be a democracy of errors."

"Oh, Andy, you've seen it!" Georgia cried.

"I never even watched the game until today. I just worked out the system because I thought you wanted it. Because I wanted to go to San Diego with you for Christmas." He blushed.

Georgia looked at him and then slowly she smiled. She reached out and took his hand. She squeezed his fingers.

At halftime Berkeley was ahead 117 to 0.

Andy and Georgia walked into the locker room where the Berkeley players were resting. Some of the boys were drinking orange pop, others were napping. In the old days Professor Deever used to give a pep talk during the half and although it never did any good they all missed it. Now he just sat silently, drinking soda pop.

"Listen, everybody," Andy said and his voice trembled with excitement. He held the piano roll of paper in his hand. "I'm sick of this kind of football. It's no fun. Even if it's my system I don't like it. Let's tear up the graph and just play football."

Professor Deever sat up straight. He started automatically to protest, but then he saw a gleam kindle itself in the eyes of the players. He said nothing.

"That's a good idea," Jacobson said.

The boys started to grin. They didn't yell or crowd around Andy or shout. They just sat and grinned, watching Andy tear the precious piano roll into shreds. And when the half period was over they went whooping back onto the field. They even yelled threats at the dejected Notre Dame players.

Georgia walked out beside Professor Deever.

"It's all right," she whispered. "Andy just had it all wrong.

And I had him all wrong. I thought he liked his system. But he didn't. He just made it for me. It was so sweet of him." She added shyly, "I guess I'll marry the silly guy if he'll have me."

Professor Deever stopped. Then he bent forward and gave her a paternal kiss on the forehead.

That second half is famous. Some say it is the best football ever played. The people who saw it never forgot it. The movie short of that half is said to be the most popular sports movie ever made. Go see it if your memory has faltered.

Berkeley kicked off to Notre Dame. It was a feeble wobbling kick that was scooped up by Woltanski, the All-American half. He had not made even a first down that day. Berkeley came yelling down the field, arms flying, whooping with joy. Efficiently, but without real hope, Notre Dame crunched into them. The Berkeley boys flew through the air and lay gasping and grinning on the turf. Woltanski got to the fifty-yard line still not believing that it was happening. Jacobson came tearing after him and took off in a long flying tackle. He was cut down in mid-air by a Notre Dame guard. Woltanski went across the goal without a man near him. The stands rose in a mighty wail of sound that carried distinctly over half of Illinois.

The Berkeley boys picked themselves up and ran down to Woltanski and pounded him on the back, delirious with joy. It was the first time Berkeley had been scored on in the Big Season.

The rest is in the movie short. But it was a wild and wonderful thing to see. Notre Dame was trying desperately to overcome Berkeley's huge lead. Berkeley played eagerly and very, very chaotically and with great pleasure. With thirty seconds to go the score was Notre Dame 116, Berkeley 117.

Notre Dame took time out with the ball on Berkeley's fifteen-yard line. When play commenced they gave the ball to Woltanski and started a long sweeping end run. The crowd keened and shrieked and yelled. The interference mowed down the Berkeley men. The Berkeley men, howling with delight, threw themselves at Woltanski, but missed. Woltanski crossed the fifteen, the ten and finally was at the five. And there he was hit very hard by Jacobson. Woltanski's momentum carried him forward, with Jacobson desperately trying to drag him down.

For a magnificent second Jacobson and Woltanski wavered back and forth on the one-yard line. Then Woltanski fell backwards and the gun went off and Berkeley had beaten Notre Dame.

That was the end of the Big Season. But when you see the movie of the game there's one thing you won't notice. You'll see that the Notre Dame players picked up the Berkeley boys and hauled them around the stadium on their shoulders. You'll see the pandemonium in the stands and hear the noise of the crowd. But you won't see a little Irish girl kissing a boy beside the Berkeley bench. They're lost in the crowd.

JANET LEWIS

Picnic, 1943

Janet Lewis, although perhaps best known as a poet, has also written fiction of great merit. She was born in Chicago in 1899, the daughter of a teacher of English, and grew up with a love of writing. She earned a Bachelor of Philosophy degree from the University of Chicago and went to California seeking health. Married in 1926 to the poet and critic Ivor Winters, she did much of her writing as a housewife in a suburb of Palo Alto while raising a family.

Janet Lewis feels that her work is true to the California experience, where strength to face life comes partially from the "health and happiness" of the physical climate. Notably versatile, she has published children's books and the libretti of four operas as well as verse, novels, and short stories. After 1960 she taught creative writing at Stanford University.

Her novels are set not only in modern California (Against a Darkening Sky, 1943) but also in sixteenth- and seventeenth-century France (The Wife of Martin Guerre, 1941; The Ghost of Monsieur Scarron, 1959), seventeenth-century Denmark (The Trial of Sören Qvist, 1947), and the Great Lakes Indian country (The Invasion, 1932).

"Picnic, 1943" contrasts the threats to noncombatants on the West Coast in World War II with a happy interlude in a verdant countryside. The story is taken from Good-bye, Son and Other Stories (1946).

They arrived at the white iron gates without getting lost on the way, although there was one confusing moment when

University Avenue turned out to be an unpaved lane, overhung by wild lilac and lustrous branches of poison oak. The two boys were waiting for them at the gates, as promised, Dmitri on the right- and Brian on the left-hand post, both with their bare brown knees tucked up under their chins, and the foliage—fortunately not poison oak this time—crowding behind them as they looked down from the green shadows. The posts were square, with architectural panelings on the side, and wide flat tops. She could tell, after one glance at them, that the house would be in the most formidable style of the 1890s, and probably painted white to match the gate.

Dmitri descended like a lizard, brown, slender, and quick, and came to stand on the running board, hooking his bare arm through the window on the right. Brian, descending more slowly, took a slow and candid look at the guests and then disappeared up the curving road.

"Straight ahead," said Dmitri. "What are we waiting for?"

"I'm afraid I'll brush you off," she said.

"Not me," said Dmitri. "My mother is waiting for you at the house. Then we go down to the stream." He peered under the roof of the car, a pointed brown face with impish flaring eyebrows above tawny golden eyes, very alert and inquiring. "You wore your old clothes? That's fine. It's not at all clean at the stream. Mud, you know. The last people who came for a picnic, they looked so beautiful, but we didn't have any fun. Too clean."

The car lurched heavily to the side as the road took on the character of a stream bed, and the brown hand tightened its hold, the small arm grew tense, but the smile remained undisturbed. When the road forked, Dmitri indicated the correct turn. They went mostly uphill, turning and twisting, and once the children in the back seat let out a cry of "The creek! The creek!" as a gleam of water showed through the tangled dark foliage on the lower side of the road. Then suddenly they emerged upon a formal graveled space, surrounded by neglected but nevertheless formal flower beds.

"To the right," said Dmitri, and there the car stopped directly in front of the steps to the veranda.

Meredith Jones got out of the car and stretched her legs.

Then she tipped up the driver's seat and let the children crawl out, a little boy of five, a girl of six, an older girl; all three of them disappeared around the end of the car to join Dmitri. Brian was already there. He had beat the car to the house.

Ted Nash let himself out, stretched his long frame, and then slumped, with his hands in his pockets.

"Picnics," he said with a sigh. "Oh well, it's good for the children, I presume."

"I only hope it's a good picnic," said Mrs. Jones. "It's a long way to come with gas what it is."

"More precious than liquor," said Nash. "At picnics we drink milk, don't we?"

"Do you like milk, Ted?" inquired Molly Leontovich. She had come out on the porch and stood there, smiling at them, a ruffled dimity apron tied on over her denim slacks, her lovely red hair and lovely Irish smile shining upon them.

Nash didn't answer. He jammed his hands deeper in his pockets and tipped his head back to look at her from under his eyelids, in the manner of the nearsighted.

Molly said, "There's some corn liquor in the kitchen. You ought to see my kitchen. It's terrific. Besides, you could peel potatoes for me."

Mrs. Jones had the impression, just before they entered the house, of more bay windows than she had ever before seen affixed to one dwelling. Within, the impression was reinforced by bay windows which enlarged each room by at least one third of its original rectangle. Doubtless a cottage in the mind of its architect, for it was only one story high, the house had yet been endowed with all possible grandeur in the way of high ceilings, deep windows, and marble fireplaces, and in all this architectural grandeur with discolored paint and faded wallpaper stood the oddest and scantiest collection of secondhand furniture that Meredith Jones had ever yet laid eyes on.

"This," said Molly, waving her hands at the discredited walls and woodwork, "is going to be beautiful. I'm going to paint it pale green with cream-colored woodwork, and have the walls frescoed with magnolia blossoms, and always keep a fresh magnolia in a green glass vase on a low table in the alcove there by the windows. Won't it be lovely?"

She looked at Mrs. Jones as if it were all there ready and visible to be admired. Meredith Jones stretched her imagination and admired it.

"And this is the horrific kitchen," said Molly. "Enter and be at home."

Ted Nash and Meredith Jones followed her into a room which barely held the three of them, the coal stove, the wooden sink, the necessary cupboards, and a table. Here the architect had lost all interest in his project. It was the kitchen for a hovel. But through the window, which was indeed large for the room, Meredith glimpsed the neglected formal garden, and, beyond it, the wall of verdure. She glimpsed also a beautiful roan mare which was wandering about the place with all the freedom of a pet dog.

"Your horse is loose," she said.

"That's Anna Karenina," said Molly, "and she wanders around like that all the time. We haven't been able to fence a paddock yet. After all, we've only been here a month."

Meredith Jones pressed closer to the window. The children had entered the picture now, and she was watching Anna drop her beautiful head affectionately over Dmitri's shoulder. Dmitri put up an arm to embrace her and went on with his harangue to the children, his other arm gesturing widely. Behind Meredith, Ted Nash was explaining:

"My wife works, the husband of Mrs. Jones works, we are the only members of the leisure class in our families—although I do labor on other days than Saturdays—and we have de-camped with the only means of transportation in our two families; therefore you need not be concerned about any respec-tive wife or husband dropping in on you at the last minute and asking for food. In fact, we are on the loose. But why such an immense number of boiled potatoes? I thought this was a picnic for the children. In fact," he continued in his gently insulting manner, "I only came in order to bring my child."

"Yes, yes," said Molly reflectively, without being insulted, "that's the way it started, but then Anton invited a few neigh-bors—I don't know just who or how many." She poured a couple of drinks in an absent-minded fashion, put down the bottle, and began to rummage in a box of knives and spoons. "I can't find anything here," she complained. "Besides, we left all the good and useful things at the house when we rented it. It's incredible how much money you can get for renting a house that's furnished down to toothpicks and nutcrackers. It's incredible too how hard it is to find a decent paring knife these days." She came upon a small knife with a red composition handle and presented it to Nash. "Drink your liquor," she said, "and then start in on those potatoes. And be careful of the knife. I had another one like it, but I broke it cutting butter. The handle broke in my hand."

Meredith said, "No drink for me."

"All right then," said Molly. "Your friend can have two."

The phone rang, and she went off to answer it. Ted Nash drank his liquor and said that it wasn't bad. He gave Meredith a chance to change her mind about the other glass. She shook her head. He helped himself to it.

"You don't explain much about these picnics you bring me on," he complained. "Who are these people?"

"You met them," she said. "At the Hendershots'."

"Yes, I know," he said. "You said they were White Russians. They came very late. But Molly—that hair."

"Molly's from south of the slot," said Meredith patiently. "Her name was Coyle. And Anton was the Czar's something or other. Not an admiral. Something on horseback. And he's very distinguished."

"I admit it," said Nash. "And now he's working in a defense plant. With the admiral. There is an admiral in the defense plant, isn't there?"

"I think so," said Meredith. She hunted out another knife and began to peel potatoes. Ted Nash began to peel potatoes also. Molly Leontovich returned from her phone call.

"That was my little stepdaughter," she said. "She's coming to supper and wants to bring some friends. I don't believe there are enough potatoes, do you? I'd better cook some more."

"How many friends?" asked Nash. "There are a lot of potatoes here right now."

Molly said, "Four or five. Ed Stebbins and his family, and someone else, some other Party member."

"Ed Stebbins!" said Nash, overcome with wonder. "And I thought you were White Russians."

Molly took her attention from the potatoes long enough to be amused at him. "Sonya is very Red," she informed him. "Very, very Red. And Ed Stebbins is very entertaining. A wonderful man."

"But what does your husband think of all this?"

"Oh, it's all right. These are Reds, not Russians. Except Sonya. And anyway, the White Russians are all so pleased now with the Bolshies. They brag about them. After all, they are Russians too, and they have been magnificent.

"And as for Sonya, you can't blame her. She's young, and she remembers being so hungry in Russia. Her mother died of malnutrition—starvation, you know—although they called it something else. And she has little pocks in the enamel of her teeth because she never got enough milk when she was a kid. The lipstick always rubs off on the edges of them. Not that it hurts her looks. She's so pretty—just wait till you see her. And so . . ."

"So what?"

"So she feels she wants to do something about it—you know, about Russian kids not getting enough milk."

"But what about your husband?" inquired Nash, determined to get to the bottom of the matter. "Is he still White?"

Molly made an impatient gesture.

"He was always White. It's like being born a Southerner. But he doesn't mind about Sonya. After all, he's an intelligent man." She suddenly remembered about the children. "Where have they gone?" she asked Meredith.

"They're with Dmitri."

Molly appeared worried. "I should go after them; I don't like such little ones down at the creek alone. Dmitri has sense—but not all the time, and the pools are still very deep. I think I'll go and see what they're up to."

"I'll go," said Meredith.

"Would you, darling?" said Molly. "I meant to have everything ready before you came, so that we could all go down together." She went to the porch with Meredith and pointed out the path to the creek. "We'll be down as soon as we get the salad made. We'll bring everything. You're an angel. And I am so glad you brought Mr. Nash. I need a man to help carry things—Anton gets home so late."

So Meredith Jones went down to the creek. The woods were very quiet and hot. The air, too dry to be sultry, seemed close, nevertheless, because it was unmoving. During the drive down the valley, on their way to the Leontovich place, she had noticed how the hills were veiled in haze that was like the day's heat made visible. It had been a hot day and she was tired, and glad to be by herself for a few minutes.

In California the creeks run full in the spring and dwindle through the summer months to a few pools or a few damp places in the sand. All the torrent-tossed rubble of the winter is left in the gullies. The secret conformations of the stream bed are exposed to the sunlight, and the children stand on the dry bottoms and look up to the high-water marks and remember or imagine how violent and fresh and lavish the stream was the winter before. The stream which the Leontovich family called theirs was better than most. Now, in early July, it still had some deep pools, as Molly had said, some shallows where the water ran with an audible ripple, and also some rocky islands and shoals, suitable for picnics, if you were not fussy about sitting upon rocks or upon the grassless earth. In the woods at this season there was poison oak, and in the fields there were foxtails, a diabolical kind of little dry, wheatlike sticker, so that, taking it all in all, a stream bed was by far the nicest place for a picnic.

When Meredith Jones reached the edge of the gully she heard joyous cries and splashing noises, and she arrived, sliding and running down the steep bank side, at the stony floor of the creek just in time to see Sally Nash totter and sit down in the shallow water.

Her own son and Dmitri roared with laughter. Sally, after the first gasp, shrieked with triumph also. Brian, solid and serious, stood on the graveled sandspit and urged Sally to get up because she was getting all wet. Meredith looked about for her daughter, who was nowhere to be seen.

There was nothing to be done about Sally for the present.

The late afternoon was still so warm that there was no danger of her catching cold. When the sun went, and the chill began to descend, they would just have to borrow something of Brian's from Molly to wrap the child up in. Brian looked more of a size with Sally than did Dmitri. Meredith Jones sat down on a rock beside the shallows and smiled at Sally. After all, what good was a brook if you couldn't get wet in it?

It was nice here. It was a long way out of the world. Meredith Jones sat and observed how the water lights reflected upward into Sally's face, and how the leaf shadows from above made her pale hair look greenish. The hair of her own son, under the same light, looked a darker brown, more nearly a chestnut than it really was, as the round head bent toward the water. Something atavistic possessed the children. Water, the aboriginal playmate, had filled them all with an excitement that was not hysterical but an abandonment, and a release. Young Jones suddenly lifted his head and looked about him with a radiant face. He ignored his mother, although he must have seen her, and after a long joyous look all about the scene, wheeled and plowed slowly downstream through the water past Sally to a narrow beach. Dmitri dashed by him, leaped to the steep bank, swung up and around a buttress of roots which the spring flood had washed bare, and curved down again and into the water.

Meredith Jones clasped her hands about her knees and leaned back to look up at the sky. The banks rose on either hand more than twice the height of her standing figure, clothed with young bay trees, bushlike, that had resisted the water, and crowned at the level of the woods with great bay trees that must have been growing there for years and years. The plumed tops swept upward, lifting the gully walls higher and higher, and leaving only a winding strip of sky that followed the journeyings of the creek. Upstream and downstream the gully turned abruptly, barring the vision. It was a wonderfully secluded and remote spot.

After a while Meredith's eleven-year-old daughter Marylin appeared, with her hands full of trophies—flowers, ferns, a spray of eucalyptus pods. She arranged a pool at the edge of the sand bar for a vase where she anchored her flowers, and then rolled up her jeans and joined the smaller children in the water. Time went by, and Meredith Jones lost all track of the passing of it. She did not know whether they had been there a long time or a short time, when Sally came dripping from the stream to complain that she was hungry. It had been so nice to sit there without responsibility, forgetting the defense plants and everything connected with them, and watch the children being happy.

Dmitri materialized behind Sally, the tawny, almost wholly naked figure akin to the rocks and water and leaf shadows, and explained, half scoffing and half consoling, that meals were always late at his house but that they always appeared in the end.

"It will be good, too, when it gets here," he said, rubbing his bare stomach and grinning.

The light, hitting sideways upon the crests of the trees, did indicate that it was past the children's usual suppertime. Meredith Jones surveyed the wet form of Sally Nash, to which the dripping garments clung like draperies in ancient Greek sculptures, and suggested that Dmitri run up to the house on a double errand: dry clothes for Sally and some information about the progress of the potato salad. He was about to leave when the soft flutter and roar of the blimp's propellers was heard, growing steadily louder and nearer, echoing down into their retreat, and he had to stay, of course, to see it go by overhead.

"How low!" he said joyfully. "She's almost brushing the treetops. You can see all the wires, and the flag!"

Indeed the blimp was very low, heading upstream almost as if following the wooded line of the creek. For a minute it was there, plain to behold, all silver and smooth, and then it crossed the line of trees at the bend and was immediately lost to them.

"So low!" Dmitri exulted. "Do you think they saw us? I waved." Then he was gone.

Marylin, dropping down beside her mother, remarked, "That was the 118. Bob Gaby's ship. He came over school one day when we were having P.E. and dropped apples down."

Her mother expressed her astonishment.

"Yeh," said Marylin. "He's one of Mrs. Cook's old boys.

Whenever he's over the school he tries to wiggle his wings at her, or whatever it is you do with a blimp. I got one of the apples."

It seemed pleasant to Meredith Jones that a friend of the children's was aloft overhead, patrolling the mountains and the coast, pleasant and safe. She smiled at the idea of apples dropping on the playground. Of course the coast had been in no danger from the Japs now for months and months, even if there were still Japs on Kiska. The real feeling of uneasiness had all died away at the end of the first summer. The wardens, it was true, had been getting some good if belated training. She had been hearing about it from their next-door neighbor, Jim Sweitzer. It did seem belated, to a mere civilian like herself. That was, she supposed, all a part of getting things nicely in order at last. The blimps, so frequent in that area of the coast, made everything seem very safe. She stretched herself and turned to see what had become of her son. The passing of the blimp had been the only landmark in time since she had left the highway that afternoon.

Dmitri was back soon, laden with dry garments and with pillows which his mother had sent to mitigate the hardness of the rocks. He came down the steep bank in three leaps and dumped everything beside Mrs. Jones. He was followed almost immediately by Ted Nash and a young woman, and another girl of about Marylin's age, both of them strangers to Meredith. Ted did not bother to introduce the young woman; he had probably forgotten her name. He brought the news that the salad was progressing nicely, and busied himself with disrobing his daughter. He seated himself near Meredith and, drawing Sally close to him, attempted to rub her dry with his handkerchief. The young woman sat down on the other side of Meredith, smiling shyly but without embarrassment, apparently willing to take Mrs. Jones on faith. Dmitri, selecting a few of the softer pillows, encamped himself by the newcomer, for once in a mood of domestication. Ted clothed his daughter, bit by bit, and young Jones forsook the stream for his mother's side.

They were all there, gathered closely into a group, as if the increasing lateness of the afternoon drew them together in a sort of home-coming gesture. Meredith heard a plane approaching from downstream, the concentrated sound so much firmer and louder, by virtue of being concentrated, than the loose roar of the blimp, and leaned back to watch it pass. The light was on the very tops of the trees now, and when the plane appeared and passed over them, almost directly above them, but not quite—a little to the left—the light actually seemed to flash upon the underside of the wings. It passed above them, just above the treetops, and disappeared completely at the turn of the gully, just as the blimp had done. But as the light had flashed on the underside of the wing, Meredith Jones saw perfectly plainly what she didn't believe she saw.

"Well, for gosh sakes!" she cried.

"Huh?" said Ted Nash, not looking up from a fastening on Sally's overalls.

"Did you see that?" said Meredith.

"What?" said Nash.

"The insignia on that plane. Do we have any planes with big round oranges under the wings?"

"Do you know what oranges under the wings mean?" said Nash sardonically.

"Jap insignia," said Marylin innocently.

"Did you see it, Marylin?" her mother asked eagerly.

"Nope," said Marylin without excitement.

"But, Ted," said Meredith Jones, "I did see it—Jap insignia. Just like those silly women at Pearl Harbor."

"What women?" said Ted, achieving the fastening and turning Sally about for inspection.

"Oh, you know, the ones that ran out shouting, 'It's all right, those planes are from California, they've oranges on their wings.' "

Ted looked at her compassionately. "My dear Meredith," he said in his best professorial manner, "your eyes need examining. There is a little red dot in the middle of a white star."

"I know all about that," said Meredith Jones with impatience. "There wasn't any star. And it wasn't a dot. It was a big round orange."

Ted Nash turned to the young woman beside Meredith and

said gently, with a motion of his head toward his friend, "Touched in the head. Sunstroke."

Meredith began to laugh, but she was embarrassed. "It sounds crazy all right, especially just after the blimp. But I did see it."

Dmitri said something then, and the young woman turned to catch it. She made him repeat it.

"What does he say?" inquired Nash.

"He says he saw it. It had big red tomatoes on the wings."

Meredith said nothing. She could not really believe that she had seen a Jap plane. She looked to Nash for an explanation.

"By me," said Nash. "Maybe the Army is sending out some fakes to test out the observers." It was a silly explanation, but it seemed to end the discussion. Dmitri, who was not at all interested, having made his contribution toward the evidence in the case, found one of those strange smooth yellow creatures known to the children as banana slugs, and was showing it to Marylin. Marylin went into shivers of horror and loathing. Dmitri, delighted at the effect of his find, immediately went in search of other slugs, and Marylin followed him, fascinated and loathing. Up the creek they went, with the cries, "Banana slugs! Banana slugs!" ringing in the air, mingled with Marylin's exclamations of disgust.

Molly appeared at the top of the bank with a crowd of people, and baskets. Supper had arrived, and the Japanese plane, or whatever it was, could not compete in interest either with the banana slugs or with the potato salad.

People whom Meredith had never met surrounded her, all acting as if they had known her always. She recognized Anton Leontovich and greeted him. Sonya, as pretty as they come, was handing about paper plates and napkins. She helped Meredith to get the smaller children settled and supplied. The confusion was magnificent, and the creek bottom seemed as populous as the Grand Central Station. In the midst of it all Meredith Jones did ask herself, "What was it I saw if it wasn't a Japanese plane? There's nothing the matter with my eyes, that I know of, and there's certainly nothing the matter with Dmitri's." Once she asked the young woman what she thought the plane could have been. The young woman smiled rather pityingly, shrugged her shoulders, and said, "I didn't see it." That was the end of it. Nobody wanted to talk about it. Nobody was interested. Nash was engaged in conversation with the great Ed Stebbins. Meredith took her plate of food to a spot near the children and ate her supper tranquilly. She forgot about the Japanese plane. It had no reality, anyway.

WALLACE STEGNER

Pop Goes the Alley Cat

Through a distinguished career as novelist, short story writer, essayist, historian, and teacher, Wallace Stegner has won a secure place at the forefront of modern literature of the American West. Born in Iowa in 1909, he lived in various places throughout the West until his family settled in Salt Lake City in 1921. After graduating from the University of Utah in 1930, he earned master's and Ph.D. degrees from the University of Iowa in 1932 and 1935, respectively, then went on to teach at the Universities of Utah and Wisconsin and at Harvard.

By the time he went to Stanford in 1945 (the next year he became director of its creative writing program), he had published five novels, the best known of which today is The Big Rock Candy Mountain *(1943), and a nonfiction work about the region where he grew up,* Mormon Country *(1942). In the ensuing years he produced another seven novels, including the Pulitzer Prize–winning* Angle of Repose *(1971) and* The Spectator Bird, *winner of the 1977 National Book Award for fiction, as well as two collections of short stories and a half-dozen volumes of nonfiction. He continues to live in California, in Los Altos Hills.*

"Pop Goes the Alley Cat" was first published in Harper's *in 1952 and was collected in* The City of the Living and Other Stories *(1956).*

Getting up to answer the door, Prescott looked into the face of a Negro boy of about eighteen. Rain pebbled his greased, straightened hair; the leather yoke of his blazer and the knees of his green gabardine pants were soaked. The big smile of greeting that had begun on his face passed over as a meaningless movement of the lips. "I was lookin'," he said, and then with finality, "I thought maybe Miss Vaughn."

"She's just on her way out."

The boy did not move. "I like to see her," he said, and gave Prescott a pair of small, opaque, expressionless eyes to look into. Eventually Prescott motioned him in. He made a show of getting the water off himself, squee-geeing his hair with a flat palm, shaking his limber hands, lifting the wet knees of his pants with thumb and finger as he sat down. He was not a prepossessing specimen: on the scrawny side, the clothes too flashy but not too clean, the mouth loose and always moving, the eyes the kind that shifted everywhere when you tried to hold them but were on you intently the moment you looked away.

But he made himself at home. And why not, Prescott asked himself, in this apartment banked and stacked and overflowing with reports on delinquency, disease, crime, discrimination; littered with sociological studies and affidavits on police brutality and the mimeographed communications of a dozen betterment organizations? The whole place was a temple to the juvenile delinquent, and here was the god himself in the flesh, Los Angeles Bronzeville model.

Well, he said, I am not hired to comment, but only to make pictures.

Carol came into the hall from her bedroom, and Prescott saw with surprise that she was glad to see this boy. "Johnny!" she said. "Where did you drop from?"

Over the boy had come an elaborate self-conscious casualness. He walked his daddylonglegs fingers along the couch back and lounged to his feet, rolling the collar of the blazer smooth across the back of his neck. Prescott was reminded of the slickers of his high school days, with their pinch-waisted bell-bottomed suits and their habit of walking a little hollow-chested to make their shoulders look wider. The boy weaved and leaned, pitching his voice high for kidding, moving his shoulders, his mouth, his pink-palmed hands. "Start to *rain* on me," he said in the high complaining humorous voice. "*Water start comin'* down on me I think I have to drop *in*."

"How come you're not working?"

"That job!" the boy said, and batted it away with both hands. "That wasn't much of a job, no kiddin'."

"Wasn't?"

"*You* know. Them old flour bags *heavy,* you get tired. Minute you stop to rest, here come that old foreman with the *gooseroo.* Hurry up there, boy! Get along there, boy! They don't ride white boys like that."

Carol gave Prescott the merest drawing down of the lips. "That's the third job in a month," she said, and added, "Johnny's one of my boys. Johnny Bane. This is Charlie Prescott, Johnny."

"Pleased to meet you," Johnny said without looking. Prescott nodded and withdrew himself, staring out into the dripping garden court.

"You know a fact?" Johnny said. "That old strawboss keep eyeballin' me and givin' me that old hurry-up, hurry-up, that gets *old*. I get to carryin' my knife up the sleeve of my sweatshirt, and he comes after me once *more,* I'm goin' *cut* him. So I quit before I get in bad trouble out there."

Carol laughed, shaking her head. "At least that's ingenious. What'll you do now?"

"Well, I don't *know*." He wagged his busy hands. "No future pushin' a truck around or cuttin' *lemons* off a tree. I like me a job with some *class,* you know, something where I could *learn* something."

"I can imagine how ambition eats away at you."

"No kiddin'!" the burbling voice said. "I get real industrious if I had me the right *kind* of a job. Over on Second Street there's this Chinaman, he's on call out at Paramount. Everytime they need a Chinaman for a mob scene, out he goes and runs around for a couple of hours and they hand him all this *lettuce,* man. You know anybody out at MGM, Paramount, anywhere?"

"No," she said. "Do you, Charlie?"

"Nobody that needs any Chinamen." Prescott showed her the face of his watch. Johnny Bane was taking in, apparently for the first time, the camera bag, the tripod, the canvas sack of flash bulbs beside Prescott's chair.

"Hey, man, you a photographer?"

"Charlie and I are doing a picture study of your part of town for the Russell Foundation," Carol said.

"Take a long time to be a photographer?" Johnny's mouth still worked over his words, but now that his attention was fixed his eyes were as unblinking as an alligator's.

"Three or four years."

"Man, that's a rough *sentence!* Take a long time, uh? Down by the station there's this place, mug you for a quarter. Sailors and their chicks always goin' in. One chick I was watchin' other night, she had her picture five times. Lots of cats and chicks, every night. *Money* in that, man."

She shook her head, saying, "Johnny, when are you going to learn to hold a job? You make it tough for me, after I talk you into a place."

"I get me in trouble, I stay over there," he said. "I know you don't want me gettin' into trouble." Lounging, crossing his feet, he said, "I like to learn me some trade. Like this photography. I bet I surprise you. That ain't like pushin' a truck with some *foreman* givin' you the eyeballs all the time."

Prescott lifted the camera bag to the chair. "If we're going to get anything today we'll have to be moving."

"Just a minute," Carol said. To Johnny she said, "Do you know many people over on your hill?"

"Sure, man. *Multitudes.*"

"Mexicans too?"

"They're mostly Mexicans over there. My chick's Mexican." He staggered with his eyes dreamily shut. "Solid, solid!" he said.

"He might help us get in some places," Carol said. "What do you think, Charlie?"

Prescott shrugged.

"He could hold reflectors and learn a little about photography."

Prescott shrugged again.

"Do you mind, Charlie?"

"You're the doctor." He handed the sack of flash bulbs and

the tripod to Johnny and picked up the camera bag. "Lesson number one," he said. "A photographer is half packhorse."

The *barrio* was a double row of shacks tipping from a hilltop down a steep road clayily shining and deserted in the rain, every shack half buried under climbing roses, geraniums, big drooping seedheads of sunflowers, pepper and banana trees, and palms: a rural slum of the better kind, the poverty overlaid deceptively with flowers. Across the staggering row of mailboxes Prescott could see far away, over two misty hilltops and an obscured sweep of city, the Los Angeles Civic Center shining a moment in a watery gleam of sun.

Johnny hustled around, pulling things from the car. As Prescott took the camera bag, the black face mugged and contorted itself with laughter. "You want me and my chick? How about me and my chick cuttin' a little *jive*, real mean? Colored and Mexican hobnobbin'. That okay?"

"First some less sizzling shots," Carol said dryly. "Privies in the rain, ten kids in a dirt-floored shack. How about Dago Aguirre's? That's pretty bad, isn't it?"

"Dago's? Man, that's a real *dump*. You want dumps, uh? Okay, we try Dago's."

He went ahead of them, looking back at the bag Prescott carried. "Must cost a lot of lettuce, man, all those *cameras*."

Prescott shook the bag at him. "That's a thousand dollars in my hand," he said. "That's why I carry it myself."

Rain had melted the adobe into an impossible stickiness; after ten steps their feet were balls of mud. Johnny took them along the flat hilltop to a gateless fence under a sugar palm, and as they scraped the mud from their shoes against a broken piece of concrete a Mexican boy in Air Force dungarees opened the door of the shack and leaned there.

"*Ese, Dago*," Johnny said.

"*Hórale, cholo*." Dago looked down without expression as Johnny shifted the tripod and made a mock-threatening motion with his fist.

"We came to see if we could take some pictures," Carol said. "Is your mother home, Dago?"

Dago oozed aside and made room for a peering woman with

a child against her shoulder. She came forward uncertainly, a sweet-faced woman made stiff by mistrust. Carol talked to her in Spanish for five minutes before she would open her house to them.

Keeping his mouth shut and working fast as he had learned to on this job, Prescott got the baby crawling on the dirt floor between pans set to catch the drip from the roof. He got the woman and Dago and the baby and two smaller children eating around the table whose one leg was a propped box. By backing into the lean-to, between two old iron bedsteads, and having Carol, Johnny, and Dago hold flashes in separate corners, he got the whole place, an orthodox FSA shot, Standard Poverty. That was what the Foundation expected. As always, the children cried when the flashes went off; as always he mollified them with the blown bulbs, little Easter eggs of shellacked glass. It was a dump, but nothing out of the ordinary, and he got no picture that excited him until he caught the woman nursing her baby on a box in the corner. The whole story was there in the protective stoop of her figure and the drained resignation of her face. She looked anciently tired; the baby's chubby hand was clenched in the flesh of her breast.

Johnny Bane, eager beaver, brisk student, had been officious about keeping extension cords untangled and posing with the reflector. By the time Prescott had the camera and tripod packed Johnny had everything else dismantled. "How you get all them *lights* to go off at *once?*" he said.

Prescott dropped a reflector and they both stooped for it, bumping heads. The boy's skull felt as hard as cement; for a moment Prescott was unreasonably angry. But he caught Carol's eye across the room, and straightening up without a word he showed Johnny and Dago how the flashes were synchronized, he let them look into the screen of the Rolleiflex, he explained shutter and lens, he gave them a two-minute lecture on optics. "Okay?" he said to Carol in half-humorous challenge.

She smiled. "Okay."

The Aguirre family watched them to the door and out into the drizzle. Johnny Bane, full of importance, a hep cat, a photographer's assistant, punched the shoulder of the lounging Dago. "*Ay te wacho,*" he said. Dago lifted a languid hand.

"Now what?" Prescott asked.

"More of the same," Carol said. "Unfortunately, there's plenty."

"Overcrowding, malnutrition, lack of sanitation," he said. "Four days of gloom. Can't we shoot something pretty?"

"There's always Johnny's chick."

"Maybe she comes under the head of lack of sanitation."

They were all huddled under the sugar palm. "What about my chick?" Johnny demanded. "You want my chick now?"

Carol stood tying a scarf over her fair hair. In raincoat and saddle shoes, she looked like a college sophomore. "Does your chick's family approve of you?" she said. "Most Mexican families aren't too happy to see boy friends hanging around."

Tickled almost to idiocy, he cackled and flapped his hands. "Man, they think I'm *rat* poison, no kiddin'. They think *any* cat's rat poison. They got this old Mexican jive about keepin' chicks at *home.* But I come there with *you,* they got to let me *in,* don't they?"

"So who's helping whom?" Prescott said.

That made him giggle and mug all the way down the slippery hill. "Hey, man," he said once, "you know these Mexicans believe in this Evil Eye, this *ojo.* When I hold up that old reflector I'm sayin' the Lord's *Prayer* backwards and puttin' the eyeballs on him, and when here comes that big flash, man, her old man really think he got the *curse* on him. I tell him I don't take it off till he let Lupe go out any time she want. Down to that *beach,* man. She look real mean down there on that sand gettin' the eyeballs from all the cats. *Reety!*"

"Spare us the details," Carol said, and turned her face from the rain, hanging to a broken fence and slipping, laughing, coming up hard against a light pole. Prescott slithered after her until before a shack more pretentious than most, almost a cottage, Johnny kicked the mud from his shoes and silently mugged at them, with a glassy, scared look in his odd little eyes, before he knocked on the homemade door.

It was like coming into a quiet opening in the woods and

startling all the little animals. They were watched by a dozen pairs of eyes. Prescott looked past the undershirted Mexican who had opened the door and saw three men with cards and glasses and a jug before them on a round table. A very pregnant woman stood startled in the middle of the floor. On a bed against the far wall a boy had lowered his comic book to stare. There was a flash of children disappearing into corners and behind the stove. The undershirted man welcomed them with an enveloping winy breath but his smile was only for Carol and Prescott; his recognition of Johnny was a brief, sidelong lapse from politeness. Somewhere behind the door a phonograph was playing "*Linda Mujer*"; now it stopped with a squawk.

Once, during the rapid Spanish that went on between Carol and the Mexican, Prescott glanced at Johnny, but the boy's face, with an unreal smile pasted on it, blinked and peered past the undershirted man as if looking for someone. His forehead was puckered in tense knots. Then the undershirted man said something over his shoulder, the men at the table laughed, and one lifted the jug in invitation. The host brought it and offered it to Carol, who grinned and tipped and drank while they applauded. Then Prescott, mentally tasting the garlic and chile from the lips that had drunk before him, coldly contemplating typhoid, diphtheria, polio, drank politely and put the jug back in the man's hands with thanks and watched him return it to the table without offering it to Johnny Bane. They were pulled into the room, the door closed, and he saw that the old hand-cranked Victrola had been played by a Mexican youth in drape pants and a pretty girl, short-skirted and pompadoured. The girl should be Lupe, Johnny's chick. He looked for the glance of understanding between them and saw only the look on Johnny's face as if he had an unbearable belly ache.

This was a merry shackful. The men were all a little drunk, and posed magnificently and badly, their eyes magnetized by the camera. The boy was lured from his comic book. Lupe and the youth, who turned out to be her cousin Chuey, leaned back and watched and whispered with a flash of white teeth. As for Johnny, he held reflectors where Prescott told him to, but he was no longer an eager beaver. His mouth hung sullenly; his eyes kept straying to the two on the couch.

Dutifully Prescott went on with his job, documenting poverty for humanitarianism's sake and humanizing it as he could for the sake of art. He got a fair shot of the boy reading his comic book under a hanging image of the Virgin, another of two little girls peeking into a steaming kettle of frijoles while the mother modestly hid her pregnancy behind the stove. He shot the card players from a low angle, with low side-lighting, and when an old grandmother came in the back door with a pail of water he got her there, stooping to the weight in the open door, against the background of the rain.

Finally he said into Carol's ear, with deliberate malice, "Now do we get that red-hot shot of Johnny jiving with his chick?"

"You're a mean man, Charlie," she said, but she smiled, and looking across to where Johnny stood sullen and alone she said, "Johnny, you want to come over here?"

He came stiff as a stick, ugly with venom and vanity. When Carol seated him close to Lupe the girl rolled her eyes and bit her lip, ready to laugh. The noise in the room had quieted; it was as if a dipperful of cold water had been thrown into a boiling kettle. Carol moved Chuey in close and laid some records in Lupe's lap. Prescott could see the caption coming up: *Even in shacktown, young people need amusement. Lack of adequate entertainment facilities one of greatest needs. Older generation generally disapproves of jive, jive talk, jive clothes.*

The girl was pretty, even with her ridiculous pompadour. Her eyes were soft, liquid, very dark, her cheekbones high, and her cheeks planed. With a *rebozo* over her head she might have posed for Murillo's Madonna. She did not stare into the camera as her elders did, but at Prescott's word became absorbed in studying the record labels. Chuey laid his head close to hers, and on urging, Johnny sullenly did the same. The moment the flash went off Johnny stood up.

Prescott shifted the Victrola so the crank handle showed more, placed Chuey beside it with a record in his hands. "All right, Lupe, you and Johnny show us a little rug-cutting."

He watched the girl glance from the corners of her eyes at her parents, then come into Johnny's arm. He held her as if she smelled bad, his head back and away, but she turned her face dreamily upward and sighed like an actress in a love drama and laid her face against his rain-wet chest. "*Que chicloso!*" she said, and could not hold back her laughter.

"*Surote!*" Johnny pushed her away so hard she almost fell. His face was contorted, his eyes glared. Spittle sprayed from his heavy lips. "*Bofa!*" he said to Lupe, and suddenly Prescott found himself protecting the camera in the middle of what threatened to become a brawl. Chuey surged forward, the undershirted father crowded in from the other side, the girl was spitting like a cat. With a wrench Johnny broke away and got his back to the wall, and there he stood with his hand plunged into the pocket of his blazer and his loose mouth working.

"Please!" Carol was shouting, "Chuey! Lupe! Please!" She held back the angry father and got a reluctant, broken quiet. Over her shoulder she said, "Johnny, go wait for us in the car."

For a moment he hung, then reached a long thin hand for the latch and slid out. The room was instantly full of noise again, indignation, threats. Prescott got his things safely outside the door away from their feet, and by that time politeness and diplomacy had triumphed. Carol said something to Lupe, who showed her teeth in a little white smile; to Chuey, who shrugged; to the father, who bowed over her hand and talked close to her face. There was handshaking around, Carol promised them prints of the pictures, Prescott gave the children each a quarter. Eventually they were out in the blessed rain.

"What in hell did he call her?" Prescott said as they clawed their way up the hill.

"Pachuco talk. Approximately a chippy."

"Count on him for the right touch."

"Don't say anything, Charlie," she said. "Let me handle him."

"He's probably gone off somewhere to nurse his wounded ego."

But as he helped her over the clay brink onto the cinder road he looked toward the car and saw the round dark head in the back seat. "I must say you pick some dillies," he said.

Walking with her face sideward away from the rain, she said seriously, "I don't pick them, Charlie. They come because they don't have anybody else."

"It's no wonder this one hasn't got anybody else," he said,

and then they were at the car and he was opening the door to put the equipment inside. Johnny Bane made no motion to get his muddy feet out of the road.

"Lunch?" Carol said as she climbed under the wheel. Prescott nodded, but Johnny said nothing. In the enclosed car Prescott could smell his hair oil. Carol twisted around to smile at him.

"Listen!" she said. "Why take it so hard? It's just that Chuey's her cousin, he's family, he can crash the gate."

"Agh!"

"Laugh it off."

He let his somber gaze fall on her. "That punk!" he said. "I get him good. Her too. I kill that mean little bitch. You wait. I kill her sometime."

For a moment she watched him steadily; then she sighed. "If it helps to take it out on me, go ahead," she said. "I'll worry about you, if that's what you want."

A few minutes later she stopped at a diner on Figueroa, but when she and Prescott climbed out, Johnny sat still. "Coming?" she said.

"I ain't hungry."

"Oh, Johnny, come off it! Don't sulk all day."

The long look he gave her was so deliberately insolent that Prescott wanted to reach through the window and slap his loose mouth. Then the boy looked away, picked a thread indifferently from his sleeve, stared moodily as if tasting some overripe self-pity or some rich revenge. Prescott took Carol's arm and pulled her into the diner.

"Quite a young man," he said.

Her look was sober. "Don't be too hard on him."

"Why not?"

"Because everybody always has been."

He passed her the menu. "Mother loved me, but she died."

"Stop it, Charlie!"

He was astonished. "All right," he said at last. "Forget it."

While they were eating dessert she ordered two hamburgers to go, and when she passed them through the car window Johnny Bane took them without a word. "What do you want to do?" she said. "Come along, or have us drop you somewhere?"

"Okay if I go along?"

"Sure."

"Okay."

In a street to which she drove, a peddler pushed a cart full of peppers and small Mexican bananas through the mud between dingy frame buildings. No one else was on the street, but two children were climbing through the windows of a half-burned house. The rain angled across, fine as mist.

"What's here?" Prescott said.

"This is a family I've known ever since I worked for Welfare," Carol said. "Grandmother with asthma, father with dropsy, half a dozen little rickety kids. This is to prove that bad luck has no sense of proportion."

Fishing for a cigarette, Prescott found the package empty. He tried the pockets of coat and raincoat without success. Carol opened her purse; she too was out. Johnny Bane had been smoking hers all morning.

"We can find a store," she said, and had turned the ignition key to start when Johnny said, "I can go get some for you."

"Oh, say, would you, Johnny? That would be wonderful."

Prescott felt dourly that he was getting an education in social workers. One rule was that the moment your delinquent showed the slightest sign of decency, passed you a cigarette or picked up something you had dropped, you fell on his neck as if he had rescued you from drowning. As a matter of fact, he had felt his own insides twitch with surprised pleasure at Johnny's offer. But then what? he asked himself. After you've convinced him that every little decency of his deserves a hundred times its weight in thanks, then what?

"No stores around here," Johnny said. "Probably the nearest over on Figueroa."

"Oh," she said, disappointed. "Then I guess we'd better drive down. That's too far to walk."

"You go ahead, do your business here," Johnny said. He leaned forward with his hands on the back of the front seat. "I take the car and go get some weeds, how's that?"

Prescott waited to hear what she would say, but he really knew. After a pause her quiet voice said, "Have you got a driver's license?"

"Sure, man, right here."

"All right," she said, and stepped out. "Don't be long. Charlie dies by inches without smokes."

While Prescott unloaded, Johnny slid under the wheel. He was as jumpy as a greyhound. His fingers wrapped around the wheel with love.

"Wait," Carol said. "I didn't give you any money."

With an exclamation Prescott fished a dollar bill from his pocket and threw it into the seat, and Johnny Bane let off the emergency and rolled away.

"What was that?" Prescott said. "Practical sociology?"

"Don't be so indignant," she said. "You trust people, and maybe that teaches them to trust you."

"Why should anybody but a hooligan have to be *taught* to trust you? Are you so unreliable?"

But she only shook her head at him, smiling and denying his premises, as they went up the rotted steps.

This house was worse than the others. It was not merely poor, it was dirty, and it was not merely dirty, but sick. Prescott looked it over for picture possibilities while Carol talked with a thin Mexican woman, worn to the bleak collarbones, with arms like sticks. In the kitchen the sink was stopped with a greasy rag, and dishes swam in water the color of burlap. On the table were three bowls with brown juice dried in them. There was a hole clear through the kitchen wall. In the front room, on an old taupe overstuffed sofa, the head of the house lay in a blanket bathrobe, his thickened legs exposed, his eyes mere slits in the swollen flesh of his face. By the window in the third room an old woman sat in an armchair, and everywhere, in every corner and behind every broken piece of furniture, were staring broad-faced children, incredibly dirty and as shy as mice. In a momentary pause in Carol's talk he heard the native sounds of this house: the shuffle of children's bare feet and the old woman's harsh breathing.

He felt awkward, and an intruder. Imprisoned by the rain, quelled by the presence of the Welfare lady and the strange man, the children crept soft as lizards around the walls. Wanting a cigarette worse than ever, Prescott glanced impatiently at his watch. Probably Johnny would stop for a malt or drive around showing off the car and come in after an hour expecting showers of thanks.

"What do you think, Charlie?" Carol's voice had dropped; the bare walls echoed to any noise, the creeping children and the silent invalids demanded hushed voices and soft feet. "Portrait shots?" she whispered. "All this hopeless sickness?"

"They'll be heartbreakers."

"That's what they ought to be."

Even when he moved her chair so that gray daylight fell across her face, the old woman paid no attention to him beyond a first piercing look. Her head was held stiffly, her face as still as wood, but at every breath the cords in her neck moved slightly with the effort. He got three time exposures of that half-raised weathered mask: flash would have destroyed what the gray light revealed.

Straightening up from the third one, he looked through the doorway into the inhuman swollen face of the son. It was impossible to tell whether the Chinese slits of eyes were looking at him or not. He was startled with the thought that they might be, and wished again, irritably, for a cigarette.

"Our friend is taking his time," he said to Carol, and held up his watch.

"Maybe he couldn't find a store."

Prescott grunted, staring at the dropsical man. If he shot across the swollen feet and legs, foreshortening them, and into the swollen face, he might get something monstrous and sickening, a picture to make people wince.

"Can he be propped up a little?" he asked.

Carol asked the thin, hovering wife, who said he could. The three of them lifted and slid the man up until his shoulders were against the wall. It troubled Prescott to see Carol's hands touch the repulsive flesh. The man's slits watched them, the lips moved, mumbling something.

"What's he say?"

"He says you must be a lover of beauty," Carol said.

For a moment her eyes held his, demanding of him something that he hated to give. Once, on his only trip to Mexico, he had gone hunting with his host in Michoacan, and he remembered how he had fired at a noise in a tree and brought something crashing down, and how they had run up to see a little monkey lying on the bloodied leaves. It was still alive; as they came up its eyes followed them, and at a certain moment it put up its arms over its head to ward off the expected death blow. To hear this monster make a joke was like seeing that monkey put up its arms in an utterly human gesture. It sickened him so that he took refuge behind the impersonality of the camera, and when he had taken his pictures he said something that he had not said to a subject all day. "Thanks," he said. "*Gracias, señor.*"

Somehow he had to counteract that horrible portrait with something sweet. He posed the thin mother and one of the children in a sentimental Madonna and Child pose, pure poster art suitable for a fund-raising campaign. While he was rechecking for the second exposure he heard the noise, like a branch being dragged across gravel. It came from the grandmother. She sat in the same position by the window of the other room, but she seemed straighter and more rigid, and he had an odd impression that she had grown in size.

The thin woman was glancing uneasily from Prescott to Carol. The moment he stepped back she was out of her chair and into the other room.

The grandmother had definitely grown in size. Prescott watched her with a wild feeling that anyone in this house might suddenly blow up with the obscene swelling disease. Under the shawl the old woman's chest rose in jerky breaths, but it didn't go down between inhalations. Her gray face shone with sudden sweat; her mouth was open, her head held stiffly to one side.

"Hadn't I better try to get a doctor?" Prescott said.

Bending over the old woman, Carol turned only enough to nod.

Prescott went quickly to the door. The peddler had disappeared, the children who had been climbing in the burned house were gone, the street lay empty in the rain. Johnny Bane had been gone for over an hour; if this woman died he could take the credit. In a district like this there might not be a telephone for blocks. Prescott would have to run foolishly like someone shouting fire.

A girl of ten or so, sucking her thumb, slid along the wall, watching him. He trapped her. "Where's there a telephone?"

She stared, round-eyed and scared.

"*Telefono?* You *sabe telefono?*"

He saw comprehension grow in her face, slapped a half-dollar into her hand, motioned her to start leading him. She went down the steps and along the broken sidewalk at a trot.

It took four calls from the little neighborhood grocery before he located a doctor who could come. Then, the worst cause for haste removed, he paused to buy cigarettes for himself and a bag of suckers for the children. His guide put a sucker in her mouth and a hand in his, and they walked back that way through the drizzle.

The street before the house was still empty, and he cursed Johnny Bane. Inside, the grandmother was resting after her paroxysm, but her head was still stiffly tilted, and a minute after he entered she fell into a fit of coughing that pebbled her lips with mucus and brought her halfway to her feet, straining and struggling for air. Carol and the thin woman held her, eased her back.

"Did you get someone?" Carol said.

"He's on his way."

"Did he tell you anything to do?"

"There's nothing to do except inject atropine or something. We have to wait for him."

"Hasn't Johnny come back?"

"Did you really expect him to?"

Her eyes and mouth were strained. She no longer looked like a college sophomore: a film from the day's poverty and sickness had rubbed off on her. Without a word she turned away, went into the kitchen, and started clearing out the sink.

As Prescott started to pack up it occurred to him that a picture of an old woman choking to death would add to the sociological impact of Carol's series, but he was damned if he would take it. He'd had enough for one day. The dropsical man turned his appalling swollen mask, and on an impulse Prescott stood up and gestured with the pack of cigarettes. The monster nodded, so Prescott inserted a cigarette between the lips and lighted it. Sight of the man smoking fascinated him.

The Rolleiflex was just going into the bag when it struck him that he had not seen the Contax. He rummaged, turned things out onto the floor. The camera was gone. Squatting on his heels, he considered how he should approach the mother of the house, or Carol, to get it back from whichever child had taken it. And then he began to wonder if it had been there when he unpacked for this job. He had used it at the Aguirre house for one picture, but not since. The bag had been in the car all the time he and Carol had been eating lunch. So had Johnny Bane.

Carefully refusing to have any feeling at all about the matter, he took his equipment out on the porch. Four or five children, each with a sucker in its mouth, came out and shyly watched him as he smoked and waited for the doctor.

The doctor was a short man with an air of unhurried haste. He examined the grandmother for perhaps a minute and got out a needle. The woman's eyes followed his hands with terror as he swabbed with an alcohol-soaked pad, jabbed, pushed with his thumb, withdrew, dropped needle and syringe into his case. It was like an act of deadpan voodoo. Within minutes the old woman was breathing almost normally, as if the needle had punctured her swelling and let her subside. For a minute more the doctor talked with Carol; he scribbled on a pad. Then his eyes darted into the next room to where the swollen son lay watching from his slits.

"What's the matter in here?"

"Dropsy," Carol said. "He's been bedridden for months."

"Dropsy's a symptom, not a disease," the doctor said, and went over.

In ten more minutes they were all out on the porch again. "I'll expect you to call me then," the doctor said.

"I will," Carol said. "You bet I will."

"Are you on foot? Can I take you anywhere?"

"No thanks. We're just waiting for my car."

It was then four-thirty. Incredulously Prescott watched her sit down on the steps to wait some more. The late sun, scattering the mist, touched her fair hair and deepened the lines around her mouth. Behind her the children moved softly. Above her head the old porch pillar was carved with initials and monikers: GJG, Mingo, Lola, Chavo, Pina, Juanito. A generation of lost kids had defaced even the little they had, as they might deface and abuse anyone who tried to help them in ways too unselfish for them to understand.

"How long do you expect to sit here?" he said finally.

"Give him another half hour."

"He could have gone to Riverside for cigarettes and been back by now."

"I know."

"You know he isn't going to come back until he's brought."

"He was upset about his girl," she said. "He felt he'd been kicked in the face. Maybe he went up there."

"To do what? Cut her throat?"

"It isn't impossible," she said, and turned her eyes up to his with so much anxiety in them that he hesitated a moment before he told her the rest.

"Maybe it isn't," he said then, "but I imagine he went first of all to a pawnshop to get rid of the camera."

"Camera?"

"He swiped the Contax while we were having lunch."

"How do you know?"

"Either that or one of the kids here took it."

Her head remained bent down; she pulled a sliver from the step. "It couldn't have been here. I was here all the time. None of the children went near your stuff."

She knew so surely what Johnny Bane was capable of, and yet she let it trouble her so, that he was abruptly furious with her. Social betterment, sure, opportunities, yes, a helping hand, naturally. But to lie down and let a goon like that walk all over you, abuse your confidence, lie and cheat and steal and take advantage of every unselfish gesture!

"Listen," he said. "Let me give you a life history. We turn him in and he comes back in handcuffs. Okay. That's six months in forestry camp, unless he's been there before."

"Once," she said, still looking down. "He was with a bunch that swiped a truck."

"Preston then," Prescott said. "In half a year he comes back from Preston and imposes on you some more, and you waste yourself keeping him out of trouble until he gets involved in something in spite of you, something worse, and gets put away for a stretch in San Quentin. By the time they let him out of there he'll be ripe for really bigtime stuff, and after he's sponged on you for a while longer he'll shoot somebody in a holdup or knife somebody in a whorehouse brawl, and they'll lead him off to the gas chamber. And nothing you can do will keep one like him from going all the way."

"It doesn't have to happen that way. There's a chance it won't."

"It's a hell of a slim chance."

"I know it," she said, and looked up again, her face not tearful or sentimental as he had thought it would be, but simply thoughtful. "Slim or not, we have to give it to him."

"You've already given him ten chances."

"Even then," she said. "He's everything you say—he's mean, vicious, dishonest, boastful, vain, maybe dangerous. I don't like him any better than you do, any better than he likes himself. But he's told me things I don't think he ever told anyone else."

"He never had such a soft touch," he said.

"He grew up in a slum, Harlem. Routine case. His father disappeared before he was born, his mother worked, whatever she could find. He took care of himself."

"I understand that," Prescott said. "He's a victim. He isn't to blame for what his life made him. But he's still unfit to live with other people. He isn't safe. Nine out of ten, maybe, you can help, but not his kind. It's too bad, but he's past helping."

"He wasn't a gang kid," she said. "He's unattractive, don't you see, and mean. People don't like him, and never did. He tries to run with the neighborhood Mexican gang here, but you saw how Chuey and Dago and Lupe just tolerate him. He doesn't belong. He never did. So he prowled the alleys and dreamed up fancy revenges for people he hated, and played with stray cats."

Prescott moved impatiently, and the children slid promptly further along the wall. Carol was watching him as steadily as the children were.

"He told me how he ran errands to earn money for liver and fish to feed them. He wanted them to come to him and be *his* cats."

Prescott waited, knowing how the script ran but surprised that Carol, a hardened case worker, should have fallen for it.

"But they were all alley cats, as outcast as he was," she said. "He'd feed a cat for a week, but when he didn't have anything for it, it would shy away, or he'd grab it and get clawed. So he used to try to tie cats up when he caught them."

Prescott said nothing.

"But when a cat wouldn't let itself be petted, or when it fought the rope—and it always did—he'd swing it by the rope and break its neck," Carol said.

She stirred the litter in the step corner and a sow bug rolled into its ball and bounced down into the dirt. "'I give them every chance, Miss Vaughn,' that's what he told me. 'I give them every chance and if they won't come and be my friend I pop their neck.'"

Cautiously Prescott moved the camera bag backward with his foot. He looked at the afternoon's grime in the creases of his hands. "That's a sad story," he said at last. "I mean it, it really is. But it only proves what I said, that he's too warped to run loose. He might try that neck-popping on some human being who wouldn't play his way—Lupe, for instance."

"Would you pop a cat's neck if it wouldn't come to you?" Carol said softly.

"Don't be silly."

"But you'd pop Johnny's."

They stared at each other in the rainy late afternoon.

Prescott told himself irrelevantly that he had not fallen in love with her on this job. Anyone who fell in love with her would have to share her with every stray in Greater Los Angeles. But he liked her and respected her and admired her; she was a fine human being. Only she carried it too far.

And yet he had no answer for her. "Good God," he said, "do you know what you're asking?"

"Yes," she said. "I know exactly. But I know you can't come with liver and fish heads six days a week and on the seventh come with a hangman's rope. You can't say, 'I gave him every chance' unless you really did."

The brief sun had disappeared again in the mist and smog. The street was muddy and gray before them. Behind them the thin woman came to the door and opened it, shooing the children in with an unexpected harsh snarl in her voice. Prescott felt disturbed and alien, out of his proper setting and out of his depth. But he still could find no answer for her. You could not come with liver and fish heads six days a week and with a hangman's knot on the seventh. You could not put limits on love—if love was what you chose to live by.

"All right," he said. "We don't call the cops, is that it?"

She smiled a crooked smile. "Let's try to get along without the police as long as we can."

The thin woman stood in the doorway and said goodbye and watched them down the steps, and the children pressing around her flanks watched too. Prescott waved, and the woman smiled and nodded in reply. But none of the children, solemnly staring, raised a hand. After a moment he was angry with himself for having expected them to.

DANNY SANTIAGO

The Somebody

For "The Somebody," Danny Santiago chooses the Eastside barrio of Los Angeles as a setting. His story reveals the proud ethnic heritage of a Mexican American, circa 1970.

Carlota Cardenas de Dwyer, the editor of the work from which this story is drawn, notes that "to Chicanos, the Fifth of May is as familiar as the Fourth of July, and the Treaty of Guadalupe-Hidalgo is as significant as the Declaration of Independence. Living on the frontiers of two dynamic civilizations, Chicanos have witnessed the evolution of two great societies and from them have created a distinct Chicano culture. The Chicano heritage is a blend of all that has come before."

Beneath the apparently lighthearted tone of this story of a day in the life of a young, rootless adventurer is a definite note of protest against the sort of life enforced upon a minority group in a great western city. One form this protest takes is gangs.

"The Somebody" first appeared in Redbook magazine and was collected in Cardenas de Dwyer's Chicano Voices (1975).

This is Chato talking, Chato de Shamrock, from the Eastside in old L.A., and I want you to know this is a big day in my life because today I quit school and went to work as a writer. I write on fences or buildings or anything that comes along. I write my name, not the one I got from my father. I want no part of him. I write Chato, which means Catface, because I have a flat nose like a cat. It's a Mexican word because that's what I am, a Mexican, and I'm not ashamed of it. I like that language too, man. It's way better than English to say what you feel. But German is the best. It's got a real rugged sound, and I'm going to learn to talk it someday.

After Chato I write "de Shamrock." That's the street where I live, and it's the name of the gang I belong to, but the others are all gone now. Their families had to move away, except Gorilla is in jail and Blackie joined the navy because he liked swimming. But I still have our old arsenal. It's buried under the chickens, and I dig it up when I get bored. There's tire irons and chains and pick handles with spikes and two zip guns we made and they shoot real bullets but not very straight. In the good old days nobody cared to tangle with us. But now I'm the only one left.

Well, today started off like any other day. The toilet roars like a hot rod taking off. My father coughs and spits about nineteen times and hollers it's six-thirty. So I holler back I'm quitting school. Things hit me like that—sudden.

"Don't you want to be a lawyer no more," he says in Spanish, "and defend the Mexican people?"

My father thinks he is very funny, and next time I make any plans, he's sure not going to hear about it.

"Don't you want to be a doctor," he says, "and cut off my leg for nothing someday?"

"*Due beast ine dumb cop,*" I tell him in German, but not very loud.

"How will you support me," he says, "when I retire? Or will you marry a rich old woman that owns a pool hall?"

"I'm checking out of this dump! You'll never see me again!"

I hollered it at him, but already he was in the kitchen making a big noise in his coffee. I could be dead and he wouldn't take me serious. So I laid there and waited for him to go off to work. When I woke up again, it was way past eleven. I can sleep forever these days. So I got out of bed and put on clean jeans and my windbreaker and combed myself very neat, because already I had a feeling this was going to be a big day for me.

I had to wait for breakfast because the baby was sick and throwing up milk on everything. There is always a baby vomiting in my house. When they're born, everybody comes over and says: "Qué cute!" but nobody passes any comments on the dirty way babies act. Sometimes my mother asks me to hold one for her but it always cries, maybe because I squeeze it a little hard when nobody's looking.

When my mother finally served me, I had to hold my breath, she smelled so bad of babies. I don't care to look at her anymore. Her legs got those dark-blue rivers running all over them. I kept waiting for her to bawl me out about school, but I guess she forgot, or something. So I cut out.

Every time I go out my front door I have to cry for what they've done to old Shamrock Street. It used to be so fine, with solid homes on both sides. Maybe they needed a little paint here and there but they were cozy. Then the S.P. Railroad bought up all the land except my father's place, because he was stubborn. They came in with their wrecking bars and their bulldozers. You could hear those houses scream when they ripped them down. So now Shamrock Street is just front walks that lead to a hole in the ground, and piles of busted cement. And Pelón's house and Blackie's are just stacks of old boards waiting to get hauled away. I hope that never happens to your street, man.

My first stop was the front gate and there was that sign again, that big S wrapped around a cross like a snake with rays coming out, which is the mark of the Sierra Street gang, as everybody knows. I rubbed it off, but tonight they'll put it back again. In the old days they wouldn't dare to come on our street, but without your gang you're nobody. And one of these fine days they're going to catch up with me in person and that will be the end of Chato de Shamrock.

So I cruised on down to Main Street like a ghost in a graveyard. Just to prove I'm alive, I wrote my name on the fence at the corner. A lot of names you see in public places are written very sloppy. Not me. I take my time. Like my fifth-grade teacher used to say, if other people are going to see your work, you owe it to yourself to do it right. Mrs. Cully was her name and she was real nice, for an Anglo. My other teachers were all cops, but Mrs. Cully drove me home one time when some guys were after me. I think she wanted to adopt me but she never said anything about it. I owe a lot to that lady, and especially my writing. You should see it, man—it's real smooth and mellow, and curvy like a blond in a bikini. Everybody says so. Except one time they had me in Juvenile by mistake and some doctor looked at it. He said it proved I had something wrong with me, some long word. That doctor was crazy, because I made him show me his writing and it was real ugly like a barbwire fence with little chickens stuck on the points. You couldn't even read it.

Anyway, I signed myself very clean and neat on that corner. And then I thought, Why not look for a job someplace? But I was more in the mood to write my name, so I went into the dime store and helped myself to two boxes of crayons and some chalk and cruised on down Main, writing all the way. I wondered should I write more than my name. Should I write "Chato is a fine guy" or "Chato is wanted by the police"? Things like that. News. But I decided against it. Better to keep them guessing. Then I crossed over to Forney Playground. It used to be our territory, but now the Sierra have taken over there like everyplace else. Just to show them, I wrote on the tennis court and the swimming pool and the gym. I left a fine little trail of Chato de Shamrock in eight colors. Some places I used chalk, which works better on brick or plaster. But crayons are the thing for cement or anything smooth, like in the girls' rest room. On that wall I drew a phone number. I bet a lot of them are going to call that number, but it isn't mine because we don't have a phone in the first place, and in the second place I'm probably never going home again.

I'm telling you, I was pretty famous at the Forney by the time I cut out, and from there I continued my travels till something hit me. You know how you put your name on something and that proves it belongs to you? Things like school books or gym shoes? So I thought, How about that, now? And I put my name on the Triple A Market and on Morrie's Liquor Store and on the Zócalo, which is a beer joint. And then I cruised on up Broadway, getting rich. I took over a barber shop and a furniture store and the Plymouth agency. And the firehouse for laughs, and the phone company so I could call all my girl friends and keep my dimes. And then there I was at Webster and García's Funeral Home with the big white columns. At first I thought that might be bad luck, but then I said, Oh, well, we all got to die sometime. So I signed myself, and now I can eat good and live in style and have a big time all my life, and then kiss you all good-bye and give myself the best funeral in L.A. for free.

And speaking of funerals, along came the Sierra right then, eight or ten of them down the street with that stupid walk which is their trademark. I ducked into the garage and hid behind the hearse. Not that I'm a coward. Getting stomped doesn't bother me, or even shot. What I hate is those blades, man. They're like a piece of ice cutting into your belly. But the Sierra didn't see me and went on by. I couldn't hear what they were saying, but I knew they had me on their mind. So I cut on over to the Boys' Club, where they don't let anybody get you, no matter who you are. To pass the time I shot some baskets and played a little pool and watched the television, but the story was boring, so it came to me: Why not write my name on the screen? Which I did with a squeaky pen. Those cowboys sure looked fine with Chato de Shamrock written all over them. Everybody got a kick out of it. But of course up comes Mr. Calderón and makes me wipe it off. They're always spying on you up there. And he takes me into his office and closes the door.

"Well," he says, "and how is the last of the dinosaurs?"

Meaning that the Shamrocks are as dead as giant lizards.

Then he goes into that voice with the church music in it, and I look out of the window.

"I know it's hard to lose your gang, Chato," he says, "but this is your chance to make new friends and straighten yourself out. Why don't you start coming to Boys' Club more?"

"It's boring here," I tell him.

"What about school?"

"I can't go," I said. "They'll get me."

"The Sierra's forgotten you're alive," he tells me.

"Then how come they put their mark on my house every night?"

"Do they?"

He stares at me very hard. I hate those eyes of his. He thinks he knows everything. And what is he? Just a Mexican like everybody else.

"Maybe you put that mark there yourself," he says. "To make yourself big. Just like you wrote on the television."

"That was my name! I like to write my name!"

"So do dogs," he says. "On every lamppost they come to."

"You're a dog yourself," I told him, but I don't think he heard me. He just went on talking. Brother, how they love to talk up there! But I didn't bother to listen, and when he ran out of gas I left. From now on I'm scratching that Boys' Club off my list.

Out on the street it was getting dark, but I could still follow my trail back toward Broadway. It felt good seeing Chato written everyplace, but at the Zócalo I stopped dead. Around my name there was a big red heart done in lipstick with some initials I didn't recognize. To tell the truth, I didn't know how to feel. In one way I was mad that anyone would fool with my name, especially if it was some guy doing it for laughs. But what guy carries lipstick? And if it was a girl, that could be kind of interesting.

A girl is what it turned out to be. I caught up with her at the telephone company. There she is, standing in the shadows, drawing her heart around my name. And she has a very pretty shape on her, too. I sneak up behind her very quiet, thinking all kinds of crazy things and my blood shooting around so fast it shakes me all over. And then she turns around and it's only Crusader Rabbit. That's what we called her from the television show they had then, on account of her teeth in front.

When she sees me, she takes off down the alley, but in twenty feet I catch her. I grab for the lipstick, but she whips it behind her. I reach around and try to pull her fingers open, but her hand is sweaty and so is mine. And there we are, stuck together all the way down. She twists up against me, kind of giggling. To tell the truth, I don't like to wrestle with girls. They don't fight fair. And then we lost balance and fell against some garbage cans, so I woke up. After that I got the lipstick away from her very easy.

"What right you got to my name?" I tell her. "I never gave you permission."

"You sign yourself real fine," she says.

I knew that already.

"Let's go writing together," she says.

"The Sierra's after me."

"I don't care," she says. "Come on, Chato—you and me can have a lot of fun."

She came up close and giggled that way. She put her hand on my hand that had the lipstick in it. And you know what? I'm ashamed to say I almost told her yes. It would be a change to go writing with a girl. We could talk there in the dark. We could decide on the best places. And her handwriting wasn't too bad either. But then I remembered I had my reputation to think of. Somebody would be sure to see us, and they'd be laughing at me all over the Eastside. So I pulled my hand away and told her off.

"Run along, Crusader," I told her. "I don't want no partners, and especially not you."

"Who are you calling Crusader?" she screamed. "You ugly, squash-nose punk."

She called me everything. And spit at my face but missed. I didn't argue. I just cut out. And when I got to the first sewer I threw away her lipstick. Then I drifted over to the banks at Broadway and Bailey, which is a good spot for writing because a lot of people pass by there.

Well, I hate to brag, but that was the best work I've ever done in all my life. Under the street lamp my name shone like solid gold. I stood to one side and checked the people as they walked past and inspected it. With some you can't tell just how they feel, but with others it rings out like a cash register. There was one man. He got out of his Cadillac to buy a paper and when he saw my name he smiled. He was the age to be my father. I bet he'd give me a job if I asked him. I bet he'd take me to his home and to his office in the morning. Pretty soon I'd be sitting at my own desk and signing my name on letters and checks and things. But I would never buy a Cadillac, man. They burn too much gas.

Later a girl came by. She was around eighteen, I think, with green eyes. Her face was so pretty I didn't dare to look at her shape. Do you want me to go crazy? That girl stopped and really studied my name like she fell in love with it. She wanted to know me, I could tell. She wanted to take my hand and we'd go off together holding hands. We'd go to Beverly Hills and nobody would look at us the wrong way. I almost said "Hi" to that girl and, "How do you like my writing?" But not quite.

So here I am, standing on this corner with my chalk all gone and only one crayon left and it's ugly brown. My fingers are too cold besides. But I don't care because I just had a vision, man. Did they ever turn on the lights for you so you could see the whole world and everything in it? That's how it came to me right now. I don't need to be a movie star or boxing champ to make my name in the world. All I need is plenty of chalk and crayons. And that's easy. L.A. is a big city, man, but give me a couple of months and I'll be famous all over town. Of course they'll try to stop me—the Sierra, the police, and everybody. But I'll be like a ghost, man. I'll be real mysterious, and all they'll know is just my name, signed like I always sign it, CHATO DE SHAMROCK with rays shooting out like from the Holy Cross.

Acknowledgments

The following stories in this book are used by the kind permission of the persons and publishers listed here.

"A Simple Genius" by Eugene Burdick. From *A Role in Manila*, copyright © 1966 by Eugene Burdick. Reprinted by permission of Curtis Brown, Ltd.

"I'll Be Waiting" from *The Simple Art of Murder* by Raymond Chandler. Copyright 1950 by Raymond Chandler. Copyright © renewed 1978 by Helga Greene. Reprinted by permission of Houghton Mifflin Company.

"Hook" by Walter Van Tilburg Clark. From *The Watchful Gods and Other Stories*, copyright 1950 by Walter Van Tilburg Clark. Reprinted by permission of International Creative Management.

"The Ghost of Billy the Kid" from *Mojave: A Book of Stories*, by Edwin Corle. Copyright 1934 by Edwin Corle. Copyright renewed 1961 by Mrs. Jean Corle. Reprinted by permission of Liveright Publishing Corporation.

"The Gutting of Couffignal" from *The Big Knockover* by Dashiell Hammett. Copyright © 1966 by Lillian Hellman. Reprinted by permission of Random House, Inc.

"Dance Mad" from *The Inland Whale* by Theodora Kroeber, © 1959 by Indiana University Press. Reprinted by permission of Indiana University Press.

"Picnic, 1943" from *Good-bye, Son and Other Stories* by Janet Lewis. Reprinted with the permission of The Ohio University Press, Athens.

"The Somebody" by Danny Santiago. Copyright © 1970 by Danny Santiago. First published in *Redbook* magazine. Reprinted by permission of Brandt & Brandt Literary Agents, Inc.

"Pop Goes the Alley Cat" from *The City of the Living* by Wallace Stegner. Copyright 1956 by Wallace Stegner. Copyright renewed © 1984

Library of Congress Cataloging-in-Publication Data
Great California stories / edited by A. Grove Day.
p. cm.
ISBN 0-8032-1688-2 (alk. paper)
ISBN 0-8032-6583-2 (pbk.)
1. California—Fiction. 2. Short stories, American—California.
I. Day, A. Grove (Arthur Grove), 1904– .
PS571.C2G7 1990
813'.010832794—dc20   90-37672
                                                            CIP
                                                             AC